THE NEW
ACHILLES

Christian Cameron is a writer and military historian. He participates in re-enacting and experimental archaeology, teaches armoured fighting and historical swordsmanship, and takes his vacations with his family visiting battlefields, castles and cathedrals. He lives in Toronto and is busy writing his next novel.

The Commander Series
The New Achilles

The Chivalry Series
The Ill-Made Knight
The Long Sword
The Green Count
Sword of Justice

The Tyrant Series
Tyrant
Tyrant: Storm of Arrows
Tyrant: Funeral Games
Tyrant: King of the Bosporus
Tyrant: Destroyer of Cities
Tyrant: Force of Kings

The Long War Series
Killer of Men
Marathon
Poseidon's Spear
The Great King
Salamis
Rage of Ares

Tom Swan and the Head of St George Parts One–Six

Tom Swan and the Siege of Belgrade Parts One–Seven

Tom Swan and the Last Spartans Parts One–Five

Other Novels
Washington and Caesar
Alexander: God of War

Writing as Miles Cameron

The Traitor Son Cycle
The Red Knight
The Fell Sword
The Dread Wyrm
A Plague of Swords
The Fall of Dragons

Masters and Mages
Cold Iron
Dark Forge
Bright Steel

THE NEW ACHILLES

CHRISTIAN CAMERON

ORION

First published in Great Britain in 2019
by Orion Books,
an imprint of The Orion Publishing Group Ltd
Carmelite House, 50 Victoria Embankment
London EC4Y 0DZ

An Hachette UK Company

1 3 5 7 9 10 8 6 4 2

A CIP catalogue record for this book
is available from the British Library.

ISBN (Hardback) 978 1 4091 7656 5
ISBN (eBook) 978 1 4091 7658 9
ISBN (Audio) 978 1 4091 7684 8

Typeset by Deltatype Ltd, Birkenhead, Merseyside

Printed in Great Britain by CPI Group (UK) Ltd,
Croydon, CR0 4YY

www.orionbooks.co.uk

For my father, Kenneth Cameron
A better author than I'll ever likely be

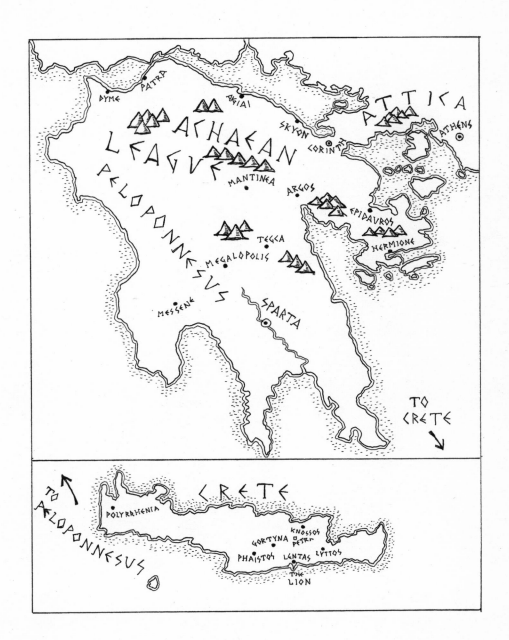

BOOK I

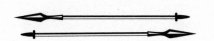

FIRST BLOOD

CHAPTER ONE

~OM~

North coast of Crete and Eastern Peloponnese

228 BCE

The Rhodian grain ship *Arktos* had endured a bad night, the last and worst of a three-day blow. She wallowed in the swell, her oars taken in, her broken mainmast still wrapped in her fallen cordage over the side, her crew struggling to cut it free in such a way that it could be saved. A relentless wind from the north drove her towards the coast of Crete, just a few stades away under a bright grey spring sky.

She only had a crew of eight and another thirty or so rowers, most of them slaves. None of them were citizens except the captain, who had given up bellowing orders from the foredeck and was now in the water, using a knife to cut the tangled shrouds one by one while his most trusted mate watched the water below him for sharks.

The ship's passengers lined the starboard side rail, watching the repairs with varying degrees of interest. The Spartan aristocrat, his red cloak flapping in the freshening wind, sneered.

'A touch of the whip would make them move,' he said. 'By the gods, what a useless lot.'

There were two women, from Kos, prosperous enough to have a slave to attend them. They were heavily veiled, their linen and wool forced against their bodies by the wind.

'You are an expert sailor, perhaps?' asked the older woman.

The Spartiate ignored her.

3

An Athenian merchant frowned. 'If I was younger,' he said, to no one in particular, 'I'd get in the water and help.'

The Spartiate glanced at him with contempt.

There was one more passenger. He'd kept very much to himself since Rhodes, and now he stood amidships, looking out into the flat glare of the clouded Mediterranean day under his hand. He was looking south, over the port-side rail, at the north coast of Crete.

'Is that Knossos?' asked the younger woman. She was at an age to find lonely young men attractive.

'I think so,' the young man said, his voice dull, as if only courtesy forced him to reply. Then he frowned. 'I think . . .'

He stepped up on the rail, balancing like an acrobat. He glanced back at his fellow passengers, uncertainty written on his features. Then he grabbed a shroud, looked again, jumped back down and crossed the empty benches and the central catwalk to lean over the side where the *navarch* was sawing away at what he hoped was the last of the movable stay that, in better times, had raised and lowered the mast.

'Navarch!' the Rhodian called. His voice was suddenly sharp and military.

'Soon, citizen,' the captain called, his voice full of the oil he needed to keep his fractious passengers at arm's length.

'There are three boats coming off the shore,' the Rhodian called. 'And we're going to touch on the beach if we keep drifting at this rate.'

Every head turned. Four sailors ran across the deck and the little galley rolled slightly in the water.

'Pirates!' yelled a sailor.

The captain swore. 'I need another man,' he called. 'Kephalos, get the boat-sail mast set. The *artemon*!'

Kephalos waved, and the navarch dived below the wreck of the mast.

The passenger who kept to himself dropped his *chiton* on the deck, drew a small bronze knife from a sheath at his neck and leapt into the water. His chest was criss-crossed with scars.

The women were watching the Cretan shore now. First one boat came off the beach, and then a second, full of men. A third boat was being readied.

'Lady Artemis protect us,' said the younger woman.

4

The older woman took a deep breath, but she released it without speaking. Her hands were trembling.

The Spartiate laughed. 'Perhaps they'll give this tub a tow,' he said.

Suddenly the deck began to vibrate like a living thing, and the whole ship seemed to shudder. Then the mast and its attendant wreckage of torn sail and trailing ropes exploded out of the water like the very Spear of Poseidon.

Now the mast floated clear of the wreck. The captain's head appeared, and he swam powerfully along the side of his ship, ducked under the mast, and looked back.

The passenger surfaced behind him.

The captain reached up, caught the low rail, and hauled himself on board.

'Get the fucking mast aboard, you whoresons,' he shouted. 'You, and Kephalos! Set the *artemon*. I told you already, you rabble.' He pointed at another man. 'Throw the weighted line. Tell me how much water we have under the keel.'

The ship was now moving more rapidly in with the land. The dragging submerged mast had been like an anchor, and free of it, the current moved the ship all the faster.

'Get that mast aboard!' he roared.

Then he leapt across the amidships platform, but he could already see the three low shapes pulling towards them, oars flashing as they left the water in perfect unison.

'Fucking Knossos,' the captain spat.

'King Cleomenes has a treaty with Knossos,' the Spartiate said. 'I'll see that we come to no harm.'

'See how you feel about that when some Cretan's pole is up your arse,' the captain said. 'Sailors, arm yourselves!'

The Spartiate stepped back before the navarch's vehemence, and the man turned as red as his cloak with anger. He put a hand on the sword he wore.

'No one speaks to me that way,' he said.

The captain wasn't listening. He stood amidships, naked, the sea-water still coming off him as if he was Poseidon risen from the waves. He was a big man, well past fifty, with grey hair on his chest, a grey beard, and equally grey eyes.

He was watching the foremast sail, the *artemon*, run up the stubby foremast. A boy not more than ten climbed the mast, reached out with a sharp bronze knife, and cut the yarns holding the sail furled. It snapped open right under him. The stiff southern breeze filled it with a crack, and the ship made way immediately, turning slightly to starboard but still making way south, dragged by the swell.

'Helm!' roared the captain.

'She steers!' called the mate at the steering oars.

The passenger was just hauling himself up onto the deck. The Athenian merchant gave him a hand.

'Poseidon's throbbing spear, you sacks of seal shit! Arm yourselves, unless you want to try mining silver on Syracusa or blowing flutes on Crete!' The captain turned, looking at the passengers. 'Women to the deck cabin. Gentlemen, you'll want to fight.'

'I won't be taken,' said the older woman's voice from under her veils. 'I've been a slave. I won't be taken alive.'

The captain bowed. 'Nor will I, *despoina*. Nor will any sensible body. But these ain't noble Knossian warriors with armour and their pick of fighters. This is some sea-scum – out of work fisherfolk and broken men. If we kill a dozen, they'll run.' His voice was firm and confident.

The younger woman burst into tears and her knees all but failed her, so she seemed to jerk in the wind. The woman who had spoken took her head, and their slave took her feet, and they carried her into the cabin.

The naked passenger came to the command platform, drying himself with his *chiton*. By the time he reached the navarch, the man had a wool *chiton* over his torso and his slave was holding a bronze *thorax* open for him.

'You're Rhodian,' said the navarch.

'Yes, sir. Born on Kos. What can I do?' But he knew what came next.

The slave closed the body armour like a form-fitting clam shell around his master and began to push the pins home to lock it closed.

'You a Citizen?'

The navarch's question capitalised the title. Citizens served at sea. They had extensive training.

'Yes, sir. I have done my service – I was a ...' He looked away. 'Marine.' The young man waved vaguely at his sea bag, lashed under

6

the port-side railing, the military way. 'I have a sword,' he admitted, as if it might be a crime.

'Best news I've heard all day. Kephalos! Javelins and a *pelta* for our young citizen.' He eyed the former marine. 'You've fought before?'

'Twice.' The young man snapped the answer, and his eyes went elsewhere.

'Excellent. Pirates are all gamon. You'll see.' The captain looked down at his mate.

Kephalos, a huge man with a fine head of red hair, grinned.

'Aye, boss,' he called.

He reached down between the benches and threw a bundle of javelins onto the main deck. Then he began to throw shields up, and the sailors grabbed them. The oarsmen looked uneasy.

The captain stood up on the command bench. Now he wore bronze greaves and the well-made bronze breastplate, and he looked even more like an image of the sea god.

'Listen up, oarsmen,' he said. 'I don't plan to fucking die, and you shouldn't either. Now take a spear, and a shield, and fight. If we're taken, slavery is the least thing that will happen to you. If we fight free, I promise every man of you ten silver drachmae, hard silver, and a word to your owners.'

The rowers were not all slaves, but they were all professionals, and they knew that pirates tended to slaughter their kind, or work them to death. One of the freemen leant over and picked up a pair of javelins and a *pelta*.

'That's the spirit, lads,' said the navarch.

'Knossos is an ally,' the Spartiate insisted.

The navarch didn't bother turning his head.

'Not to Rhodes,' he said. 'Not this year.'

The Rhodian put the strap of his sword belt over his shoulder and half-drew the weapon.

'Not bad,' the captain called out.

The original work party had managed to get a purchase on the butt of the mainmast, put a rope around it, and hauled it inboard without staving in the side or turning turtle.

'Two points to starboard,' he called to the helmsman, then turned to the Rhodian passenger. 'Pray for a wind change.'

But the grain galley was too big to be driven solely by her boat-sail, and they were still making way south while the rising wind drove them west. The three smaller boats were on converging courses.

'Who did you serve under?' the navarch asked the Rhodian passenger.

'Orestes, son of Alexander, sir. *Asklepios.*'

The young man saluted, one arm held stiffly out parallel to the deck.

'By Artemis! Were you in the fight last autumn? With the Aegyptian?'

'Yes, sir.'

The navarch looked at him and said nothing. Perhaps he bowed his head slightly.

'And your name?'

'Alexanor, son of Philokles.'

Even with a hundred pirates clawing after them in a long chase, the navarch managed a smile.

'Philokles the Victor? The Olympian? Well, Alexanor, son of Philokles,' he said. 'I hope you can fight as well as your father. Is that his sword?'

The sword in question was hanging over Alexanor's shoulder. It had an ivory hilt, banded with gold, and the image of Poseidon was set into the pommel. Alexanor's father was a merchant, but also a well-known hero of the older generation, an Olympic champion in boys' *pankration* and triumphant in a dozen sea-fights as well.

Alexanor nodded. 'Yes,' he said.

The navarch looked back over the goose head at the stern.

'They'll be up with us in an hour. But every stade we make will give them less light to take us, and I don't intend to slow or turn. The pity of it is that with our mainsail up, we'd leave them in our wake.'

'Any chance we could get the mainmast up?' Alexanor asked.

The navarch looked around the deck. With the wind almost directly astern, there was nothing more the rowers could do, and the storm had cost them half a dozen sweeps, anyway. Two rowers were badly injured, their ribs broken by their own oars, from a rogue wave that had struck them in the dark.

'Better if the wind would change to blow from the south,' he said. 'But let's have a go, anyway.'

Alexanor looked north, towards Mount Olympus, and began praying that the King of the Gods would order the winds to blow from the south.

The navarch was more direct. 'On me, you ruffians. Listen, then! Fighting is the last resort. Let's try and get the mainmast up.'

There was a murmur of agreement.

But the execution of the idea was much harder than Alexanor had imagined. He'd only raised a mainmast from the deck in open water before, with all the raising tackle laid along by professionals. It was a different matter with all the side ropes torn away, and the mainmast an inert mass along the ship's centreline. If its weight shifted even a foot or two off the centreline it was enough to make the ship fall off course if shifted abruptly. He didn't even want to think of what the mast would do to the deck if the ropes let it go.

Alexanor, who had taken very little interest in anything since leaving Rhodes, took a deep breath and prayed to Poseidon. And then, with two Persian slaves and an Athenian rower, he took hold of a rope and pulled when he was told to.

The pirates, if they were pirates, drew closer.

Overhead, the boy and two Aegyptians rigged a cradle of ropes to the *artemon*'s mast at the navarch's orders, and then everyone hauled away. The mast rose, a handspan and then another.

A gust of wind made the *artemon* crack and flap, and the mainmast swayed, and the men on the ropes were dragged two steps along the deck.

'Steady there!' the navarch called. 'Two points more to starboard.'

The boat-sail flapped and then was still as the ship turned to run north by west.

'Someone has a line to the gods.' The navarch smiled at Alexanor. 'By Poseidon, one breath of the wrong wind ...'

The Rhodian looked back over the stern. The three pirates were hull up and halfway from the horizon; their low boats had colour now, the hulls black with pitch, and he could just make out faces. They were perhaps five hundred paces away.

'Heave!' called Kephalos, and the mast rose again.

'Heave!' he called again.

At each heave, the waterlogged mast crept higher. The navarch stood at the butt with four heavy wedges at his feet and a maul in his hand.

'Heave!' called the mate.

An arrow clattered against the goose head that decorated the stern and fell harmlessly to the deck.

'Heave!' roared the mate.

Alexanor was covered in sweat. When he looked across the deck, he could see the older woman from Kos and her slave had clapped on the port-side rope. Her veils were wrapped around her head like a turban and she had strong arms. She looked at him, and then back at her work.

'Heave!' begged the mate.

The mast went up, and then up again. And again. It was now at such a steep angle that it almost looked erect. There were parties of men on either side holding belaying ropes that kept the mast from swaying ... much. But as the ship rolled, the mast swayed with it, and it was all six grown men could do to hold it.

The navarch's face gave away the looming disaster.

Alexanor looked back and saw the prow of the nearest pirate boat just a hundred paces aft, and gaining, the pirate's oarsmen pulling like men racing for a prize. An arrow zapped in like a vicious insect and struck one of the Rhodian oarsmen with a sound like a butcher cutting meat. The man fell and emitted a thin scream.

'Fuck,' spat the navarch. 'So *close*.'

'Hang on!' called Alexanor.

He could see it in his head. The mast; the roll of the waves. It was almost impossible, but if it worked ...

The navarch looked at him.

'Drop the mainmast on the lead pirate,' he said.

'Stupidest thing I've ever heard,' spat the navarch.

Alexanor considered just roaring out the orders. He could see how it could be done, how tight the time was ...

But he was a veteran, and he knew that no man could cross a captain on his command deck. No one would obey him.

'It could work,' he said softly.

The navarch made a face. And then a minute shrug that barely moved his armoured shoulders.

'Let's try it.'

He clapped his hands together and raised his voice.

'Listen to me, you lot. When I say "Let fall!" all the belayers let go. The mast will swing to starboard as we turn. When I call "now", every fucking one of you on the stays lets go. Got it? Don't fuck this up. You there, on the gangway. You have a *stay* in your hand. Got that? "Let fall" is for those of you holding belaying lines. "NOW" is for those amidships. Got it?' He looked forward. 'Oarsmen, to your benches. Ready to row on command.'

He looked around. He didn't wait for an answer.

'Hard to port,' he called.

The man in the steering oars didn't believe him.

'Hard to port!' the navarch screamed.

The man in the oars obeyed.

As soon as the turn began, the nearest pirate boat surged forward. As the merchant turned, the pirates were racing to catch the merchant amidships and board.

'Belay!' the navarch roared, and the men at the rails let go their ropes.

Instantly, the masthead leant out to port with the sudden turn. The men holding the tall monster were pulled forward, and the swell under the turning ship heeled her over still farther.

The pirate galleys didn't have rams; they were *lembi*, coastal boats for fishing or routine trade. Or rape and murder. The men in the bows had leather armour and spears. They were close enough that men were getting ready to leap aboard.

'Now!' The navarch's voice was like a trumpet.

The mast fell like an axe. Smashing the low railing of the *Arktos* and descending on the pirate like a Scythian's axe. The end of the falling mast went through the lead boat's side; the force of the blow broke her back, and suddenly the seawater was full of men, some swimming and some already going down.

The merchant's turn had slowed her, and the mast over the side turned her again, so that her bow pointed up into the wind, due south.

'Here they come,' called Kephalos.

'Cut the mast free!' called the navarch.

Alexanor had time to put his *pelta* on his left arm. He had two javelins, and he ran to the port side of the merchant ship, near the bow, and leant out, even as, deep in his mind, he thought *here we go. Again.* The pirates were coming up both sides now, but they were going too fast; the merchant's sudden turn had caught them by surprise, and they were racing past.

The first javelin went into a man standing in the bow. An arrow shattered against the rail next to Alexanor, and then a sling stone buzzed by like a wasp. The pirates were throwing grapnels on ropes, but the merchant sailors were cutting them as fast as they came aboard. The mast was cut free and the ship seemed to come alive, no longer bound to the mast or the sinking pirate vessel.

A man was drowning beneath Alexanor's feet, sinking away into the depths as though being pulled by a hand. His eyes were open and his mouth, too, as if he were screaming as his lungs filled with salt water.

Alexanor leant further over the rail, his eyes on the dying man, and then he made himself raise his head to the fight, and caught sight of the enemy steersman. As the enemy stern came even with the merchant's bow, Alexanor threw with a step and the full power of his hips.

The javelin went into the man's belly, and he doubled forward, hands clutched to the wound. He fell to his knees, and the oars fell with him, and suddenly the pirate boat was turning to port, away from the merchant – turning, turning …

'Ware!' roared Kephalos.

Alexanor turned to find that the pirates on the port side were boarding. He drew his father's sword straight up into a parry, using the strong steel spine of the *xiphos* to turn a spear before stepping in close to finish his man with a thrust, exactly like a drill on the deck of the *Asklepios*.

Exactly like the other fight.

He pushed the dying man back into the arms of his mates. A spear licked out of the enemy mass and caught him in the shin. He had no armour, and the needle point hurt, but the leg held, and the spearman whipped his weapon back. Alexanor held his shield out at arm's length, strapped against his left arm, so the little shield was edge-forwards, almost invisible to his enemies, and he went forward into their spears, regardless of numbers, because that's what he'd been trained to do.

They flinched. Only one blow came at him, a hasty spear thrust that he caught on his shield. Then it was just fighting, close and terrible – and he had no helmet and no armour. He was hit, who knows how many times. He didn't really feel the pain, and his father's sword left a red path to death written across half a dozen foes until it broke in his hand, and all he had was a stump of iron. His right arm was red to the elbow and his head throbbed.

Exactly like the other time. Bodies like gutted fish. The stench of everything inside a man; the terror, the animal rage, the animal fear. Black, and deep, and horrible.

And then he was standing against the bulkhead of the bow, panting like a smith's bellows, and Kephalos was handing him a clay flask full of fresh water.

The redhead had as many cuts on his arms as Alexanor had himself. Indeed, he was bleeding from a dozen wounds – some just dull aches from spear-shaft blows which had not broken a bone – but he had three cuts in his right forearm, a gouge taken out of his shin, and a puncture in his right thigh that was leaking blood. His father's beautiful sword, stolen in anger from its place on his father's wall in the *andron* at home, pattern welded by the expert sword-smiths of Colchis, was a stump, stuck to his hand by sticky, congealing gore.

How symbolic, he thought, bitterly.

His vision tunnelled, and he thought he might be sick.

'By Zeus above and all his thunder,' the redhead spat. 'Oh fuck, here they come again.'

Those were his last words, as a thrown javelin caught him in the back of the neck and he went down like a sacrificial ox. The boat that had lost its steersman had now returned to the fight, but her crew seemed less willing, less ferocious. Alexanor put a man down with the javelin that had felled Kephalos, and then he made himself stand with the navarch and the other sailors on the command platform, watching the vessel approach. The sailors pushed him into the front rank.

He was next to the navarch, flexing his right hand, trying to get feeling to return to it.

'If we kill five of them, they'll run,' the navarch said in a matter-of-fact voice.

'My king has a *treaty* with Knossos!' the young Spartiate said petulantly, though he sounded less sure of himself. He had a fine breastplate on, an *aspis* on his arm and his sword was red-brown.

'Where's Kephalos?' the navarch asked.

'Dead,' Alexanor said.

The navarch turned, and his grey eyes looked old inside the bronze of his helmet.

'Damn.' He shrugged his shoulders, as if indifferent to his mate's fate, or perhaps he was just settling the weight of his armour on tired shoulders.

Alexanor bent down to collect two javelins. He also killed two wounded pirates while he was about it.

Black.

The pirates came up both sides, all together, at a horn call. But they stopped just as the spears crossed, hesitant to close. Alexanor had to make himself stand tall. His knees wanted to fold. He felt as if he'd run thirty stades. *And it was all happening again. The deaths. The waste.*

'Give us your grain and we'll leave you to go,' called a voice.

'Come here and die,' growled the navarch.

'If you are men of Knossos—' called the Spartiate.

'Shut up,' the navarch spat. 'Rhodes makes no deals with these scum.'

'Maybe …' muttered one of the oarsmen.

A sailor shuffled back. The pressure on Alexanor's back lessened, as if the rear rank was considering flight.

There's nowhere to go, he thought.

Alexanor ignored the pain in his right arm and the fatigue and his near despair. The last thing he wanted to do was to kill, but training held, and his hand went back, almost without his willing it. He threw like Zeus flinging lightning from heaven, and one of the pirates – one of the few with a breastplate – fell screaming, the iron point lodged in his belly right through the bronze.

The pirates, despite odds of three to one, hesitated.

And then, as if pulled by unseen strings, they turned, all together, and fled into their boat.

The woman who had hauled on the ropes put a hand on his arm. Her hand was covered in blood, and he realised she had been fighting too.

'Don't touch me,' he said dully. She flinched away.

He sat suddenly, in his own blood, and then …

Two days later, as dawn raced across the surface of the sea, the merchant galley, running lightly west with a jury-rigged mainmast and just ten oars in the water, crept past the rocky crags of the island of Agistri like a wounded water bird and then wallowed slowly onto the beach of Epidauros.

Alexanor thought that he was ready to go ashore on his own legs, but he was still exhausted, and his hands gripped the ship's rail just to keep him upright as the oarsmen manoeuvred towards the beach. He had a wound like an angry mouth in his thigh, and his shin still leaked blood. He still had encrusted gore under his fingernails.

The other passengers left him alone at the rail.

The town rose on the promontory to the right, with fine red-glazed tile roofs, white buildings and a magnificent Temple of Apollo on the headland.

The navarch was braver than his passengers, and he came and stood with the scarred passenger.

'What will you do here?' the navarch asked. 'Your wounds aren't *that* bad.'

Alexanor knew that the older man intended to help, but he had no interest in a conversation.

'I've come to take my vows,' he said. 'I'm going to be a priest. We're hereditary priests, in my family. Priests of Asklepios.'

The navarch was watching as a bale of dyed Carthaginian hides came out of the maw of his ship.

'You? A priest?' He laughed. 'You're a killer.'

'Yes.' Alexanor shrugged, aware that the other man had meant his comment as praise, not damnation. 'I'm not interested in being a killer any longer,' he said, with more vehemence than he'd intended.

He thought of the deck when the pirates broke; and his mind flashed back to the other time, when the men he'd trained with had died. Corpses like gutted fish, white in death.

The elder of the two women, a matron of perhaps thirty, came forward and put a daring hand on his arm.

'Why study here, so far from home?' she asked. 'Kos has a fine Asklepion, if you want to be a doctor.'

'I come from Kos, *despoina*. Kos is too close to Rhodes.' He turned away from her.

'Perhaps—' she began.

He turned a little too suddenly, as if he meant to attack her. She started back, but he merely bowed.

'I'm sure that you only mean to help,' he said. 'But I do not intend to go back to Kos, or to Rhodes. For any reason.'

The woman backed away as if he'd stung her.

And later, when he'd gone cautiously over the side with his bag and the hilt of his father's broken sword and splashed ashore in the warm water, she glanced at the navarch.

He was watching the young man as he walked up the beach. A tall, white-haired man in a long white robe came down and spoke to him, and then a slave came and took his pack.

The navarch looked back at her.

'What a waste,' he said.

The woman had her veil back over her head, and a straw hat over that, but she met his eyes.

'I agree,' she said softly. 'Someone has hurt him.'

The navarch shrugged. 'That's the world. Right, you lubbers! Corinth! Get the anchor stones in!'

Alexanor bowed to the older man. 'Alexanor, son of Philokles of Kos,' he said.

'I am Chiron,' the priest said. 'You may call me by my name, or you may call me "Hierophant".' He gave the Rhodian a little grimace, as if the title amused him. 'Let me see your arms. You are injured. Your hands are filthy. You smell of death.' The older priest's voice was impersonal. 'This is not the way aspirant priests usually appear. Come with me.'

They walked to a booth at the top of the beach, where two other younger priests were greeting pilgrims from a Corinthian trader. Inside the wicker construction were two stools, four low beds, and a variety of phials and clay containers neatly labelled on shelves. An overweight man lay on one of the beds, deeply asleep.

'Sit down,' Chiron said, brusquely.

'I'm ...' Alexanor began. *I'm not here as a patient.* 'I'm here to study to be a priest.'

'Are you?' Chiron said. 'Please sit down.'

'I assure you ...' Alexanor hated the petulant tone he took. *The tone he used when arguing with his father ...*

'Do you always find obedience this difficult?' Chiron asked. 'Sit down. I'm going to look at your arms. You were fighting?'

'We were attacked by pirates.'

'You have fought before,' Chiron stated.

'Yes, sir,' Alexanor returned. 'How do you know?'

'If you stay with us, you will learn to read a man's body like a scroll. Who dressed this arm?'

'A lady of Kos,' Alexanor replied.

'Well trained,' Chiron said. 'And yet she didn't wash the blood from under your nails. What was her name?'

Alexanor knew a moment of shame as he realised he had never asked the woman her name.

'I don't know,' he admitted.

Chiron paused for a moment in his examination. He sniffed.

'Interesting,' he said. 'You are a very lucky young man. Raise your forearm. Like this. Over your head.'

Alexanor did as he was told.

Chiron shook his head. 'This cut should have severed the tendon. You would have been crippled for life. As it is, it will take a long time to heal. The tendon is like a rope on which you pull to move the arm. Do you understand?'

'Yes,' Alexanor said. 'I have read Aristotle and some Polybius.'

The older man's eyebrow twitched. 'Interesting. Do you realise that we ask for a gift, a fairly sizeable gift, before we allow you to enter as an initiate novice?'

'Yes,' Alexanor said.

His family was rich; he had the gift in his bag, a gold lamp worth as much as the rest of the ship's cargo.

He allowed his impatience to show, but really . . .

Chiron nodded. 'This will hurt,' he said, his tone sharp.

By the time Alexanor emerged from the booth, the sun was high in the sky, and the sound of the doves had died away. The old priest had washed and scrubbed his arms until they both bled again, and then wrapped them in clean white linen after applying a salve that smelt of roses.

'What's in the salve?' Alexanor asked. Roses reminded him of Aspasia.

Her hair smelt of roses, and her neck. Kissing her neck, the taste of her salt sweat, the smell of roses.

Oh, Aphrodite, let me be.

Chiron looked at him for a moment, and then shrugged.

'Four drachmae of rose petals. Dry them and then grind them to powder and mix with two drachmae of saffron, with a small measure of spikenard – that particular oil is best – and a quarter drachma of powdered opium. A little gum acacia, carefully warmed. Add rainwater until the mixture becomes a paste.' He indicated the road. 'You will have to walk to the sanctuary. It's a long walk.'

'I'll manage,' Alexanor said.

'I'm sure you will.' The priest seemed amused. 'But I'll come with you, nonetheless.'

Once they were clear of the port and climbing the hills, Alexanor glanced at the priest.

'It must be expensive,' he said. 'Rose petals, saffron, spikenard ... opium. All rare.'

'You are from Rhodes,' Chiron replied. 'I suppose you would know.'

'Spikenard comes from India,' Alexanor said. 'Which is beyond Persia. My father is a merchant.'

Just speaking of his father brought it all to mind, and he paused for a moment. Aspasia. His father.

Lord Apollo, let me be free of what is past.

Chiron stopped on the path.

'It is all very expensive,' he said. 'We ask pilgrims to make a donation. But mostly we depend on the extravagant donations of the very rich – the Ptolemies, the Agiads, the Antipatrids. You have been to Kos?'

'I am from Kos,' Alexanor said. 'My family lives in Rhodes now. I was educated on Kos and I was healed at the Sanctuary there.'

He remembered the columns, the magnificent temple, and the calm. *It is the calm I seek.*

'Why didn't you stay on Kos to be trained?' the priest asked.

'That is my business,' Alexanor snapped.

'Interesting,' Chiron said.

They walked on for perhaps half a stade, and Alexanor was surprised how well the older man dealt with the steep hills and rocky ground, moving like a man much younger. They topped a ridge, the priest slightly ahead, and suddenly the ground fell away, and they had a vast vista before them.

The sun was beginning to set in the west, over the Peloponnese, and the mountains of Arkadia showed in the distance, like temples built by the gods themselves. The beauty of it penetrated Alexanor's fatigue and his boredom and his despair.

He stopped, and he had to make himself take a breath.

'Oh, gods,' he said aloud.

Chiron smiled broadly, for the first time that Alexanor had seen.

'Good,' he said. 'But, young man, if you plan to stay among us as a patient, much less as a priest, let me tell you that everything is my business.'

They started down the ridge. At their feet, glowing pink and white in the late afternoon sun, was the temple complex of Epidauros, the healing Asklepion famed throughout the world. The older priest pointed out the buildings as they walked down towards the formal gateway: closest, the portico of Kotys, where the priests were housed; then the central Altar of Asklepios by the *Abaton*, the sacred dormitory, where pilgrims were sent to receive dreams from the god; the Temple of Artemis and the magnificent tholos tomb of Asklepios, and then, in the distance, the *palaestra* and the stadium, the magnificent *Hestiatorion* in which pilgrims were fed, and the four square courtyards and *stoae* of the pilgrim hostel, the *Katagogion*. Beyond lay the baths, and then, set in the hillside, the largest theatre that Alexanor had ever seen.

'It's not the largest theatre,' Chiron said with humour, as if reading his mind. 'Merely the best.'

Alexanor felt himself moved, despite everything, by so much beauty.

'Building in marble is also very expensive,' the priest said. 'And money leads us quickly into politics, at least the politics of patrons. Patrons and politics lead us to rivalries – Illyria and Rome, Sparta and Achaea, Aegypt and Macedon. This is not a place for one man, one city, one country. This is a place for all people. Do you understand?'

Alexanor was breathing the pine-scented air and watching the glow of the late sun on the marble below him. He felt …

He took a deep breath.

The old priest suddenly put a hand on his shoulder, and Alexanor almost collapsed as it all fell in on him. Without a conscious thought, he was weeping.

Like a summer storm, it passed, and he backed away from the old priest, humiliated.

The man in the white robe stepped off down the trail as if nothing had happened.

The next morning, Alexanor awoke from the best sleep he had experienced in a year. He lay on his pallet for perhaps two hundred beats of his heart, thinking of nothing. It was all still there: the dead comrades, the loss of his love. All there, but a little farther away.

A boy, a slave, knocked gently at the door to his cell.

'The priest Sostratos says you are to serve this morning,' the boy said, in the sing-song voice of a memorised message.

Alexanor lay still, listening to the sound of the doves outside.

He was trying to imagine a life here.

Or, really, any life at all.

The boy cleared his throat, obviously undeterred by late sleepers, and Alexanor rose, slowly, feeling every bruise and every cut anew.

He put on a plain brown *chiton* that he found hanging on the back of the door and went out into the new day. He followed the boy along a curving path, past the *Abaton* with patients' beds, and down the hill towards the great temples of Asklepios and Apollo.

Chiron waited in a spotless white wool *himation* with another man in white, younger, short and broad.

'You're right,' said the younger priest. 'He looks like a soldier.' The man smiled. 'Greetings. I am Sostratos, priest of Asklepios.'

Alexanor bowed and introduced himself.

'Alexanor of Kos. I was a marine,' he said. 'A Rhodian marine. My citizen duty.'

Sostratos nodded. 'I was a mercenary. Strictly business.' He grinned and showed a mouth full of missing and broken teeth.

Chiron waited. 'Let me see your hands,' he said.

Alexanor frowned. 'They're clean.'

Chiron held out his hands. 'Let me see.'

Alexanor sighed and held out his hands. Chiron took them and sniffed.

'Filthy. Never come to the god with your hands dirty. You must wash them at every opportunity.'

I have fallen among madmen, Alexanor thought. *You washed my hands yourself yesterday.*

'Go and wash,' Chiron said. 'And hurry.'

When he returned, only Sostratos awaited him.

'Come, we'll make the morning sacrifice. Are you pious, lad?'

Alexanor shrugged. 'I worship the gods.'

'You have to be a little more pious than that to be a priest, boy.' Sostratos seemed to find him amusing, and Alexanor fought anger. 'Have you made a sacrifice before?'

'Yes, sir,' Alexanor said, stiffly.

'Don't "sir" me – all men and women are equal before our god.'

They were at the foot of the steps to the temple, and Sostratos led the way up.

'Good morning, Bion,' he called to an older slave who was cleaning moss out of the cracks in the marble.

'Morning, Sostratos! May the light of the god shine on you!'

Sostratos indicated the Rhodian. 'This is Alexanor, from Kos. He'll be joining us.'

The slave rose, wiped his hands on his smock, and bowed.

Alexanor returned his bow, vaguely pleased that the priest had said *he'll be joining us.*

They entered the outer sanctuary and Sostratos began to sing a prayer. Alexanor didn't know it, so he waited.

'We'll sacrifice at the outside altar,' Sostratos said.

'Where is the animal?' Alexanor asked.

Sostratos smiled. 'Barley cakes, my young soldier. Most of the priests here are Pythagoreans. We don't kill animals unless we must. Some of us do not even eat meat.'

'Pythagoreans?' Alexanor asked.

'Followers of Pythagoras. We have a dozen philosophers with us at any one time. You might do well to spend some time listening.'

'I want to be a priest. To ... heal.'

'To heal instead of killing, you mean?' Sostratos took a slim wick and began lighting oil lamps along the edge of the sacred space. 'Here, you see how it's done? You light these and I'll fetch a censer.'

Alexanor lit all the bronze lamps. There were a dozen silver lamps hanging suspended from the marble vault above him; he looked up and was again struck with an awe that snapped him out of his despair. A lattice of marble vaulting hung above him, imitating wood. The central panels were painted in lapis blue, decorated with carved rosettes magnificently gilded, and the silver hanging lamps were like stars in the heavens.

A young man of his own age or a little older came up and inclined his head. He was tall and so thin that he looked as if his bones might come through his skin. He wore the same brown *chiton* that Alexanor wore.

'May I help you lower the lamps?' he said. His form of address indicated that he was a slave.

'Thanks,' Alexanor said. 'I need all the help I can get.'

The slave, if he was a slave, managed half a smile. Together they went to the wall, and the other man showed Alexanor where the chains that held the lamps were fastened, and how to lower them. There were cunning winches concealed in the walls. As he turned one, he could hear the sound of drums turning and ratchets taking the strain. When the lamp had descended fully and he went to light it, he discovered that it was very heavy.

'I'm Leon,' the other man said.

Alexanor offered him a warrior's handshake, which the other man accepted, a firm clasp hand to wrist.

'Alexanor, son of . . .'

Leon smiled. 'No patronymics here.'

Together they lowered and lit all the lamps before Sostratos returned, swinging a silver censer. The smoke billowing from the silver ball smelt of frankincense and spikenard and something even rarer, some hint that Alexanor could barely catch.

He and Leon went around the altars with the incense, singing a hymn, and Alexanor began to learn the refrain as they walked. Then the three of them went outside, collected the slave Bion, and went to the altar, where they lit a ritual fire and burnt a dozen barley cakes. Leon and Bion excused themselves, and Alexanor was left alone with the priest.

'Is Leon a free man or a slave?' Alexanor asked.

Sostratos nodded, as if a question had been answered.

'Why do you ask?'

He began to walk to a low wooden building.

Alexanor was taken aback. In the world from which he had come, a man's status – slave, freedman or citizen – was as important as gender. It was a definition.

'Leon has been with us for almost five years. He has learnt a great deal. He can do amazing work on his own, and he reasons well, but he struggles with reading. He is a slave, but that has little meaning among us – men and women can rarely control their freedom, and much of what you might call "freedom" is illusory.' The priest turned away, as if the subject wasn't particularly interesting. 'Now, this building is called the skeuotheke; our storehouse for sacred items and our sacristy. Almost all of the temple's supplies are housed here.'

He hung the censer from a hook that was clearly just for this purpose, and began putting away the ritual implements.

22

'Leon will be freed in a year or two. With luck, and a patron, he will eventually be a priest.'

'I have a great deal to learn,' Alexanor said.

'I'm glad you realise that,' the former mercenary said. 'How do you feel about work?'

Alexanor smiled. 'My … father would say I'm lazy,' he admitted.

Sostratos nodded. 'We'll soon fix that.'

A week later, Alexanor knew ten of the hymns to Apollo and two of the hymns to Asklepios. He attended his first *diagnosis*, and he was taught to oversee the needs of the pilgrims at the baths. For a citizen from a rich family, it was degrading work: he was, in almost every way, a bath-house attendant, and the hours were long and the patients very demanding. He fetched hot water, carried towels, responded to demands from men who clearly imagined themselves his superiors, and fought the urge, every day, to put one in his place.

'When I ask for a towel, I mean immediately, *pais*,' said one older man with a pot belly and a red nose. *Pais* was a word usually reserved for very small children and slaves. No one had called Alexanor *pais* since he was eight years old.

'Is this the cleanest you could make my *kline*?' asked one woman. 'Please, clean it again, *pais*.'

After a week, he presented himself to Sostratos.

'Am I being punished?'

'Not really.' The priest shrugged. 'Well, perhaps a little.'

'I am not a slave!'

'You are, in fact, a slave of the god. Best to come to an understanding of this, or leave us. Let me add that you still don't seem to understand how seriously we take cleanliness. Use the bath-house to learn about the goddess Hygeia.' He smiled. 'It's just work. You want to heal people. People are often dull, rude and dirty. It's our job to ignore the dull and the rude, and to heal the sick. Learn what you can.'

Alexanor kept his back straight and went out into the sunlight. He spent the rest of the morning thinking of finding the high priest, Chiron, and quitting, but just when his sense of injustice was peaking, Leon came to the bath-house and began stacking towels.

'I love working here,' Leon said.

23

Alexanor made a face. 'You do?'

'It's clean,' Leon said. 'Would you rather be growing vegetables or cleaning chamber pots?'

'Lord Apollo. I hadn't even thought of chamber pots.'

'Listen, the same fat old man who wants so many towels also eats too much, with the usual consequences.'

'Thanks for that image,' Alexanor said, and they both laughed, the first laugh he could remember in some time.

But that night, as he lay on his narrow pallet, he thought of Aspasia: of her body in the moonlight; of kissing her in her father's yard; of walking to the temple, hands touching as often as they dared … The hardness of her stomach under his hand, the touch of her cheek …

'Stop it,' he said aloud, to the gods.

So instead he thought of home – his brothers, his sisters …

And his dead. A dozen *epheboi* who had trained with him, their bodies fish-belly white in death. Even as his eyelids fluttered, *a hand reached for him* and he started awake.

'Stop it!'

He rose, and went out into the night to run. Running silenced all the voices – the betrayal, the death.

He ran until his legs were too tired to go on, and the next day he worked silently, and was too tired to respond to patrons who made demands. He didn't even have to bite back his retorts. And that evening, instead of staring at his dead friends in his mind's eye, he began to help Leon with his reading.

A month passed. By now he knew all the hymns. He sang them to himself when he could not sleep. He had moved from working in the bathhouse to the *Xenon*, or the *Katagogion*, sometimes at the *Abaton* itself; he emptied chamber pots and folded towels and sheets, and turned patients who needed to be turned. Some were model patients, some were touchingly thankful, and a few were difficult and surly.

Some days he went running at the end of his day, or practised *pankration* in the *palaestra*. The priests of Asklepios had their own forms of *pankration* and they were different from the ones he knew on Kos. Alexanor found himself taking an interest. He learned to eat quickly; to listen for the call of any of the priests; he learnt to wash his own dishes, or everyone's dishes, depending on need; he learnt to be clean whenever he was working. He learnt that Leon had a real problem in reading – that following words left to right and right to left could confuse him – but many of the texts had been copied by a scribe who worked them 'as the ox ploughs' and he needed to follow them wherever they led.

Despite which, they made progress.

But it was in his third month, when he was working in the fields where the temple grew both vegetables for feeding patients and many herbs and medicines, that a boy came and called his name. Sostratos came down into the field.

'What's that?' he asked, pointing at the white bulb with shooting green stalks at his feet.

'Fennel,' Alexanor said, glad that he'd been working on something he knew.

'And this?' Sostratos asked, stooping to pluck a sprig of something from the raised earth of an herb garden shaded by the taller fennel.

'Mint,' Alexanor said, but his voice betrayed his hesitation.

'Specific to …?' Sostratos asked.

Alexanor frowned. 'I don't know. My mother said it was good for the stomach.'

'Your mother is a clever woman. Go and bathe quickly and put on a clean *chiton*.'

Sostratos turned and walked off down one of the paths beaten through the stony fields.

Alexanor told the slave overseeing the fields that he had been called and went to bathe, and then went to his cell, where he found a spotless white wool *chiton* hanging on the back of his door.

His heart beat faster. He slipped it on and went to the gate, and Sostratos waved him on, towards the Temple of Asklepios. There, for the first time since his arrival, he saw the high priest. Waiting by him was Leon.

'We are raising Leon to the status of Initiate,' Sostratos said. 'You will be initiated together.'

An hour later, he was an initiate, a novice healer. Sostratos and Leon both embraced him, as did several other novices with whom he'd worked.

And then he went back to his patch of fennel in his sweat-stained brown *chiton*. He whistled the ancient *paean* of Apollo while he worked, and that night, he slept well enough.

A year later, Alexanor was just beginning to learn the ways of physical healing. Priests of the god Asklepios were divided in their philosophies, and heated arguments could erupt over diagnosis and treatment. The more conservative priests both preached and practised that all healing flowed from the gods, and especially from Asklepios, hero and demi-god; that the best cure for a patient was to sleep in the *Abaton* and receive dreams that would themselves reveal to a priest the best path to healing.

But many of the younger priests, and some of the professional doctors that trained with them, from the veteran midwives who served Asklepios and Artemis, to the surgeons who cut into living bodies to remove tumours or arrowheads, had begun to preach a different path: that the god guided training, and influenced his priests and every patient, yes; but that there were strictly empirical reasons that some drugs cured some illnesses – that willow bark and willow root alleviated pain, for example, whether administered by your mother or a priest. Alexanor learnt that radical healers in Alexandria and Athens even broke the very laws to cut up the corpses of criminals.

Then a letter from home punctured his new life like a sword wound. It was not so much the news as the manner of it – the casual way his father described the happiness of Aspasia with her new husband. Filial piety warred with feelings of betrayal.

Alexanor put the letter down, the fine Aegyptian papyrus fluttering in the lightest breeze.

> *As I explained to you, a woman as young as Aspasia needs a steady hand and an older head. She has settled to her role now.*

Alexanor's hands shook with anger, and the darkness he'd avoided for so long fell on him like a familiar blanket. His father had taken his love and given her away as an object to one of his business partners.

Alexanor found that he had crumpled the papyrus. He struggled to breathe, aware from his training that he had flushed, his heart was racing, and all from an external impulse.

He made himself breathe the way they were taught in *pankration*.

26

Alexanor hadn't even looked at a woman in a year. There were women in the sanctuary: pilgrims, even young, attractive patients; there were female slaves, and there were several female priests. And each day Alexanor expected his lust, at least, to reawaken. But nothing moved him: not the naked breasts of Sappho, the small African slave who handed towels to the female patients in the baths; not the fine figure of a young matron come to pray for sons.

Nothing.

He wondered if he had offended Aphrodite, or if Eros was lost to him. And he knew in his head that Aspasia had had no control over whom she married, that she would be trying to make the best of her lot. Just as he knew in his head that it was no fault of his that he was alive while a dozen of his fellow *epheboi* were dead. But his heart felt differently, and after a year of peaceful sleep, his nights were again haunted, and his days full of waking dreams of his lost love and his dead classmates. He ran with Leon, he worked and he did *pankration*, he read his texts, ate thin soup and worked his body as hard as he could, but sleep was elusive and his dreams were dark.

Two weeks after his father's letter arrived, he stood with Chiron and watched helplessly as his first real patient, a young man called Nikeas with an arrow wound in his leg, gradually grew worse. It was frustrating, and it had a nightmare-like quality, in that no matter what Alexanor did, the man grew worse. Alexanor washed the wound as often as he dared; he prayed until his knees and hips burned, he made incense, read entrails, and went to the altar with his invocations.

None of it mattered.

After three days, the leg had to be amputated to prevent the spread of the infection. After the amputation, performed by Philomenes the surgeon, removed the poisonous limb, the young patient turned his face to the wall and refused food.

'Talk to him,' Sostratos said. 'This is the crisis.'

'And tell him what?' Alexanor demanded bitterly. 'That the leg will grow back?'

'Without hope, he will surely die. And the crisis is the moment when the patient decides if he lives or dies. Oh, I'm sure the gods play a role. But if that young man decides ...'

'I have no hope to give him,' Alexanor said. 'I'm not really a man who believes in *hope*.'

Sostratos raised an eyebrow. 'Best learn some, then. We rely more on hope than any other medicine.'

Two nights later, while Alexanor slept fitfully on a chair by his bedside in the *Abaton*, Nikeas died.

Alexanor rose and composed the body carefully. He was unhurried in his movements, his rage carefully in check, as he washed the now-familiar body one more time, and laid the man's hands on his chest and put the linen sheet over him. Then, the fire of his anger untouched, he strode through the night to where Chiron sat, working by the light of a dozen oil lamps.

'I cannot be a healer,' he spat. He'd hoped to be composed and simple; instead, his anger leapt out of him and he snarled, 'I can only kill.'

Chiron was sitting at a table, writing with a stylus on wax tablets that Leon, the former slave, was copying slowly on papyrus. Leon looked away.

Chiron sat back. 'You want to leave us?' he asked.

Alexanor blinked. 'Yes,' he said.

Chiron nodded. 'Interesting. Leon, give us a moment, eh?'

The thin man got up. On his way out, he put a hand on Alexanor's shoulder.

'Don't go,' he said.

Chiron steepled his hands. 'So, Alexanor,' he said. 'Why doesn't the god heal *all* sick people?'

Alexanor was frustrated, and very tired. And he didn't really like Chiron. So he shrugged.

'No idea,' he said dismissively.

Chiron nodded. 'Me neither. Here's the important thing, though. It's not your fault. When they live, you may have played some small role – the right medicine, the right diagnosis. Or not – many we heal here might have healed at home. We know so little, Alexanor. And when they die?' The old man spread his hands. 'Who knows why they die? Who knows why Nikeas was hit with an arrow? He and his brother were shooting at marks.'

'All I know is that he died,' Alexanor said. 'I am a killer.'

Chiron nodded. 'Bullshit,' he said.

Alexanor's head snapped back as if he'd been struck.

'Listen, *pais*.' Chiron's voice was different. He was angry, too. 'I know that you like to make yourself responsible for anything that happens. Up to a point, that's laudable – beyond that, it's *hubris*. You are a proud man – far too proud. And you like to wallow in your emotions. I'll guess you were your mother's favourite. *So intelligent*.'

Alexanor literally writhed at those words.

'If you want to leave, leave. Don't come and tell me so. There are no bars on our doors – even the slaves can just walk away.'

Alexanor started to stand, and was ashamed and humiliated that hot tears were coming from his eyes. Angry words crowded to his lips.

'But I think you should stay,' Chiron said. 'You're going to be a brilliant priest, if we all survive your training.' He smiled. 'By Apollo, *pais*. I've lost enough patients to crew a warship in Hades. Get over yourself and get back to work.'

Even then, with Chiron's words burning in his ears, Alexanor was moved by some spirit of self-destruction to leave – to flee. He made it as far as the side gate, the gate that looked west into the mountains, where distant villages showed in the darkness as tiny pinpoints of firelight, and he stopped, and stood there in an agony of indecision.

He heard the sound of running feet, and turned to find Leon, his long body gleaming with sweat.

'Don't leave,' Leon said. 'I'll have to run all by myself.' He put a hand on the taller man's shoulder. 'And you're teaching me to read. And frankly, you are the only rich man who's ever taken an interest in me. I need a patron. Stick it out, boss. Don't quit.'

Alexanor managed a smile, and went back to his room. He prayed a little, and then he lay down, and slept without a dream – haunted neither by love nor death.

CHAPTER TWO

⚍ ⚍

Sacred Sanctuary of Asklepios, Epidauros, Northern Peloponnese

223 BCE

'Let me see your hands,' the old priest said.

Alexanor hid a smile. Once he might have bridled; no man training seriously for the priesthood of Asklepios would dare to bring dirty hands to the temple. But five years had changed him: five years of discovering that the great Asklepion was full of the sons of rich men who were visiting to drink wine and chase fine young bodies. Only a handful of the novices were serious. And sometimes they came to the temple with dirty hands.

He held his out.

The older priest looked at them.

'Dirt under your nails can kill a patient,' he said, for the thousandth time. 'Old blood can carry the arrows of Apollo from one visitor to another.'

Alexanor nodded politely. 'Yes, Hierophant.'

Sometimes he worried that Chiron was too old, and repeated himself too often.

'Don't "Hierophant" me,' the old priest muttered.

It was early, very early; the great temple complex was silent. The magnificent temple to the God of Healing rose among the pines, its innumerable pillars of milk-white marble as superb today as they had been on the evening of Alexanor's arrival five years before. This

30

morning they were touched with pink as the sun rose; Apollo's chariot had not yet crested the eastern hills, and the light had a presence.

Alexanor loved serving the god in the early morning. He loved being alone at the altar ...

'Fetch some incense, will you, *pais?*' the old man snapped, interrupting his reverie.

The term *pais* no longer rankled. Alexanor had learnt many things in five years at the temple: to run like the wind; to fight with his hands; to open a man's body and remove his impurities; to balance four humours; and to know when to take no action at all. He'd learnt to forget, as well – to forget his home, his brothers and sisters. *Aspasia. The dead.*

The last rule, the great unwritten rule of all the followers of Pythagoras and Hippocrates and Apollo's son Asklepios himself, was one that applied not just to the crisis of treatment but to everyday life, to speech and action. He knew that the old priest meant no insult; hence, there was no reason for him to take insult.

As if reading his mind, the older priest made a wry face.

'Apologies, Alexanor. But the new slaves have not put out the water or the censer. I'll fetch the water.'

'Yes, master,' Alexanor said. And when he said the word master, he meant it.

He went back down the long aisle of the temple, his white leather sandals making a rhythmic sound on the floor that echoed up into the coffered ceiling.

Doves cooed. The pink light of morning seemed to radiate from the marble, pulsing like the beat of a divine heart. Alexanor paused at the top of the temple steps, overwhelmed. There was something bubbling in the world – something immanent. He extended his arms in an attitude of prayer.

But the moment passed. He folded his arms and trotted down the steps, intent on his duty.

He was tempted to run, once he was down the steps. It was a magnificent morning, but then, almost every morning at the Temple of Asklepios was superb, and five years had not robbed the mornings of wonder. The sun was just rising over the hills away to the east; the mountains to the west were tipped in gold and orange. The light was like the hand of Apollo gilding the world, and changed subtly from rose pink to golden.

Running would make him sweat, and sweat was dirt in the eyes of the god. Good dirt, honourably earned when you played a game, but not for serving at the altar in the first light of Apollo's sun. He walked briskly, settling his *himation*, a garment unsuited to athletics at the best of times.

The skeuotheke was familiar ground now, the small wooden building by the temple that housed all the things a priest didn't want to intrude in the temple: stores of clean white linen cloth; spare vases and metal ewers; spare braziers and fine charcoal and incense – not the ones of solid gold and silver, given by the great donors like the king of Macedon or the king of Aegypt. They lay in wood shavings in the treasury under the floor, behind the altar, cased in white marble. Here were the plainer ones of bronze for every day. Alexanor took a silvered-bronze censer from its hook and moved it to the narrow window built for just this purpose; he opened the shutter and hung the censer's chain, and then used tongs to move small chunks of charcoal into the censer. It was quicker, he knew, to use his hands – quicker and much dirtier, and wearing a milk-white *himation* was difficult enough on the very easiest day. All of them had brown *himations* for work, but white for serving at the altars.

Alexanor half-filled the pierced silver ball, and then lit it from the oil lamp that burnt all year: a sacred fire brought down from a lightning bolt of Zeus on the slopes of Olympus and passed from temple to temple. He thought of his family home on Rhodes; of the slave who had taught him to kindle fire on Kos. He held one coal in the tongs over the flame until it snapped and popped, and then dropped it into the others and blew gently until all the coals were burning well. Then he added a spoonful of incense, saying aloud a prayer for the intercession of his god, and only then, after all was billowing smoke out of the window, did he close the top of the censer, singeing his fingers in the process.

He took the lit censer by the chain, and swinging it softly, he walked back out of the skeuotheke and up the steps of the great temple. His eyes were drawn, as they always were, to the painted figures in the pediment, Greek men and Amazons fighting a brutal but beautiful battle. Just over his head, a magnificent woman on horseback thrust a spear through a naked hoplite who lay on the ground.

What a savage wound that would make, he thought.

Alexanor passed into the temple. Chiron and Leon were the only men present; the complex of fifty buildings seemed as silent as Alexanor imagined the underworld to be. Chiron had the water ewers filled for purification and Leon, working with him, had lit the oil lamps from another branch of the sacred fire. The master priest took the censer from Alexanor with a regal bow and censed the altars. They offered barley cakes as a sacrifice, and together they sang the service of the dawn to the rising sun, and a hymn to Epidauros, son of Apollo, and then the *paean* to the god Apollo.

Alexanor loved ritual, and he let his mind float away amid the incense and the song. It was faster than meditation; his thoughts died away and he was still, alive with his sense of the immanence of his god. His thoughts turned to the terrible wound dealt to the fallen Greek by the mounted Amazon. He considered them, and it came to him, a vision from the god: *the sudden onset, felt the dirt under his body, the horse rearing over him …*

There was a loud metallic *crash*. He snapped into reality, saved from the downward stroke of the Amazon's spear. A pair of slaves had entered the south end of the temple and had begun to wash the floor, apparently unmoved by either the sacred or the aesthetic. One of them had kicked over his bronze bucket.

Chiron finished the morning invocation as Alexanor stood as confused as a man newly awakened from a dream. The two men stood side by side in the perfumed smoke for perhaps ten beats of their hearts.

They bowed to the images of Apollo and his sons, Asklepios and Epidauros, in whose name the hospital had been built.

'Do you ever …?' Alexanor was embarrassed the moment he opened his mouth. He flushed.

'Speak, lad,' the older priest said. 'Do I ever? Ever what? Wash?' He laughed.

Alexanor smiled. 'No, master. Do you ever have dreams so real …?'

'I am a priest of the god,' Chiron said. 'Of course I have dreams that are real.'

Alexanor was looking off into the middle distance beyond the temple. He sighed, annoyed with himself. Closer to, Bion was admonishing the two new slaves. Their lowered voices carried, echoing through the sacred space.

'Well,' said the older priest, understanding his silence. 'Shall we change out of these robes and see who has come to be healed today?'

He handed the censer to Leon and swept out of the temple.

Almost no one came to be healed early in the morning. It was twenty stades to the port and forty or more to a good town. Men either came by ship, to the town on the coast, or via Hermione or Troezen, or by land, coming down through the Peloponnese from Corinth or Isthmia by easy stages; after all, most of the visitors were sick. New guests came in the heat of afternoon; veteran guests came in early evening, when the shade was cool and the dinner was ready to be served. The great temple had beds for two hundred guests, maintained by enormous donations from the distant kings who tried to control Greece with armies and bribes: Antigonus Doson, king of Macedon, and Ptolemy of Aegypt, whose ambassador to Athens lay on one of their beds, recovering from an operation and dreaming, Alexanor hoped, of the god.

Alexanor put away the ritual vessels and went to his cell, where he changed his spotless white *himation* for the plain brown wool *chiton* and a light *chlamys*; the *chlamys* was more an expression of his youth and status as a junior priest than it was a necessary garment. In the month of Agrianios – being Rhodian-born Alexanor always thought in the Rhodian months, even in the Peloponnese – it was always hot. Not the brutal heat of the Attic plain, where his father had estates; more like the sea-cooled late summer of the Aegean islands, Rhodes or Lesvos, where he had grown to manhood, and Kos, where he had begun to dream of medicine and the gods.

He untied his white sandals, something only priests and rich women wore, and changed them for good Laconian shoes, a style favoured by soldiers and men who had to walk. He emerged from his cell to find Chiron standing in the long hall of pillars, the *stoa* of Kotys, off which they lived, looking out of the window. It was cool under the shade of the high roof, even on the second storey, where the priests slept.

Chiron was watching a dust cloud to the west. Visitors on horseback were often visible stades and stades away; the sanctuary had been placed where it was to provide a beautiful view for initiates, guests, and the gods themselves. In the busy time in spring, sharp-eyed slaves and young under-priests would sound trumpets from the hillside to announce important visitors, whose purple clothes and gold horse trappings would show ten stades away.

Today's visitors glinted more bronze than gold. Alexanor knew the colour.

'At dinner last night the Aegyptian was saying there was trouble in the west,' the older man said.

'That is your diagnosis, sir?' Alexanor asked. 'That the trouble is coming here?'

Chiron smiled. 'Men are riding to us swiftly, and behind them comes another group, larger, also riding swiftly.' He shrugged. 'One does not have to be Plato to guess that trouble is coming here. Come – let us greet them.'

But the old priest paused at his cell and took from the peg on his door, not the sword that hung there, but his stainless white *himation*, which he put back on, and he picked up the staff of his rank.

He rapped on the door of the next cell with his knuckles.

'Sostratos!' he called. 'Trouble.'

'On my way,' came the answer.

Sostratos was now a senior priest – old, wise, and humble, quicker with a joke than Chiron but lacking something of his dignity. Alexanor had long since learnt that Sostratos had fought the Gauls in his youth, taken a wound that should have been his death, and been healed by a priest of Asklepios.

A woman's voice floated through the door; a squeal, and a protest, and the door opened. The old soldier was naked, the scar of his near death an angry brown line like a trench that ran from the top of his groin to his ribs. He slipped a sword-belt over his shoulder, snapped a *chlamys* off the door and came out on to the portico of the *stoa*.

Chiron led the way down the stairs at a rapid rate; down from the upper level of the *stoa*, then along the path past the altar of Asklepios, out past the stadium to the edge of the sacred precinct, where there was a large courtyard, stables, and two wine shops which operated with the toleration, if not the approval, of the priests. A foreigner, a northerner, someone's slave with ugly white skin and pale hair, sat in the dust with a carpet covered in amulets – tin hands; bronze feet;

a penis, a vulva – and a variety of statues in pale yellow pottery: an Athena, far from her home; several Aphrodites, and a veritable phalanx of Apollos and Asklepioses.

He didn't glance at the two priests emerging from the gate.

Empedocles, the steward, hurried towards them from the gatehouse. 'How can I help you, Alexanor?' he asked.

He was more efficient than servile. He was as Greek as Alexanor himself, or more so; he'd been sold to the temple as a child, to pay his father's gambling debts, it was said.

Chiron put a hand on his arm.

'Maybe trouble,' he said. 'Maybe I'm an old fool. But close the inner west gate and warn the guests. Put a guard on the *Propylon*.'

'At once!'

Empedocles bowed deeply and, hiking his long robe, ran for the gatehouse.

'I'll see to the Epidauros,' Sostratos said.

The Epidauros was the hospital itself, dedicated to the son of the god.

Chiron slapped his shoulder and walked towards the road. There was an outer gate, where the road came into the stable yard.

Alexanor had never seen the outer gate closed. It was only a wooden bar across the road.

'Master? What is happening?' he asked.

He had never seen the way of the pilgrims barred, and something in Chiron's posture unnerved him.

Chiron raised an eyebrow. 'I have no idea.'

'Will you close the outer gate?' Alexanor asked.

The older priest gave him a wry smile. 'What is the first rule?'

Alexanor nodded. 'Commit no *hubris*. Do no harm.'

'It applies even here. We will receive these visitors and see what the god has sent us.'

Chiron turned to the open outer gate.

The horses were audible now: a steady patter of hoof beats like rain on a roof. Perhaps a dozen horses, ridden hard. A boy ran into the stables and a pair of slaves emerged. One brought water and began to fill a horse trough.

Chiron leant on his staff. It was nothing but a long stick of cornel wood, as tall as his shoulders, bent at the top, no more than any shepherd in Arkadia would carry. But, in any of the forty Asklepions around the Greek world, the staff marked a master priest, and it had become Alexanor's dearest wish. Even if it was twenty years away. He was not yet a full priest; he had far to go.

The patter of hoof beats became a roar; the earth seemed to tremble.

The horsemen seemed to flood into the courtyard. There were only nine, but they came in at a fast trot, and one pulled his horse up so sharply that the big creature reared; it was certainly a military horse. Two of the men had armour on, confirming his diagnosis. One horse had a corpse tied over its back.

'You take the first party,' Chiron said with a gentle inclination of his head. 'I will await the second.'

'Master,' Alexanor said.

It was a privilege to be entrusted with guests. Alexanor went forward even as the big man on the biggest horse slipped to the ground. He had bright red hair, was a foot taller than Alexanor, and had muscles on top of his muscles.

'I need a priest,' Red-hair snapped.

Alexanor walked past him. On the next horse was the corpse, face down over the horse's back. But something told Alexanor that the man was not dead.

He raised the wounded man's head gently. He put his cheek by his mouth, as if waiting for a kiss.

'Is he alive?' Red-hair asked, anxiously.

'No thanks to you,' Alexanor said.

One was not supposed to say such things, but it was insane; the man on the back of the horse, who had long, dark hair like a Spartan, was badly wounded. He'd lost so much blood that his skin had the pale look of a corpse, and Alexanor held himself still inside, so as not to flinch. But his own dead were years behind him; those wounds were scarred over, no longer tender.

The worst wound in the man over the horse that Alexanor could see was a long gash in his arm, but as he locked an arm around the wounded youth to move him, he saw a puncture in the abdominal cavity.

'You should not have moved him at all,' Alexanor went on.

'Fucking Spartans would have killed him if I left him,' Red-hair said. 'Kleostratos! Take the horses!'

A Thracian slipped from his mount and began gathering reins. Slaves moved to help him.

'You may have killed him just as effectively.' Alexanor turned. 'Bion!' he called. 'Get this man down where I can examine him. And *be gentle.* You know the drill.' Alexanor turned to the stable boy, the *pais* who ran errands. 'Get a stretcher from the baths. Run,' he snapped. 'Bring more slaves.'

Red-hair watched the big slave untie the wounded man. Now that Alexanor had a moment and there was less dust, he could see that all of them had wounds: slashes to the forearm; cuts to the shoulder; or contusions and abrasions that he knew came to men who wore armour – lacerations under the armpits and at the neck, for example, where a mounted man's cuirass bit into the soft flesh. He saw them on every man.

'Spartans are right behind us, priest,' Red-hair called. 'You are a priest, right?'

Bion lifted the wounded man, grunting at the effort. The victim was tall, and very strong, and Alexanor had to catch his legs and feet to prevent Bion from dropping him. Laid on his back, the man was as tall as a Titan, with as much muscle as Red-hair and a strong face, the kind of face Alexanor associated with athletes and boxers: handsome, blunt.

'You are?'

Alexanor directed his comment to Red-hair, but he was already kneeling in the dust by the wounded man. Patient. Guest. He didn't look at Red-hair. His eyes were on the guest's wounds, which were, as he expected, all the result of combat.

'I am Dinaeos. I am a citizen of Megalopolis. The men of Sparta attacked us in the night and stormed our city. Their king, Cleomenes, has sworn to wipe us out.'

He seemed to be making an effort to speak slowly; to sound rational. The priest could tell he was on the edge of panic; exhausted, probably. No sleep, wounds, a friend dying ...

'We fought until the end,' the man said with pride. 'We held the gate so that the citizens could escape. *He* wouldn't have left even then.'

Alexanor could see the man's exhaustion, and the dried blood all the way up his arm. He actually *felt* the man's tiredness, as if for a moment he was in the wounded body, not his own.

'You all need rest and treatment,' he said.

'Not without my friend,' Dinaeos said.

'Dinaeos,' he said, looking up, 'the best favour you can do this man is to go immediately to the baths. Every one of you.'

Alexanor spoke with authority. He was a priest of the god, a doctor, and an aristocrat; the tone of command came easily to him.

Dinaeos shook his head. 'When he goes in, I go in. I told you, the Spartans are right behind us.'

'You speak well,' Alexanor said. 'Your friend is in the hands of the god, as you should be, too. Go and bathe!'

The Achaeans with Dinaeos began to sag; three of them turned, avoiding slaves coming out of the temple precinct, and went in. Dinaeos stood his ground.

Two slaves ran up, big men with a wooden stretcher on their shoulders.

'Easy there,' Alexanor said.

He put a hand directly on the wounded man's side and held the wound as the man was lifted and carefully rolled onto the stretcher, his fingers holding the sides of the puncture steady. It was bleeding, but there was no abdominal fluid that he could smell; the only hope the man had was that his intestines had not been pierced.

'Straight to the Epidauros. Go!' Alexanor said. He was thinking of the wound.

The slaves grunted. Even for two, the wounded Titan was a heavy load.

They started for the gate.

The second party came into the wide yard at a canter, scattering horses and slaves; one of the Achaeans was ridden down, and Bion was struck with a javelin stave.

The newcomers were all professional cavalrymen; Alexanor thought that they looked like mercenaries, with soft boots and wide-brimmed hats, and dust coating every surface of their bodies. One man glanced at him, and Alexanor knew him for a killer; his eyes had that look. Contempt for life.

'Halt!' called a Spartan voice. 'No one move!'

Alexanor shoved one of the slaves carrying the wounded man.

'Ignore him. Go.'

They went.

Dinaeos drew the sword he wore under his arm, covering the slaves. They had only a few steps to go to reach the closed gate of the sanctuary. They were strong and quick, and Alexanor noted their courage. Slaves who were brave deserved reward.

The gate opened for them; someone was sharp.

One of the mercenaries rose on his horse to throw a javelin. His arm went back and he threw.

Dinaeos stepped past Alexanor. Raising his short cloak as a shield and covering the young priest, he cut the javelin out of the air with his sword. The head bit into the sand and the shaft came up and struck Alexanor a stinging blow to the shin, but he shook it off.

The Thracian man who had taken the horses emerged from the stable, took the javelin out of the ground as if he'd planned such a thing all along, and stepped up beside Dinaeos. The other men who'd ridden in first were shuffling. One, the youngest, with a bloody bandage on his head, whimpered and ran into the grove, but the others closed up around Dinaeos.

The Spartan pointed at the running man.

'Get him,' he said.

One of the mercenaries followed the running man at a trot into the sacred grove.

The Spartan dismounted. He didn't seem tired. He was as tall as the wounded Titan, thin-faced and black-bearded, his scarlet cloak like a banner in the sun. He looked straight at Dinaeos.

'Where is he?' he asked. 'Don't tell me he's still alive.'

'Come and find out,' said Dinaeos.

The Spartan shrugged. 'Very brave. I assume he was on that stretcher. And now in the Asklepion.' He turned to Alexanor, but Chiron emerged from the dust cloud – a tall old man in white, with a staff. 'Just save me the time. Is he dead or alive?'

The old priest pointed. 'Halt,' he said.

'Answer me,' spat the Spartan, to the red-headed Achaean. He ignored the older priest as a person of no consequence.

'Stop your impiety or take the consequence,' the priest said.

His tone carried conviction; one of the Thessalian mercenaries shuffled his horse back, and another made an avert sign.

'Open the gates, and no one gets hurt,' the Spartan said. 'Well, almost no one,' he added with nasty smile, and one of the mercenaries laughed.

Alexanor was beginning to be afraid. But the part of his mind trained to think kept going. *Thessalians*, he thought. *These are Thessalians; trained killers.* Their clothing and their horses identified them, and the habit of diagnosis was strong, even in moments like this.

'No,' Chiron said. It was the kind of 'no' you said to a child, or a slave with a foolish, time-wasting idea. 'The precinct is sacred, even to Spartans.'

'Keep your superstitious crap for the peasants,' the Spartan said. 'Open the gates or I'll open them, and there will be blood.'

'There is always blood,' the old priest said. 'Bodies are full of it.'

'Stupid old fool,' the Spartan said. 'I am here on the business of the king of Sparta. Let me past.'

The stupid old fool stood his ground. He raised his hand and slammed his staff into the ground so that it seemed rooted in the earth.

'No,' he said.

'Out of my fucking way,' the Spartan growled, and he reached for his sword.

Chiron moved forward. He didn't seem to move fast; it was almost as if he floated, his white *himation* hiding his limbs, the superb fabric like a cloud. His left hand pinned the Spartan's sword arm against his chest as he reached to draw; his right hand shot out, and the palm of his hand struck the Spartan on the nasal of his magnificent helmet. Still he went forward. The Spartan's head snapped back, and suddenly he was thrown full-length in the dust. The old man kept hold of his sword hand and turned him into the throw, then knelt by the fallen Spartan, holding his arm behind his back.

It happened so fast that it was only in retrospect that Alexanor realised he'd heard the man's elbow break.

'Ride away or I kill him,' the old priest said to the Thessalians. 'Ride away now. I assume he's your employer. Or stay and be shot down by my archers.'

He looked at them. The Spartan made an attempt to escape, and then gave a scream.

The old priest was unrelenting. 'I care little. Your man has committed an impiety and *hubris*, and my god will rejoice if I practise a little anatomy on him. Did you know that this soft spot here, just forward of the ear, is the perfect place to kill a man if you want to avoid spoiling his face?' The old man's voice was calm and level.

The Thessalians looked at each other.

'Don't do it!' half-screamed the Spartan. He was brave enough; he tried to keep the pain out of his voice, but his elbow was in agony. 'Kill them! Gods damn you, priest.'

'Me?' the priest asked. 'Me? I have not offered impiety at the precinct of the god. You have.'

'Hypocrite! Pious fake!'

The Spartan was face down in the dust, but he was trying to fight. Even with the priest's hand at his neck, he was moving; even with an arm behind his back in a submission hold, he writhed against the pain in his elbow.

'Do not be foolish and make me kill you,' said the old man. 'Ride, you mercenaries. And do not return.'

Alexanor had watched the whole drama from the safety of the red-haired cavalryman's cloak. Now he turned and knelt by his teacher and passed him his knife, which the older priest immediately pressed to the Spartan's throat.

The officer's writhing stopped. He felt the knife and he sagged.

The Thessalians turned their horses. One looked at the sacred grove, where the lone Thessalian had chased the fugitive. He looked a moment for his partner, and then shrugged, looked at the gatehouse walls, and turned his horse.

'Oh, you are the fucking *king* of doctors.' Dinaeos managed a laugh. 'Please let me kill him.'

'No,' Chiron said in the same peremptory tone he'd used to the Spartan. 'By the great god Apollo, you men come to us dirty with your foolish violence, Greek against Greek. I feel polluted just being with you.'

He rose.

The Spartan was on his feet in an instant – a remarkable feet of gymnastics for a man with a broken elbow. He stepped back and reached, left-handed, for his sword.

Chiron followed him, his *himation* floating behind him, and pinned his arm again.

The Spartan gave a choked scream.

'Let go of your violence,' Chiron said. 'Come inside and let me set your arm.'

'Fuck you. Fuck you, you charlatan. Come inside so you can poison me? I'd rather sleep in a den of vipers. I will come back here with an army and loot this place to the ground. I will find your family and kill every one of them, or sell them to brothels. I will burn your home to the ground, and I will …' The fear and the hate boiled out of him; his face was ugly with pain and anger.

'You refuse treatment?' Chiron's voice was loud. 'Then be gone.'

He let go of the Spartan's arm, and the weight of the man's hand dragged at his elbow and he screamed with pain and fell to his knees.

Chiron turned his back. He pointed at Dinaeos.

'Sheathe that sword,' he said.

Dinaeos obeyed.

The remaining Thessalian emerged from the sacred grove, his horse's head up, ears back.

'You speak Greek?' the old priest snapped.

Dinaeos had his sword out again, and Alexanor was watching the Spartan struggle for composure. He could see that Chiron's casual humiliation of the man had been an error; he could see that the Spartan would never forgive what had just happened.

He was trying to rise again.

Alexanor thought he must be very strong and very brave. With a sprained shoulder and a broken elbow, most men would lie and whimper.

The Spartan got one foot under himself and tried to rise. He was trying to get at the sword under his left armpit with his left hand, and in the effort he dropped the weapon.

The Thessalian nodded. 'Of course I speak Greek.'

'Then take your officer and ride,' Chiron said.

The Thessalian was older than the others, in a fine cloak with a purple stripe.

'Or?' He didn't threaten. He sounded relaxed.

Alexanor stepped past the Spartan officer and snapped up the sword before the man could do it himself. He noted the beautiful work on the man's helmet: the tall crest, and the strap under the chin, which held the two cheek plates together under the man's beard. He was trained to see all these things, and others: the redness in the man's eyes, from dust and pain; the missing tooth; the signs of dehydration.

'Or we fuck you up,' said Sostratos, from the gate.

He had four priests with him and a dozen slaves, all carrying staves

43

or spears. They filled the stable yard, and the Thessalian nodded.

'No!' bellowed the Spartan.

The Thessalian came to a decision. He backed his horse, turned it, and then plucked the Spartan off the ground with an arm around his waist, like a centaur taking a Lapith woman, and rode away.

Chiron sagged to one knee. 'You took your time, Sostratos,' he said. 'I am too old for this.'

'I stopped for a cup of wine,' the former mercenary said with his usual sarcasm. 'All right – everyone take a wounded man. Here we go. Put those weapons up! You! What are you, an Achaean? Sheathe. Alexanor, what the hell is that in your hand?'

Alexanor realised he was still holding the Spartan's sword.

He turned to Dinaeos. 'Who was that man?' he asked.

Dinaeos looked as if he might collapse in the stable yard, but he managed a feral smile.

'That's Nabis,' he said. 'The Spartan king's enforcer. A bad man and a worse enemy.'

Alexanor got an arm under the redhead's shoulder and supported him. The young Achaean seemed to be made of stone – particularly heavy stone. But Alexanor was not weak; he used his back and held the big man up.

'Come on,' he said. 'I ordered you to the baths, and I meant it.'

As soon as the Achaeans were in the healing houses with attendants to look at their wounds, Alexanor ran to the Epidauros to look at his principal 'guest'. He found Chiron standing over the young giant's bed.

'A fine specimen,' Chiron said, as Alexanor ran up. 'No need to run, young man. If the ride here didn't kill him, he'll live until the infection takes him.'

'What is your diagnosis, Hierophant?' Alexanor asked.

'Mine?'

The old doctor smiled, just a little. Alexanor could see that, despite his bold face, he was shaken: his lips were pale, his eyes a little too wide, pupils dilated. Alexanor knew he would be showing these signs himself. He had been afraid, and he had been forced to act while full of the daemon of the god of war, that influx of power that seemed to flow along with fear.

He had a moment to reflect that once he would have channelled all that fear into violent action. He smiled.

The old man met Alexanor's smile with his own, and it was steady. He put out a hand and rested it on Alexanor's shoulder.

'I told you this guest was yours, Alexanor, and I meant it. I saw this in the smoke of dawn. This one is for you. If he lives, he will make your reputation; if he dies, it is the will of the god. So, what is *your* diagnosis?'

Alexanor wanted nothing more than to go to his narrow bed; by now, his room slaves would have made it. Crisp white linen and a thick, white wool blanket ...

Fear makes you tired. Alexanor knew this, both from scrolls and from experience. He looked at the young man on the bed.

Young he might be; between twenty-five and thirty, fully bearded. His skin was smooth, and he was heavily muscled. But the muscles were those of a man who worked on a farm and not those of someone who only knew sweat in the gymnasium. But his size, and the health of his hair, proclaimed him a rich man, as did the gold ring on his left hand.

His left arm had two wounds – superficial, but deserving of Alexanor's immediate attention. Both were long slashes: sword cuts to a mounted man's bridle hand. The long gash under the man's right arm had been inflicted while the arm was up. The puncture wound in his right side, though ...

'I believe he was stabbed while he lay on the ground, unhorsed,' Alexanor said.

As he said the words he thought of the Amazon and the Greek on the temple pediment, and he felt the presence of his god. *Ahhh, now I understand.*

'Interesting, and highly probable, although I can't say that such a guess will help him in any way. What caused this wound?' Chiron asked.

Sostratos appeared and began to examine the Aegyptian ambassador to Athens, who lay three beds away. Two slaves fanned the ambassador while he was watching the priests and the wounded man with avid curiosity.

Alexanor narrowed his eyes and bent low, sniffing at the wound.

'Not a spearhead,' he said. 'A spike, or perhaps a *saurauter*. Perhaps a cavalry spear, reversed.'

'Agreed,' Chiron said.

'It is possible that it has passed between the coils of the intestine.'

'Unlikely.'

'The edges of such spikes are rarely sharpened,' Alexanor said.

Chiron raised an eyebrow, but Sostratos interrupted.

'He's right, you know. Don't be a stick, Chiron. If this boy got pricked by a *saurauter*, his intestines may be whole.'

'There is no smell of the fluids of the abdomen,' Alexanor said.

Chiron bent down and sniffed.

'So? What do you propose to do for the puncture?' he asked.

'I will clean and bandage the outward wounds – indeed, I will have them bathed, coated in boiled wine, and wrapped. But the puncture wound?' Alexanor shook his head. 'I will do nothing.'

Chiron nodded. Sostratos nodded.

'Is that right?'

Alexanor thought about Nikeas, dying in the night. He'd lost twenty more patients since young Nikeas, but the first remained the hardest.

Chiron shrugged. He looked at his peer, who smiled.

'I have no idea,' he said. 'He is your patient, and he will live or die at the whim of the gods. What is your reasoning?'

Alexanor's turn to shrug.

'I have no idea what has happened inside the abdomen,' he said. 'I do not want to introduce anything foreign. Even food could kill. So I will take no action and do no further harm. But I will say, with … caution … that if there is no smell of abdominal fluid after a twenty-hour ride, it seems possible that he will live.'

Chiron frowned. 'There is something in what you say. I will leave you to your washing and bandaging the lacerations. He is a healthy young hero, and if he survives the crisis, he may yet live, as you say.'

Alexanor was trying to imagine what it had been like – the young man lying, unhorsed, already wounded, and a man over him on horse-back stabbing down, over and over. Did the victim scramble free only to be stabbed, in the end, before he could get to his feet? Or was he lying stunned from his fall?

He imagined it like the pediment of the temple. He looked at the young man's back, but found no exit wound, so the blow had not been hard enough to pin him to the earth.

He nodded respectfully to his teachers.

'Excuse me. I'll fetch what I need.'

'Send for Leon,' Sostratos said. 'You two always work together – he needs the practice.'

Sostratos glanced at the wounded man when Alexanor stepped into the room where practical supplies were kept. He glanced at Chiron.

'You know what this means?' he asked.

Chiron nodded. 'It means that if Alexanor is correct, and the young warrior lives, we must raise him to the rank of full priest.'

Sostratos winked at Alexanor's back, visible through the narrow doorway.

'Far too soon,' he said. 'Let him sweat another fifteen years. No, I mean that Sparta has attacked Megalopolis, and thus, the Achaean league. And been successful.' He looked back at the Aegyptian ambassador.

Chiron made a sign of negation. 'This is nothing to do with us.'

'Apollo's beard, how old are you? There was a Spartiate in your outer yard willing to defile the sanctuary. We are not immune from the politics of this peninsula.' Sostratos shook his head.

Chiron frowned again. 'He was young and foolish. His king—'

'Is young and ambitious. Surely ...'

Alexanor returned with the tools of his trade and two slaves bearing wine and honey and a little box of drugs. He sat on a stool and began to wash the wounds on the left arm, first with clean water, then with olive oil.

The wounded man gave a cry and tried to roll over.

Alexanor was perfectly still for a moment.

The young man's eyes fluttered open and then closed.

'Interesting,' Chiron said. He held up the man's right hand, coated in dried blood, and with blood under the nails. 'He reminds me of someone,' he said, and nodded. 'Report to me if there is a change.'

When the other Achaeans were clean they were carried to the Epidauros. Aristaenos, the youngest, was in the worst state. Alexanor sat with him for a while, but Aristaenos turned his face to the wall and refused to speak.

Dinaeos, when questioned, lay back on his bed.

'He ran from the fight in the courtyard. He is ashamed.'

'Shame can kill a man,' Alexanor said.

'He cut and ran when his friends needed him,' Dinaeos said. 'Maybe death is the kindest thing.'

Alexanor was cleaning his scalpel. He paused.

'I take it you have never betrayed anyone out of fear, or failed a friend?' he said, as mildly as he could manage.

'Fuck no,' Dinaeos said. 'Do I look like a coward? When you're born with red hair, you learn to fight. I *like* to fight.'

'Perhaps young Aristaenos has never fought before.'

Alexanor used pumice to clean his scalpel to mirror brightness. For some cuts, he would use obsidian from a volcano, but here ...

Dinaeos sighed. 'I know what you are at. I've seen it too. Men get ... taken ... by fear. Good men. But hungry, wet, cold, and tired, suddenly they are afraid. You think it is that? And not that he is base-born, because his mother fucked some slave?'

'That seems an odd notion,' Alexanor said. 'And a terrible thing to say of a man. Do you always say such things?'

'You talk like *him*.' Dinaeos shook his head. 'Yes, I'm a fuckwit. I say whatever comes into my head. No life of politics for me!'

Alexanor nodded. 'Some men are braver than others, I allow. But I don't see much sign that it is due to birth, but rather, to inclination and training. Who are the others? The man with the sword cut on his thigh? And the tall man with the puncture wound in his side?'

'Lykortas, son of Thearidas, took that sword cut in the agora of Megalopolis, defending a gaggle of women and children. He's not even one of us – he's a student at the Academy in Athens.' Dinaeos leant over the wounded man, who was conscious.

'You ... exaggerate my role,' the wounded man said. 'I was trying to run, and Spartans kept getting in my ... way.'

Alexanor knelt by the man and looked carefully at the wound. Despite a lot of dried blood that the slaves hadn't cleaned away, it was a neat slice. The boy had no fat, and the blade had done little damage to the muscle.

'You'll be with us for a while,' Alexanor said cheerfully. 'But with the help of the god and a gentle touch from Hygeia you'll have a pretty scar and nothing more.'

'That's wonderful,' the young man said. His eyes sparkled as if he had a fever. 'I really only came for the pretty scar.' He winked.

Alexanor winked back.

'You're very attractive, doctor,' Lykortas said wickedly. 'Or am I just happy to be alive?'

'Lock up the altar boys,' Alexanor said to Leon. Leon smiled carefully.

'And the badly wounded man?'

Alexanor began cleaning the student's wound as he spoke. Leon handed him a soft brush, and then a length of boiled linen.

'He's the bravest man in our city,' Dinaeos said. 'By Ares, doctor. The Spartans were in the streets – they surprised us in early morning ... I've lost track. Was this two days ago?'

Alexanor was giving them all a little poppy.

'You rode here straight from Megalopolis?' he asked.

He moved from Lykortas to Dinaeos, and began to examine the man's bandages.

'They attacked us during a truce. And he got his companions mounted and fought back. He didn't even have his armour, and he fought. Brilliantly. You should have seen him – like a centaur, clearing the agora, one of us to ten of them. Every blow put a Spartan down.' The man's eyes closed.

Alexanor leant forward to draw the blanket over the man, but suddenly his eyes opened and he bolted upright in the bed.

'Spartans! Ares' dick. They weren't Spartans, they were all fucking mercenaries. There are no *Spartans*, any more.'

'Calm, calm,' Alexanor said, pressing his patient back onto the blankets.

'Tell me, doc. Will he ...? Is he ...?'

Dinaeos started up again. One of his wounds was bleeding through the bandage, and Alexanor realised how tired the man was, and he knew that the forearm wound ought to be bandaged again. But healing started in a man's mind, or in a woman's. He knew that from repeated experience.

He leant down.

'He's still alive. I cannot say more. I expect the crisis soon. Then perhaps we will know more.' He forced a smile. 'What is the name of this new Achilles?'

Alexanor pressed the big red-headed man back down into the bed again.

The red-fringed eyes fluttered closed.

'Philopoemen.' The Achaean smiled. 'Like Achilles – yes. The best of the Achaeans.'

Alexanor's struggle with Philopoemen's wound was like a labour of Herakles. The wounds on his arms closed in time, but the puncture wound continued to weep a strange, clear fluid that didn't stink. The edges of the wound grew angry and red, and Alexanor prepared for the crisis, sitting by the wounded man's bedside as he had sat by Nikeas five years before, and dozens of pilgrims since. He read aloud from plays of Menander, and from the works of Hippocrates. He sang, and he washed the man's body, and he became increasingly convinced that he should attempt some intervention in the puncture wound. It would not close. Only the patient's superb physique kept him from an early death, but as days turned to weeks, the man's heroic constitution began to erode, and his fever mounted.

Night was falling outside, and autumn was in the air. A brazier burnt in the Epidauros, and the air was laced with incense.

'Take no action,' Chiron said. 'Let him go to the gods, if that is their will.'

Alexanor washed his hands in a basin held by a slave and said nothing. But when his teacher was gone, he rolled the man with the slave's help and while Leon, who was also a skilled nurse, held the wounded man's arm, Alexanor looked over the wound again. It was like an old friend or an old foe, by then, and its refusal to heal or show the slightest sign of closing was infuriating.

It *had* changed, though. After the first few days a curious line of inflammation, like the decorated border on a garment, had appeared, running from the wound in the man's side down towards the hip. Today, Alexanor could follow a whole line of bad tissue down the wounded man's side; there were bright red lines, new ones, radiating from something like a scarab of infection a hand's breadth below the wound. He put his thumb on it, very cautiously; the wounded man groaned. He had been awake, several times, but never to any purpose; he'd soon passed back into his feverish coma.

The scarab was very hot. Soft, full of blood.

Alexanor sat back on his stool, estimating what this could mean in terms of the humours. Hot, and wet. And far out of balance.

He rose and went looking for Chiron, but found Sostratos. The old soldier was chatting with the Achaeans; they all seemed to get along well enough. Aristaenos had made a recovery, and that was due in no little part to the former mercenary, who'd talked to him about nothing, and everything.

They were all lying on *kline*, with shawls over them, watching the sunset. Alexanor could smell the wine.

'A word, master,' Alexanor said.

Sostratos groaned, but he rose smoothly to his feet like a much younger man and stepped in off the portico. Alexanor took him by the arm and led him down the hallway to the wounded man's bedside.

Sostratos sat, winked at Leon, who was still patiently holding the Achaean, and looked.

'See this?' Alexanor said.

'Hmm,' Sostratos said, interested.

'What is it?' Alexanor asked.

Sostratos poked at it. The patient whimpered. His eyes fluttered open.

'*Sing*,' he muttered, '*O Muses* ...'

'What?' asked Alexanor. 'Is that the *Iliad*?'

Sostratos nodded to Leon, who let the patient relax.

The older man stepped back out of the long room full of beds, his head tilted to one side like a good dog listening to a distant master. Sostratos beckoned to Alexanor.

'I have a theory, but for once, we needn't rely on guesswork. Come.'

He led the way back to the drinking party.

'Why don't they leave?' Alexanor asked. 'Are they waiting for him to die?'

'That, and other things,' Sostratos said. 'They love him, and hope for a miracle. And the Spartans have taken their city. They are in shock. Where can they go?'

Alexanor exhaled slowly, and then they were out on the portico.

Sostratos waved the others to silence.

'Tell me,' he said. 'When your friend Philopoemen fell, what was he wearing?'

'Just a *chiton* of wool his wife made him,' Dinaeos said. 'He had no time to put on armour.'

Sostratos looked pleased. Alexanor understood immediately.

'There's cloth in the wound,' he guessed.

'Thank the gods it is wool and not linen or cotton,' Sostratos said. 'Where are you going?'

'I know what to do. What I would have done yesterday, or a week ago.'

Alexanor went back down the hall. Sostratos followed him but said nothing. With Leon's help, they put a sheet of thin wood under the patient's side and covered it in sea-kelp.

'You are sure?' Sostratos said.

'Yes.'

Alexanor took a small knife with an obsidian blade held in a masterfully crafted bronze and silver handle. It was a tool for removing tumours and warts.

Leon raised the patient's arm.

Alexanor looked at the scab again. And then he made a single incision along the flank of the red pustule, and it burst. Blood and bile flowed, and Sostratos mopped at it with a sea sponge, and then pounced with tweezers and held up an obvious scrap of bloody wool.

'Get it all,' Alexanor said, rather unnecessarily. He realised he'd just admonished his senior, but Sostratos was grinning.

'Yes, master,' he said with gentle sarcasm.

Leon barked a laugh.

Alexanor looked at the line of infection, which seemed paler already, and frowned.

'How did the cloth get way down there?' he asked.

Sostratos, with both hands on the wound, still managed a shrug.

'When you have done this as long as I have, young man,' he said, 'you'll realise that we know *nothing* about how the body functions. Perhaps the gods put it there for us to find. Perhaps the body has subtle protective mechanisms to move alien objects out to the surface of the skin – think of a splinter. Perhaps the cloth floats on the fluid of the body.' He stared down into the wound. 'Perhaps little pink men run about inside us and do all these things.' He tossed the tiny, blood-soaked tuft of wool into the dish Leon held with his free hand. 'That's all I see.'

Alexanor was a little appalled by the level of his intrusion into the body cavity. He could see the muscle under the skin. Dissection of any kind was an abomination, or so most of his teachers told him, but he had seen dead men before, and so he had some idea of how the abdomen worked.

He shook his head. 'Close him up?'

Sostratos washed his hands in a bowl of hot water. The Aegyptian ambassador had come over and brought a stool; now the great man held a washbasin.

'I'd say wash the wound and wait a little,' Sostratos said, 'if you are asking my opinion. Sometimes I think we are too fast to close.' He shrugged. 'Soldiers often keep wounds open to let them breathe.'

Alexanor nodded. 'Let us keep it open, then. I will pray.'

In the morning, the infection was down. The patient's eyes opened as soon as Alexanor ordered him rolled, and for the first time, they were clear.

'I am not dead?' the man asked.

His heavy, blunt features might have caused him to be taken for a mere bumpkin, or one of those empty, handsome men sculptors loved. But when he smiled, his features changed, and he radiated *charisma* like the sun.

'Not so far,' Alexanor said.

'I had *such* dreams,' Philopoemen said.

'Dreams are good,' Alexanor said. 'I am Alexanor of Rhodes, a priest of the god. Tell me your dreams – they will speed your healing. Often the god sends men dreams about their cure. I am trained to interpret them.' He paused. 'You have had both lotus flower and opium, which give richer dreams.'

'I wondered. The colours were . . .' The young Achilles fell silent.

'I had a waking dream about you and your wound, before you came,' Alexanor said.

Philopoemen managed a wry smile. 'The spear went right into me. How am I alive?'

'The grace of the god,' Alexanor said.

'Your skill, too, I imagine.' The Achaean lay back. 'Zeus, I am tired. All my muscle will rot away. The only dream I remember was all fire and snakes. I think I *was* a snake. There was a fire, and I was a snake and I went through the fire and then I was burnt. And then there was another fire, and a rat, and I ate the rat and went through the fire, and I was burnt again.' He raised his eyes. 'It doesn't sound like much.'

'It sounds very much like a dream from the god. How many fires did you pass through?'

'Oh, seven or eight. And I swam through water, deep water, to an island, and there was fire there, too.'

'Deep water can have many different meanings,' Alexanor said. 'Sex, usually.'

'Hah! Sex ... Save that for ...' The man's face closed. His body went rigid, and his breathing changed. 'Oh, Zeus, father of gods ...' he said.

He rolled suddenly, as if trying to avoid something; he rolled over his wound, and he choked.

'God! That hurts.' He muttered a little and was gone.

But only to sleep.

Another month passed, and there was snow on the distant hilltops. No more pilgrims came, and most of the beds were empty. The nine Achaeans and the Aegyptian ambassador were almost the last men left in the sanctuary. A deputation came to the sanctuary from King Cleomenes of Sparta, bringing a talent of gold and promising further reparations. The officer was a different man, a languid youth with long hair and cosmetics on his eyes.

'The king proclaims an amnesty to any Achaean citizen and bids you return to your city of Megalopolis, which he will return to you,' he said in tones of bored pomposity. 'His amnesty covers all those who served in arms against him, even Philopoemen and his friends.'

Sostratos received his scrolls and his sacrifice and sent him on his way. He repeated the speech over dinner, acting the part of the thin Spartan to perfection.

'You should have been an actor and not a soldier,' Chiron said. 'I hear we're putting on a Menander in the spring – perhaps you can have a part.'

Sostratos took a long drink of wine.

'Medicine and drama are both gifts of Apollo,' he said. 'I wanted to be an actor, but my father said it was as worthy a profession as selling my arse on the street in Athens.'

'So you killed people instead,' Chiron said.

Sostratos shrugged. 'Strictly business.'

The wounded man recovered enough to take exercise, and then enough to begin to excel at exercise. Indeed, Alexanor had seldom seen anyone recover so quickly. The transition from bed-bound patient to enthusiastic athlete was sudden and took Alexanor by surprise. One day he found the Achaean stretching at the magnificent, empty *palaestra*.

He had got to know the Achaean's body as a doctor. He estimated that Philopoemen was twenty-seven or twenty-eight years old. He had shoulders as broad as an ox, and yet a waist as slim as a woman's and a delicacy of movement like a gymnast. His heavy features hid a sharp mind and he could speak, at length, about many things. But he would not stop moving, and his restlessness hid something.

Most of all he seemed to love horses; in matters of literature, he was old-fashioned, preferring the *Iliad* and the works of Xenophon.

'I love the old bastard, even if he hated Epaminondas, the best of men,' Philopoemen said.

It was cold, but not too cold for exercise.

'It's true, he never mentions Epaminondas,' Alexanor said.

He stripped and began stretching. Then he lifted some light weights, as much to stay warm as to build muscle. They had all the sands of the magnificent training area to themselves.

'Exactly. His sons were both killed by Theban cavalry. He never forgave the Thebans.' Philopoemen looked away sharply. 'Nor will I ever forgive the Spartans. May Apollo witness my oath.'

Alexanor, who, as a priest, had heard many oaths of revenge, merely continued to lift his weights and watch his patient.

Philopoemen stretched and then groaned.

'By Apollo, sir. Will my side ever loosen up? Every time I reach with my right arm ... Damn it!' he said, suiting action to word and flinching. 'Some spearman I'll be.'

'By spring, you will be free of pain,' Alexanor said. 'In two weeks, I will encourage you to stretch that ligament and the wound a little further. Right now, you are endangering your healing.'

'Good,' the Achaean said. 'I have plans for spring. I need to convince the exiled men not to return to our city.'

'Really?'

'Yes. Cleomenes just wants us to come back so that he knows where we are. He'll leave a garrison, and hostages will be taken.' Philopoemen picked up a weight-stone. 'May I exercise in ways that do not stretch the wound?'

Alexanor considered. 'Yes, as long as I am with you.' He watched the bigger man lift a ten mina stone with apparent ease. 'You are very strong,' he added.

'I'm a farmer. I have cattle, and olive trees, and a vineyard. And I haven't lain on my back for a month since I was a newborn.' Philopoemen continued to lift his stone: left arm, then right arm, left arm, then right arm. 'Farming seems less a waste of time than empty exercise,' he said with a smile. 'At least there's wine and olives at the end.' He lifted again. 'I need exercise, friend. I need ... oblivion. Is there a drug you can give me, so I will not think too much?'

'Wine?' Alexanor said, trying to be humorous. He had seen patients succumb to the darkness, but had not expected it in this young warrior.

'I had hoped for something stronger,' the man said, meeting his eye. 'You mentioned lotus flower, and opium?'

'No,' Alexanor said, and there they were, eye to eye.

'Cleomenes took *everything* from me. I do not want to think, for a while.' Philopoemen looked away, and then back. 'I know you probably don't understand—'

'I probably do,' Alexanor said. 'I was a Rhodian marine. My ship was almost taken by Aegyptians – all the other marines on board were killed. All my ... friends.'

Philopoemen smiled. 'Well, there's my foot in it, then. I thought you were some soft-handed priest.' He smiled, but the smile couldn't hide his pain.

'You make Cleomenes sound like the very personification of evil.' Alexanor allowed his tone to carry a little scepticism. He found that he was not immune from a competitive spirit; he picked up a ten mina stone, too, and lifted it.

Philopoemen's eyes flashed. 'Listen,' he said. 'I am well taught – I have been to the Academy and the *Stoa*, and I have read Plato and even Aristotle. Ekdelos and Demophanes were my teachers – I know enough to doubt everything, including my doubts. But Cleomenes is a tyrant. He wants to re-enslave the helots and recreate a Sparta that never was. Sparta, the real Sparta, was built by heroes who obeyed the

Law of Lycurgus and put the welfare of the state above their own. This is a boy playing at war with money provided by strangers who use him as a tool.' He glanced back at the Epidauros. 'Aegypt is paying his bills now. And he has taken from me ...'

Alexanor was as surprised as if his pet cat had delivered an oration.

'Well spoken,' he said. 'I haven't heard you say so many words all together since you recovered your wits.'

Philopoemen gave him half a smile.

'It is not just rhetoric. I hate him, I will not hide it. He has made war on us for five years, for no better reason than that Aratos and the Achaean League would not bend their knees to Sparta. He killed one of my stepfathers in cold blood – even then, I helped arrange a truce. *They attacked us during that truce.* And then his mercenaries killed my ... my ...'

He had begun to speak quickly; his reserve was cracked, and his face grew red with anger. He turned and faced Alexanor as if they were about to fight, and then, with a visible effort, he mastered himself.

'I am done with doubt, and caution. I will do what must be done to defeat Cleomenes and destroy this rump of Sparta.'

Alexanor might have smiled; a wounded man, not even in the prime of adulthood, promising the destruction of the Spartan state. Instead he raised his eyebrows in astonishment, but not at the man's statement; merely his assurance.

'My father warned me against war,' Philopoemen said. 'He told me that it simplifies, and destroys, and no good ever grows from it.' He shrugged, looking out over the sand of the *palaestra*. 'But it seems to me that war is about to come.' He pointed at hand wraps. 'Will you box?'

Alexanor thought for a moment.

'Let us try.'

It was an odd bout. The Achaean was recovering. His endurance was poor, and he had trouble moving his right arm correctly. On the other hand, he was almost a head taller and Alexanor was aware from the first that a single blow from those arms, even the left, would send him to the dust.

He knew how to beat the Achaean: simply by wearing him down, moving, moving, using up his short wind.

He didn't like to do it, however, because he was not the man's sparring partner. He was his doctor.

He danced in, blocked a weak right jab . . .

And the Achaean was helping him up, full of apology.

'Oh, by the gods, sir. I am so sorry! I am out of practice. Is your jaw broken?'

Alexanor opened and closed his mouth several times.

'No,' he said, hesitantly. 'No. Damn it. I am accounted a fair boxer. And as a physician I should certainly know how long those arms are.' He rubbed his jaw. 'Damn,' he muttered again.

'If it is any consolation, my side hurts like fire,' Philopoemen said with a wry smile.

'That pains me twice – I am a poor follower of Hippocrates if I allow you to indulge in a sport for which you are not sufficiently healed, and the worse for losing to you!' But Alexanor laughed. 'When you are healed, we will try a few falls of *pankration*.'

'That would suit me,' Philopoemen said, with more enthusiasm than he had shown for anything but hating Sparta. 'I love *pankration*.'

Later in the afternoon, Alexanor found Leon putting clay labels on medicine pots.

'Make sure the opium and the hellebore and lotus are secured,' he said.

Leon nodded. 'The Achaean?'

'Has he been by?' Alexanor asked.

Leon smiled. 'I wasn't born yesterday.'

That night, they sat in the *tholos*, all their couches circled, with wine flowing freely. Philopoemen drank more than Alexanor would have liked, and yet it didn't seem to affect him much. It was a symposium, although not so formal as some; even Chiron attended. It had been a difficult year at the sanctuary, and the autumn had brought hundreds of pilgrims. The Achaeans had only been the harbingers of a flood of refugees and sick.

They drank to the healing god, and the *kylix* circled the couches. Chiron directed that wine be allowed to the slaves serving them.

'We should speak on worthy subjects,' suggested Philopoemen.

'We should lie here and drink until we are drunk,' Dinaeos said. 'That's as worthy as I feel. I haven't been drunk in two months. Say, doc, is there a woman anywhere in this place?'

Alexanor was lying with Philopoemen.

'A woman? Of course. Dozens – in the woman's sanctuary. There are priestesses ...'

Dinaeos grunted. 'You know what I mean.'

Philopoemen laughed. 'He probably does not, our dear doctor,' the Achaean captain said.

'I'm from Rhodes, not Olympus,' Alexanor said. 'I know what you want. You want a slave *porne*. We do not allow any such here.'

'Because it wastes the humours?' Dinaeos asked. 'I *want* to waste some humour.'

Chiron lay with Sostratos. He sat up.

'Because the trade in flesh is ignoble,' he said. 'The mind governs the body as aristocrats govern lesser people. Yes? And when you take people and make them slaves, force them to copulate, humiliate them, you injure their minds as surely as a sword injures their bodies.'

Dinaeos shook his head. 'I don't plan to *injure* anyone,' he said, expecting a laugh that didn't come. He sat back and sighed. 'Fine,' he muttered. 'Prudes.'

The Aegyptian ambassador nodded. 'Surely this is a very ... *heretical* thought? And you are very strict?' He was a small man for a Macedonian, with blond hair and bright blue eyes undimmed by a life of excess. He lay by Dinaeos. 'The whole world runs on slavery, surely? This temple, if you will pardon me, has hundreds of slaves.'

Chiron lay back. 'We have hundreds of slaves who are trained, treated humanely, and most of whom earn their freedom. None of them are ever forced in sex.'

The Aegyptian raised a cynical eyebrow. 'They remain slaves. A slave is a slave.' He shrugged.

'Why?' Chiron asked. 'Is the contrary also true? Is a free man always a free man? Since he can so easily be made a slave by any pirate, by war, by chance? And once he is made a slave, is that slavery eternal? Or can he return to being a free man?'

'Like all philosophers, you ask difficult questions,' the Aegyptian said. 'I have never been a slave. I'd rather die.'

'Perhaps you would not have the opportunity to die?' Sostratos asked. 'Come – you have been a soldier.'

The ambassador shrugged again.

As a Rhodian, Alexanor was stung, because the Aegyptians were too often the enemies of Rhodes.

'Aegypt benefits from slavery,' he said without thinking. 'Aegypt supports the Cretan pirates.'

'Aegypt supports the cause of freedom,' the ambassador said smoothly.

'By paying hard cash for Greeks seized from weddings and fishing boats and forced into the lowest forms of slavery!' Alexanor said.

Philopoemen listened attentively but said nothing.

Chiron raised an eyebrow. 'You are too spirited, young man.'

Alexanor took a breath. 'I am from Rhodes,' he said. 'I have served as a marine. Our navy faces the pirates every day. Every Rhodian knows someone who has been seized as a slave – women made whores, even boys.'

He blinked, and thought of all the ways to do harm, and forced his thoughts away from the dead young men and the Aegyptian ship. He closed his eyes and calmed his breathing. He almost missed the Aegyptian ambassador's next sally.

'Perhaps they should find a stronger protector. Perhaps they need to stop pretending to independence and admit a royal garrison that could protect them.' He smiled nastily.

Alexanor met his eye. 'Rhodes? Submit to Aegypt? Never.'

'Speaking of slavery,' the Aegyptian said with an intent to insult. 'Did you hear that the Achaean League sent envoys to Antigonus Doson, king of Macedon, for aid against Sparta? And yet King Cleomenes still was able to sack Megalopolis with impunity.'

Philopoemen bridled. 'That was ill said.'

'I have said nothing ill,' the Aegyptian reassured him. 'Weak states should submit to protectors. It is my master's policy. Only the strong can protect the weak.'

'You suggested that the Achaeans make themselves slaves,' Philopoemen said.

'To Macedon, yes,' the Aegyptian said. 'Better you had approached my master, Ptolemy. He is the richest lord in all the world, with the money to put armour on your hoplites and garrisons in your fortresses. Now Macedon will own you.'

Alexanor could feel his companion by his side – his muscles rigid, and then gradually loosening as the Achaean made an effort of will to relax.

'I really know little about it,' Philopoemen said. 'But if the *hegemon* of the Achaean League chose to approach the regent of Macedon, I assume he knows his business. Aratos has been the *strategos* of the Achaean League since I was born, or thereabouts. He probably does not think your master's reach is long enough.' He glanced around the room. 'And surely it would be uncomfortable for your master to have both Sparta and the Achaeans as horses in his stable?'

'We could land ten thousand men on these shores . . .' the Aegyptian said. 'We may yet.'

'And feed them?' Philopoemen asked.

All the other eyes were on him, and suddenly his thick features did not seem so brutish. Alexanor admired the way he did this; from the sleepy sword-brute to the statesman in one change of expression.

Philopoemen sat up and took the *kylix*.

'May I counsel you, sir? There was a time, and not so long ago, when there were just three powers in the world – the Ptolemies of Aegypt and their allies, the Seleucid kings and *their* allies, and the kings of Macedon and their allies. And Greece was your battlefield and your stage, where you could build fine theatres and fight your surrogate wars.' He drank.

The room was silent, and so was the world outside.

He handed the *kylix* to Alexanor.

'But the world is changing. Epiros and Illyria; the Aetolian League; Rome and Carthage. Once there were three powers, and now there are ten, or twenty. If the *hegemon* has gone on one knee to Macedon, it is because they have the power to help us and their throne is far enough away that we might not fear oppression. Aegypt might send troops, but they would demand concessions, and I do not imagine that the Seleucid king would allow an Aegyptian fleet to pass west of Crete without a fight. Do you?'

The Aegyptian ambassador could not have been more surprised if a dog had sprouted wings, than by the Achaean captain speaking so exactly about issues of politics.

'I would maintain that Macedon is close enough to be your master,' he insisted. 'But I admit there are more powers now than there were in my father's generation. But Rome? A city of barbarians and the merest oligarchy.'

'Beggars cannot always choose,' Philopoemen said bitterly. 'As men without a city, Macedon may simply be the daemon we know.' He glanced at the other men. 'And what I hear of Rome suggests to me that they are very strong.'

'An interesting point of view, I'm sure,' the ambassador said. 'Tell me when they have a fleet, and perhaps I'll be interested. What I see is a barbarian state that struggles to overmatch a mere colony of Tyre.'

Chiron nodded. 'Philopoemen, before you came, we had a visit from a Roman nobleman who sought to learn our skills.' He shrugged. 'You never heard more superstitious nonsense than this man spouted.'

Philopoemen subsided. He nodded to Chiron and bowed to the ambassador.

'I am still a young man. Perhaps I know little. But I will remind you, gentlemen, that the Romans imposed a treaty on the Illyrians, with their fleet. I find that … amazing.'

'Barbarians fighting barbarians!' the ambassador said, his voice rich with contempt.

'Rather like Greeks fighting Greeks,' Chiron said. 'Pointless and wasteful. I propose we change the subject.'

As morning dawned over the snow-capped mountains, a messenger arrived from Messene. Cleomenes had issued an ultimatum to the Megalopolitan exiles, and the citizens were going to vote on whether to return to their city and accept Sparta's terms, or fight on under the king of Macedon.

'I must be there,' Philopoemen was saying. 'Men will listen to me.'

'You need another month to heal,' Alexanor said, but he knew it was a waste of his breath. Dinaeos was already tacking up horses; Lykortas was collecting scrolls and Aristaenos was collecting food from the kitchens.

Alexanor tried again with Lykortas, as he was in many ways the most interested in medicine.

'Your wound is almost healed,' he said, 'but Philopoemen—'

'I'm afraid you waste your breath, sir,' Lykortas said stiffly. 'My own father is proposing that we accept these so-called "terms" from Sparta. I would walk barefoot across the snow to dissuade him.'

In the end, all Alexanor could do was walk out with the Achaeans. A light snow was falling, and the breath of the horses rose into the air. Philopoemen's charger stamped, its hooves striking the earth like hammers.

'Never worry about me, brother,' Philopoemen said.

He mounted with a wince, and circled his mount once.

'You called me brother,' Alexanor said.

Philopoemen smiled. 'You saved my life. And then you very carefully fenced me off from all the drugs. Don't think I didn't notice,' he added, smiling. 'We've boxed and we've argued. Are we not now brothers?'

Alexanor reached up and clasped his hand, and the Achaeans rode away into the snow.

A day later, Lykortas returned to collect their armour and spare horses. He got all of the horses into a paddock and ordered a pair of slaves to pack the armour in baskets, and then set himself to currying all the horses like a man possessed.

'He'll do himself a mischief,' Sostratos said, reporting the event. Behind the older priest, Leon nodded. 'Go talk to him, lad. He won't listen to me.'

Alexanor went out to the paddock by the sanctuary entrance, poured a libation to Hermes, god of travellers, and then found Lykortas with the horses.

'You couldn't wait to have your armour back?' Alexanor asked in a light tone.

'I couldn't watch my father and that fool Cercidas try to betray our city and the League,' he said to Alexanor. 'They proposed that we ... surrender to Sparta. *Join* Sparta. As if we Arkadians have forgotten.' He was tacking up a horse; the bridle was on. He was fiddling with the reins. 'But Philopoemen swayed them. He gave a speech and called them traitors.' Lykortas shook his head. 'My father is a traitor.' He picked up a saddle cloth.

'A cup of wine and a good night's sleep will make it a little better,' Alexanor said, putting his hand on the younger man's shoulder. 'You cannot ride all the way back tonight.'

Lykortas stopped, as if he hadn't given the matter any thought. He held the saddle cloth in his hands, and he was looking at one of their big military horses as if he'd never seen a horse before. He had deep lines in his face and Alexanor recognised all the signs of exhaustion: dark smudges under the eyes, like bruises, and deep lines in a young man's face.

'Come on,' Alexanor said. 'I have some good wine.'

The younger man bit his lip.

Alexanor was unused to the role of counsellor, as opposed to physician, but he put an arm around the other man's shoulder and pulled, almost like wrestling.

'We need to see to the horses,' Lykortas said. 'Fuck, I'm not even making sense.'

Alexanor looked back at Leon, who had two of the temple slaves behind him.

'The horses and all your armour will be ready in the morning,' he said. 'Come on.'

'My father was just going to sell us to the Spartans,' Lykortas said. 'My *father*.'

Alexanor, who was well used to living in the shadow of his famous war hero father, sympathised with the young man. He had left Rhodes to leave his father behind. The man could be difficult – domineering, overbearing, blustering … But he had never betrayed his city, nor anything like it. Alexanor couldn't imagine what the young man was experiencing.

But he did have good wine. He sat the boy down with Sostratos, and they heard it all: the speeches, the denunciation.

And in the end, he said, 'I ran away and left my family.'

Alexanor shrugged, as if it could happen to anyone.

Lykortas gazed at him, aghast.

'You, sir?' he asked.

'Our parents are often a disappointment.' Sostratos laughed, but no one else did. 'Perhaps your father did what seemed best at the time, lad,' he went on.

'Why did you leave?' Lykortas asked.

Alexanor gazed into the fire on the raised hearth. He shook his head.

'Many reasons. My father believed me a coward, and so did …' He broke off. He thought of Aspasia for the first time in a long time. And smiled. 'I couldn't forgive him. I can now.'

'I don't like the choices my *father* is making,' Lykortas said. 'He's a traitor!'

'We all love Philopoemen,' Sostratos said. 'But disagreeing with him is not treason.'

'Cercidas will never forgive Philopoemen,' Lykortas said. 'But Philopoemen won. The men stood firm and refused to accept the Spartan yoke.'

'What happens now?' Alexanor asked.

Lykortas looked at him as if he was a fool.

Sostratos, the former mercenary, put down his clay wine cup.

'Now the Spartan king will send his mercenaries to destroy the temples and cut down more olive trees and rape the women,' he said. 'That's how it's done.'

Alexanor shuddered. 'You did these things?' he asked.

Sostratos met his eye. 'I did. It seemed perfectly reasonable at the time – it is the way of the world.'

'Apollo, Lord of Light, stand with us,' Alexanor said.

Lykortas leant past him, his face animated for the first time in an hour.

'What changed your mind, sir?' he asked.

Sostratos looked away. 'Listen, boy. I always knew what I did was evil.' He was looking off into the distance. 'I told myself fucking stories about how my life as a mercenary was noble and virtuous and how the peasants we destroyed had it coming. One day the stories weren't enough, and I knew it was all bullshit, and we were bad men.'

Lykortas nodded, although his fatigue was beginning to show in drooping eyelids and slack features.

'And then?'

'And then I walked a long way. I came to a little shrine in Boeotia, up on the flanks of Kithaeron. A tomb to one of the men who fought at Troy. I dedicated my shield and had a long talk with the priest there, and he sent me here.' Sostratos smiled crookedly. 'And here I am, pretending to be good.'

'Maybe pretending to be good is as good as we ever are,' Alexanor said. 'I was a marine, for Rhodes. I, too, have seen some … shit.'

Lykortas shook his head; he was almost asleep sitting up. He turned to Sostratos.

'Will my father … ever realise that he was wrong?'

Sostratos frowned. 'No one is good at that,' he said. 'But I promise you, you won't change your father's mind by yelling at him.' He glanced at Alexanor, as if to make sure that the younger priest was aware of their patient's exhaustion. 'You are studying at the Academy in Athens at the moment?'

'Yes, sir.'

'Let our slaves take the horses and armour back to Megalopolis. You go on to your studies. When you read Plato, think of your father.'

'When I read Plato, I think of Philopoemen,' the young man said, and the name *Philopoemen* seemed to wake him. 'We need a Herakles to clean the Augean stables, and Philopoemen is the best we have. Men like Cercidas and my father want money and power, and care nothing for the means they use. Philopoemen ...'

With that word on his lips, the young man fell asleep. Alexanor and Sostratos carried him to a bed in the heated room, and tucked him in.

'I hate even thinking about it,' Sostratos said to the darkness.

'War?' Alexanor had been thinking of Aspasia. 'It's far enough from here.'

In his mind, war was about rope and seawater and the sound of gulls, far from the peace of the groves of Epidauros.

Sostratos sighed. 'No,' he said. 'War is coming. That young man is the herald of Ares.'

CHAPTER THREE

―⟨∾∾⟩―

Sellasia – 55 Stades from Sparta

SUMMER, 222 BCE

Alexanor was less than three hundred stades from the sanctuary at Epidauros. He sat on the back of a gifted horse and watched the king of Macedon bring war to the Peloponnese.

He was with the great man's staff: a dozen officers; as many courtiers without obvious military office; the great man's Macedonian physician, who glared at Alexanor whenever he thought he was unwatched; a male concubine named Phaex, who wore a sword he'd clearly never drawn and wasn't comfortable on horseback; and a dozen women including an Athenian *hetaera* and her servants. They were halfway between Megalopolis and Sparta, and apparently the king of Sparta had erected fortifications across the one good road. Ahead of them rose two hills, conical, like a young woman's breasts, and behind the hills ran a ridge that was taller than either, like a woman's shoulders above her breasts. The king of Sparta occupied all three heights. A river, the Oenus, flowed rapid and shallow across the front of the hills, and the road crossed it at a ford to the left of the Allied position, which consisted of a low ridge and the Oenus that ran, very shallow, but with deep cut banks, along the ground below them.

To Alexanor, the Spartan position appeared impregnable.

The king of Macedon had camped well away, almost thirty stades distant, with the river Oenus between them. Alexanor had never seen a war on land before; he was surprised at the tents and all the baggage, and surprised again to be treated by the Macedonians as if he was roughly equal in importance to Phaex, the male concubine.

Alexanor thought that his presence was the direct result of his age, and his military experience. When they understood that the king of Macedon was coming to the Peloponnese in person to prosecute the war against Sparta, the priests of the temple of Asklepios hadn't imagined that they would be involved in any way. But as the spring wore into summer, the king had sent gifts, and requests that were very like commands; he wanted a priest to attend him. A liver complaint, or perhaps a stomach disorder.

At the festival of the Spring Equinox, Alexanor had been made a full priest and an initiate of the highest degree of the order; he was shown the sacred signs, and asked to volunteer to attend the king of Macedon. As he was now the youngest full priest, he accepted. Indeed, he had already begun to experience the change in his relations with his peers. It was one thing to be the best of the students, but another to be the first to be promoted to priest.

Philopoemen, busy in the north playing politics, had sent him a horse as a gift. A damn good horse, with word that he had been appointed commander of the Megapolitan Exile cavalry.

Alexanor had ridden over the mountains with Leon and a mule loaded with surgical instruments and drugs, to find that the king of Macedon didn't seem to know anything about him, so that today he had ridden along behind the great man, his escort, and his courtiers from hilltop to hilltop without yet being recognised. He'd left Leon with the main army.

'Well,' the king said.

He was perhaps the most powerful man in the world – certainly the most powerful in Greece. Now he was standing two horse lengths away, pissing on the ground. He looked up and his eyes met Alexanor's for the first time.

'Who the fuck are you?' he asked, his voice polite.

'Alexanor, son of Philokles,' he said. 'You sent for a priest from the temple of Asklepios.'

The king pulled his *chiton* down over his hips and then raised his cavalry breastplate and let it down, shrugging his shoulders to seat it.

'Huh,' he said. 'Did I? Antipater, how far does his flank run down that hill? Don't they look like a woman's tits?'

'Great tits.' Antipater was a young cavalry officer, also clearly a favourite. 'Most tits sag when a woman lies on her back. Not *Gaia*.'

Most of the men laughed.

The king smiled. 'I did order up a priest, at that. When I was pissing blood this spring. You know anything about stomach problems?'

Alexanor considered a host of answers.

'Perhaps,' he said.

The king nodded. 'Where's Prince Alexander?'

Antipater waved into the valley of the Oenus River at their feet. 'He went down to look for fords.'

The king shook his head. 'That's a beautiful position Cleomenes has there, and we're going to lose a lot of boys from Pella taking it.' He walked over to Alexanor and put a hand on the borrowed horse's bridle. 'Nice horse. Thessalian?'

Alexanor shook his head. 'No, my lord. He was gifted me by a friend – I really don't know the breed.'

The king of Macedon patted the horse's head.

'There, my friend – there's a fine fellow, open your mouth for the king.'

The horse opened his mouth and gave a little shudder.

The king stepped away.

'A fine gelding. Too good a warhorse for a quack. Who's your friend? The king of Syria?'

Alexanor smiled. 'No, my lord. The *Hipparchos* of Megalopolis. Philopoemen.'

'Oh.' The king turned to his cavalry orderly, Antipater. 'Who's Philopoemen?'

Antipater winked at Alexanor. 'An officer of Megalopolis,' he said. 'Commanding the Exile cavalry.'

'The Achaean League?' the king asked.

Antipater shrugged. 'My lord, I cannot keep track of all these pissant little Greek states.'

King Antigonus, known as 'Doson',' laughed.

'Who can?' he asked. 'But the Achaean League has its uses. Do you know the man, Antipater?'

'He did a lot of scouting the last two weeks. Alexander says he's got the stuff. The balls.' Antipater looked around and then back at the king. 'They took a raid right to the gates of Sparta, or so Alexander said.'

'Ah,' the king of Macedon said. 'He's a good judge of horseflesh, too. Right. Get me Alexander, and tell Demetrios to take the Illyrians and clear the middle ground. Get all those crap *psiloi* and *peltastoi* out of the river bottom. We'll do this one step at a time, like peeling an onion.' He looked up at the two peaks, which were dense with the enemy's phalanxes behind earthworks. 'By the rage of Ares, though, gentlemen – this is going to be a tough nut.'

The sun climbed through an empty sky, and the pleasant air of early morning gave way to the forge heat of the full weight of the sun, which fell on every man like the strokes of a hammer. Eventually Alexanor dismounted; he was not such a veteran rider that he really wanted to spend all day on a horse, no matter how highly praised the beast was. But he had no groom and he had to wander the hillside with his reins over his arm until the *hetaera*, a tall, thin woman in perfectly respectable riding clothes, called out to him.

'Are you the priest of Asklepios?' she asked.

Her face, under the veils she wore against the sun like any rich Athenian lady, was beautiful; her skin was like the finish on the finest Athenian pottery, her red lips so crisply defined that they might have been made by the chisel of a master sculptor, and her eyes a vivid green-brown. Her smile was not predatory or vulpine, merely friendly.

'I am, *despoina*.' He bowed.

'Let Thais here take your horse. What a beauty. My father raised them. I've seldom seen a better head.' She flashed her magnificent smile at him.

He was surprised at his own response. *Hetaerae* were known to be clever, but they were merely women, and often dissolute women at that, and here he already wanted to win her good opinion.

It was a long time since he had sought a woman's good opinion.

'The king of Macedon thought so, too,' he said, and then thought that sounded pompous. 'What I mean is, yours is the second compliment today. I am merely the horse's custodian.'

'I heard.' She turned her head so that he could see her profile, her pert nose and long neck under her enormous straw hat. 'Thais, my sweet, get the horse out of the sun. He doesn't fancy it any more than you do.'

She suited action to words, taking Alexanor by the hand and leading him into the shade of a silk parasol that her ladies had erected. As soon as his head was out of the sun, Alexanor felt better.

He also realised that he'd just been very gently reprimanded.

'You await the king's pleasure?' he asked.

She laughed. 'I await the king's sexual pleasure. You are a doctor – surely I can use the term "sexual" with you?'

He flushed. 'Yes,' he said.

She shrugged. 'I am distressing you.'

He shook his head. 'I do not have many chances to discourse with women.' Especially about sexual matters,' he added, hoping he sounded worldly.

She nodded. 'Well, we'll do what we can to save you, won't we, Artemis?'

She addressed another of her women, who poured him a plain, earthenware cup of sparkling red wine that must have been iced, it was so cold.

'My lady, I am in your debt.' He bowed.

She smiled. 'Listen, you are not here of your own will, are you? I'm going to guess that he asked for a man from your temple, and you drew the short straw.'

Alexanor could not help but be moved by her sparkle.

'There's some truth in your assertion,' he conceded.

'You sound as if you are debating with Socrates,' she said.

'You know Socrates?'

She smiled wryly. 'Well, he's been dead for almost two hundred years, but I've heard of him. Something to do with clouds, I think.'

'You are mocking me,' Alexanor said.

'Yes,' the *hetaera* said. 'Shall I continue?' She smiled again. 'I only mock men I like. I'm exceptionally polite to other men.'

At their feet, the battle had started, or so it seemed to Alexanor. Long lines of men, each perhaps a spear's length from the next, rolled down their ridge towards the river. To his right, Macedonian cavalry in purple and blue went forward where the ground was not so steep. The king of Macedon stood on the volcanic outcropping just to his left and watched them.

Alexanor took a sip of his wine, which was delicious.

'Phila!' the king called. 'You asked what a skirmish was. Well – have a look. This is skirmishing.'

The *hetaera* rose and walked down the rock, jumping lightly from crag to crag, until she stood by the king. In the valley, men were running; at first, there appeared to be no order to their movement.

Alexanor watched with interest. Almost no one came to close combat; men ran up to an invisible boundary and threw javelins, or stones, and then danced back, like boys playing at fighting, except that there were already bodies lying in the dirt amid the scrubby bushes along the riverbank.

A corps of archers appeared on the Spartan side of the river. In two volleys of arrows they drove the Macedonian light infantry off the riverbank.

'Fuck,' Doson muttered. 'Cleomenes must be made of money. My Agrianians are hard to beat. But he has *Cretans* ...'

The *hetaera* glanced at him. 'I am told that the king of Aegypt was his ally, but has now cut him off,' she said.

'Who tells you these things?' the king asked. 'Lovers?'

She shrugged. 'Friends,' she said, evasively.

'Well, honey, those are Cretan archers, and they are worth their weight in silver, which is about what they charge.' He held up his hand to shade his eyes. 'Antipater, tell Demetrios to get this done. Tell him to use the Illyrians. Those Achaean skirmishers down there aren't worth a fuck.'

'Aye, my lord.'

The young officer saluted, leapt onto his horse without apparently using his hands, and set off down the steep hillside at what appeared to the watchers to be a suicidal gallop.

'Terrible cavalry country,' the king said. 'Probably why Cleomenes has chosen it.'

He held out his hand and a Persian slave put a large straw hat into it. He put the hat on his head without taking his eyes off the fighting.

'That's right!' he called as a clump of his Agrianians advanced in a dense mass, threw their javelins and then dashed forward to the riverbank and began to cross. 'Someone has some guts.'

The Cretans loosed arrows and Agrianians died. They responded by using the river's far banks for cover, squatting down in the swift water.

Spartan *psiloi* went forward to the riverbank to fend them off and died on the spears of the Macedonian *peltastoi*. Not many of them, though. They were helots and didn't seem particularly keen to push the contest.

Young Antipater reached Demetrios of Pharos, the Illyrian commander. He raised his shield, which in the fierce sun seemed to be made of solid gold.

'Illyrians are the worst soldiers in the world,' Doson said. 'No discipline, no logistics, no tactics.'

There was a roar, like a peal of thunder, echoes from all the hills, and a thousand Illyrians ran forward. They had no particular formation: they seemed to hug the ground like desperate wolves moving in a pack against easy prey, eager for the kill and a mouthful of flesh and blood. They ignored the hard-won salient where the Agrianians had crossed and leapt into the river directly opposite the Cretan archers.

The Cretans loosed, all together.

Fifty Illyrians went down. The rest were in the river and splashing their way across. The fastest men were already clambering up the far bank.

The Cretans turned and ran, all together, like a flock of birds turning in flight.

The Agrianians rose out of the river and pushed forward. Even at this distance, Alexanor could see men stooping to collect rocks or pick up spent javelins.

All the helots and all of the enemy's mercenary *peltastoi* turned and ran from a thousand Illyrian highlanders who were now all out of the river and baying like hounds, charging across the open ground.

'I mean, they're the greatest *assault* troops in the world,' the king said, with a grin at the *hetaera*. 'Otherwise, they're completely useless. Too stupid even to know when they are outclassed. Well, that's that.'

'So we've won?' she asked.

'Oh, Zeus Pater, not at all. Now we simply hold both banks of the river, so Alexander and I can ride over and look at the entrenchments he's built on the hills. I see how to do this now. It won't be fun.' He looked at Alexanor. 'I have a moment, priest. Can you talk to me about my gut?'

Antipater was riding back up the escarpment with as little concern for his horse or himself as he'd shown riding down.

'At your service, my lord,' Alexanor said.

He walked out onto the rock, which was a little like being a sardine thrown on the grill; the stone was hot, and the sun was brutal.

'I didn't used to have any troubles,' Doson began. He glanced at his slave and snapped his fingers, and the Persian man handed him a heavy wineskin from which he took a long pull. He looked embarrassed. 'Now everything seems to make me ... fart. And squirt. All the fucking time. I can't enjoy anything. Once I pissed blood. Eumenos, my doctor, claims it is an imbalance of the humours.'

Phila rolled her eyes behind the king, and it was all Alexanor could do not to laugh at his patient.

'I will need to see everything you eat,' he said.

The king looked at him. 'Of course.'

'Will you change your diet if I say so?'

The king nodded. His eyes were back on the valley.

'I'd be a fool not to, wouldn't I?'

'You have other physicians,' Alexanor said. 'They may not agree with me.'

'But you are right and they are wrong?'

Alexanor shrugged. 'Honestly, my lord, I can have no idea until I have examined your diet and your stool.'

'Apollo's beans, lad. What a fine job you have,' the king said. 'Right. Darius there is my body-slave. He handles ... everything. Sometimes I think *he's* the fucking king of Macedon and I'm the slave.'

Darius smiled.

'At any rate, get him to provide you with ... whatever.' The king beamed at Antipater as the young officer crested the ridge. 'Well ridden, by all the gods.'

The Illyrians were still going, right up to the enemy on the far side. They hadn't stopped, and by this time the Achaean skirmishers and the Agrianians had caught up to them – maybe three thousand men moving up the opposing ridge and its two outlying hills.

'The left-hand hill is called Olympos and the right-hand is called Euas,' Antipater said.

'Hmm,' the king said. 'Says who?' He glanced back. 'Wine,' he snapped.

'Philopoemen of Megalopolis. He scouted all this two days ago

74

before the Spartans dug in. He's keen.' Antipater paused. 'I like him. He's like one of ours, not Greek at all.'

Doson walked back to the very edge of the volcanic outcrop, leaving Alexanor with Phila.

'What a very noble job *you* have,' she said. 'Looking at his chamber pot and his undigested food.' She smiled, though.

He knew she was testing him. So he smiled back.

'I agree,' he said. 'All things considered, it might be easier to have sex with him.'

'See?' she said. 'I knew you'd come around. Anyway, he's polite, he pays gloriously well and on time and in gold. And mostly he wants Phaex over there, anyway. He might settle for you, though. You are pretty.' She looked over the valley. 'Really, I came of my own free will. A king for a lover, even if he's older than dirt, *and* a military campaign. Always wanted to see one.'

Alexanor had never been called pretty before, and wasn't sure what to make of it.

'That has never been one of my desires,' he said.

'What, sleeping with a king?'

'Nor that,' he agreed.

'Now you are going to tell me that you are a Cynic,' she said.

'No,' he said. 'I am not a follower of Diogenes, although I confess to a liking for his works.'

He received a radiant smile from young Thais, who was brown enough that she didn't bother to wear her hat, and poor enough not to care. She gave him his reins.

'A Stoic?' she asked.

'Better a Stoic than a Sceptic.' He tried not to look surprised that a slave girl knew the difference between a Stoic and a Sceptic.

'Really?' Phila asked. 'Have you been to the Academy?'

'I have never had the pleasure,' he said, while thinking *I am on the edge of a great battle, debating philosophy with two women.*

'Mmm.' She looked back at the king, who was waving.

'Wine,' he called, as if it was his war cry.

'I begin to see what might be wrong with my patient's innards,' Alexanor said.

*

75

Between the sand and gravel in his blankets, ants, camp noise and the endless sound of horses' hooves, it was the most uncomfortable night Alexanor could remember. He rose as soon as there was enough light to see and visited his horse and the mule, which both seemed to have been more comfortable, and certainly had more straw than he'd had.

Then he walked across the camp. The Macedonian camp was neat and orderly; the Achaean camp was not so much disorderly as chaotic. The other, smaller contingents' camps were like slums of a big city: mostly, hungry, tired men huddled among rocks under their cloaks.

He found the Macedonian military hospital by the cook-fire line. No one stopped him, so he went in and found wounded men, mostly Illyrians and Agrianians from the day before, lying on dirty straw on the floor of the tent. The sun had not yet crested the horizon and the wounded men were already plagued with flies.

The army had two Athenian doctors and a Macedonian named Antigones. He introduced himself and offered his services.

'Can you do an amputation?' Antigones asked.

Honesty was called for.

'I know the theory,' Alexanor admitted, 'but I've never practised it.'

'Can you kill a man who's beyond saving?' Antigones asked.

Alexanor flinched.

The Macedonian nodded. 'Listen, lad. You are here for the king. I'm sure you are a dab hand at gut ailments. But this is nasty business. Mostly, we cut things off that will never work again – arms, legs, lives. Tomorrow and the day after, there'll be more ... time ... for the Hippocratic method.'

'Diagnosis? Massive stab wound,' one of the Athenian doctors mocked. Then he relented. 'I'm Creon. I don't mean to be a prick. We could use the help if this is as much a mare's nest as we've heard. Ever deliver a baby?'

'Yes,' Alexanor said.

'Well, a military hospital after a hard fight is roughly like two thousand women all delivering babies together, and you have two friends to get it all done.' He leant over and opened an Illyrian's bandage. The man sat, grey faced, and made no sound. 'This one will live.'

'Come back when the fighting has started,' said the Macedonian. 'I'm serious. If you want to lend a hand, we'll be fools not to take you.'

'I've treated arrow wounds,' Alexanor offered.

'You have arrow spoons?' the Macedonian asked, suddenly eager.

Alexanor nodded. 'I brought a set made of silver.'

Antigones nodded as if bowing from the waist. 'Well, that's a mercy. Good – we'll need you, then.'

Alexanor went and fetched his tools, and moved them to the tent. Then he woke Leon and asked him to find food.

He met Thais when she was fetching horses for her mistress and the other women.

'My mistress asks, have you and your slave eaten?' she said.

'Leon is not my slave,' he said. 'He was freed a few years back. He probably knows more of medicine than I do.'

Thais nodded. 'I love it whenever one of us is freed.'

'As to food, we have none,' he admitted.

Thais took him to the women's tent, which was guarded by no fewer than four royal guardsmen. He left again with bread, wine, cheese, oil, and a pomegranate, which he shared with Leon, who had come back empty-handed.

Then he joined the *hetaera* and walked his horse to where the king of Macedon stood, watching his army form.

The Macedonian phalanx was more formidable than anything Alexanor had ever seen – more formidable than a squadron of Rhodian warships. There were ten thousand men, or so Phila told him: nine thousand of the Macedonian regular infantry and a thousand of the king's royal guard, who bore shields embossed in silver and gold like so many versions of Achilles. Their equipment was as good as that of the officers in other contingents: bronze breastplates and greaves; helmets with cheek plates that formed almost full face protection; and great horsehair crests that seemed, together with their helmets, to double their height.

'Look at them,' a deep voice said at Alexanor's elbow. 'Magnificent. That is how hoplites should appear.'

Alexanor turned and saw Philopoemen, armoured from head to foot in bronze cavalry armour, and they embraced. The Achaean looked like a different man. At the Epidauros he had distinguished himself by the plainness of his clothing; here he wore beautiful armour.

'How's the horse?' the Achaean asked.

'Superb, as you well know.' Alexanor nodded. 'Yesterday the king of Macedon complimented me on it. And that lady there.'

'The concubine?' Philopoemen said casually. 'What would she know?'

'She grew up with horses,' came the woman's voice from under her enormous straw hat. 'And asses.'

Philopoemen bridled.

Alexanor laughed. 'You had that coming. Phila, this is Philopoemen of Megalopolis. Where did you grow up with horses?'

'Thessaly, sir. And thank you for asking as if I was a real person.' She flipped her hat back.

Philopoemen blushed. 'Ah, *despoina* ...' he began, and then failed to find words.

'Philopoemen!' shouted a magnificently armoured Macedonian on a tall white horse. Alexanor turned his head. The Macedonian officer was waving at the Achaean.

Alexanor watched his friend turn his horse as if thunderstruck and shook his head.

'Sir?' he called.

'Get your people down on to the plain. Tuck right in behind the phalanx where you'll be safe.'

Philopoemen saluted with his fly-whisk riding whip and turned back to Alexanor.

'Care to come and kill some Spartans? Probably the greatest battle in our generation.'

Alexanor nodded. 'I would like to come. I will not kill anyone unless I have no choice.'

'Can you fight?' Philopoemen said.

Alexanor shook his head. 'Not from horseback. Nor from conviction, if it comes to that.'

The Achaean nodded. 'Fair enough. Come along and see anyway.'

He waved his whip at the *hetaera*, who waved back. Alexanor walked his horse over to her as the Achaean called orders.

'That's your friend who loaned you the horse?' she asked.

'Yes,' he said.

She shook her head. 'Don't die. You provide good conversation.' But her eyes were on Philopoemen. 'He's like Achilles.'

Alexanor felt a pang.

Alexanor had to struggle to control his mount as a dozen horses went by at a gallop. Then he got in behind Philopoemen, and together they started along the road.

'Was that Alexander? The cavalry commander?' Alexanor asked.

'Yes,' Philopoemen said. His eyes were already watching the far ridge.

'He has a high opinion of you, I heard yesterday.'

'First I've heard of it,' the Achaean said. 'I've been on this horse for ten days, or so it seems to me. Serving under Alexander is not like serving under Aratos.' He shrugged. 'Aratos has been the *Strategos* of the Achaean League since I was born, or thereabouts.' He sounded wistful.

'Who is the boy in the golden armour?' Alexanor asked.

Philopoemen turned his head, away from the ridge. 'Prince Philip. He'll be king, someday, as opposed to Prince Alexander, who's a member of the royals but not in line. It's all a little barbaric.'

'Have you met Philip?' Alexanor asked.

'Yes. But they protect him as if he was made of Aegyptian glass. I'm out skirmishing all the time. But I've got to know Alexander pretty well. Not what I had expected.'

'How are they different?' Alexanor asked. 'Prince Alexander and your Aratos?'

Philopoemen's head had turned back to the events on the distant ridge line.

'Stay around and you'll see,' he answered. 'Alexander swears like a trooper, that's the biggest difference. Tells the truth from time to time.'

'Damn, it's the priest,' said red-haired Dinaeos. He cantered up as if he and the horse were one creature and slapped Alexanor on the back hard enough to make him cough. 'How's Epidauros?'

'Not as exciting as it was when you were there,' Alexanor said.

He was not an effusive man, but he could see the Thracian, Kleostratos, smiling, and other men he knew in the ranks of the Achaean cavalry, and it made him very happy to be so easily accepted.

The Achaean Exiles looked very much like the Macedonian cavalry. They had armour: most of them had helmets, good ones, although almost all without plumes, and breastplates; long boots, and heavy spears and javelins. They all had matching cloaks of heavy wool in a dust-brown.

'Aratos is a brilliant politician and philosopher, but I've learnt more about making camp and guarding it in a week with Alexander,' Philopoemen said. 'And patrolling.'

'And swearing. Don't forget swearing.' Dinaeos laughed. 'I'm sick of patrolling. That's all Alexander thinks we're good for. In fact,' he confided in a mock whisper to Alexanor, 'everyone is sick of it except our *hipparchos*. He's in love. With his horse.'

Men laughed. Alexanor had enough knowledge of men to know that the mockery directed at Philopoemen was a form of respect.

Then they were slip-sliding down the steepest part of the road. Alexanor might have been terrified except that he was surrounded by men who chatted as they slid, as if going down a steep slope on horseback was part of life. He leant so far back he felt as if he might be standing straight up, and at one point his legs seemed more around his horse's neck than its belly, but he made it to the bottom of the steepest stretch still mounted.

He was surprised to see that the Exile cavalry was still in ranks and files. They were almost three hundred strong.

'I don't think—' Dinaeos began. A sling stone struck him in the torso and unhorsed him. He went down, leaving his horse to stand, terrified.

Alexanor heard another sling stone go past him with a low *whirrr* like a huge insect and he ducked his head. Something brushed his scalp, and he was bleeding.

'Skirmish order! MOVE!' bellowed an enormous voice.

The man's voice was so loud he made Alexanor's teeth vibrate. The priest turned to see a big man in bronze armour atop a very big horse. He roared the order again like the whole of a chorus at a play. The giant figure was Philopoemen, and he seemed to have grown in stature to the size of a Titan.

Dinaeos was up, a deep dent in his *thorax*.

'Broke a rib,' he said.

Another sling stone whispered by.

'Stay with me,' Philopoemen said. 'I was worried that they'd come back over the river in the darkness but no one ...' The Achaean used his knees clamping the horse's back to lever himself up and get a longer view. 'Ready?' he roared.

In the few heartbeats since the first sling stone went past, the cavalry had formed four deep in a line at irregular intervals.

'Forward!' Philopoemen ordered.

The cavalry line went forward.

Men with slings appeared in the tall grass ahead of them. A trooper was hit and came off his horse; a horse was hit and dropped like an ox felled at a sacrifice.

'Charge!' Philopoemen roared.

The cavalry burst forward. The slingers turned to run, but too late. They died on the Exiles' spears, or else lay cannily under the hooves of the horses and waited for them to pass, except that the Achaean cavalry knew the trick. Two ranks halted and began to kill men lying on the ground while the front two ranks carried on, flushing a big clump of *peltastoi* with long shields and heavy spears from the high grass by the riverside. The *peltastoi* made a stand; their officer ordered them to form close. Alexanor could hear every word.

Most obeyed but some did not and the order of the *peltastoi* had gaps and flaws in it.

'AT THEM!' Philopoemen roared in his superhuman voice.

Alexanor watched Philopoemen ride into one gap, striking with his spear over men's shields, his horse pushing forward. Suddenly he had, alone, split the *peltastoi* into two groups, and a dozen cavalrymen followed him into the gap. There were shrieks and screams. Fifty of the Achaean horse halted, watching the rising dust as if they were watching a play or a race, and the rest surged forward.

The rear ranks, having massacred the *psiloi*, came forward.

The *peltastoi* collapsed into the Oenus behind them, men dropping their shields and fleeing down the steep bank.

Philopoemen followed them down the bank and so did his cavalrymen.

The *peltastoi* tried to cross the stream and were caught. Again.

Alexanor didn't want to watch any more. The contest had become murder. The river was suddenly red-brown in the bright sunlight. Philopoemen's spear was like a judgement of Zeus. Alexanor turned his head so he didn't see the number of light-armed men the Achaean killed.

He looked back up the ridge that he'd ridden down a few minutes before. Now the Macedonian cavalry was descending. Off to the army's right were the Illyrians and other light troops; they, too, were encountering resistance all along the front.

Dinaeos trotted along the front of the Exiles that hadn't followed Philopoemen into the water.

'Hold, hold,' he called. 'Let the *hipparchos* play. Watch his flank, boys.'

Behind them, perhaps two hundred paces, a Macedonian cavalry squadron halted and began to form a wedge.

From behind it came the king. He was on a big black horse, perhaps the biggest horse Alexanor had ever seen. He rode out from behind his cavalry and across the bloody grass with a dozen officers and as many guardsmen.

Philopoemen came trotting back out of the river bed, his javelin unbroken, blood running down the shaft and over his hand. When he saw the king he sat back on his horse and saluted with his javelin. Blood flicked away as the salute ended.

Doson trotted up so that they met a few yards from Alexanor's horse.

'Thracian mercenaries,' Philopoemen said. 'My lord.'

'All across the fucking plain,' the king said. 'That'll cost us an hour. How much money does this bastard have? And where's Alexander, lad?'

If Philopoemen disliked being called 'lad', he didn't show it.

'Off to the right, covering the Illyrians, my lord,' he said.

'And you are?'

'Philopoemen, my lord, *hipparchos* of Megalopolis,' he said. 'Alexander calls us the Exiles.'

'Megalopolis? If it is such a big city, why doesn't it send more cavalry?' He laughed. 'Very well, I only think I'm funny because I'm king ... Get off to the right, *Hipparchos*. I need this ground for the phalanx.'

'And those are the thanks of kings,' Philopoemen said without much malice as his troopers filed off to the right.

They had one dead and one man unconscious and carried to the rear. The *peltastoi* had lost almost half of their men and more had surrendered. Dinaeos had sent two files of cavalrymen to guard the hundred prisoners.

'You took prisoners,' Alexanor said.

'I'm not a barbarian. I don't kill without reason.' Philopoemen gestured at the captured Thracians. 'It might be my turn next time. Besides, the tall fellow with the dyed red hair and the starburst tattoo is a Getae noble.'

'I thought Thracians never surrendered,' Alexanor said.

'Maybe when they fight each other,' Philopoemen said.

He snapped a salute at the Getae, who nodded. Then he waved and rode off into the dust on the right, leaving Alexanor to Dinaeos.

The Megalopolitan Exile cavalry reformed in its ranks, this time in a wedge. It took time.

'Everyone's tired,' Dinaeos said.

Alexanor nodded.

'If we had remounts,' Dinaeos said, 'we'd be in better shape. Macedonian cavalrymen mostly have two horses.'

He slipped to the ground and stretched his legs, then went off a few paces and raised the hem of his *chiton* to piss.

'Dismount and rest your horse,' he called.

'I'm afraid if I get off I'll never get back on,' Alexanor said.

'I'll help you up,' Kleostratos said. 'Come on down, sir.'

Alexanor allowed himself to sort of collapse off his mount. He wasn't wearing armour and he was already very tired. But, off his horse, he stretched, the same exercises he would do at dawn back at the temple, and the muscles in his thighs and buttocks began to give him a little grace.

Off to the right, he could see the Illyrians coming forward. They were tall men, mostly blond, a few red-headed or black-haired, all in fine armour; linen *thorakes* or bronze, and many in the new maille armour from the north. They carried all manner of shields, from crescent-shaped *peltoi* to the old-style *aspis*, three feet across, to the new-style *aspis*, only two feet across, and some even had long, narrow shields in the Celtic style. One man looked at him and he had very light eyes and a deep tan, so that his eyes seemed to glitter with menace. The man wore a fortune in gold on his arms and had tattoos across his face and his linen *chiton* was woven in patterns.

Alexanor held his gaze.

The man turned away and waved an arm. A thousand warriors raised a cry.

Philopoemen came back, walking his horse carefully in the stony field. There were a dozen men with him; one had a purple cloak.

'My lord Alexander,' Dinaeos said, bowing in the saddle.

'Dinaeos!' Alexander said. 'Regular as the oracle, our Philopoemen. Why do I ignore him?' He smiled. 'Maybe too much wine?' He turned his horse to face Antipater, the king's aide. 'Philopoemen said that the Spartans would put their skirmishers back into the river valley during the night, and look, they did. Credit where credit is due.' He turned back, looked at the ford and the river, and shrugged. 'The king is going to take the phalanx straight up the slope of Olympos and into the Spartan king. That's the battle. We're a sideshow. Don't die, that's my advice. This is the worst terrain for cavalry I've ever ridden across.'

'We can ride across it all day long,' Philopoemen said. 'All of Arkadia is like this.'

'I should rent you all to Seleucus to fight the Parthians, then,' Prince Alexander said. 'Just stay here and don't move. I'm going to ride over to the king and see what our timings are. The valley being full of *psiloi* may have set us back a day.'

He touched his helmet and his horse sprang away, followed by his staff and Antipater, who waved a salute at Philopoemen.

'They're fine horsemen,' Philopoemen said contentedly.

'They put too much stock in big battles,' Dinaeos said. 'Are you all right, Phil?'

The helmet turned, and the eyes inside seemed to shine with their own light.

'Of course,' he said.

Dinaeos looked away. 'I worry about you.'

Alexanor looked at him.

The *hipparchos* shrugged, his armoured shoulders rising and falling.

Then both men turned to look at the Illyrians. The tall man with the light eyes and the gold arm rings was chanting. It sounded like poetry.

'What's that mean?' Alexanor asked.

'Honestly? I don't know.' Philopoemen shook his head. He looked back to the west, where the king could be seen talking to Prince Alexander. 'I don't know much. But that man is Demetrios of Pharos, their chief. They say he fought the Romans. I want to meet him.'

The Illyrians gave a great, hooting roar, a sound not unlike the sound a wave makes crashing on a rocky shore.

The Macedonian phalanx answered them with a roar like a crash of thunder.

Off to the left, another phalanx was forming. They were coming down a separate trail from the camp above – another eight thousand men or more in dark red cloaks, and then a big contingent in grey cloaks.

'The Boeotians in blood red and the Achaean phalanx in grey,' Dinaeos said. 'Under fucking Cercidas.'

'Cercidas the poet?' Alexanor asked.

'Cercidas the fat traitor?'

'Dinaeos,' Philopoemen chided gently. 'Let us keep our family quarrels for ourselves, eh?'

Far away on their left, Alexanor could see what they were watching: the Spartiates, the cream of the Spartan army, in their matching scarlet cloaks, were moving into position on the hillside. There were four thousand of them, and their brilliant red cloaks seemed to cover the slopes of Olympos in neat lines.

'Would you at least like a sword?' Dinaeos asked.

Alexanor shook his head. 'Once the fighting starts, I'll go back to the hospital. I have a sword in my baggage.' He shrugged.

Philopoemen nodded, once, as if that was a logical, correct thing, which in fact it was. But he was watching the Spartans with the same professional intensity that Doson had watched the skirmishing the day before.

'See?' He pointed. 'There is Cleomenes, up on Olympos with his elite infantry. Here is his brother Eucleidas, just above us on the other "breast" – he has all their mercenaries.' He was watching the enemy lines the way a predator watches a herd of deer. 'Now where is their cavalry?'

'It must be on the flank, with the king,' Dinaeos said.

Philopoemen shrugged. 'There's a rubble-field of volcanic stone on the right flank and the southern slopes of these hills are murder, even to me. Surely he'll place his cavalry in the centre between the hills, as we did?'

'Maybe Cleomenes doesn't have anyone as smart as you,' Dinaeos said.

'I think you are mocking me.'

Dinaeos nodded. 'Yep.'

Dinaeos turned to the priest.

'Years ago, when he came back from his time in Athens, he gave me a lecture about philosophy,' he said. 'I decided that I'm a Skeptic. I only care about what works and most theories are so much shit.'

'There is more to Skepticism ...' Philopoemen began.

Dinaeos shook his head. 'I'm a pragmatist. I just want to get the job done. Perhaps I could start a philosophic school in Athens that taught people to cook and fix broken water mains and things.' He laughed. 'And drink. I believe in wine. But then, I'm a wine merchant.'

'I'm a farmer,' Philopoemen said. 'But— Damn. What ...?'

The last was occasioned by a roar from the right, where the Macedonian phalanx started forward. The very left of the line was the King's Companions with their magnificent shields; then, echeloned behind them, came the main body of the phalanx, eight thousand men, in files sixteen men deep and just five hundred men wide, their twenty-foot *sarissae* erect on their shoulders. They went down into the stream bed, losing their order completely, and Alexanor saw one man knocked unconscious or killed by the casual swing of another man's pike as he slid down the bank. A file leader struck him; orders were called.

Alexanor moved without volition; rode to the fallen man's side and dismounted. The whole side of the fallen man's bronze helmet was dented as if he'd been hit by a sling stone. A Macedonian file-closer with an elaborately dyed horsehair plume paused.

'Fucking Erinida,' he said, indicating the man who'd swung his spear so inexpertly. 'Useless fucking fuck. Meleager was ...'

'Is,' Alexanor said.

Men were passing on either side of his horse, struggling down the riverbank. Alexanor could imagine what it would have been like if the river had been held against them. He took a knife from around his neck and cut the man's cheek plate cord. The cheek plates sprang apart and Alexanor slipped the helmet off his head. He'd used a sponge as the padding in his helmet and it had clearly taken some of the blow, but now it was full of blood.

Alexanor ran his fingers over the contusion. The skin was swollen, and he could feel fluid under his fingers, as if the scalp had absorbed some of the sponge. But there was no fracture; the skull did not give under his gentle pressure.

86

'Move him into the shade,' Alexanor ordered.

Two pikemen laid their long weapons on the riverbank, picked up their comrade, and carried him like a sack of grain into the brush.

'He's the lucky one, ain't he?' said the first, a scrawny man who seemed too small to be one of the fearsome Macedonian pikemen. 'I hear it's gonna be murder up that hill.'

'Stay in the shade, that's my plan,' said the other. 'Fuck, now Antenor can see me.'

Both men hurried to their weapons as under-officers pressed every man into the phalanx; a file-closer gave Alexanor a long look, as if suspecting him of malingering.

Alexanor collected his own helmet and rode back to the left. The Achaean cavalry had moved another hundred paces, keeping with the left flank as it moved. A gap was opening in the Allied centre.

Two hundred paces further off to the left, the Boeotian and Achaean phalanxes began to move forward. Their efforts to cross the stream were even less organised than the Macedonians' had been. Alexanor tried to make out what he was seeing, but the whole Achaean phalanx seemed to turn into a mob; men pushed other men into the water.

'Poor Cercidas,' Philopoemen said.

'Cercidas is your political enemy and he is a fat, traitorous slug. Stop being all noble – it only pisses me off,' Dinaeos said.

He pointed. A man in a magnificent, gold-plated helmet with a huge transverse crest had his helmet well back on his head as he roared at the Achaeans in a powerful, trained voice, like a *rhapsode* or an actor.

'That should be you.' Dinaeos shook his head.

Alexanor looked at him.

'Cercidas only won the election for *taxiarchos* by three votes,' Dinaeos said. 'The League phalanx is fucking hopeless. We'd do better to take a few thousand slaves and criminals and train them up, the way the Macedonians do. Our so-called citizens are more useless than tits on a boar.'

The men at the back of the mob kept pushing and sliding down the riverbank, which was steeper on the left than on the right.

Then stones and arrows began to fall on the mob in the river.

Prince Alexander galloped up, trailing a dozen Macedonian knights.

'What the hell ...? What is Cercidas playing at?'

'The enemy *peltastoi* and *psiloi* have come back down the hillside,' Philopoemen said. 'See, my lord?'

Even as the Achaean spoke, dozens of unarmoured men appeared on the near flank of the Boeotian mob and began to rain missiles into the river bed. They were relatively ineffective; a hundred javelins killed perhaps five men.

But the Boeotians were knee deep in water and taken by surprise. And one of the first men to die was their Boeotarch, the commander of their phalanx. He took a dart in the neck, over the top of his fine bronze *thorax*, and he fell forward into the shallow stream, dead, his dark red cloak floating on the water.

'I could ...' Philopoemen was bristling like a dog at the sight of a lion.

'You will stand your ground,' Prince Alexander said. 'You will wait here with my reserve. Damn it all, you Greeks are the worst *fucking* soldiers I've ever seen.'

Alexanor was shocked at the Macedonian commander's invective, but Dinaeos merely turned and winked.

'In a mood,' he mouthed.

Philopoemen turned his horse in a circle, then rode, almost unwittingly, closer to the riverbank.

Cercidas had got his front rankers together, and now, in a bold move, he led a small, well-armed group forward – almost three hundred men in good armour, all athletes. They got across the stream; a few fell, victims of the slippery, weed-covered rocks. Then the Achaean infantrymen were climbing the far bank, which was head height and as steep as a wall.

In armour.

The *psiloi* stood and threw rocks down on them, but then one brave man made it to the top, eviscerated a naked rock-thrower with his short sword, and the rest of the helots turned and ran, with the fastest of the Achaeans running along behind, cutting down the laggards. The Achaean mob gave a roar of approval and began to cross again.

'Does Cercidas think that was a great feat of arms?' Alexander muttered. 'Zeus the Judge hear me! Let many days pass before I have to watch—'

A galloper handed him a message.

'Fucking Greeks,' he said again, watching the hillside.

He read the message and turned, looking off to the right.

There, high on the shoulder of the hill called Olympos, was the Macedonian phalanx in their buff and blue cloaks. It was a third of the way up the hill, and even from five hundred paces away every observer could see that the Macedonians were being attacked in their shielded flank by little knots of *peltastoi* who were in the rocks of the hillside, rolling rocks down, throwing a javelin or covering a slinger, giving ground and then suddenly rushing back. The Spartan positions, with fortified hilltops and the ridge above, virtually guaranteed that every Macedonian attack could be taken in the flank.

'Sir, we need to clear the centre,' Philopoemen offered. 'I can do it with the Achaean horse.'

'Like fuck you can,' Alexander said savagely. 'Stay in reserve, damn your eyes. Stand here and do not move!'

He turned his charger and galloped away to the left, to the Macedonian wedge. As soon as he rode up they could hear him shouting orders. The wedge began to evaporate, the leader turning and following the prince as he rode back towards the left so that the wedge ran out like equine sand from a military hourglass, into a long file of horsemen moving quickly along the path behind the river.

Right in front of Alexanor, the enemy foot soldiers were growing bolder, coming in close to throw javelins at the flank of the Achaeans now across the river. Cercidas, still distinguishable by his superb crest, was waddling up and down his front rank trying to get his phalanx formed. The man was clearly already tired.

The Boeotians had been driven all the way back across the river, on to Alexanor's side, and they were a huddled horde and not a formed phalanx. Some men had thrown away their spears; a few, their shields.

'These are the Plataeans who stopped the Persians? And the Thebans who defeated Sparta?' Philopoemen said. 'Epaminondas would kill himself.'

'Maybe you should go tell 'em that,' Dinaeos said.

Philopoemen smiled. 'Perhaps I should, at that. You are in command. I'll be back.'

He turned his horse on its haunches and set out at a canter for the Boeotian tangle, where a dozen men in good armour were haranguing their phalangites.

Alexanor followed him after a glance at the slopes of Olympos. The

Macedonian phalanx was halted, locked with the Spartan phalanx so that the men were helmet-crest to helmet-crest with the Spartiates. But the Spartans – reputed the best infantry in the world – were higher and had a palisade of stakes and a trench covering their front, so that the Macedonian phalangites had to cross the trench to get at the Spartans. The odds looked very long.

It occurred to Alexanor for the first time that the Macedonians could lose the battle. He had not given any thought to what might happen afterwards, and now he was worried: worried for Leon, alone and dismounted in the Macedonian camp; worried for Phila and her women, who would be badly treated.

Worried for himself.

Still, he followed Philopoemen into the wreck of the Boeotian phalanx.

'Boeotians!' his friend called. His voice was still supernaturally loud, and mounted as he was, he was bigger, taller, and more imposing than any other man. 'Boeotians!'

There was half a breath of silence. Men turned; men who were yelling paused, and Philopoemen struck into the silence like a swordsman finding a flaw in an adversary's defence.

'The Achaeans are counting on you to hold their flank! You Boeotians are the heroes of a hundred fights – your Thespians helped hold the pass at Thermopylae! Your Thebans defeated Sparta! Your Plataeans faced the Persians at Marathon!' He pointed with his drawn sword. 'The river is nothing! Come on!'

He had pushed deep into their ranks with his horse, and now he emerged, riding for the riverbank.

Alexanor's horse offered him no choice, and followed the horse it knew.

A dozen men followed, and then a hundred. A man in fine armour began roaring in the Boeotian dialect, something about following young Achilles, and they were off, into the river bed. Alexanor's gelding gave a great roll as he lost his footing and then caught himself, cat-like. Alexanor only held on by a miracle, and then he was across.

The Boeotians streamed across behind. All of them must have come, and they came at a run, and raised spray like children playing in a stream.

'Achilles! Achilles leads us!' called the rear-rankers.

'Now form your ranks! Form your ranks!' Philopoemen was calling, his voice like a trumpet of bronze. 'Where are your officers! Where is the Sacred Band?'

This last was a purely historical allusion, and Alexanor knew it, but it seemed to put iron into the older men and they pushed forward, the best armoured and the richest. A dozen of them had already bloodied their spears on the *psiloi* who tried to hold the riverbank, and the phalanx began to form like bread rising.

'Achilles! ACHILLES!'

Alexanor felt enlarged – spiritually awakened. It was like meditation and prayer and athletics all together. Some of the Boeotians, as if attuned to his thoughts, caught up the *paean*. But when he turned to congratulate Philopoemen, he saw the sparkle of the sun on bronze in the distance, and a nodding of plumes.

'Cavalry!' he shouted.

Philopoemen reined in and turned in the saddle, looking back over his shoulder.

There, on the slope below the Macedonian phalanx, was the Spartan cavalry. And almost directly to the front of the Boeotians, the Spartan mercenaries under Eucleidas were forming in front of their redoubt, clearly intending to come down the hill and smash the Achaeans and the Boeotians.

Philopoemen looked back and forth between them.

'A very good plan, Cleomenes,' he said aloud. He glanced at Alexanor. 'Would you be so kind as to fetch me Dinaeos and the Megapolitan *hippeis*? The Exiles?' He glanced up the hill. 'And ... can you tell a lie? In a good cause?'

Alexanor shrugged. 'I have told a lie or two in my time.'

'I need Demetrios the Illyrian to go forward.' Philopoemen looked back across the stream. 'I could explain ... Never mind, there is no time. Will you go?'

'Why me?' Alexanor asked. But he'd already turned his horse.

'Everyone saw you with the king yesterday. You don't think I know how to win this, do you?'

Alexanor was watching the Macedonian phalanx.

'Our first law as doctors is to never take action unless we are sure,' he said. 'How can you know more than the king of Macedon?'

Philopoemen showed frustration, but he made himself sit up straight on his horse.

'He is with his phalanx. Prince Alexander went to support the phalanx. They are Macedonians – they cannot imagine that the crisis of the battle could be anywhere but where they are.'

The word 'crisis' was the deciding blow. Alexanor knew about crisis – the moment in a disease when the cure either succeeded or failed. It was the right word for Philopoemen to use, and it went right through Alexanor's defences.

'Very well,' he said, and saluted as he had seen other men salute.

He got his horse back across the stream, and then, amazingly, up the far bank. His thighs were burning, his arse hurt and he was lathered in sweat. A javelin skidded along the grass in front of him like a lethal snake, and his horse shied. A sling stone struck his horse's withers, and another hit his thigh, leaving a bright red mark that the doctor knew would deepen to a black bruise with time. Even at long range they were targeting him. The enemy *psiloi* knew he was a messenger.

But the sling stone that stung his horse prompted the gelding to an explosive gallop, and before Alexanor could think of what to do, he was riding clear of the shower of missiles.

He leant forward over his horse's neck and got the gelding down to a canter. He stayed there, leaning forward like a jockey, thighs closed on the horse's back like a jeweller's vice, until he saw Dinaeos. He managed to sit back and use his reins in such a way that did not humiliate him; his gelding came to a stop head to head with Dinaeos' larger stallion.

'*He* says to take the *hippeis* across immediately,' Alexanor said.

'On me!' roared Dinaeos.

He didn't even look back, or acknowledge the priest at all; his entire being was focused on the stream crossing.

'I'm ordering the Illyrians across too!' Alexanor called.

Dinaeos paused, looked back and then forward at the width of the easy ford in front of them.

'Halt!' he roared.

The Achaeans halted in confusion.

'Then get them fucking moving!' Dinaeos called. 'I want them in front of me, not coming in behind.'

The *hyperetes* was calling orders and men were aligning themselves, grumbling in frustration.

Alexanor got his horse to a trot, and then a canter, and rode down the line to the Illyrians, who faced a difficult crossing and an almost empty vale between the two hills.

'Forward!' Alexanor called as soon as he was close to the pale-eyed chieftain.

The Illyrians heard him. They didn't wait to hear their king translate the order. They went forward. There were perhaps two thousand of them, and they put their heads down and ran. The left of their line crossed the ford in front of the Achaean horse, and kept going up the hill. They didn't wait for the rest of their line, either; the Illyrians were not so much a phalanx as two thousand individual warriors.

Their appearance immediately changed the battle in front of the Achaean phalanx, though. Like the lid being taken off a boiling pot, the pressure on the front of the barely formed Achaeans was released. Hundreds of *psiloi* ran for their lives to avoid being spitted by half a hundred Illyrians, and the Boeotians finally pushed forward into that space and began to coalesce into a fighting group and not a mass.

Now the Allied left began, for the first time, to press forward.

Over to the left on the slopes of Olympos, the Macedonian phalanx was lower on the hill than it had been, and it had hundreds of infantry clawing away at its shielded flank. Cretan archers loosed shafts and helots dropped rock after rock. The Macedonians would not give more than a foot here and another there.

The two kings were locked, spear to spear, helmet to helmet. The Spartans had every advantage. The Macedonians were the better soldiers.

Alexanor could see the Spartan cavalry and some broad-hatted Thessalians coming down into the vale between the hills. With them came a small horde of light-armed men; many stopped pelting the Macedonians and turned into the valley, looking for easier targets.

The Illyrians were across, and scrambling up the hillside into the waiting pikes of Eucleidas and his mercenaries, some of whom were as Macedonian as the men on the other hill. Alexanor could now see, as if written in a medical text, what Philopoemen had seen five minutes earlier – that the crisis of the battle would come in the centre between the hills.

The Illyrians struck the front of the mercenary phalanx at its front right corner – an oblique blow, as the Illyrians were more like a tide than an army – and went straight up the valley instead of matching frontages with the Spartan mercenaries, who were torn by the first impact, and men died in heaps. But then both bodies flinched and pivoted, going forward where they had no resistance, back where they were stopped.

The Spartan infantry began to drive the Macedonian phalanx down the hill on the left.

The Achaean phalanx hesitated, just a few paces off the front of the Spartan mercenaries, and then, urged on by their poet-commander, they went forward. They did not charge; they seemed to stumble forward, as if the rear ranks pressed the front ranks into contact. It was scarcely a fearsome attack. Through most of the front, men huddled behind shields and thrust feebly with long spears that were yet barely long enough to strike a blow on their adversary's shields. Most of the Achaeans were armed in the old way, with shorter spears and narrow, Gaullish shields, and they were very vulnerable in a close fight, especially as most of them had no armour.

Alexanor was following Dinaeos, who himself followed the Illyrians across the ford and then looked for a place for his horsemen. But Alexanor had no such concerns and he continued to follow the fight just to his left.

Philopoemen came riding across the back of the pike fight.

Dinaeos waved. 'Good,' he said quietly. 'You decide.'

Alexanor was watching the Spartan cavalry come from the right.

'They will attack the Illyrians,' he said.

Dinaeos shrugged. 'So? I don't know any Illyrians. Most of them are thieves and rapists.'

'If the Illyrians are beaten –' Alexanor was surprised to hear himself – 'aren't we going to lose?'

But Philopoemen saved him the effort.

'Half-wheel to the right,' he snapped as he rode up.

'So nice to see you too, Philopoemen!' Dinaeos said.

The light-armed men with the Spartan *hippeis* swept forward, or were impelled, and they fell on the shieldless flank of the Illyrians. A dozen men died.

Then a hundred died.

'Wedge!' Philopoemen told his *hyperetes*.

A trumpet sounded.

'Oh, the gods are with us,' Dinaeos said. 'It's fucking Nabis!'

He was using his knees to get his horse into its place in a dense wedge. Alexanor *almost* wanted to join them. He looked up the vale between the hills, and he, too, recognised the magnificent helmet and fine horsehair plumes of the Spartan officer who had attempted to violate the sanctuary.

The Exiles' wedge was forming fast.

The right end of the Illyrian line was collapsing. They were not formed close, and the light-armed men cut down any without armour, and now the Spartan cavalry was coming to finish the job.

'He can't even see we're here! Dinaeos said with an aggressive satisfaction.

Indeed, although the Achaeans could see the Spartans over the distant combat, the Spartans showed no sign of having discerned that the Illyrians had any friends.

Philopoemen was at the point of the wedge. His helmet shone like gold; his red plume marked him.

He raised his spear. 'Ready! Right up the hill and into the Spartans and then straight on until we crest the ridge.'

His cavalrymen cheered. The Achaean phalanx took up the cheer. The Boeotian calls of 'Achilles' rang out, and suddenly the Achaean phalanx caught it up.

'A-chill-es! A-chill-es!'

Alexanor saw heads come up among the Spartans and among the Illyrians.

'Walk!' the bronze-lunged *hyperetes* called.

The hillside was rocky, but the ground was not too bad for horses. The wedge started forward.

The Spartan cavalry were in four ranks, in a line like an equine phalanx. They were coming for the Illyrians. But the Illyrians had hundreds of war tricks and now they played one: the men facing the Spartans turned and sprinted down the hill. Some just lay flat; most ran off to the left, swelling the ranks of their friends. The Spartan charge fell on just a few, and butchered them …

The Exiles' wedge went forward, its order nearly perfect despite the slope and the stones.

Philopoemen raised his hand and the *hyperetes* called 'Trot.'

The noise increased dramatically.

Alexanor didn't want to turn his head, but he had to know. He glanced to his left.

The Achaean phalanx had been pushed back ten paces, flinching away from the contest but not yet broken, and the rear rankers were shouting for their Achilles. The Spartan mercenaries were losing their order, but they were winning, except where a corner of their phalanx was helmet to helmet with the Illyrians, who fought like madmen. Or barbarians.

Alexanor thought that there were just about twice as many Spartan cavalry as Achaean.

The order 'charge' came, clear as a hawk's call, and the wedge seemed to *fly*. The acceleration from trot to gallop was so sudden that it seemed as if a rope had dragged the head of the wedge forward, a stage trick, like the *deus ex machina*.

'What the fuck is he doing with my reserve?' Prince Alexander bellowed from close to Alexanor's ear. He almost lost his seat. 'Gods damn him. Ares' balls, you fuckwits!' The prince set about abusing the Megapolitan Exiles.

The wedge struck the Spartan horse and cut through them like an axe cuts a chip from soft wood. The front of the Spartan cavalry seemed to collapse as if they'd ridden over a tripwire – two dozen men killed or wounded at the impact – and the Achaean *hippeis* continued, momentum preserved. They went right up the hill, and the Illyrians turned and went with them – the men who'd lain amid the volcanic rock and the men who'd run to join their mates. Every unengaged Illyrian turned like a barn-swallow and joined the cavalry going up the vale. The Spartan cavalry had no chance. Hundreds were unhorsed in the first moments, either by the spears of the Exiles or by the panic of their mounts.

'Achilles! Achilles lives!'

Alexanor could see Philopoemen's scarlet helmet crest, deep in the onset. He watched with awe as the Achaean stabbed a Spartan horseman over his shield, a perfect stroke into the neck, then threw his spear into the next Spartan, deep into his body, then put his arm around another man's neck in the close press and threw him to the ground off the back of his horse. His right hand emerged from the throw with the man's long *falcis*, with which he beheaded the fourth man in the file and then he was out the back, his red plume flying behind him. His big charger knocked a smaller horse to the ground and trampled him, and Philopoemen turned back. One glance, and he cut, underhand, at a foe behind him, and his rising blade caught the man's chin and cut up through the bone of his skull, killing him instantly.

Five men downed in five deep breaths. Alexanor had never seen anything to equal it, even from the famous Rhodian marines.

'Achilles! ACHILLES!'

The survivors were running, but the Illyrians were on them like wolves on a fawn, and the Exile horse rode clear, their wedge intact, if slightly more open.

'Well,' Prince Alexander said. 'Spartan cavalry never were worth shit.' He looked at Alexanor. 'I ought to kill the bastard.'

He watched the Achaeans headed diagonally towards the crest of Olympos, clearing the hillside as they went with their Illyrian allies.

'Of course, he's won the fucking battle,' Alexander said with an odd smile. 'And man to man, he's like a fucking Titan. So maybe I'd do better to thank him.' He laughed. 'He *is* like fucking Achilles, except he never sulks.'

Alexanor looked up the left-hand hill, where Philopoemen's red-crested figure was disappearing into the press. The Macedonian phalanx was still helmet to helmet with the Spartiates, but now, their flanks finally clear, they surged. For the embattled Spartans, the sudden loss of their cavalry and the sight of the Achaean horse coming up their flank rattled them and they began to give way.

Alexander was grinning. 'I'll just deliver the killing blow. Otherwise the Achaean bastard will think he's important.'

Alexanor bowed, and rode for the hospital.

CHAPTER FOUR

—⟨ɷɷ⟩—

Sellasia and central Peloponnese

222 BCE

It was getting to be too dark to see. Men said it was a great victory, but there were always more wounded being brought in from the field, and Alexanor was in demand, first extracting arrows from Macedonian pikemen, and then looking at broken skulls. Eventually he was faced with an endless series of the same wound: skulls broken by heavy sling stones.

'Don't these men wear helmets?' he asked.

He had more than a dozen men whose skulls were actually broken. He was covered in blood. The light was bad for detailed examination.

'They have helmets,' Antigones said. 'The bronze doesn't stop a heavy stone.'

Alexanor just wanted to go to sleep. The man under his hands was very young: brown haired, with pale eyes made shallow by pain. The boy's breathing was bad.

'I could try a trephine,' he said.

Antigones shrugged. 'Maybe tomorrow,' he said callously, turning away and beckoning for the Rhodian to follow him. 'The light is going. I need you to look at another case anyway, before I ...' He looked back.

Alexanor had stopped. He was looking at two dim figures carrying a third.

'Dinaeos!' he called out.

'It's the priest!' the Achaean said, as if he'd just found a new-minted gold piece. 'Alexanor, it's Philopoemen. Please have a look at him. He ...'

They had the cavalry commander sitting on a spear between them. They put him gently on a blood-smeared table.

The big Achaean had spear wounds in both thighs. The wounds were torn and one bled heavily.

'He cut the head and pulled the shaft through,' Dinaeos said. 'With some gods-damned notion of returning to the fighting.'

The Achaean *hipparchos'* face was very pale in the last light of day.

Alexanor turned to the Macedonian doctor. 'What case did you want me to look at?' he asked.

'Another arrow wound,' the Macedonian said, 'but—'

'No, I'll do that first,' Alexanor said. 'Philopoemen, can you hear me?'

'Yes.' The Achaean tried to smile, but his lips only trembled.

'Get me a six-wick oil lamp,' Alexanor snapped. 'There's one in the *hetaera*'s tent. She has four ... No, wait. Dinaeos? Ask her if I can operate in her tent. Be quick.' He turned back to Kleostratos, the Thracian. 'Put your thumb right there,' he said, placing the man's thumb on a gurgling vein. 'See how it stops the bleeding? Good. And on this leg? Right there. Good. I need you to keep him just like this for ... a few minutes.'

The Thracian nodded. 'Yes, lord.'

'Good. I'm not a lord.' Alexanor turned back, snapped up his roll of arrow spoons, and hurried to the new patient. 'Leon?'

'Yes?'

'Carry him outside,' he said.

Leon was a big, strong man. He lifted the wounded Illyrian as gently as he could, but the man gave a scream.

The tent was full of screams. Alexanor shut them out and followed his patient out into the last light of day.

He knelt by the Illyrian, who was blond and green-eyed and smooth-skinned. He had an arrow deep in his left thigh. His eyes met Alexanor's and they were full of pain and trust. He *knew* he was safe.

'This is our high-priced help,' the Macedonian doctor joked to the mercenary. 'He costs more than you do. He'll get that shaft out.'

Alexanor ran a hand down the back of the young man's thigh. Someone had cut the shaft to save the man from the vibration of the shaft in the wound; but the shortened shaft made it more difficult for Alexanor to work out the path of the wound.

He prayed. The arrowhead was right against the artery that ran along the bone. Usually arrowheads were dull enough, except at their points. He tugged a little at the arrow.

The man screamed, a shocking noise.

'Barbed,' Alexanor said.

Antigones shrugged as if to say, 'I could've told you that.'

Alexanor opened the two halves of the spoon and began to work them into the wound on either side of the shaft. Leon put a piece of cane between the patient's teeth. The man bit down so hard he splintered the cane. Then he whimpered.

Alexanor knew better than to hesitate.

He pushed. The spoon would not budge, and then there was an elasticity. And then it gave; there was a gout of blood . . .

And then more blood. Blood everywhere. A massive flow of blood, like a sack emptying.

Alexanor sat suddenly, as if his tendons had been cut.

Out loud, he said, 'I killed him.'

Antigones was already cleaning the spoons. The Illyrian was already dead – bled out in a few beats of his heart.

'Damn it!' Alexanor said.

'Yes,' the military doctor said.

Dinaeos came up. 'She has cleared her tent,' he said. 'It's much brighter.'

'Asklepios,' Alexanor said softly. 'Oh, Apollo. Oh, fuck.'

He couldn't make his limbs move. He was sitting in the grass, and he had the dead Illyrian's blood all over him. Some had spurted onto his face and the warmth was horrible.

He was sitting on the deck, and his chiton was red with blood. Philip's head was in his lap. They were all white and dead, like gutted fish.

'Come on,' Antigones said. 'Come on, man. Your friend needs you.'

'Maybe I'll kill him, too,' Alexanor's self-disgust was evident in his voice. 'You do it.'

The Macedonian physician grabbed his hand and levered him to his feet.

'I don't even know what you plan to do,' he said. 'I didn't even know there were pressure points to stop bleeding in the thigh. So, I suggest you get your shit together and go and save your friend.'

Alexanor frowned. 'Very well.'

He shook himself, and followed Dinaeos to the women's tents.

Phila, the *hetaera*, was looking at Philopoemen, who lay across four low benches, bleeding on a white linen coverlet. The Thracian had done his best, but blood had flowed.

'Will you use fire?' Antigones asked.

Alexanor felt he was seeing it all from very far away.

The *hetaera* was looking at him with unconcealed horror and she flinched, and then stood her ground.

'Thais!' she said. 'Warm water and a towel for Master Alexanor.'

Alexanor stood over the Megalopolitan *hipparchos*, trying to sort his thoughts: the foolishness of men's attempt to heal; the utility of taking no action against the almost certain death the Achaean faced if he did not attempt ... attempt ...

'Linen thread, well waxed with beeswax,' he said. 'And water to wash. My hands are filthy.'

'You will sew the wound?' Antigones asked.

Dinaeos, so bluff, so confident, looked at him with a trust that Alexanor knew he did not deserve. It made him feel like a fake. The Illyrian had had the same trust.

'No.' Alexanor took a breath.

Phila appeared with an ivory cross wound round with linen thread. She uncoiled a length and ran it through a piece of wax and then bit it off.

Alexanor snatched it. He made a noose of the end and laid it over the wounded man's chest.

Thais appeared with a bowl of hot water. Alexanor took the time to wash his hands and face, to dry his hands on the towel, to sing a hymn to Asklepios and another to Apollo while he washed. His voice grew steadier.

'Now,' he said, with a confidence he didn't really feel. 'We need to find the source of all the blood. Yes?'

Antigones nodded. 'You don't work in a field hospital all your life without learning about blood vessels,' he said.

'You may know more than I do,' Alexanor said. 'We are forbidden dissection.'

Antigones shrugged. 'I hear we too are forbidden dissection,' he agreed. 'But the gods send me an infinite supply of barbarian bodies, already dead.' He washed his hands in the same bloody water. 'Let me try this leg. There – I have it. I didn't know the pressure point, but surely this is the vessel.' He turned, as if they were alone. 'You should try dissection. Really.'

Alexanor ignored him. 'See the flow of blood? Timed with the beat of his heart? So slip the little noose over the end and pull it tight,' he ordered. 'Excellent. See the bleeding stop?'

'Won't this whole leg die?' Antigones asked.

'This is purely empirical, but so far, I've never seen it happen. I think it is like ... It is like the countryside. There are many roads to carry the blood. This leg is not nearly so badly damaged, and I'm going to guess that if I wrap this well ... My dear, may I have some very clean linen? Splendid,' he said as the slave-woman presented him with a strip of white linen. He began to wrap the leg. He coated the wound in honey and Leon drove off the flies. Then he examined Antigones' work, put wine and honey on the wound, and wrapped it. 'Well done,' he said.

The Achaean had uttered no more than a moan.

'Are you awake, my friend?' he asked.

'Yes,' the Achaean whispered.

'Can you take nourishment? You have lost a great deal of blood.'

'I ...' The Achaean paused.

'I'll give him food,' Dinaeos said.

'Broth,' Alexanor said. 'Full of meat.'

The *hetaera* waved her hands and slaves ran.

'I swear ...' Philopoemen said.

Alexanor bent low to hear him.

'I swear I don't get wounded every fight,' the Achaean whispered. He smiled.

His eyes closed.

'Yes, he does,' Dinaeos said. 'Every gods-damned fight. Fuck, doc. Is he going to die?'

Alexanor was looking at his hands, newly coated in blood. All he could see was blood. He had been working on broken bodies for eight hours. When he closed his eyes, he saw blood, and wounds. Torn skin. Death.

'Did we win?' he asked.

Dinaeos sighed. 'Oh, yes. We won. Cleomenes is broken, if he's not dead. The Spartiates were wiped out. Our hero had to dismount to fight them.' He sounded bitter. 'We were done. We won the fucking battle, but he had to dismount, to do more.'

'The king,' Thais said from the doorway of the tent, and there was the king of Macedon and Prince Alexander.

'Is he dead?' the king asked.

'No, my lord,' Alexanor said.

'I understand this young man saved the centre,' the king said. 'Pray the gods he lives – he has the head of a great commander. I will make him famous.'

The king nodded to all and turned to Phila with a bow.

'My lady, thanks for letting your tent be used for the wounded. You … That is …' He shrugged. 'Thanks.' He looked at Antigones. 'How many dead and wounded?'

The Macedonian doctor shook his head. 'My lord, I'm sorry – I have no count yet. The Illyrians lost heavily. The phalanx, perhaps two hundred.'

'A dead Illyrian is an Illyrian I don't have to pay,' the king said. 'I feel for the boys from Pella more.'

Alexanor thought of the trust in the dying Illyrian's eyes, so like the trust in Dinaeos' eyes – and how easily the highlander had bled out.

Outside, in the warm summer air, Alexanor took a deep breath.

'How do you do it? How do you handle it? When it is so *fucking* pointless?' he asked, expecting Antigones, but it was Phila who stood behind him.

She handed him a flask of unwatered wine.

'I drink too much,' she said. 'I recommend it.'

He took the flask and Thais, the slave, handed him a light cup, Athenian ware, he noticed in a detached way. Phila was more than a *porne*; everything was beautiful, from the linens to the cups. Her tent was like the well-appointed home of a very rich, very accomplished Athenian, and even through the curtain of blood before Alexanor's eyes, the care she lavished managed to penetrate, steadying him.

He poured the cup full and drank it off.

'I haven't really had anything to eat,' he said. 'That was ungracious,' he muttered unsteadily. 'I only mean—'

'Fetch our heroic doctor some food. Meat. Some of the broth we're making for the Achaean cavalryman. Bread.'

She waved at Thais, and then fetched him bread with her own hands.

Alexanor shook his head. 'I should go. I must pray, and wash . . .'

'I say you will not go until you are fed.'

She took an iron pot, worth a small fortune, off the brazier and poured water into a deep bowl.

Alexanor, who felt that he was moving in a fog, wondered how a deep ceramic bowl made it over the passes and across the Isthmus unbroken. He washed his hands like an automaton, but there was always more blood. Up his arms, past the elbow . . .

He was standing with his weight forward. Like he had fallen. His arms were on the low table that held the hot water, and he couldn't move, and the red, red blood had tainted the clean water, so that the bowl seemed to sparkle with blood. He gagged.

Her hand, warm and confident, touched his bare chest under his *chiton*. She opened the pins at his shoulder and the buttons and pulled it away, leaving him naked. And then she began to wash him. She sang a little, and the song, a hymn to Demeter, seemed to run all around his head and leave room for nothing else. Demeter, the Mother. Demeter, who lost her child. Demeter, who brought peace and not war to men.

She sang the hymn in a light voice, and he, unbidden, began to hum the tune, which he knew. Thais came in, put down a tray that smelt of lamb and broth, and went out, to return in a few heartbeats with more hot water, another bowl.

Phila washed him as if he was a child. At some point he took a linen towel from her and completed the task himself – as if at some point his mind returned to being master of his body – and he took the bowl of soup and drank it off like wine. There was bread, and he ate it, more animal than man, and he felt his body take the nourishment like a drug, so that aches in his shoulders and legs from riding, from a day of cutting men's flesh, vanished.

Phila was gone; he could hear her in another portion of the tent, is-suing orders. Thais came in, nodded to him, and refilled his soup bowl.

Phila came back in. 'Your Achaean is sleeping. Unless dying men snore.'

'Snoring is not always a healthy sign . . .' Alexanor said automatically.

He rose and went through the curtain of wool to the next room of the tent. But on inspection, the *hetaera* was correct; the young Achaean was deeply asleep, and he, too, had been washed clean of blood.

Alexanor took a deep breath, aware that some nameless apprehension had hung over him, and was dispelled. He followed Phila back into the other room. Almost without his volition, his right hand took the refilled bowl of lamb broth and he drank it off, greedily, like a small boy.

Phila laughed. 'Really? Do men require a woman to make them eat?'

Alexanor was embarrassed by his poor manners.

'*Despoina*, I am sorry. I can only plead . . . fatigue. My manners are terrible – my mater would have me flogged. You have been so kind – your tent . . .'

He wanted to say something elegant about how it was like a beautiful home, not some dreadful brothel, but nothing came to him that wouldn't offend.

Her smile broadened and she stepped up close to him.

'I'm not done with you yet,' she said. 'I, too, am a healer.'

He was still naked – a natural state to a priest of Asklepios. But this time, as she stepped close and put a hand on his chest, his whole body responded. The response was explosive, and as involuntary as the second bowl of soup. He held her so hard she might have cried out. Her long *peplos* overgown fell to the floor, and her linen underdress was so fine as to be transparent in the brazier light; but Alexanor noticed none of this. He was urgent, immediate, hungry.

She laughed, exposing her throat to his kisses. She wrapped her legs around him as if she meant to climb him, and they were entwined, standing, and he walked to the long *kline* and laid her down.

'We're going to need more towels,' she said, a little later. She laughed and climbed over him. He watched her body . . .

'Who is Aspasia?' the *hetaera* asked. 'Don't be embarrassed. In my profession, we're used to being called other names.'

Alexanor tried to relax, but he was flushed and his breathing was too fast.

'My ... first love.'

'Was she wonderful? What happened?'

She was sitting on the edge of the *kline*. Naked. Alexanor was transfixed.

Thais appeared with a pair of linen towels. Alexanor was watching the *hetaera* – as a physician, as a priest, as a man. Her body was fine – thin and muscular, not lush. He could see that she had borne a child, and that she danced and exercised regularly. He could see that she had taken a bad wound in her youth, a cut up her side that left a scar from her hip to her breast. Her breasts were those of a maiden, high and small; her throat and shoulders those of an Amazon, her back packed with subtle muscle.

'I loved her. My father ... forbid me to wed. And she ...' Alexanor looked away. 'Thought me a coward. I left Rhodes. She married someone else.' There it was, in a sentence. Words he had not spoken in five years.

She looked at him. Her face was remarkable, her eyes huge, her cheekbones high, her teeth perfect and white, her lips strong and ...

'I very much doubt that anyone ever mistook you for a coward,' Phila said. 'I think you are leaving something out.'

Alexanor was amazed at what he'd just said.

'I ...' he began, and then he was kissing her again.

'My,' she muttered when he began to nuzzle her neck. 'You *are* a hero,' Phila said, running a hand up him as she lay back down.

Again, it was like the soup. Alexanor watched himself from afar, as he took her – shocked at the animalistic urge of his passion. He was not untutored in the arts of sex; he had known a beautiful woman before, with carefully controlled ...

He was gone.

Much later, she lay with one arm over the back of the *kline*, her diaphanous linen enhancing rather than hiding her. He was sitting, eating candied almonds.

'You over-value your control,' she said. 'I agree that it is important. It makes us Hellenes. But it is important to know when to let the daemon free.'

'A priest of Asklepios must always be in command of his body,' he said, although he smiled.

'Even if the gods command otherwise? Do you think I might have a few of my own honeyed almonds, or must you eat them all?'

He handed her the bowl. 'Who made you so wise?'

She shrugged. 'Motherhood? Prostitution? Half the men who buy you would do better with a chat than a fuck.' She shrugged again. 'Or both. Sex is very healing.'

'You have just made a correct diagnosis and delivered a powerful treatment. The patient is healed.' Alexanor shook his head. 'If I'm not killed by the king of Macedon. Will you be ...?'

She shook her head. 'The king chose his boyfriend for the night of his victory. In fact, I'm mostly here as decoration. And you are not leaving. When I left the world of leaning against the theatre walls to service my clients, I swore that no man would have me unless he spent the night in my bed. So you will sleep here. I'll make it right with the king.' She smiled. 'And you are not telling me everything about this woman. You are no light o' love. When did you last have sex?'

Alexanor finished the almonds.

'I am deeply in your debt ...' He shrugged. 'Doctors make poor patients,' he admitted. 'Many years.'

'Exactly. Did she really think you a coward? And if she's such a fool, why do you still love her?'

Alexanor ran a hand across that marvellous, muscled back.

'I ...'

She laughed. 'I can't help myself. I am almost to my diagnosis, but you are working on another bout of exercise.'

'Perhaps I could help with your stomach ailments,' he murmured, kissing her hard stomach.

'Yes, well, any girl likes free medical care,' Phila said. 'Do not, I pray you, get your sticky hands on this linen. You know where the wash bowl is.'

Alexanor washed, checked one more time on his patient, and lay down by the *hetaera*. She put her head on his shoulder and curled against him, and he marvelled at her, and at himself, and he was almost instantly asleep.

*

He awoke to the oddest sensation. After a moment of disorientation, he remembered it all: the blood, the Illyrian, the sex. The woman who was sleeping at his side.

Alexanor had never *slept* next to a woman. He smelt her hair and pulled her closer and went back to sleep. But then he dreamt of Aspasia, walking up the hill to the temple of Apollo in the dawn.

The next morning, clean, neat, and dressed in a plain brown *chiton* borrowed from one of Phila's slaves, Alexanor reported to the hospital. Before the sun was a hand's width above the horizon, he and Leon had performed two trephines on men with fractured skulls.

Leon held the head of the third patient perfectly steady while Alexanor cut.

'Now that you are a full priest ...' Leon said.

The sharp teeth of the round saw cut into the man's head.

'Yes?' Alexanor said.

His hand was steady. He felt ... clean. Rested.

'I'd like to stay with you. As your assistant. And eventually be promoted myself. Take my full vows.'

Leon continued to hold the man's head, his thighs like a clamp.

Alexanor's hand never wavered, although his heart soared.

'You would stay at the temple?' he asked.

Leon was silent, and just then the skull gave very slightly and Alexanor relaxed his fingers, gave a twist, and the broken patch of skull came free. A long splinter went down into the pink-grey matter.

'Apollo,' Leon breathed. 'He should be dead.'

'But he is not,' Alexanor breathed.

His roll of instruments was open on the bloody sand next to him. He reached out and took a pair of tweezers, long tweezers of shining bronze.

'Not a move, now,' he said.

He reached in with the tweezers, took the protruding nub of the bone splinter, and drew it smoothly out along what he guessed was the path of entry.

'Oh, mother!' the man cried. 'Oh, mother, I never meant to hurt you! I lost the spoon!'

A drop of blood appeared on the cranial matter, but no more.

At the hospital they had wafers of pure gold to cover holes in skulls.

He'd taken three. He slipped one under the dangling scalp and attached it with two tiny pins as he'd been taught, and folded the scalp
back across the skull. In a dozen careful stitches, he had the scalp
back in place, and then he and Leon finished, each taking one of the
cross cuts until all the slack was out of the scalp. There was a lot of
blood – scalp wounds always bled copiously.

'I guess that man will never be poor again,' a Macedonian said.

Alexanor got to his feet. His leg was cramped. He used the trephine
sitting like a tailor, and Leon was trained to hold the patient's head
between his powerful thighs. Both men got slowly to their feet to
find that they were surrounded by Macedonian officers, and several of
the Achaeans. Cercidas the poet was there, as was Doson. Alexanor's
concentration had been so great that he hadn't noticed.

'That was his brain? The inside of his head?' the king asked.

'Yes, my lord,' Alexanor answered.

'He cried for his mother when the bone was removed.' The king's
eyes gleamed with a hard intelligence.

'Or perhaps,' Alexanor shrugged, 'I think he had a memory, perhaps
trapped by the splinter and released by its removal.'

'And now he'll always have a gold piece,' the king said with a broad
grin.

Alexanor was sticky with blood. But today, it bothered him not at
all, and he smiled at himself, at the fragility of the mind, and at Phila's
powers of healing, all while glancing at the king.

The golden young man, Prince Philip, stood with Doson.

'You did it beautifully,' he said. 'Will the man live?'

Alexanor liked the young man instantly; his eager curiosity and his
good manners. He raised his bloody hands in an attitude of supplica-
tion and prayed.

'With the will of the gods, he may live,' he said.

Philip pressed closer. 'How many men have you saved?'

Alexanor shrugged.

'Ask him how many he's killed,' spat one of the Macedonian officers. He was a big man, as big as Philopoemen, with dirty blond hair
and a knowing smile.

Again, Alexanor shrugged. 'I killed a man last night. My arrow-
mould slipped.'

Philip was fascinated. 'But surely you do not blame *yourself*? You were not the cause of his death, merely the agent.'

'Perhaps a surer hand than mine would have saved him,' Alexanor said.

'Maybe he'll kill Philopoemen,' Cercidas said.

Alexanor turned to look at the man, appalled.

'You heard me, foreigner,' the Achaean *Taxiarchos* said. 'He's a danger to his friends and his community. Feel free to make a "mistake" on him.'

The king shook his head. 'No, my friend. I saw the speed of your cut – the way you pulled the bone splinter. I have a *hoplomachos* – a weapons teacher. His movements are like yours – sure, quick, like an eagle stooping on prey.'

Alexanor was unused to praise. He flushed.

Doson nodded. 'Your efforts here will not go unrewarded. I have to settle with the Spartans – then I'm for Argos. I would appreciate it if you would accompany me at least to the Isthmus. Besides, you might enjoy the trip. I hear you are a fine rider.'

Alexanor bowed. 'I will be happy to accompany you, my lord. But a fine rider? I think not.'

Doson laughed quietly. 'And on my *own* mare,' he whispered.

Alexanor froze, but the king was laughing loudly.

His laugh cut off like an extinguished candle, and the king turned on Cercidas.

'Philopoemen won the battle where you almost lost it,' he said. 'Your comments are of a piece with your incompetence, Cercidas. Philopoemen is the best officer your fucking Greeks have. And you want him *dead*?'

'There is more to politics than war, my lord,' Cercidas said. 'I'm sure that the young man excels at *war*.'

'If you do not excel at war, someone conquers you. Begone, Cercidas. Don't appear before me again until someone tells you it's safe.'

Doson appalled the Achaean League by releasing all the Spartiate prisoners and forbidding the sack of the city of Sparta. His own phalanx was none too happy, to judge by the grumbling of the wounded men under Alexanor's care; Sparta was a rich city and they had all expected loot. Philopoemen and his friends were livid.

'That wily bastard ...' Dinaeos spat.

Philopoemen, who was, again, recovering faster than any physician would have believed, was sitting on Phila's couch, leaning back with his feet up.

'He planned this all along,' Philopoemen said bitterly. 'He gains the reputation for clemency with the other Greek cities, and he puts shackles on the Achaean League.'

Another of his companions, Aristaenos, who had fought bravely in the battle, shook his head.

'But our city is restored,' he said. 'Our farms, our people. Megalopolis is free.'

'Free,' Philopoemen nodded. 'Until the Spartans attack us again. Free for Doson to make our foreign policy. Free to be taxed to support his armies.'

'You sound like Cercidas,' Dinaeos said.

'Just because he hates me doesn't mean he is altogether wrong,' Philopoemen said.

'We have our own army!' Aristaenos said. 'The Achaean phalanx did well enough, and everyone says ...'

Phila smiled from her chair. 'You all have such good manners. Everyone says the Megalopolitan cavalry saved the battle.' She waved. 'You. The Exiles.'

Philopoemen nodded. 'Everyone says so a little too loudly,' he said. 'Cercidas will hate me all the more.'

As it proved, it only took Doson four days to settle the affairs of Sparta. The king, Cleomenes, fled into exile, boarding a ship in the south with his Royal Companions. Doson settled the government on the other king of Sparta; as Phila said, it was convenient for everyone that the Spartans always had two.

And Doson had other problems, as a steady stream of *causia*-wearing Macedonian messengers brought news of new Illyrian incursions into Western Macedon as they journeyed towards the Isthmus.

'I thought that all of the Illyrians were fighting for us?' Alexanor asked Kleostratos. The Thracian was the best horseman Alexanor had ever seen, managing his horse with no apparent effort.

Kleostratos barked a laugh. He was tattooed over most of his body and had gold studs in his nose and gold cuffs in his ears. His beard was bright gold, and he had a huge smile.

'Fucking Illyrians,' he said. 'They all fight each other. We have our Illyrians, at least as long as we pay them, and then the Aetolians have their Illyrians, as long as they pay theirs, if you take my meaning. Fucking barbarians.'

This from a man covered in geometric tattoos.

He grinned.

Alexanor realised he was being mocked.

Kleostratos shrugged. 'Really, they are worse than Thracians. When we're bought, we stay bought.'

'Aetolians?' Alexanor asked.

Philopoemen appeared from behind him. He reined in.

'Aetolians?' he asked.

'They have a confederation, do they not?' Alexanor asked.

Philopoemen put out a hand, like a physician taking a pulse.

'Are you feeling well, friend? Are you losing your memory?' He laughed. 'The Aetolian Federation is our true enemy.'

Alexanor shrugged. 'For myself, I have no enemies.'

Philopoemen laughed. So did Kleostratos. The Thracian pointed at him.

'I heard you bare your teeth at the Aegyptian ambassador. You all but went for him, the pious windbag. Pirate! Slaver!' the Thracian said, in a fair imitation of Alexanor's Rhodian accent.

Philopoemen nodded. 'Aye, my friend,' he said, 'so don't tell us how you have no enemies. The Aetolians are our bane. They send money to Sparta, they raid our coasts, and they send mercenaries to help the pirates.'

'I'm sure they love their children,' Alexanor said.

'Don't be sure of it,' Philopoemen said.

'Probably sell them into slavery. For more armour,' said Kleostratos.

'Even now, Macedonians are marching north to fight Illyrians who are taking Aetolian silver,' Philopoemen said.

'You can't know that,' Alexanor said.

Kleostratos shrugged. 'The king of Macedon needed a rapid solution to the Spartan problem. He wouldn't listen to Aratos or Philopoemen or any of the other Achaean leaders – he said he "didn't have time".' The Thracian smiled mirthlessly. 'So by paying off the Illyrians, the

Aetolians have saved their butt-boy, Sparta, from a whipping.'

Alexanor shook his head.

Philopoemen smiled grimly. 'How long have you served at Epidauros?' he asked.

'Almost six years,' Alexanor answered.

'The sacred wall must cut off more than infection,' Philopoemen said. 'Every peasant in Achaea knows this. Listen, my friend. Just as the kings – the Seleucids, the Macedonians, the Aegyptians – pour their money into the Peloponnese to show their riches ... do they not?'

Alexanor had only to think of the magnificent theatre at the temple, the second-largest in the world. Built by the king of Aegypt.

'Yes,' he said.

'They also like to fight their surrogate wars here,' Philopoemen said bitterly. 'They pay the gold, and we die, so that various tyrants can proclaim themselves the "Liberator of Athens" and the "Liberator of Olympia" at parties.'

Alexanor looked back and forth between the two horsemen.

'If you have such a low opinion of the kings,' he asked, 'what are you doing here?'

Philopoemen nodded. 'Good question. Aratos ordered me to obey Doson, and Doson commanded that my cavalry escort him north.' He shrugged. 'We'll see. My suspicion is that we're hostages.'

The Thracian clapped a broad hand on Alexanor's back.

'Welcome to the game, priest,' he said. 'The game of kings.'

Alexanor bridled. 'I think I understand the game, as you call it. In Great Alexander's day, my city, Rhodes, was an ally of Athens – later, of Macedon. When Demetrios attacked us, we turned to Ptolemy of Aegypt for aid. When other Ptolemies began to use the Cretan pirates to undermine us, we found other allies. That is the way of *politics*.'

'Yes,' agreed Philopoemen, 'and for us, the Achaean League was under the heel of Macedon until Aratos freed us by taking Corinth – the greatest military feat of the age, I assure you. And now we are back under the Macedonian yoke because we cannot face Sparta with her Aegyptian money and her Aetolian allies. Not unaided. Someday, I swear, if the gods spare me, I will make men fear the name of the League, and no Spartan kinglet will disturb men who wish only to till their farms and be free.'

They rode along in silence, until Dinaeos laughed.

'What a politician you will be, Phil, when you're done playing war! You make beautiful speeches. But no one will ever fear the name of the Achaean League – look!'

He was pointing at a bend in the road, where the Achaean phalanx, homeward bound, had tangled where two roads crossed – the northern road to Arkadia, and the eastern road to the coast. Listening to the angry voices, it was clear that the coastal men wanted to go home, while the northern members of the League wanted the phalanx to march to Megalopolis before they dispersed.

A group of men in red caps and grey cloaks gathered their slaves and walked away down the road to the coast while officers bellowed at them.

'Look,' Dinaeos said with contempt. 'The Achaean League.'

More and more men were picking up their shields and walking off down the coast road. The *Strategos* of the League – the highest elective office in the Peloponnese – watched helplessly as half his men trickled away.

'If I was in command, I'd crucify half a dozen of the bastards right now, and this would never happen again,' Dinaeos spat, eyes hot with anger.

Philopoemen nodded. 'You and Cercidas would agree, then,' he said softly.

The *Strategos* stood in the middle of the crossroads, shaking with rage.

Dinaeos turned on his friend.

'I have nothing in common with that pompous windbag,' he spat.

Philopoemen didn't back down, or smile. He sat on his horse like an equestrian statue: calm, but stern.

'You would give an order without *knowing* that it would be obeyed,' the cavalry officer said. 'Who, exactly, would hold six fishermen of Hermione to crosses? Hmmm? What men could you trust to perform these executions? I say nothing of the ethics of the act, my friend. Merely the practicality. Although they are related. I, for example, would not obey you.'

Dinaeos scratched his beard. Alexanor expected hard words, but he nodded.

'Yes. It is a fantasy of anger. I'm sorry.'

Philopoemen shrugged. 'The time to fix this problem would have been yesterday, or the day before. Either the *Strategos* should have won the agreement of his hoplites in camp, that we would all march together, or he should have accepted their decision and dismissed them with the thanks of the League. Right here.'

'But then he would be giving in to them!' Dinaeos said.

Philopoemen smiled. 'You have served with me three times, Dinaeos, and still you imagine that an officer can just give orders and be obeyed? Even among the Spartans, the king is only first among equals, and the "Peers" can comment, even disobey – read your Herodotus! An officer can only lead by the consent of the led, like any government. The only place where a commander's authority is absolute is on the battlefield, like the powers of a *Strategos* granted by an emergency session of the League parliament.' He looked back at Dinaeos. 'Even then, that trust must be earned.'

Alexanor smiled and looked away. Something in the Achaean officer made his heart seem heavier in his chest, and he counted slowly and put a finger on his pulse, to see if the idea of liberty actually raised his heartbeat. His eyes met those of the Thracian, Kleostratos.

The man nodded. 'You see why we follow him? For me, I would kill whomever he told me to kill.' The Thracian looked away and caught sight of something he didn't like. 'Cleander? What the fuck are you doing?'

The man in question had ridden out of the column and was creating chaos as other men tried to ride around him. He was fiddling with his bridle, oblivious to the consternation of his mates. Kleostratos rode off to deal with him.

Dinaeos turned back to Philopoemen.

'You see? Kleostratos would kill for you,' he said. 'I, too, would do as you said. If you told me to crucify six farmers, I'd do it, and so would most of the rest of us, I'll wager.'

Philopoemen sighed. 'What a terrible power. And what a burden you lay on me – to carry the weight of all your moral decisions, which you cede to me? No thanks.' He seemed angry, and he rode a little ahead.

Cercidas was still in the road. He stood in silent rage; his sons stood by him, leaning on spears and tugging at their beards.

He saw Philopoemen and his rage broke.

'You!' he shouted. 'Take the *hippeis* and ride down those traitors!'

Philopoemen reined in, probably lost in his own thoughts.

The League *Strategos* raised an arm.

'Get your head out of your arse and obey me!' he shouted.

The Achaean was in his armour. The wounds on his legs were bandaged but didn't seem to hurt him; his back was straight. The *Strategos* wore no armour; he stood in the road in a cloak with gold embroidery and a long *chiton* over walking sandals, like a rich traveller and not a soldier. Indeed, almost none of the Achaean hoplites wore any part of their military kit. Slaves were carrying it, a huddle of them flocking like sheep just off the road.

The mob of angry hoplites was blocking the road, and the phalanx of Macedon was visible coming around the shoulder of the mountain behind them.

Philopoemen affected not to have heard the *Strategos*.

Cercidas put his hands on his hips.

'You! Philopoemen! Get down that road and force those fishermen back into the ranks!'

Philopoemen frowned. He waited for a long time, but, as Cercidas drew breath, he finally answered.

'No,' he said.

'I am your *Strategos*!' Cercidas spat. 'Obey!'

'No.'

Philopoemen held out a hand and motioned, and the cavalry went from four files to two; not quite as neatly as Macedonians, but it was a creditable performance, and the two-wide column began to thread the mob of angry hoplites filling the road.

Alexanor pressed in behind the cavalry officer, so that the big warhorse ahead made a hole in the crowd that he could follow.

'Best get your men moving,' Philopoemen said to the *Strategos*. 'The king of Macedon is no friend to indiscipline.'

'I order you ...' the *Strategos* said. 'I will see you never, ever hold office in the League, you *fucking* ingrate.'

Philopoemen nodded. 'Sir, with respect, I am not serving the League. Megalopolis raised three hundred cavalrymen from her exiled citizens. As a city. Not for your League.' He looked around. 'Indeed, I think that you have a *hipparchos* of your own, and the League voted to keep the cavalry home.'

'A lawyer's quibble,' snapped the *Strategos*.

Philopoemen had turned his horse aside, and Dinaeos led a long file of cavalrymen past. Kleostratos was pushing along the far edge of the road, through the slaves.

'No,' Philopoemen said, his reserve cracking. 'No, it is not. If I were to obey your foolish order, the League would explode right here. Arkadians against the Coast.'

Cercidas snapped around as if he'd been struck.

'Did you just call my order foolish?' he asked.

'Foolish. Ill-advised. Impossible to carry out. Yes, all of those things.'

Philopoemen was enraging the man by sounding like a schoolteacher. Direct, like a man giving children a lesson. And edging towards frustration.

Alexanor, who was used to the soldier being a man of near perfect control, was amazed to see Philopoemen seeming to expand with anger.

He put his heels into his marvellous horse and pushed forward. Then, as Cercidas stumbled back, he managed some mostly pretend flailing, as if he'd lost control of the big gelding, who turned in circles because Alexanor had his left heel pressed into the horse's side. Round and round they went, and Cercidas ducked away, and his sons both struck the horse with spear shafts, confusing it more, until Philopoemen got the bit in his right hand and dragged Alexanor, horse and all, clear.

'Don't go back,' Alexanor said, as Philopoemen turned his horse again. Behind them, a Macedonian officer was bellowing at Cercidas. 'Just keep riding.'

'You are right,' Philopoemen said, the annoyance peaking in his voice. 'But it angers me that the League sent such a fool to war. The divisions are deep. Fucking idiot. Traitor.'

The vulgarity was the first that Alexanor had ever heard from the young Achilles. It was uttered as the Macedonian column simply drove through the unarmed Achaean hoplites, who were driven off the road. The Macedonians marched in open order, with their slaves between the files, but all of them wore their armour, which gleamed in the autumn sun, and carried swords. They punched right through the Achaeans, their supposed allies, and marched on. Dinaeos had to look sharp to keep the Megalopolitan cavalry ahead of the Macedonian phalanx.

'What did he mean, he'll keep you from holding office?' Alexanor asked.

Dinaeos shook his head. 'That was a mistake, Phil. He's still spitting.'

Philopoemen rode off, silent.

Dinaeos shook his head and ordered the Megalopolitan cavalry on down the road.

'Where's he going?' Alexanor asked.

'He doesn't like to show anger,' Dinaeos said. 'I think he tried too hard. Anyway, he's no doubt embarrassed at his outburst. He'll ride alone for a while. No, leave him! He won't thank you.' He shrugged. 'The sad part is that he craves public honours, and Cercidas will now make sure he is denied them.'

'Craves public honours?' Alexanor looked back at the lone figure riding somewhat recklessly down the long slope instead of taking the road. 'He seems above all that, surely?'

Dinaeos grinned. 'You may be Apollo's favourite medico, but you have a lot to learn about people. He isn't just called the new Achilles. He wants to *be* Achilles.'

Three days later, and they were at Argos, its citadel rising over the plain. It had been an easy march from the Isthmus, and the summer games there were drawing to a close. There were twenty thousand Greeks from all over the Peloponnese, as well as Attica and Boeotia, camped on the plain. The stadium was packed, and there were people outside the stadium too, in among the olive groves. Outside the stadium was the old racecourse for horses, and it was there, on the perfectly flat ground, that Doson paraded his phalanx in full view of the spectators, and they cheered.

'He's a very able politician, for a king,' Philopoemen said, looking on.

The Megalopolitans looked like young gods; all their bronze was polished, and their fine red *chitons* and scarlet plumes made them visible across the plain.

The head of the Macedonian phalanx halted, and the files at the rear flowed forward, so that in the time it took the black-robed Nemean judges to come forward from the stadium, the whole phalanx had formed to the front, sixteen ranks deep and almost a hundred men wide.

'You see how good they are,' Philopoemen said.

'Yes,' Alexanor said.

'And yet, how little space they occupy. Twelve thousand men, and not much more than sixty paces wide.' He shrugged. 'I wonder ...'

One of the Macedonian noble messengers was riding towards them, across the flat plain of Argos, from where the king sat on horseback with his officers at the edge of the olive grove.

Philopoemen smiled and turned to Dinaeos. 'Could this be for us?'

Dinaeos raised an eyebrow. 'We can hope, eh?' he said, a little too casually.

The messenger trotted up and threw Philopoemen a salute – a crisp one, the kind of salute that Macedonians gave each other and not usually their inferior 'allies'.

'The king requests that the *hippeis* of Megalopolis come to the left of the phalanx and join the line. The *Agema* will come to the right of the phalanx.'

Philopoemen raised his arm to return the salute.

'Column of fours,' he said. 'We will form the rhomboid on me as we come into line.'

Dinaeos snapped his hand to the visor of his helmet.

'Yes, sir.'

Alexanor was struck by the speed with which the Megalopolitans went from a society of equals to obedient soldiers. In one comment, Dinaeos expressed casual disinterest; in the next, he sparkled with obedience.

I do, indeed, have much to learn about men, the physician thought.

'Ride with me,' Philopoemen said to Alexanor. 'When we approach the king to salute him, you can ride over and join his staff.'

'I wasn't asked,' Alexanor said with a smile.

Philopoemen was looking back over his column, which had formed well, although two men were wrangling over a place in the sixth rank. Kleostratos cantered down the lines, jaws working behind the moustached bronze cheek plates that hid his face.

Philopoemen nodded. 'You don't have to be asked,' he said. 'You are on his staff. I promise you this is true.'

'Oh,' said Alexanor. 'Should I have been there all morning?'

'Yes.' Philopoemen flashed the Rhodian a brilliant smile. 'But I'm glad you were here with us.'

He's nervous. A man who opened a hole in the Spartan ranks and fought on with a spear through both legs, and he's afraid of the crowd. Or is that too simple?

Philopoemen looked back again. The column was now formed well; the horses shone like children of Poseidon, their riders alert, heads up.

The king of Macedon had dismounted and now stood with the Nemean judges, a purple and white figure with eleven black ones. Prince Alexander was well off to the right, emerging from the olive groves with the Macedonian Companion cavalry; the magnificent *Hetaeroi*, once Alexander's bodyguard.

'Olympic salute,' Philopoemen said over his shoulder to Kleostratos, who made a face.

'Are you sure?' Dinaeos asked quietly. 'Think of Cleander and what an awkward sod—'

'The gods are with us.' Philopoemen smiled.

Kleostratos bellowed the order. The column began to move forward.

Alexanor rode aside, to be clear of the column, and then trotted past the king to where his staff waited in the burning sun of the Argosian plain. Alexanor had time to realise how much better his riding had become in three short weeks, and then he slid to the ground and looked back.

The Megalopolitans, four wide and more than seventy deep, were just drawing abreast of the king. A trumpet sounded, and three hundred hands raised their spears, straight up into the heavens, so that the sun burned like fire on their tips. And then three hundred arms came down, and the spears pointed sideways. The men's arms extended to the right, parallel to the ground, a dangerous manoeuvre in close order and ten times as dangerous on horseback.

Several of the Nemean judges applauded. Doson extended a hand in the Macedonian salute. The Megalopolitan Exile cavalry went by in a rattle of horse harness and a flash of scarlet plumes. The spear points went back up as the last files passed the judges and the king. The cavalry wheeled sharply to the left, rode along the flank of the phalanx, heading away from the king, and then whirled, wheeling through half a circle to come straight back at the judges.

Philopoemen rode out of the dust cloud, raised his spear, and sang out a command.

Dinaeos and Kleostratos emerged behind him and each of them

put their knees behind his, their order very close – so close that the flanks of the horses touched. Like a flock of starlings settling on a tree, the rest of the *hippeis* settled in behind them. Even if Cleander and one or two others rode too far and had to haul their reins, the whole formation was creditable, and it came together so quickly as to draw spontaneous applause from the spectators.

Doson shook his head, but he was smiling.

'Not bad, not bad,' he said softly.

The Macedonian household cavalry appeared from the opposite direction. They didn't form a wedge or rhomboid; instead, they wheeled by squadrons from column into line, forming to the right of the phalanx. While nowhere near as showy as Philopoemen's manoeuvre, theirs had an effortless perfection that spoke of long hours of training, of men who had spent years together.

Doson spoke to the judges, and then he turned and received some cheers from the crowd of spectators. Then he beckoned to one of his *hypaspists*, who ran forward with his horse. All the rest of his staff mounted, so Alexanor followed suit.

Young Antipater glanced around, saw the physician, looked him up and down, and smiled.

'You'll do,' he said. 'Ride with me. Stay right next to me and do what I do.'

'What's happening?' Alexanor asked the young Macedonian noble.

'The Nemeans and the other Peloponnesians have asked the king to enter the stadium and receive a wreath,' Antipater said, looking at the staff. 'We'll ride at his heels, and then Prince Alexander with the *Agema* and then your friend Philopoemen with his Greeks.' He made a face. 'Apparently it's a great honour.'

'You don't think much of Greeks, do you, Antipater?' Alexanor asked.

The Macedonian smiled. 'Oh, you Greeks are fine. Great artists. Marvellous philosophers. Medicine. All that.'

He locked his knees on his horse's back and raised himself, looking back behind them.

Alexanor could hear the word 'but' coming.

'But?' he prompted.

'Crap soldiers,' Antipater said. 'All the real men must have died fighting the Persians.' He made a face. 'No offence.'

Alexanor was surprised at the depth of the resentment he felt, but he didn't allow the anger to register in his face, and besides, they were entering the stadium.

If he had thought the cheers of the spectators loud on the plain, here, inside the stadium, which held *another* twenty thousand people, the noise was deafening. His horse started, ears laid back, eyes rolling, but Alexanor put a hand on the gelding's neck and hummed, as Kleostratos had taught him, and the gelding's ears went forward again.

Doson rode through the gate, waving to either side, and then went slowly around the course. The men in the stands were all citizens of various states; they were on their feet, and the handful of women attending, mostly senior priestesses, added their cries.

As he entered the closing stretch, the *Agema* entered the stadium from the open end. There was more cheering, and Prince Alexander saluted the crowd as the cavalry rode by, their purple cloaks moving like wings in the breeze.

The cheering seemed more subdued.

Doson, led by one of the judges, turned aside at the end of the track, and his staff followed him. They all dismounted and *hypaspists* took their horses. Alexanor found himself next to the king.

Philopoemen entered the stadium, his red cloak flashing behind him, his bronze helmet making him look as if he was crowned in light.

The crowd roared. And they roared more as the Megalopolitan cavalry came in behind.

'*Hellas!*' shouted someone in an upper tier. In a few heartbeats, it was a chant.

'*Hellas! Hellas! Hellas! Hellas!*' they called. And voices cried, 'Achilles, Achilles for the Achaeans!'

Doson raised an eyebrow. He glanced at Alexanor, and his eyes danced with amusement.

'Greeks,' he said. 'If I gave them their so-called freedom on a platter, they'd have lost it by the next Olympiad.'

His cynicism stung Alexanor the way his orderly's comments had.

'They cheer young Philopoemen as if he was their god. But in fact, most of these very same men voted *not* to send the League cavalry to aid me.' The king of Macedon shook his head. 'And if the League *had* sent me its precious cavalry, they would have been led by Mikkos of Dyme, who can't find his arse with both hands.'

Alexanor had no idea what to say, so he bowed.

Doson shook his head. 'Aratos, their usual *Strategos Autokrator*, is a meddling busybody. Good politician – terrible soldier.' He watched Philopoemen. 'This young man, though ... I'll take him. He belongs in Macedon.'

Alexanor wondered why the king was telling him these things.

Philopoemen came by them, face aglow from the cheers. Every man in the stadium was on his feet, roaring for Greece. The Macedonian cavalry was filing out at the far end of the theatre.

'My boys just saved these useless fucks from the Spartans,' Doson said. 'And they cheer for the Megalopolitans. Greeks. Really.' He smiled. 'You can see how I might find this tiresome.'

Again, Alexanor could think of nothing to say.

'What kind of reward would move him? Your friend? Estates? Gold?'

'I don't know.'

The cheers went on and Alexanor wasn't sure that the king heard him.

'Perhaps I'll give him a year of Phila's contract. Enough reward for any man,' the king said without turning his head. 'Don't bother to look offended. You cannot afford her, and I'm paying her. Mercenaries are mercenaries, young man.' Doson nodded and raised his arm, returning the salutes of the last ranks of Greek cavalrymen, and then he turned to the judges. 'My thanks for the ovation.'

They rode out, past a huddle of *pankrationists* preparing to compete. Alexanor, alone of the Macedonians, saluted them. They, in turn, ignored the Macedonians.

That night, after watching six bouts of *pankration* in the stadium, Alexanor was invited to dine with Phila and the king. After Leon had fussed over him, he found himself sharing a couch with Philopoemen at a Macedonian banquet. The drinking had started before Alexanor arrived, and most of the Macedonian officers were drunk already, staggering from couch to couch. Someone had given them all wreaths of wild celery, the reward of victors in the Nemean Games, which only served to make them appear even more like satyrs. On couches farther from the king, a dozen couples rutted away, as if public sex acts were routine matters in Macedon. Two men wrestled, their purple officers' *chitons* ripped away to reveal scarred bodies and new blood. Serving slaves moved quickly, with averted eyes, hoping to avoid reaching hands.

It was the most dangerous party that Alexanor had ever attended: he saw a shoulder dislocated; a slave was thrown over a couch and broke his femur; a man beat a flute girl, lacerating her back and shoulders with a branch that had been part of the decorations, even as his brother officers cheered him on.

'Do her!' one roared. 'Get her!'

She turned to run, and her abuser tripped over his own *himation* and fell, cracking his head against the stone floor. The terrified girl slipped away into the *stoa* and vanished. The spectators applauded and several threw their crowns of wild celery after the girl with various lewd suggestions.

'If they terrify all the slaves, we'll never get any wine,' Philopoemen said.

'I'm going to—' Alexanor put his feet on the floor.

'They'll tear you to pieces,' Philopoemen said. 'Don't.'

'Apollo!' Alexanor called for aid. 'Divine musician, save these people.'

'This is the way, with Macedon,' Philopoemen said. 'Everything goes to the strongest. It is their whole system of government.'

Alexanor shook his head, and rolled over to look at the ceiling, which was magnificently decorated with scenes from the war of the Lapiths and Centaurs.

'I can't watch,' he said. 'There's a man killing another man ...'

'Both Macedonians,' Philopoemen said, after a glance, 'and neither one of them would thank you for intervening.' He stiffened and Alexanor looked at him.

'Look sharp,' he said. 'It's Prince Philip.'

The young heir of Macedon was walking through the party like a priest through a temple. As he passed, men looked wary or stood at attention, but as soon as the young prince was out of earshot, they would return to gambling, drinking, fornicating.

Philip smiled when he saw Philopoemen. He inclined his head, and Philopoemen sat up and bowed.

'The prince of Megalopolis,' Philip said.

'We have no princes,' Philopoemen said. 'My lord, this is my friend, the priest of Asklepios, Alexanor son of Philokles.'

'Philopoemen, you had more cheers today than my father,' Philip said. 'How do you think my father liked that, sir?'

'You are determined to be difficult.' Philopoemen lay back. 'Why can't you Macedonians have a civilised party?'

Alexanor realised that the two of them knew each other well enough to engage in a bout of needling.

'What kind of party is civilised?' Philip asked. 'A dull party.'

Philopoemen laughed. 'A good answer for a young man. But I don't think your father is any better pleased than Alexanor here.'

Philip shrugged. 'I admit they all drink too much. When I am king, I will be sober.'

'And virtuous?' Alexanor asked.

The prince's eyes fell on him, and he saw that they all but burnt with intelligence. Alexanor wasn't sure what he had expected, but it wasn't this.

'What is virtue?' Philip asked.

'Strength of character,' Alexanor said.

'Why is a man who strangles his appetites stronger than a man who satisfies them? They are soldiers. They take what they want. I'm sure it is different for Greeks – it is so long since they were proper soldiers.' Philip didn't sneer outwardly, but the disdain was there.

Philopoemen smiled pleasantly. 'I think it is time I went back to my farm.'

'You know I don't mean you,' Philip told the Achaean.

'And yet, I am a Greek,' Philopoemen said. 'And so are most of these slaves.'

'Islanders.' Alexanor was rigid with anger.

'They are merely slaves,' Philip said. 'You needn't worry about them. There's more where they came from.'

Antipater appeared by Philip.

'Prince, your father says this banquet is not for you.'

Philip stood. 'I'm not sure I agree,' he said. 'Maybe I want a flute girl.'

Philopoemen rose. 'I'll walk you to your tent,' he said.

'I don't need a nursemaid,' spat the prince.

'Your father—' Antipater began.

'Fuck off,' the prince said. 'Didn't I fight? At Sellasia? Am I not a

Macedonian? Why does that not make me a man? If I want to plough some slut's furrow, why not?'

Antipater looked around, as if someone might save him.

Philip reached out for a woman moving past him. He reached his hands around her from behind and grabbed her breasts.

She stamped down on his instep, twisted, and slammed the palm of her hand into the underside of his jaw, so that he fell full-length across Alexanor.

The woman was Phila.

'Next time I'll cut your dick off,' she said. 'Friend of yours?' she asked Alexanor.

Philopoemen smiled. 'So neatly done,' he said, with obvious admiration.

'I've been to a couple of Macedonian parties,' the *hetaera* said.

'You know this whore?' Philip sputtered.

Philopoemen looked down at the fallen prince.

'This is the *Hetaera* Phila.' He laid a slight emphasis on the name.

Philip was angry. 'Striking the son of the king has penalties.'

'Grabbing Phila's tits has penalties, *pais*,' she said, her voice level. 'I'm not just any whore.'

Antipater grabbed the prince.

'Don't,' he said. 'Your father ...'

Philip pushed the other man away, slipping Antipater's sloppy grip with a *pankration* break-hold that Alexanor knew immediately. His face was livid; his lips pulled back in a snarl. And then, like a serpent shedding his skin, he put it away. He straightened, his face softened, and he breathed out.

Alexanor had risen, ready to protect Phila, who, for all her skills, was a head shorter than the Macedonian prince, but the boy had his hands at his sides, and he bowed his head, the way a man might before a statue of a god.

'I apologise, *despoina*,' he said.

She favoured him with a wry smile. 'You apologise? Or you'll have me raped by slaves later?'

Philip flushed. 'No!' Then, more calmly, he said, 'No, lady. I was in the wrong and I acknowledge it.'

She sank into a deep reverence.

'My lord does me too much honour,' she said, with just a hint of sarcasm.

Philip smiled. It was a false smile, but whether it was false because the prince was not actually contrite, or false because he was controlling himself, Alexanor could not judge.

'It is past my bedtime, and my royal father has decreed that the party is too much for me. And perhaps I have proven him right.' He bowed again. 'And Philopoemen will think less of me.'

'More of you, for the manner of your apology,' Philopoemen said. 'But grabbing women at parties is grotesque.'

Philip blinked. 'Goodnight.' He allowed Antipater to lead him away.

'He knows who I am,' Phila said. 'He did that on purpose.'

'Did you know who he was?' Philopoemen asked her.

She shook her head. 'No, I'm not insane.' Her hands were trembling, and she sat down suddenly.

Alexanor was watching the prince being led out of the hall.

'I have never seen a man master himself so quickly,' he said. 'And I have seldom seen rage take a man so suddenly. It's as if he's two men.'

Philopoemen tugged at his beard. He reached out and scooped a *krater* full of watered wine from a passing slave and sat back. He took a drink and handed the *krater* to Phila.

'You are very beautiful,' he said to Phila.

The simple, direct statement seemed to surprise her. She smiled in genuine pleasure, and a slight blush reached her nose.

She raised the *krater* as if toasting him. 'I didn't know you even admired women, Achaean.'

He looked away.

'I wasn't sent here to practise my boxing with the prince,' she said with a smile. 'The king wants to see you, Philopoemen.'

She turned to Alexanor and smiled brilliantly, and he flushed with warmth. He was painfully aware that the *hetaera* was not for him, and yet she captivated his senses; her smile brought him an instant burst of joy. No woman had ever caused such intense reactions; the scientist in him wanted to measure his pulse against her beauty, her *charisma*. He observed himself as if from a distance, and smiled ruefully at his reactions. Moreover, he knew that she had reawakened something in him; he suddenly saw other women ... all women. *Oh, Aspasia.*

Philopoemen rose with a smile at both of them and walked between the couches to where the king reclined.

'Will you come to me tonight?' Phila asked quietly.

Alexanor's inward observer noted that he appeared to have been struck by lightning. The outward man mumbled something.

Phila laughed. She lay down by him, full length on the *kline*. She was smaller than him, and took up very little room, even facing him.

'The king is about to ask Philopoemen to serve him as a cavalry officer,' she said softly.

Alexanor tore his eyes away from her and looked over his shoulder. Philopoemen was standing by the king's couch, and then, as the king invited him, he sat, leant over, laughed obediently at some witticism.

'I don't know ...' Alexanor began.

'It will make his career. Oh, in Athens we have no great love for the king of Macedon, but Philopoemen needs a wider theatre than the tiny stage of Pelops, don't you think?' She looked into Alexanor's eyes. 'Don't fall in love with me, darling. Your mother wouldn't let you marry me anyway.'

Her tone was light, but Alexanor's inner observer wondered if her words weren't true.

'My mother would like you,' he said.

She smiled. 'That's a much better compliment than being told that I'm beautiful.'

'The king said he would give Philopoemen your contract,' Alexanor said, a man set on wounding himself.

'Ah!' She smiled. 'That would be a real pleasure. I would like to help form a hero.'

'But ...' Alexanor said.

She put a hand on his chest. 'My friend,' she said softly, 'if you use your arts to cure one man, must all your other patients be jealous?'

Behind her radiant face, Philopoemen sat straight for a moment. The smile on his face vanished. He said something, and the king sat up. The two men looked at each other with something like enmity.

Phila rolled over, exposing one beautiful naked shoulder as her linen caught on the couch.

'What in Hades has he done?' she asked.

Philopoemen rose with angry dignity and inclined his head to the king before walking towards them, so stiffly that he appeared to be injured. The king made a gesture and began coughing. Slaves hurried to him.

'I'm going back to the king,' Phila said, rolling off the couch and straightening her *peplos*.

Philopoemen brushed past her as if he didn't see her. He nodded to Alexanor.

'I have to go,' he said, and walked off.

A few paces away, a Macedonian cavalry officer threw a punch at his mate, and knocked the man back over their drinking couch. Philopoemen avoided the falling body with a twitch of his hips, stepped over the downed man, and continued into the *stoa* and out into the night.

Alexanor followed him. He stopped to look at the man lying on the floor.

'Fuck off, Greek,' the man who'd thrown the punch said.

'I am a doctor, and a priest,' Alexanor said.

He thumbed back one of the man's eyelids, looked into his eye, and then raised his eyebrows.

'Fuck off, I said,' the Macedonian spat.

'Help me get him onto the couch,' Alexanor said.

'Didn't mean to hit him so hard,' the drunken Macedonian mumbled, suddenly contrite, and came around the *kline*. As if he'd never uttered a threat, he took his mate's feet and the two of them lifted the unconscious man onto the couch.

'Keep him awake,' Alexanor said. 'He may have a concussion.'

'Didn't mean to hit him so hard,' the Macedonian said again.

Alexanor raised the man on the cushions, and then took a piece of charcoal from the nearest brazier, holding it in tongs. He waved it under the unconscious man's nose until the man began to cough. His eyes opened.

'Keep him awake. No more wine.' Alexanor made himself smile at the drunk Macedonian.

'Sure,' the man said. 'Never meant to hit you so hard, Alexos.'

Alexanor tossed the burning coal back into the brazier and hung the tongs by it, where they belonged, and walked out under the line of columns. But he'd waited too long. Philopoemen was gone.

*

Alexanor rose in the morning, after watching Phila sleep. He watched her too long; he was afraid to leave her, too conscious that he would probably never lie beside her again.

But eventually, he wriggled off her couch. His clothes, neatly cleaned and pressed, were piled on a stool. He dressed silently, drank a bowl of warm broth that Thais provided, and looked out over a magnificent Nemean morning. He was tempted to ask the young slave why ... *Why does your mistress receive me in her bed? Why am I here? Why doesn't the king care?*

Thais frowned at him. 'Your friend, the Achaean hero, has already left.'

Alexanor looked at her, a hollow forming in the pit of his stomach despite the warm broth.

'Left?' he asked.

'Yes. The whole *hippeis* of Megalopolis mounted and rode away shortly after dawn. I was washing clothes.' She smiled.

Alexanor ran a hand over his throat and wondered where Leon was, and whether he felt abandoned, and where he'd left his razor.

'Why? Some mission?'

'Oh, no.' The slave began to fold laundry from a basket. A male slave appeared, unfolded a small table, and vanished silently. 'Mistress told me last night. The king asked him to serve, and Philopoemen refused.'

'Yes, I saw that,' Alexanor said. 'I wandered around trying to find him.'

The slave girl shrugged. 'Who refuses a king?'

BOOK II

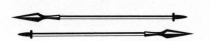

THREADS
OF FATE

CHAPTER ONE

—◦◦◦—

Megalopolis

221 BCE

Alexanor rode his horse into the courtyard of the roadside inn, and Leon came behind with their pack mule and closed the yard's gate. They were on the edge of night; winter was not far away, and the wind seemed to blow through Alexanor's heavy cloak and the wool *chiton* beneath it like a knife of ice cutting to his bones.

'I'll be happy to pour some warm wine down my throat,' Leon said. 'In fact, I might prescribe two cups.'

Alexanor laughed, and slid from his charger, wincing as his hip socket gave him a painful twinge. An Illyrian spear had caught him below the waist two months before; the wound was healed, but the muscles would not knit properly, and cold weather didn't help.

Slaves emerged from the warm light within and took their horses, cursing at the number; two men with four horses and a mule.

'I'll make sure they do their job,' Leon said. 'Go and get warm.'

Alexanor shook his head. 'I'll go when you go,' he said, and the two men helped the slaves tend to the animals. It wasn't so much that they wanted to help as that both of them had enough experience of roadside inns to want to make sure that their horses were actually fed, watered, and rubbed down.

Inside, the central hearth of the inn was piled high with logs and the fire roared, although no warmth seemed to get below waist level.

The owner came to them as Alexanor ducked his head to get in the low door. He liked what he saw: the low room was hung with oregano and thyme; he could smell soup from the kitchen; best of all, the place was almost empty.

A slave girl brought them a bench to sit on and stools for their feet, and the two men sat back, soaking in the warmth and drinking a *kykeon*, in this case hot wine with grated cheese and a little boiled barley.

'You like it?' the slave girl asked. She smiled.

Both men nodded and gulped greedily. She ladled more into their cups.

'Where are you gents from?' the innkeeper asked.

'Epidauros,' Leon said.

'Illyria,' Alexanor said.

The innkeeper looked back and forth. 'Well, which is it, gents?'

'We're both servants of Asklepios at Epidauros,' Alexanor said. 'We have been with the king of Macedon in Illyria.'

'Oh, may the gods bless him!' the innkeeper said.

'You approve of the king?' asked Leon.

'Spartans burnt this inn twice in six years. King Antigonus put an end to that, eh?' the man said. He polished out two fine Athenian cups and placed them on a low table. 'Are you gentlemen wanting dinner and some good wine?'

'What do you have?' Alexanor asked.

'Lamb, killed yesterday, stewed with herbs. Some good cheese. The best olives in the world.' The man smiled. 'Did you meet the king? In person?'

For a moment, Alexanor was back there, attending the king, who was coughing and spitting blood on a purple camp bed.

'Yes,' he said. 'I saw him every day.'

'You never did!' the innkeeper said. 'You know the king?'

'Knew him,' Alexanor said. 'He's dead.'

The innkeeper turned to his household shrine and made a sign to avert evil.

'The king is dead?' he said. 'That's the worst news I've heard in months.'

Alexanor looked at the fire and said nothing.

'Oh, by Apollo, gents? Were you his doctors?' The innkeeper rubbed his hands together like a mouse. 'Oh, I'm so sorry.'

Leon shrugged. 'Alexanor was his physician, but he had Macedonians as well.'

No one would listen to us, Alexanor thought.

'Oh, aye, I imagine the Macedonians ain't much in the medical line.' The man shrugged. 'Good at fighting, though.'

'I thought you Megalopolitans were members of the Achaean League?' Leon asked. 'You seem awfully fond of Macedon.'

'The League ain't worth a fart, begging your pardon. Can't protect us from the Spartans, can't protect us from the Aetolians. Can't do shit, pardon me. Rather pay my taxes to the king. He seemed a decent old fellow.' The innkeeper shrugged. 'I could show you fifty gentlemen around here of my mind. You know, our cavalry went and fought for the king.'

'At Sellasia,' Alexanor said. 'I was there.'

'You were? So was my eldest. He rode with Philopoemen.'

The man spoke with pride, and he pointed at a fine *kopis* hanging over the door.

Alexanor made the sign of Apollo.

'Now, you must be god-sent,' he said. 'I am seeking Philopoemen, and you'll know where I can find him.'

The man smiled. 'Let me just see to your dinners, and I'll give you directions for the morning. He has a fine farm, just around the mountain. Lamb?'

'Lamb,' they answered.

The morning was cold and clear, and the wind had died. There was snow on the slopes of both peaks of Mount Lykaion, and smoke rose from the great altar of Zeus high on the hillside. An eagle soared over the altar, and both Alexanor and Leon made the sign of the lightning bolt.

'No better omen,' Leon said.

Philopoemen's farm covered the lower slopes of the sacred mountain. As they crossed the shoulder of the steep rock, all of it was laid out for them to see, the outlines of the walls clear in the winter sun. Up above them, Alexanor could see shepherds and flocks; down in the valley, a dozen slaves were gleaning the fields in which barley stubble stood like hair on an unshaven man. Stone walls ran along the roadsides, topped with wooden fences, and at every field corner there was a small shrine.

'Our Philopoemen is richer than Croesus,' Leon said.

Alexanor agreed, but his sharp eyes saw the signs of Spartan occupation: a sheepfold burnt, its stone wall scorched black; a roadside shrine reduced to white marble rubble, the severed head of Artemis reverently placed on a tall stone pending some repair; a blackened stone barn with a fallen-in roof. Men were working on the stone barn, clearing the fallen roof tiles and working on the stone. They passed a wagon on the road with logs of beautiful, sweet-smelling white pine and, closer to the barn, another wagon full of red roof tiles stood at the gate.

Leon rode over to the gate, where four men were working.

'Can you point me to the house of Philopoemen?' he asked.

The youngest labourer looked up. 'Certainly, sir,' the boy said with the clear, unaccented speech of Arkadia. 'The master's house is at the end of this road. You cannot miss it, although it is covered in scaffolds now. But master is right here – he's on the barn.'

'I see him,' Alexanor said, and put his horse at the wall.

A full season campaigning with the king of Macedon and his riding skills had improved immeasurably; his military gelding jumped the low wall almost from a stand, and he waved.

Philopoemen turned. His grin was visible fifty paces away.

Alexanor reined in and looked up to where the former cavalry officer was standing on a charred beam, his *chiton* unpinned, naked to the waist despite the cold.

'I didn't expect to find young Achilles working on a barn,' Alexanor said.

'I expect Achilles didn't own a farm,' Philopoemen called down.

The man leapt back to the recently repointed stone wall of the old barn and then leant down, caught the charred beam, and lifted one end slowly out of its socket in the scorched stone wall. He placed the end on the top of the wall for a moment, changed his grip, and then dropped it, so that the damaged beam fell away into the interior.

Philopoemen jumped down, following the beam, and walked out of the damaged barn's entrance. He wiped his sooty hands on his dirty *chiton*, and Alexanor slipped from his horse and embraced him.

'I had not expected to see you here,' Philopoemen said. 'No one comes to Arkadia, except Spartans.'

'The king of Macedon is dead,' Alexanor said. 'He sent me with a message before he died. I was supposed to come a month ago, but I was wounded.'

'Wounded? You lot are supposed to cure wounds, not take them.' Despite his words, he looked concerned.

Alexanor nodded, rubbing his hip. 'I was with the king in Illyria. We all thought the Illyrians were beaten. They weren't – they ambushed the baggage train.'

Philopoemen nodded, his eyes on the barn.

'Diocletes!' he called, and a heavyset man appeared from behind the roof tile wagon. 'I'm going back to the house with my guests. Try and get the new beams in.' Philopoemen waved.

Diocletes waved back and returned to negotiating with the roof tile man.

'My stepbrother,' Philopoemen said. 'Let's go to the house. This way.'

The former cavalry officer didn't seem to have a horse. He began to run. He was very fast, and Alexanor had to trot his charger to keep up. He didn't jump the wall again; this time, the men at the gate cleared away respectfully. He turned his trot into a canter as he entered the road between the stone walls, but Philopoemen went over the wall like an athlete and began to sprint up the lane.

Leon laughed. 'I had forgotten what he is like,' he said.

Both men had to ride hard to keep up.

The house was indeed covered in scaffolding. It was a large country house, with a variety of outbuildings under construction, and Alexanor, as an islander, couldn't imagine what they were all for. The house itself had a roof so new that no moss had grown into the tiles, nor had their colour faded. A dozen men were putting stucco over the new stone, and behind them on the frame, a younger man was painting a fresco in the wet stucco.

The second storey was clearly women's quarters, with a long *exedra* like a city house, so that the balcony came out over the yard. A pair of servants or slaves were hoisting new shutters on pulleys – elaborately carved shutters, with flowers and nymphs splendidly worked into the wood.

A young hunting dog came out into the yard, barking madly and then circling his master playfully.

'What a fine house!' Alexanor exclaimed.

It was of noble proportions; something about it suggested both opulence and practicality, elegance and comfort.

'You like it?' Philopoemen asked, clearly pleased. 'I'll show you around. I designed it myself, on the principles of Aristotle.'

'Your wife must be proud,' Leon said.

'My wife is dead, and my sons. The Spartans killed them all. And my dogs and my horses,' Philopoemen said, his voice flat. And then, as if nothing remarkable had been said, he went on. 'Shall we look around?'

Leon made the sign of Pluton. Alexanor put a hand on Philopoemen's shoulder.

'He didn't know,' he said. 'By Artemis, brother. You never—'

'Nor should you know of my personal issues,' Philopoemen said, pleasantly enough. 'This is my winepress. I probably made it too big, but all of us in the valley have had such good harvests the last two years that it seemed better to go too big than too small.'

'Is that a hypocaust?' Alexanor asked, understanding that Philopoemen's dead family was not to be discussed. The winepress seemed to have a heated floor – an unheard-of luxury.

Philopoemen nodded. 'Yes. One system for all the buildings, and the warm air is pumped along. It doesn't work as well as I had imagined, but it's good in here, and in the workshop.'

'You designed the hypocaust as well?' Alexanor asked.

'Yes,' the Achaean said. 'I like to be busy.'

Alexanor looked at the man, remembering his drive for oblivion, even as a patient. Now he was bustling across his yard to show them the workshop. *And what will you do when the buildings are all finished? Plough your own fields? The Spartans killed everything you loved, and you are here, rebuilding it quietly, because the king of Macedon has made peace.*

Later, sitting in his own kitchen while slaves and free servants bustled over their food, Philopoemen looked at Alexanor.

'How did the king die?'

'Old age. Fatigue. Bad food, little sleep, a dozen things.' Alexanor's frustration seeped into his voice even though he tried to control it.

'You loved him,' Philopoemen said.

'Love is too strong. I liked him. He was ... genuine, somehow, in a way I never expected from a king.' As he said the words, he watched the Achaean.

Philopoemen nodded. 'I liked him too. And he was a pleasure to serve – as an officer, I mean. Lately, the League officers have been idiot politicians. It's all faction, and no skill.'

'But you didn't like him well enough to serve him.'

Philopoemen shrugged. 'You don't really know Arkadia,' he said easily enough. 'Here, try this wine – it's not mine, the Spartans destroyed all my stocks. It's from Dinaeos. Remember him?'

'Of course. The redhead.'

'Exactly. Several of his barns escaped, whereas they had to destroy all of mine.' Philopoemen nodded. 'Tell me what you think.'

'I think you are full of shit,' Alexanor said.

Philopoemen looked at him a moment, stunned.

'Why are you working so hard to pretend that it is nothing to you, that the Spartans burned your farm and killed your wife?' Alexanor asked. 'I speak as a physician. It costs a man, to hide his feelings like this.'

Philopoemen shrugged and looked away. 'We are at peace now. The king declared that there would be no reprisals.' He turned back and looked at Alexanor. 'What would you have me do? Howl at the moon? Sacrifice a Spartan boy on the hillside?' His normally mild eyes were virtually afire. 'I thought of it, you know,' he said, as if such thoughts were normal, like discussing philosophy. 'Perhaps three boys for each of mine, and ten women for my wife.'

Just for a moment, his hate, his rage and his despair were right there, like palpable presences – the closest Alexanor had ever come to seeing the Furies.

Alexanor had to work to cover the shock of his horror. He swallowed, and then met the Achaean's eyes.

'Is that why you declined the king's offer?' he asked.

Philopoemen shook his head, once more in control. 'No. He was offensive. He asked me to serve Macedon as a *satrap*, first there, and eventually here. We are priests of Zeus, in my household. Men obey us. But he knew that my stepfathers gave their lives to fight Macedon and its surrogate tyrants. All over the Peloponnese, whenever men began to speak of liberty, Macedon would install a tyrant. My stepfathers ...'

He shrugged. 'I forget you are a foreigner from Rhodes. Do you know the name of Megalophanes?'

'No,' Alexanor said.

'I will show you his grave monument later today. In Arkadia, men called him the "King Killer". He deposed three tyrants in three different cities, and killed two of them with his own hand. He was my sword teacher, my second father. He fought Macedon all his life.' Philopoemen shook his head. 'I am not the man to serve the king of Macedon. He mistook me, that's all. He imagined that I ...'

Alexanor raised an eyebrow.

'Remember the spat with Cercidas?' he said.

'On the road to Argos?' Alexanor asked.

'Exactly. He heard it reported. He knew that Aratos was no friend of my father's.' The Achaean shrugged. 'He imagined that I would serve him because of my dislike for Aratos.' He shook his head.

'Aratos?'

'Surely even on Rhodes you have heard of Aratos?' Philopoemen asked.

'Say rather that in six months with the king I got to know him well enough. He was virtually Doson's prime minister. Philip listens to him. Philip will be king now.' Alexanor raised an eyebrow.

Philopoemen nodded. 'Well. Aratos is no friend of my family. But Philip had excellent steel in him. He will be a good king, I think.'

Alexanor nodded agreement. 'Nonetheless, before the king died, he suggested that I approach you on his behalf.'

'Why you?'

Philopoemen poured water from a pitcher into a low *krater* of wine and poured for both of them. As it was morning, the quantity of wine was a little surprising. Most men drank watered wine in the morning, but Philopoemen poured a day's ration.

'The wine really is quite good, but you are drinking too much,' Alexanor said. 'Listen, then. You'll see why the king sent me in the end.'

'I'm all ears.'

Philopoemen sat back and drank off half his wine in three gulps.

Alexanor sighed, because now that he was to the point of making his pitch, he felt awkward.

'The king is asking the League to send a force to Crete,' he said. 'He'd like you to command it.'

140

'Aratos and Cercidas will not let me command a League force,' Philopoemen said. But he leant forward as he said it.

Alexanor smiled. *Aha, my friend. You are interested.*

'You underrate the King, and Philip,' the priest said. 'And me, for that matter.'

Philopoemen began to drum his fingers on the table.

'Ahh, Aratos and Cercidas want me out of Arkadia!' he said.

Alexanor shrugged. 'Yes. Aratos said so in just so many words, not a month ago.' He shrugged again. 'Everyone knows you received an ovation at Argos.'

'It was for all the League troops, not for me,' Philopoemen said.

'That's why they shouted "Achilles, Achilles". For all the League troops.' Alexanor smiled.

Philopoemen folded his hands modestly. 'I didn't hear that.'

Alexanor sat back, sipped his wine, and laughed. 'Didn't you, though? But never mind your vanity. Aratos wants you out of the Peloponnese.'

'How many men?' Philopoemen asked.

'Five hundred at the cost of the League. The king seemed to think that you, personally, could raise more, and contract for them.'

Philopoemen leant back, tucking his broad shoulders into a corner of the wall.

'Crete,' he said. 'Why Crete?'

Alexanor nodded. 'Because Macedon is looking to re-enter the game of kings,' he said. 'To re-establish naval power. To challenge Aegypt. Because Crete is incredibly rich.'

'There's Aegyptian money flowing back into Sparta,' Philopoemen said. 'And the Spartan king, Cleomenes, is in Aegypt. Sparta gets men and money from Crete, I know it.'

'There's a war on Crete—'

'Oh, I know. Gortyna and Knossos against the rest of the island.'

Philopoemen put wine cups down as if they were opposing warriors.

'You seem to know a great deal,' Alexanor said.

'Arkadia may seem isolated, but the priests of the sanctuary here come from Crete and Cyprus, and Olympia is only a day's ride away. Everyone comes to Olympia. We get news here, probably faster than the king of Macedon.

'At Pella, the war on Crete sounded more like newly enriched men against old aristocrats. And perhaps Macedon against Aegypt.'

141

Philopoemen poured both of them more watered wine.

'Which side is Macedon taking?'

'The new men. And the "Federation".'

Philopoemen sat back. Then, suddenly, he leant forward, and pushed one of the new shutters. The window, paned in horn, opened, and suddenly Alexanor had a breathtaking view of the mountain towering above the olive trees.

'Some men say Zeus was born on Lykaion,' Philopoemen said. 'But most local priests say that Zeus came here from Crete. Most of us have guest-friendships with Cretans. In my family, we are guest-friends with noble families in Gortyna and in Knossos.'

The cold air washed over them.

'I can raise perhaps fifty cavalry here,' he said. 'I'd have to get the rest elsewhere. I can probably find Thracians in Athens. Thracians would be best.' He swirled wine in his cup and then set it down. 'I suppose this has to be approved by the League.'

Alexanor nodded. 'Yes.'

The Achaean looked at him carefully. 'What's in this for you? A Rhodian? Serving Macedon?'

'I serve my god.' Alexanor hoped he didn't sound too pompous. 'I suspect Chiron sent me to the king of Macedon to learn some humility. But the king has arranged ... Anyway, I'm to be promoted. I will be the new high priest of the Temple of Asklepios at Lentas.'

'I am not alone in my vanity, am I?' Philopoemen asked, raising his wine cup in salute.

Alexanor sat forward, hesitated, and then laughed at himself.

'True enough. And I'm only to be acting high priest. And it's all politics, anyway – Kos and Epidauros disagree over which mother house owns Lentas. It may come to nothing, or it may be my step to master priest.'

'You are ambitious,' Philopoemen said.

Alexanor shrugged. 'I was going to have a different life. But now that I have found this one, I might as well make the most of it.'

'You are a very private man,' Philopoemen said, swirling the wine in his cup. 'Here, have some more wine and tell me why you became a priest.'

Alexanor started to raise his hand to refuse the wine, but then accepted it. He was still negotiating, and Philopoemen seemed serious, in a lightly drunken and somewhat dangerous way.

'I lost the woman I loved,' he said. 'And my father ...' He looked away.

'You lost your father?' Philopoemen asked. 'I have been an orphan for as long as I can remember. But with a pair of wonderful step-fathers.'

'No, no.' Alexanor drank more wine. 'I don't even like to think about it.'

'Tell me about it.' Philopoemen looked out of the window. 'I don't like to think about much of anything, brother.'

'I was to wed a woman, Aspasia. I knew her well. I loved her. We virtually grew up together. I went on my ephebe cruise as a marine. We met a heavy Aegyptian pirate and fought.' Alexanor looked away, out of the window. 'All my ... friends ... died. Except me.'

He shook his head. Shrugged again, started to speak, stopped, and looked at Philopoemen. Who met his eye.

'They all died. The friends of my youth – the men I hunted with, ran with, flirted with girls in the market with, got drunk with. Went fishing. Went running ... In a quarter of an hour, they were all dead, and I still lived. It took me six months to recover, at the Temple of Asklepios on Kos.'

He looked away again, and blinked to rid his eyes of the sight. *Gutted like fish.*

'I went home to find that my father had arranged for Aspasia to marry his business partner. All my friends were dead in the ship fight. I lost the woman I loved,' Alexanor found he couldn't stop. 'She thought ... My father thought ...'

'Tell me,' Philopoemen said gently. His hand was on Alexanor's shoulder.

'My own fucking father thought that I fled and left them to die,' he said, and the release of bitterness was like the gout of blood from a death wound. Or the release of the lancing of a boil.

'Your father?'

'And then her father refused to let me wed her.' He was silent a moment.'But I could look in her eyes and see ...' Alexanor took a deep breath. 'By the gods, my friend, I thought that I'd put this behind me.'

Philopoemen came and put a hand on his shoulder.

'Oh, Alexanor,' he said.

'My father asked me why I had come home alive, when the other boys died.' Alexanor was weeping, where the deaths of the twelve friends had not made him weep. 'He's a war hero. He thought I turtled.' This through tears, against a ball in his throat like a burning apple.

'Apollo!' Philopoemen spat. 'I am an arse. I sit here and assume that I am the only man in the world who has troubles.'

He poured more wine for Alexanor, and the priest drank it off greedily. He waited for a long time – time enough for the sun to move in the heavens.

'I want to ask another question,' Philopoemen said.

'Ask me anything,' Alexanor said, his eyes dry. 'You are the first man I've told that story to. At least, the whole story.'

'You loved her?'

'More than the gods.'

Philopoemen nodded. 'And yet, you ... Tell me what you did to recover.'

Alexanor shrugged. 'The temple saved me. I was always busy – I had a clear goal.'

'I dream of them every night,' Philopoemen said. 'My children. Sometimes I lie all night in my bed imagining how they died.'

Alexanor nodded. 'A year or so,' he said. 'Hard work, exercise ...'

'Wine,' Philopoemen said, pouring more.

'No. It's a false argument. Drugs cover but they do not cure. The cure is time, and the will of the gods, and some worthy activity. So here's the fucking truth, my brother. I'm willing to play the game and fight to be acting high priest because it keeps me awake and alive.'

He reached out and slapped the wine cup off the table. It broke on the tiled floor.

Philopoemen nodded slowly. Then he rose to his feet, picked up his own wine cup and the *krater* of wine, and threw them out of the window. When he turned back to Alexanor, he was smiling.

He went and fetched water, and handed a cup to Alexanor.

'To Crete,' Philopoemen said, looking out of the window. And then he turned back, and he was thoughtful. 'Lentas, the Lion. A port just south of Gortyna.' He sounded like a man in a dream, and then he turned, suddenly, and his eyes were focused. 'Surely you'll be the youngest high priest—'

'That anyone can remember,' Alexanor admitted. 'Yes. Well, Doson made a huge donation to the temple. And demanded my promotion.'

'You are the clever one,' Philopoemen said with a grin. 'I'll watch myself, with you.'

'Yes,' Alexanor said, allowing himself to return the grin.

Philopoemen fingered his beard. But then he sat back, almost like a deflated wineskin.

'No,' he said. 'Aratos will never let me go.'

Alexanor leant forward. 'Am I your physician?'

'Of course,' Philopoemen said. 'You have healed me. Twice.'

'Then listen, brother. My prescription for you is that you leave this house and this valley and go out into the world of men and affairs. Wage war and make peace. Live. And I am so committed to this prescription that I have taken a few devious actions of my own to make it very difficult for Aratos to block it.' The priest sat back.

Philopoemen tugged at his beard. He looked out of the open window at the mountain above them; at the eagle still in the sky, and the column of smoke from the ash altar of Zeus. He drank, and then looked down, at the field closest to the house.

There were four small marble stelae there, all in a row. Alexanor knew them immediately as graves.

Philopoemen looked at them for a long time, as long as it might take a man to sing the whole *paean* of Apollo.

'Yes,' he said. 'Let's do it.'

CHAPTER TWO

─⟨⟨⟨⟩⟩⟩─

Temple Grove of Zeus Unifier, Aegio, northern
Peloponnese, capital of the Achaean League,
Athens, and Thrake (Thrace)

221 BCE

'You are not particularly good at waiting, I find,' Alexanor said.

They were standing in the cool shade of the magnificent pines forming the sacred grove from whence the Achaean League was ruled.

Philopoemen wore the white *himation* of a priest of Zeus and had a sharp knife in his hand. He was pouring water from the sacred spring over the bloody blade.

'On the contrary,' Philopoemen said with a smile. 'I merely occupy myself while I wait.'

'Aratos wishes to see you,' Alexanor said.

'Since when are you his errand boy?'

'Since Chiron of Epidauros sent me as his representative to the Achaean League,' Alexanor said.

Philopoemen ran a thumbnail along a patch of gristle and then wiped the gleaming Chalcedonian knife on a spotless linen towel.

'How was your sacrifice?' Alexanor asked.

'He died well, if that's what you mean. And was propitious.' Philopoemen bowed to the temple servant, who returned his bow and turned away with the knife. 'I'm ready for Aratos.'

Alexanor bit back various comments and led his friend across the temple sanctuary to where the *Hegemon* and *Strategos* of the Achaean League stood chatting with his *hipparchos*, or cavalry commander,

Demodokos, a man so fat as to be almost round, and Cercidas, the poet and former *Strategos*, who was heavy, but not fat.

Aratos continued to speak to Demodokos as the two younger men stood in the colonnade, waiting. Cercidas protested.

'I won't have it! He's dangerous, like his father!'

Aratos raised a hand and said something, his tone soothing.

Philopoemen glanced at Alexanor and raised his eyebrow.

'Be patient,' Alexanor said quietly.

Aratos patted his commander's back, with a little more drama than was necessary. Cercidas frowned and moved away. Aratos shrugged and then turned, as if seeing Philopoemen for the first time.

'Ah, the young hero. Walk with us,' Aratos said to Philopoemen. 'And you, Alexanor. I know that young Philip has included you in his councils.' His tone suggested that he knew everything.

Alexanor bowed. The tone Aratos adopted was aristocratic, hearty, and all-knowing, as if the man was playing Zeus in the theatre. Alexanor wanted to writhe with embarrassment.

Philopoemen's face was like stone.

'I know that we do not always see eye to eye, young man,' Aratos said. 'And you certainly have a number of people who dislike you. But in this case, I hope that you will allow yourself to be guided by me. The king wishes to see the League provide military support on Crete. And you have made quite an enemy in Cercidas, just when he is likely to follow me as *strategos* again, eh? A little foreign service with the League ought to put the shine back on your armour and put you in a position to resume your political career on your return. And perhaps, if you share some small successes, Cercidas will come to forgive you eventually.'

Philopoemen said nothing.

Aratos went on, 'Young men always think of war, and of course, I hear you are quite the warrior. Crete ought to suit you – the Cretans do nothing but fight.'

'What is the League's objective?' Philopoemen asked quietly.

'Objective?' Aratos asked.

Demodokos glared at the younger Achaean. 'Objective, lad? Our objective is to be seen to support Philip of Macedon.'

'Pardon me, *Strategos*, but if we send a thousand men ...' Philopoemen began.

'Two hundred, I think,' Aratos said thoughtfully, as if he'd just decided the number. 'And you can provide a hundred cavalry of your own, can you not? Your *fathers* must have left you very rich.' His eyes flashed.

Philopoemen paused for a moment. 'Two hundred men cannot accomplish anything,' he said.

Demodokos laughed coarsely. 'Who said you were to accomplish anything?'

Alexanor saw his whole plan disintegrating before his eyes.

'I believe the young king hopes that Gortyna and Knossos will be defeated, and the old aristocrats replaced with a more moderate government,' he said.

Demodokos smiled smugly. 'The boy king can hope all he wants,' he said. 'Knossos has the backing of Aegypt and Sparta and the whole Aetolian Federation. We can't match that. So we send a symbolic force ...'

Aratos looked discomforted. 'My *hipparchos* speaks a little too broadly,' he said, his voice smooth. 'Philopoemen, your military reputation is such that we all hope for great things from you.'

'What is the League's objective?' Philopoemen asked again.

Aratos stood straight. He was a fit man. When he drew himself up, Alexanor could see his youth; could see that he was the man who'd stormed Corinth and led armies.

'Our objective is the creation of a federal government of Crete, ruled by moderate lawgivers, who will be allies of the Achaean League and the king of Macedon,' he said solemnly.

'And to accomplish this mission, against the armies of Aegypt and Knossos and Gortyna and the Aetolian Federation and Sparta and Rhodes, you are giving me two hundred men,' Philopoemen said.

Aratos frowned.

Demodokos smiled nastily. 'You got it, hero.'

Aratos turned to admonish his *hipparchos*, but Philopoemen merely smiled. He looked at Alexanor, and then back at Aratos.

'I accept,' he said.

'I've already raised my tenants and borrowed some good men from my stepfather,' Philopoemen said. He was writing carefully on a wax tablet while his groom, Laertes, waited with his reins over his arm.

'I'm just sending a note to Dinaeos, will join us at Mytiline with our tenants. First, though, I'm off to Athens to buy another fifty cavalrymen. More, if I can afford them.'

'I am so sorry,' Alexanor said. 'I was used. I'm not as subtle as I thought ...'

Philopoemen shrugged. 'It's worse than you think. The League won't actually vote on these two hundred soldiers until later in the cycle, and then they'll have to vote on how to apportion them among the member states. Should take all summer. Then a lot of fat old men will vote the minimum funds for their equipment and pay, and then each member state will have to vote, and then choose the men – who won't be real citizens, I promise you, unless they are bankrupt debtors.'

'This is shameful!' Alexanor said, feeling a stab of guilt. 'You must decline!'

'Never in life. Listen. You are right in the important thing. I need to leave the graves ... of my dead ...' He forced a smile. 'I need to go out into the world. The happiest I've been since ... she died ... was at Sellasia. Maybe killing is my business. Maybe I'll die.' He smiled. 'But by the gods, if I come back from this alive and with my reputation intact, Aratos will rue it.'

'Will he work against you?'

Philopoemen shrugged. 'Who cares? Cercidas might, but—'

'Why do they alternate?' Alexanor asked. 'Perhaps this is a foolish question from a Rhodian, but why is Aratos not always in power?'

'The rather brilliant men who founded the League made laws to protect us from tyranny. One law is that no man can be *Strategos* two terms in a row.'

'Ahh, that is good.' Alexanor nodded.

Philopoemen raised an eyebrow. 'It certainly is, but a faction can still hold the office for years ... Anyway – listen, brother. I'm leaving for Thrake from Corinth. Care to come?'

Alexanor had business for his temple at Corinth. But Thrake was a world away ...

On the other hand ...

'Yes,' he said.

'Good,' Philopoemen said. 'Because I'll probably get wounded.'

*

They rode east from Aegio, along the coast road, with magnificent mountains rising on their left. As they rode, Philopoemen told Alexanor the myths and tales of Achaea: tales from the Trojan War; stories of the gods of the peaks and valleys, of nymphs, satyrs, and battles. They camped in the valley of Pitsa and rode on into a glorious morning, with the sun shining on the Bay of Corinth. Kleostratos threw his spear in the air, a great turning bar of sunlight, and caught it. Then Philopoemen had to do the same, and cut his hand practising, and they all laughed and rode on to Corinth. Alexanor noted that Philopoemen's servants were as well mounted as he, and none of them were slaves.

Leon commented on them.

'Local lads,' he said. 'Arkas and Lykon, both Arkadians. His own people, except Syrmas, the one with scars. He's another Thracian. Your friend freed him as soon as he purchased the man. After Sellasia.'

'A noble act,' Alexanor said.

Leon gave him a look.

Lykon was the cook, an older man. He purchased supplies in towns and then dismounted to gather herbs on the roadside, constantly fussing about the food. But the results were meals so excellent that Alexanor began to wish they'd travel for ever. But after three days they reached the Isthmus, and rode around the town, heading for the port and beaches facing the Aegean.

'I need to go to the Temple of Apollo,' Alexanor said.

'Let's find our ship and see our horses aboard first,' Philopoemen said.

They rode down on to the beach, and then they rode up and down the shore in the grilling sun, past a hundred hulls either moored stern first, or pulled well up the shingle, or anchored just off the surf, but none of the little ships at the commercial end of the beach was *Cyrine*, a freighter that Philopoemen had hired.

'When I was younger, and my fathers were alive, I shipped all our produce off this beach,' Philopoemen said. 'I know the factors. I'll find our ship.'

'Tell me of these "fathers",' Alexanor said.

Philopoemen shrugged. 'Two tyrannicides. Two philosophers who were prepared to kill to change the world. Revolutionaries. I loved them both. When my father died, they took me in.' He shrugged. 'As they loved each other, they had no sons, and hence, some people will tell you, I had the fortune to inherit three great legacies and not just one. My stepbrother is my mother's child by her second marriage. We are different, but close.' He looked at Alexanor. 'See? Eventually you will know all my secrets. Come, let's ride.'

But an hour later they were sweating like athletes, and still none of the merchant factors on the beach had any news of the *Cyrine*.

'If she's not available by tomorrow night, we'll hire someone else,' Philopoemen said. 'I have a guest-friend here, a Corinthian. We'll go impose on him. He'll welcome us.'

Alexanor wondered if anyone would truly welcome half a dozen armed men with a string of horses, but Nicanor, the Corinthian, came out into his yard to receive them, and his wife, a very small woman, led them to bright, painted rooms herself, while a dozen slaves took their horses.

'Nicanor is a good man,' Philopoemen said.

'His slaves adore him,' Alexanor said. It was obvious; a house full of smiles and careful service. 'Have you ever considered that slavery itself might be an evil?' he asked, while a young woman served him a pomegranate and took his riding boots.

Philopoemen threw himself on a couch.

'I think about it all the time. I listened when your Chiron spoke, back at Epidauros. But ... one evil at a time. Something as big as slavery would have to be tackled from a position of power – eminence, even.'

'But you might take it on?' Alexanor made room for Kleostratos, who smiled and began to peel another pomegranate.

Philopoemen smiled. 'Can we go to Crete first? And let me ask you this, my idealistic friend. What do we do with all the slaves? Just kick them off our farms?'

'No,' Alexanor said. 'No, there would have to be careful manumission, with funds ...'

Philopoemen nodded. 'Citizenship?'

Alexanor cringed. 'Of course not. Not in the first generation. They wouldn't know how to engage in the democracy.'

'Wouldn't they, though?' Philopoemen lay back and looked at the ceiling. 'What if I told you that I think most of the men who vote at the Achaean Assembly are unworthy of their citizenship. Rich fucks who pretend to read philosophy and talk a lot about food.'

Their host came in. He embraced Kleostratos like a long-lost brother, kicked off his sandals and sat with Philopoemen.

'He's a dangerous radical,' Nicanor said. 'Don't listen to him.' He grinned. 'Wine, anyone?'

His wife, Penelope, sat down. It wasn't unheard of for a woman to join men; rare in Arkadia, but common in Athens. Alexanor understood immediately from her presence that Nicanor was also a radical.

'He's contending that most of the men who exercise the franchise of Achaea don't deserve it,' Penelope said.

'Military service,' Kleostratos said. Just the two words.

Penelope nodded.

Philopoemen shook his head. 'War is not so important. And what of good men, brilliant men, with club feet or misshapen hands or what have you?'

Kleostratos smiled quietly. Nicanor made a face.

'But of course, Kleostratos reminds us that in Thrake, such men would be strangled at birth anyway.' He nodded. 'Thus solving the problem of the franchise.'

'Women,' Kleostratos said.

'Surely you aren't suggesting that *women* be included in the citizenship?' Alexanor asked.

Penelope glanced at him.

'Among the Getae and the Sakje, the women fight, and participate in councils,' Philopoemen said.

Nicanor laughed. 'I'd better pour some wine, or your priest is going to run into the street and report us to the garrison as madmen.'

Alexanor shook his head. 'I had no idea you were such a ... progressive,' he said to Philopoemen. He had a thought of Phila rising in an assembly to speak. It wasn't so outlandish; she knew more about politics than any woman he'd ever spoken to. He grinned. 'You are a radical, after all.'

'My stepfathers wandered Greece killing tyrants,' Philopoemen said. 'Do you understand now why Aratos fears me?'

The next morning, Alexanor rose early to go to the Temple of Apollo. He had penned a long report on papyrus the night before, a little bleary from wine, and he gave it directly to the high priest.

'You are on your way to your posting on Crete, yes?' the priest asked.

'Yes, Hierophant.'

The high priest frowned. 'I mistrust this intrusion of Macedonian politics into our order. It is bad enough to have a Macedonian garrison here.'

Alexanor bowed. 'Hierophant, I am a Rhodian – I am no friend of Macedon. Nonetheless, the needs of the Order are being served. Chiron ordered me to this task.'

The priest nodded. 'You are too young for your office. You know that?'

Alexanor bridled, but then, after a moment, calmed himself and forced some humility.

'Yes,' he admitted.

'Good. Go with the god, my son. Here – we are about to make the morning sacrifice. Come and join us.'

In Corinth, none of the priests were Pythagoreans, and the sacrifices were animals. After the meat had been distributed to the poor, Alexanor changed into his street clothes and walked about the agora. He made purchases and used a public letter-writer to send a note to his father on Rhodes.

He found himself looking at a table of swords; most of them were simple, cross-hilted *xiphoi*, but there were two longer swords, the curved bladed *kopis* favoured by mercenaries.

Philopoemen appeared out of the crowd.

'Fancy meeting you here,' he said.

'I thought that I might buy a sword,' he said. 'I broke my father's. And I can't bring myself to use the sword I took from Nabis.' He shrugged. 'Who knows where it's been?'

The slave keeping the stall was utterly uninterested.

Philopoemen drew one of the *xiphoi*. 'Nice. Look at the blade – folded steel. Good work. A little chip at the point – not a major flaw.' He drew another. 'Inferior. There, that's what I thought. All iron. I could bend it with my hands.'

'I was thinking of a *kopis*.'

'Too long,' Philopoemen said. 'Cavalry fights get to be wrestling matches, like a fight in a phalanx.' He smiled at his friend. 'Do you know how to use a sword? Of course you do,' he answered himself.

'Oh, I've held one or two.' Alexanor liked the patterns in the folded steel. 'How much for this one?'

The slave stood up. 'One hundred drachmae,' he said.

'I could buy a ship for that,' Alexanor said.

He put the sword back on the table and turned away.

'It's not a bad price,' Philopoemen said. 'It's probably from Amphipolis or one of the Thracian cities. They make the best swords – so does Macedon, now.'

'Too rich for me,' Alexanor said. 'How was your morning?'

'I found our ship,' Philopoemen said. 'I was on the wrong beach. It's on the Corinthian side, at Lechaeum.'

'Surely that's no use to us – we're for Athens.'

Alexanor was watching a group of soldiers come into the agora. They shoved a slave and then a freedman from their path. They were obviously drunk.

A priest of the Temple of Poseidon approached them. He was in his formal robes, and Poseidon was the patron of the agora; Alexanor guessed the man was the *archon* of the market.

'You'd be surprised,' Philopoemen said. 'It will be ready to sail in four hours.'

'But we have to wait for it to go all the way around the Peloponnese.'

The priest was ordering the soldiers from the market. Alexanor was not surprised; in most cities, the agora was for citizens only.

'It is such a pleasure to know something you don't know,' Philopoemen said. 'Watch out!'

His last exclamation was the result of one of the soldiers knocking the priest to the ground.

People scattered.

'Fucking sheep,' roared one of the soldiers.

'Baaa!' called another.

Philopoemen didn't move, and Alexanor stood next to him. As almost everyone else in the market ran, or hid behind bales of merchandise, this had the effect of leaving them facing the soldiers.

'Run away, little sheep,' said the Macedonian *dekarch*. His breath stank of cheap wine.

'You should probably go back to your barracks and sober up,' Philopoemen said, reasonably.

'Oh, oh! A scary citizen of the League of Sheep! Fuck off home, before we all decide to piss on you, little sheep.' The man's tone was derisive.

Philopoemen sighed. 'I told you I'd get wounded,' he said to Alexanor.

'I think we can take them without getting hurt,' Alexanor said, loudly enough to be heard. 'They're drunk.'

Philopoemen turned and gave him a warm smile.

'I knew I liked you,' he said.

Then, without preamble, he stepped forward, caught a soldier's arm, and broke it, throwing the man into a garlic seller's cart.

The Macedonian soldiers were surprised, to say the least. But even as Philopoemen grappled the second man, the third and fourth men were drawing swords.

Philopoemen rotated his man into the swordsmen. Alexanor passed between them like smoke, took a sword hand, and kicked his opponent in the head while holding his wrist. The wrist broke with an audible snap, and the man roared in pain and then screamed as the shattered socket continued to rotate. Alexanor threw his man so that he collided with Philopoemen's victim.

The fourth man cut at Philopoemen, drawing a line of blood down his right arm. The Achaean's head snapped back, and then he flowed forward into the tempo of the passing blade, and his left hand found the man's elbow as his powerful right took his shoulder. Philopoemen's left hand pushed ruthlessly, raising and rolling the other man's sword arm and shoulder, over and down, until the man was face down in the street and screaming.

Alexanor took all four swords from their prone owners.

Philopoemen gave him an odd look. He released the last of the soldiers. The man stayed down.

'Let's just walk away,' Philopoemen said.

Two of their opponents were screaming and moaning by turns. Alexanor was already trying to set the wounded man's wrist.

In one of the town's watchtowers, an alarm trumpet was blaring. The Macedonian *dekarch* was screaming obscenities and trying to rise. He had a knife, and he went after Alexanor, and Alexanor snap-kicked him as he passed.

'I've seen you box,' Philopoemen said. 'I had no idea you were such a lion.'

'Oh, I've never been much of a boxer,' the physician said. 'The Temple of Asklepios teaches a different *pankration*.'

'So I see.'

People were emerging from covered stalls and houses; there were a hundred men crowded on the portico of the Temple of Poseidon. Alexanor hurried to the priest, who lay on his side, his robes soiled by the mud.

The man was holding his head. Alexanor spoke to him quietly while Philopoemen watched the crowd and the distant tower.

'It won't be healthy for us to stay around,' he said.

Alexanor was raising the priest to his feet. The man muttered something.

Philopoemen retrieved the priest's staff and put it in his hand. The man smiled at him; his face was stiff, and he was having trouble focusing his eyes.

'We need to go,' Philopoemen said. 'Right now.'

'I should help these men,' Alexanor said, pointing at the injured Macedonians.

'No,' Philopoemen said, and started away. 'That would be stupid.'

Alexanor looked at the priest, nodded, and followed Philopoemen, who began to walk briskly across the agora towards the Temple of Aphrodite. A dozen young women were peering out from the pillars.

'Don't run. Look busy. Imagine you have an appointment,' Philopoemen said.

Alexanor glanced over his shoulder.

'Don't look back,' Philopoemen said.

'You make a practice of fleeing the authorities?' the Rhodian asked.

'My stepfathers certainly did. Tyranny and foreign garrisons go together like bread and *opson*.'

Philopoemen trotted up the steps of the Temple of Aphrodite like a man in a hurry. Alexanor followed him.

In among the columns, dozens of young men and women were gathered in groups, and a line of temple servants stood just inside the *pronaos* with clubs.

'Temple prostitutes,' the Achaean said.

'I know,' Alexanor returned. 'I've visited before.'

Philopoemen turned and Alexanor smiled. 'I'm a disappointment, I can tell.'

The Achaean shrugged. 'No. I erred in thinking you more of a ... Stoic.'

'A Stoic?' Alexanor was admiring a young woman in a gauzy *himation* and little else. 'I thought all that nonsense was refuted by the Academy?'

'No. We are not stopping, brother – you needn't flash your eyes at that young woman. We need to get to the beach and get under sail.'

'I'll be happy to help get your mast up, love,' said a dark-eyed beauty. 'And I can take you places no ship will take you.'

Alexanor was delighted to see the Achaean blush.

'Another time,' Alexanor said, 'But you can help us get our ship together.'

The blonde woman laughed. 'How so?'

'A ship needs oars,' Alexanor said. 'And so does a sailor.'

The women laughed. 'We have a whole temple of oars,' the raven-haired woman said, and Alexanor walked along the *naos*.

'Don't tell me you are a prude, brother?' Alexanor said, leading the way down the steps on the far side of the temple. The magnificent structure now stood between them and pursuit.

'I'm not interested in paying to rut with some woman forced into sexual slavery,' Philopoemen said. 'It's rape.'

'It is not! And who forced them?'

'You said yourself – the Cretans, the Aegyptians, all the pirates. I heard you say it.'

'But temple prostitutes are sacred ...'

'Really? Or are they just more of the same?' Philopoemen was looking behind him.

Alexanor frowned, and the two men hurried on, down the long hill to the gate on the Saronic Gulf side of the city proper. But as soon as the gate came into view, they could see that it was packed with Macedonian soldiers.

'I know another way out, through the tanneries,' Philopoemen said.

'Right behind you,' Alexanor said.

The two men turned east, into ever narrower streets, until they were passing open sheds that stank worse than a two-day-old battlefield. There were tanning sheds on both sides of the narrow street, and it was clear from the smell that the workers pissed into the little gutter that ran down the middle, and so did every cat in the city.

'This way,' Philopoemen said.

The two walked into one of the sheds, where a hundred slaves were treading dog manure into the skins of cattle and sheep.

'By the gods,' Alexanor said, holding his hand to his nose. 'Hygeia herself could not clean this place.'

'Imagine if one of these slaves has a cut on his foot,' Philopoemen said.

'The infections . . .' Alexanor shook his head.

They came out from under the shed, crossed a dirty stream that smelt of blood and scrambled up the other side.

'Follow the little path,' Philopoemen said.

'How do you know this?' Alexanor said.

'I told you, I grew up with rabble-rousers and revolutionaries. I know how to get out of Corinth.'

'You are a Stoic?' Alexanor asked.

'Yes,' Philopoemen said.

'I thought you people just waited around for fate to decide. I thought you just accepted what happens.'

They followed the path up and over a mountain of cow dung. The path had beaten the dung into a hard trail, and even polished it. They came down the other side to rows of low houses, some of crumbling mud-brick, some neatly painted in whitewash or garish colours. The smell was still terrible.

'This is the poorest section of Corinth,' Philopoemen said. 'And there's the *Diolkos*, the ship road across the Isthmus. That's our ship on it.'

Directly below them, a dozen stades away, a ship was being hauled across the Isthmus. A small freighter, it had reached almost the top of the grade, and the slaves were reversing the ropes to let the ship run down the far side.

'I've never seen anything like that,' Alexanor said.

He realised that he had heard of it; someone on Rhodes had mentioned it, or bragged about sending his ships across. It was different to see it in action.

'It's over three hundred years old,' Philopoemen said. 'Come on, before someone sees us.'

The two men walked purposefully down the slope toward the tanners' gate. There were guards, but they stayed inside their tower, as they were hated by the lower-class population. Only the colour of their cloaks were visible on the wall. Philopoemen, with his gold seal ring and red *chiton*, stood out like a pearl in a bowl of barley.

'You stand out,' Alexanor said.

'At least I'm not carrying four stolen weapons,' Philopoemen said. 'We need to be rid of the swords.'

'I was going to keep one.'

'A death sentence if you are caught. Maybe not, as you are a priest, but it could be made very bad.'

'Shall I throw them in the ditch back there?'

'Never waste a weapon, brother. Come over here. Give them to me.'

Philopoemen paused at a cross-street shrine and asked directions of a small boy, and then led the way to a wine shop with sagging walls and a pair of unpainted wooden benches outside. He went in and emerged soon after with a skin of wine, from which he took a drink and then offered the skin to his friend.

'Not bad!' Alexanor said, surprised.

He was watching two cats fight over the head of a very small fish. Philopoemen now had a long, dirty *chlamys* over his scarlet *chiton*.

'There's good wine to be found here, if you know where to look,' Philopoemen said. 'And I found good homes for the swords.'

'They won't be found?'

'It would take the whole garrison to search the lower town, and there'd be trouble. Let's get going.'

They went back towards the gate. The soldiers were still up on the wall and were watching the temple area. There was a signal burning high up the Acrocorinth to the west.

They went through the gate.

'Halt!' called a voice above. 'You with the dark hair. State your business.'

Alexanor looked up and saw an opening in the arch above him.

'Got work!' shouted Philopoemen in a Corinthian dialect.

'Halt, I say,' said the Macedonian.

'Fuck off,' snapped Philopoemen. 'I got work, an' I got to go!'

He kept walking.

Alexanor felt as if a sword blade was being pressed between his shoulders, but there were no further shouts, and they walked out of the lower gates into the slum at the foot of the tanners' quarter.

'No local would ever stop,' Philopoemen said. 'There's no garrison at ground level, so it's foolish to wait for them to come and get you, right?'

They walked out past the slum of temporary shelters, some no more than two or three thin hides held on a few poles, and then they were walking down through fields.

'There's our ship,' Philopoemen said.

He pointed to the ship, now well along its journey from the Gulf of Corinth to the Saronic Gulf.

'Is it a road?' Alexanor asked.

'Come and see,' Philopoemen said, and they climbed the shoulder of the ridge.

Alexanor was stunned by what he found.

Cut stones had been laid, one after another, and neat grooves cut into them.

'So the wheels ...'

'Fit the grooves, yes. They can't pop out, so that all the slaves have to do is pull. It isn't cheap, but it's fast – two hours to get a ship across the Isthmus. Three hours for a trireme. When I was very young I used to follow them.' He pointed to the axles. 'Three sets for a small ship like this, up to six for a military trireme.'

'You lived in Corinth?' Alexanor asked.

'Corinth and Athens and Megara. My fathers were always being exiled.' He smiled. 'I loved Corinth. Aratos freed her from the Macedonians, and now he's sold her back ...' Philopoemen shook his head.

They were climbing down the ridge on the Saronic Gulf side, and as they passed the crest they could suddenly see all the shipping on the beach, and their own small round ship on the last stade of the *Diolkos*.

'And Athens?' Alexanor asked.

'I was there for school. I went to the Academy for a while. I enjoyed fighting in the *palaestra* and I loved the theatre, but I found the Academy to be too ...' He paused. 'It's hard to say. Everyone was richer than me.'

'You do not seem to me to suffer from any deficit of wealth,' Alexanor said.

'I agree, and that's why I found them remarkable. Rich, and full of themselves, teachers and students alike.' He shrugged. 'One day, a young woman took me to the Painted Stoa to listen to Chrysippus. I never went back to the Academy.' He smiled.

'And the young woman?' Alexanor asked before he thought.

'She's dead now,' Philopoemen said, his face suddenly set.

They walked to the ship in silence.

Their little vessel was not one of Poseidon's beauties racing across the waves: it stank of newly tanned leather in the sunlight, and in fact it took hours for four sweating slaves with long oars to work the ship off the beach and out into the wind, and even then Philopoemen and his entire retinue had to take turns at the oars. The ship was a fat tub of a small merchant, pierced for six oars a side, fully laden and heavy as a lead ball.

But they had a beautiful day and a calm night, and they got the mainsail up and left it there, wafting slowly along, with a ripple under the forefoot of the little vessel, and morning saw Aegina off the bow and the great bay of Salamis opening to the north. Before the evening swell began to change the currents in the channel of Salamis, they were past the Dog Island and into the harbour of Piraeus. The little ship tied up to a pier in the military harbour and the captain paid a fee, or a bribe, to unload his passengers and their horses right there. Alexanor heard him swear by Poseidon that only the passengers would unload, and then watched as the whip-crane on the mast unloaded the horses, their baggage, and then a dozen bales of newly tanned leather which was taken away instantly by longshoremen, big men who could carry heavy loads.

'You have our olive oil for Aegina?' Philopoemen asked, and the captain nodded.

'Yes, sir. I will deliver it tomorrow and be back the day after. Our people are raising a cargo for Mytilene.'

The captain was a small man, a freedman. Only then did Alexanor fully realise that Philopoemen owned the ship, and the cargo.

Philopoemen slapped the captain on the shoulder.

'Good man.' To Alexanor, he said, 'Might as well turn a profit while I'm on this errand. I have friends in Athens. I hope they can find me twenty Thracians.'

'Soldiers?'

'Slaves. I'll buy them and free them for service. It's expensive, but it builds loyalty quickly, I promise.' Philopoemen smiled a crooked smile. 'I'll probably need a week.'

'My ... father ... rents estates along the coast,' Alexanor said. 'If we are here for long, I will visit them.'

'For your father?'

'I've been thinking about him ...' Alexanor admitted.

Philopoemen nodded. 'Good,' he said. 'I think you have at least five days. But I'd rather hoped to show you Athens.'

Alexanor waved to Leon, who was leading out their pack animals.

'Then I'll meet you ... where?'

'The Painted Stoa? I tend to end up there, whenever I visit,' Philopoemen admitted. 'You know Athens at all?'

'Not at all,' Alexanor admitted.

'Well, hurry about your business and I'll show you around. It is a magnificent city, even if you find their monuments a little tasteless.'

Alexanor thought the last comment remarkable as he rode north between the decaying Long Walls, looking at the distant Acropolis and the gleaming, ethereal figure of Athena Nike and the noble perfection of the Parthenon. But he led Leon out of one of the east gates, riding under the new artillery towers and into the brilliant sunlight.

They had to ask directions frequently, but afternoon found them on a plain of olive groves and barley fields. Alexanor found his father's factor in a shed, watching a smith rebuild a broken cart, and the man took him around the farms with a confidence that impressed him. The next day, the factor took him to the other set of farms down by the fortress at Sounion, and Alexanor wrote his father a long letter praising the man's industry. He was preparing to send it from Piraeus, but the factor told him there was a Rhodian warship in the harbour at Sounion.

'The choir is warming up,' the ship's captain said to him. His name was Menestaeos, and his brother Orestes had been Alexanor's commanding officer. 'We're heading for another war. You should come home.'

Alexanor shook his head. 'I have a mission for my temple. And then I'm for Crete. Please tell my father that I've been promoted to high priest.'

The captain, an older man, nodded. 'Good for you, lad. Never doubted you'd succeed, whatever you turned your hand to. But ... people talk, and the talk is you're serving Macedon.'

Alexanor smiled thinly. 'Yes. So it would appear.' He shrugged. 'The talk used to be that I was a coward.'

Menestaeos frowned. 'No one ever believed that shit, Alexanor. We need lads like you.' He looked as if he was going to say more, but then shook his head.

Alexanor nodded. 'I do what I can,' he said. 'Send my greetings to my father.'

The Rhodian captain had to accept this.

'Well, I'll see your pater in a dozen days,' he said. 'I'm sure he'll be happy to hear from you.' He smiled, and even added a small bow, as if Alexanor was a man of consequence.

'Will he, though?' Alexanor asked the air.

Alexanor thought that he was prepared for Athens, but he was not. Rhodes was a great city, with high walls, a determined garrison, modern weapons, and a fine navy. It had magnificent temples and had once been dominated by the Colossus, one of the most remarkable statues of the ancient world.

Nothing on Rhodes was to the scale of Athens. Athens had thirty temples as grand as the grandest temple of Rhodes; but it wasn't temples that struck the priest with awe. It was the agora and the *stoae*; the public buildings, gleaming white and edged in blue and gold and bright vermillion; the remarkable profusion of first-rate statues, which seemed to be everywhere, so that the streets and the agora seemed to teem, confusingly, with unmoving people. The *Kerameikos*, which he walked past, was so crammed with marble stelae that it appeared that the ground had indeed been sown with marble dragons' teeth. The agora itself was beautiful, well laid out and cool, filled with goods from every quarter of the world – Persian spices, eastern cottons, barbarian bronzes, Spanish swords – in deeply shaded porticos and well-roofed rows of columns.

'It's like a forest of marble,' Leon said.

'And this a hundred years after the fall of her empire,' Alexanor said, awestruck.

Leon nodded. 'She is still very great.'

Alexanor made his way to the so-called Painted Stoa, which was as beautiful as the other *stoae* and didn't seem any more painted, at least from the outside, but once in under the mighty colonnade, Alexanor and Leon were surrounded by magnificent paintings of Athens's greatness – colourful and enduring, untouched by sun or smoke. Here, Theseus defied the Minotaur; there, Arimnestos of Plataea thrust his spear into a Persian officer at Marathon. A cavalry battle swept across the great arch at the end of the *stoa*, and battle scenes, scenes of gods and men and women attracted the eye in every direction.

'This is where the poor Stoics meet?' Alexanor breathed. 'It is not plain or dull. It's beautiful.'

'Beauty is a weapon,' said a voice. 'We can use it, like any other. Even we poor Stoics.'

Alexanor turned and saw that, in entering, he had missed a dozen young men clustered under one of the columns. They stood around a man of medium stature who radiated both *charisma* and intelligence. He was beginning to lose his hair on top in front, and his eyebrows were as bushy as olive trees in spring. In fact, Alexanor thought that he looked almost like a parody of a philosopher, drawn by the hands of the gods, except for the man's obvious intelligence, and his smile.

'A weapon?' Alexanor asked.

The philosopher nodded. 'Every man must struggle against the world – to survive, to be himself, to achieve anything, to lead an excellent life. We are very nearly slaves to our basest, animal selves – the urge to sex, the urge to violence, the charm of the irrational. We must struggle to force ourselves to be more than animals. Beauty is one of the great weapons in our hands. Beauty reminds us of awe, and a world full of things greater than we ourselves. Understanding of the greatness of other men's achievements can serve the same purpose, to remind us not to lose our way. The *stoa* shows us both.'

He spoke directly, even though he stood twenty feet away, and his words echoed through the *stoa*.

One of the men standing by the philosopher was Philopoemen. He smiled.

'Master Chrysippus, this is my particular friend Alexanor son of Philokles, of Rhodes, a priest of Apollo and Asklepios. And his freedman and fellow initiate, Leon of Arkadia.'

The philosopher was famous enough that Alexanor blushed not to have known him, and he stepped forward with his hand extended.

The other man took it in both of his, a clasp of human warmth that seemed at odds with the Stoic doctrine of emotional distance.

'Any friend of our Achilles is welcome here,' Chrysippus said. 'And you, Leon. We know no social distinction, and we count slaves and freedmen as our equals. After all, we are all slaves to our bodies, a harsher master than any.'

Leon smiled crookedly. 'I'm not sure I'd agree,' he said.

Chrysippus paused. 'Speak frankly, brother,' he said.

Leon shrugged. 'I know these urges of which you just spoke. Indeed, as a doctor, I see when men eat to excess, or suffer from diseases caused by extreme behaviour. But ... these are things that they themselves have willed. I have been beaten by a harsh master. It is another thing entirely.'

Alexanor looked at his freedman in astonishment. He'd never heard the man speak so many sentences all together.

Chrysippus looked at him thoughtfully, as if preparing his counter-arguments. But then he surprised them both with a shake of his head.

'I think you are correct,' he said simply.

Alexanor frowned. 'Just like that?'

Chrysippus shrugged. 'Leon is right. I have no lived experience of slavery – I should be careful what I say.' Cautiously, he went on, 'Yet, let me say in response that I have known men and women to lead excellent lives as slaves, to strive every day to overcome the limitations of their conditions, whereas other men, even rich, powerful men, fall to the tyranny of their bodies. You, yourself, brother – were you better for being beaten, or worse?'

'Far worse, I assure you,' Leon said, and his delivery was such that every man present laughed.

'And yet here you are, a free man, in the Painted Stoa in Athens, wearing a good robe, living, I sense, an excellent life.' Chrysippus nodded, as if indicating that Leon should dispute.

But it was Philopoemen who spoke.

'Chrysippus, I dote on your every word, and when you are gone, I'll suggest you be deified, but in this ... Imagine our friend Phila were here. What would she say? And surely a man, or woman, who is brutalised daily, has almost no chance to meditate, to think, to rationalise?'

Chrysippus nodded.

'You may be right. Zeno maintained it, but we didn't actually admit slaves ...' He smiled. 'In fact, we may perhaps be guilty of saying an empty and untrue thing, merely to make a point, like Sophists.' He nodded. 'I will consider this.'

'And *that's* what makes him a great man,' Philopoemen said as they walked through the agora an hour later. 'He admits when he's wrong, he makes no pretence of being infallible, and we constantly examine our own principles and those of the founders, instead of enshrining them as some sort of received, godlike wisdom, the way they do at the Academy with Plato and Aristotle.'

'He was impressive. I could see immediately how he would win the argument ...'

Leon nodded. 'I expected him to argue that even the punishment of my worst master was merely pain inflicted on me by my body,' he said. 'Outward pain that affected the outward body.'

Philopoemen smiled. 'Yes. And that is, probably, a valid argument. But Stoics are practical, and we seek to understand the world, not to win arguments.' He shrugged. 'It is readily apparent that a slave who is regularly beaten, humiliated, raped, even, is experiencing a different order of tyranny than a man who drinks too much.' He looked at Leon. 'But it is a useful simile, when you want to shock a new student into some understanding of the reality of the human condition.'

'Useful for rich, free men,' Leon said. 'Possibly offensive to slaves.'

'Understood,' Philopoemen said. 'You have taught me, or reminded me, of something important, Leon.'

The Achaean took them out of the agora and out through the Dipylon gates. They discussed the new heavy torsion engines on the towers.

'Macedon is threatening Athens,' Philopoemen said. 'Athens no longer has a mighty fleet. She has to take precautions.'

'By Apollo, I heard enough rhetoric against Athens at Pella,' Alexanor admitted.

He was looking at the graves of famous Athenians along the sides of the road – the magnificent tombs were often very moving.

'Here Athens commemorates defeat,' Philopoemen said. 'There is something refreshingly honest about Athens having monuments that admit to failure, like this one.'

'What is it?' Leon asked.

'It's the tomb of the citizens killed in a famous military disaster, when Athens attempted to defeat Thebes in the time of Pericles, or close to it.' Philopoemen glanced back at it.

He led them to the Academy Gymnasium, amid the tall pines.

'The grove of *Academe*,' he said. 'Even the Spartans were too cultured to destroy it. May it grow forever.'

He led them up the marble steps and through the portico into the *palaestra*. Men were wrestling on the sand; two were boxing.

Twenty or thirty young men sat among the columns, most of them stripped for athletics. Young or old, they all appeared very fit. Philopoemen was looking for someone, even as he took them on a tour, describing the columns, the statues, and how Socrates, the Athenian war hero, had started young men on the study of philosophy among the columns of the *palaestra*.

'Socrates was a war hero?' Alexanor asked. 'I suppose I imagine him as an old Sophist or debater, like your Chrysippus.'

'How shall I answer you?' Philopoemen said. 'Chrysippus is no Sophist, although I wouldn't mention his name here! And he, too, has held a spear. But Socrates – he stood alone against the Thebans at Delium. He held his ground, and slew a dozen Theban hoplites, and other men fell in around him, until a rearguard was formed and shamed the *hippeis*, the cavalry of Athens, into coming back and rescuing them. And he was no general, nor even a front-ranker – he was too poor. He was in the third rank when the phalanx broke. Here they say he was the best spear in Athens – that he practised constantly – and it was his fame as a hoplite and as a warrior that allowed him the freedom to speak his mind on political matters.'

Leon shook his head. 'I have never heard this!'

Philopoemen nodded. 'Plato wanted his Socrates to be a mature aristocrat, not a penniless swordsman.' He pointed. 'There's our friend.'

Lykortas, whom Alexanor had last seen mounting a horse at Epidauros two years before, lay on the smooth marble, his head propped on the base of a column. He was reading from a five-fold wax tablet he held up to his face. He was still naked, covered in sweat, and wearing boxing straps.

'You will ruin your eyes,' Alexanor said.

'Already ruined,' Lykortas said, leaping to his feet with every sign of pleasure. 'Phila said you were coming. I hope you will let me be your host, sir, as you saved my life.'

Alexanor was looking around. The *palaestra* was the finest of its kind he'd seen, except perhaps the smooth sand at Epidauros; the level of physical training he saw around him was remarkable. Men were lifting stones and pulling at heavy Scythian bows.

'I think I'd like to take some exercise here,' he said. 'If only to say that I'd been on the sands of the famous *palaestra*.'

Lykortas smiled. 'I'm sure some gentleman will oblige you, sir,' he said.

'I will,' said Philopoemen. 'I saw you in action in Corinth. I want to try you at *pankration*.'

Alexanor looked at the young giant, who was half a head taller. He smiled.

'Of course,' he said easily.

A slave led them to one of the changing rooms, and the two men stripped.

One of the Gymnasium officers came and introduced himself. He was polite to Lykortas and civil to Philopoemen, but when Leon was introduced, he shook his head.

'No freedman can exercise here,' he said. 'There are places for such as you in the city.'

Alexanor frowned. 'Why, exactly?' he asked.

The man shrugged. 'The taint of slavery is never lost. Besides, this place is for citizens. You foreigners are welcome because of Lykortas, but only because you are gentlemen.'

'My friend,' Philopoemen said, in the act of folding his *chiton*, 'you have reminded me why I left this place and went to learn in the *Stoa*. Alexanor, I am sorry. We will have to have a bout another day.'

Alexanor was also dressing. 'I am completely of your mind, brother,' he said.

The officer shrugged. 'Your loss, foreigner.'

Outside, Lykortas was profuse in apology, and Philopoemen shrugged.

'In fact, I was very close to tossing that ... man ... on his head,' Philopoemen said.

'But you didn't,' Alexanor said.

'I'm a Stoic. Sometimes it's really annoying.' He grinned.

'Let's go see Phila,' Lykortas said.

They walked back through the mighty Dipylon gates and up the side of the hill facing the Acropolis, past the Aeropagus. On the hillside were a number of fine homes, and Lykortas led them into the courtyard of one. Alexanor knew a pang; he hadn't thought of Phila in a year. At the expiration of her contract with the king of Macedon, she'd returned to Athens.

Thais met them at the stairs and took them into the *andron*, the fine, mosaic-floored room with couches that men used for entertaining.

The *hetaera* was seated in a heavy Aegyptian chair, combing wool, while two of her women spun it into yarn.

'The noble matron,' Lykortas said.

Phila laughed, placed her wool carefully in a basket and stood. She kissed Lykortas on both cheeks, and then greeted Alexanor. She looked into his eyes for a moment.

'Am I less a matron for being a *hetaera*?' she asked. 'I have two children, after all.'

He couldn't help but smile, and she responded to his smile with one of her own. And then she smiled at Philopoemen.

'You again?' she asked.

He laughed. To Alexanor, he said, 'We've eaten here every night since we came.'

Alexanor had a single, lightning-bolt-like strike of jealousy.

'I've learnt a great deal about your Thracians,' she said to Philopoemen, as a dozen slaves began to set tables. Thais took Alexanor to a couch, and he was delighted to find that Phila lay down next to him to dine. 'And some other matters near to your heart.'

Philopoemen lay by himself, and Lykortas lay with Leon. There were no other guests.

'That's good, as I cannot find even one.' Philopoemen shook his head. 'I spent the day with Chrysippus. I haven't found a single cavalryman in this city.'

'A friend says that Macedonians won't sell any Thracians into Athens, for fear they'll be used as soldiers,' Phila said. 'I'm sorry. I was told to tell you that you might find Thracians at Amphipolis or Zone, on the coast of Thrake. But you won't find them here, or even at Delos.'

'So Macedon is determined to attack Athens?' Alexanor asked.

She rolled on an elbow and looked at him. 'Perhaps. This sort of harassment is routine.'

Alexanor nodded. 'It's the sort of thing Aegypt does to Rhodes. Will we sail to Amphipolis?'

Philopoemen ate some grapes and lay back.

'I'll have to ask my captain,' he said. 'Alkaeos knows most of the Aegean ports – he knows what we can do and what we can't.' He sighed. 'The gods do not want to make this easy.'

Alexanor felt a pang of guilt. 'I'm sorry I've got you into this.'

'It's worse than you think,' Philopoemen said with a smile. 'It's pretty clear to me that every state in the Middle Sea is recruiting. Carthage is going to fight Rome again. The Seleucids are looking at Aegypt. Everyone is backing someone on Crete.'

'Why?' Alexanor asked.

Phila laughed. 'Too many old men died. In this case, Doson in Macedon and Seleucus Ceraunus in Antioch. Ptolemy Euergetes in Aegypt. The board has been wiped clean.'

'The old board,' Philopoemen said. 'Rome and Carthage and Rhodes and the Aetolian League and even little Achaea are all on the board now.'

'Achaea …' She smiled, and shrugged.

'Speak your mind, *despoina*,' Philopoemen said. 'It is your house, and I am a guest.'

'That is why I will not offend you,' she said.

'She means, Achaea is but a province of the Macedonian empire,' Philopoemen said, and there was bitterness in his voice.

Alexanor noted that while he could keep himself from showing hostility to a domineering fool at the Gymnasium, he couldn't bear to hear Achaea spoken of as part of Macedon.

'Regardless,' Phila said, 'every empire is now ruled by a new king. No one knows what is next, but everyone is arming for war.'

'And there are no Thracians to be had,' Philopoemen said. 'Unless we go to the barbaric north, and recruit them ourselves.'

Lykortas grinned. 'I'm ready,' he said.

'You?' Philopoemen said. 'You are not one of my people, Lykortas. You are a student at the Academy.'

'I'd rather visit Thrake than deal with another day of the pompous fucks at the Academy. Who knows? Maybe I'll end up a Stoic?'

'He seems more a Cynic than a Stoic,' Alexanor whispered in Phila's ear. 'I can't see Lykortas denying his body anything.'

'That makes him an Epicurean, not a Cynic, my dear,' she said. 'Although to be fair, the Epicurean notions of pleasure aren't exactly like my own. They hate the Stoics, though.'

'He is nonetheless a pleasure-loving man,' Alexanor said.

'And yet he asked to share a couch with your freedman, so that Leon would know that Lykortas did not harbour any of the prejudice that the Gymnasium had,' Phila said. 'He is a noble man. He is merely young.'

'And you are so old,' Alexanor said.

'I'll be thirty soon enough.'

She rose, and served them all wine, mixing the wine and water as the host did. Alexanor had never been at a party hosted by a woman, and it had an odd edge to it, but both Lykortas and Philopoemen seemed completely relaxed. Leon, who was used to eating with slaves and servants, was enjoying the tutelage of Lykortas, who showed him what to eat and when, mocking the customs of the Greeks and not his couch-mate's ignorance.

'Do you have armour? Cavalry armour?' Philopoemen asked the younger man.

Lykortas smiled. 'No. But I'll have it by the time you sail.'

'War is not like a bout on the *palaestra* floor,' Philopoemen said.

'More egalitarian?' Lykortas asked. But he put away his dramatic gestures, and his eyes grew serious. 'I know, Phil. I know. It will be brutal, and I will probably be too soft for it. But I can't take any more of the gilded cage. I want to do something. I'm not even sure what I want – what side I'm on. The world is going to Hades – at least *you* are doing something.'

Philopoemen shook his head. 'Don't, I pray, make me responsible for your ethics.'

'Listen, sir. Do you ever lie in bed in the morning, wondering why you should rise? Wondering why you even exist?' Lykortas was not relaxed now.

Philopoemen nodded. He handed the wine cup to Leon and sat up.

'Yes. I know this feeling *very* well.'

'You?' Leon asked. 'I've watched you work on a barn with your own hands.'

'When I learnt of how my wife and sons died,' Philopoemen said simply, 'I thought of suicide. And I didn't want anything. Food. Sleep. Wakefulness. Thought. Nothing. I wanted *nothing*.'

There was a moment of silence. It was clearly not the answer Lykortas had expected.

'I'm sorry, sir. I hadn't meant … Bah. I'm sick of it. I want to *do* something.'

'Do something worthy?' Philopoemen asked gently.

'Yes!' the young man said.

Philopoemen smiled. 'How do you know what I propose is worthy?'

'Tell me then, sir. Tell me what are we going to do with these Thracian mercenaries?' Lykortas sat up.

'We'll attempt …' Philopoemen paused. He looked around. 'Shall I tell you what young Philip of Macedon wants? He wants Crete in a state of chaos, so that he can start building a navy while Rhodes is busy with Crete. Shall I tell you what Aratos wants? He wants me to fail, of course, but if I succeed, he merely wants me to march around a bit, so that Aratos and the Achaean League can be seen to support their ally of Macedon.' He looked at Lykortas. 'Does that sound worthy?'

'No,' Lykortas said. 'But that's not what you're going to do.'

Philopoemen tried to hide his own grin, and ended up with a lopsided smile. 'No,' he said. 'I'm going to find a loose thread in the alliance of cities that rules the island, and I'm going to pull until it unravels.'

'What loose thread is that?' Alexanor asked.

'I found him one,' Phila said.

'And then?' Alexanor asked, moved. He sat up too.

'And then we'll conquer Crete, and give them good government, and just laws,' Philopoemen said.

'That's worthy,' Lykortas said. 'By the gods …'

Philopoemen's eyes were shining. 'And that is only the beginning. I don't want to conquer the world. I want to make it *better*.'

Just for a moment a chill touched Alexanor, as if one of the gods had brushed his sleeve.

The coast of Thrake came up slowly – a long, flat coast with high ridges behind it, covered in trees. The freighter had a fair-sized wave at her bow; a steady wind pushed the mainsail, and the oars were in and stowed amidships.

'Thrake,' Syrmas said. 'But not my part. I'm an Odrysian.' He pretended to shudder. 'These are tame Thracians, Greek-lovers.'

'Not like you,' Lykortas said. 'You hate Greeks.'

The Thracian laughed. 'Fuck your mother,' he said.

Lykortas shrugged. 'Too old,' he replied.

Alexanor winced, but the other men on deck laughed. Lykortas' youth often took the form of a desire to shock.

'There's Zone,' Syrmas said, pointing. 'Not a big place, but rich enough. Slavers bring men there, and when bands of mercenaries want to hire out, they camp in the ditch and wait for a customer.'

'That sounds uncomfortable,' Lykortas said. 'Why camp in a ditch?'

'Not a ditch, *the* Ditch,' Philopoemen said. 'The fortress walls are high, and to make them higher, there's a deep ditch hewn directly into the rock. It's as wide as a street and deep – probably a good place to camp. And, of course, it keeps the mercenaries out of the city.'

'How do you know these things?' Syrmas asked. 'You have never been here!'

'Phila told me,' Philopoemen said. 'I like to know what I'm doing. And what I'm getting into.'

Alexanor had another pang of jealousy.

'This is a good place to practice Stoicism, gentlemen. A slave town is a rough place – one slip and we'll find ourselves serving wine to some Roman magnate.' Philopoemen nodded at the shore. He was sharpening his sword.

Alexanor smiled. 'I'll at least be his physician. But yes. Anyone can be enslaved here. We should trust no one.'

'You'll be the first Rhodian to ever set foot in this place, I'm guessing,' Philopoemen said. 'Shall we say you are from Epidauros, instead? Looking for some slaves?'

Lykortas pursed his lips. 'Why the subterfuge?'

'Rhodes is in a permanent state of war with the slavers,' Alexanor said. 'If they knew I was Rhodian – if they knew I'd been a Rhodian marine ...'

'Right. We won't let that happen, will we, friends?'

Philopoemen had a way of expressing a command as a polite request. Alexanor admired it.

'We will not,' Lykortas said. 'If anyone gets in our way, I'll ...' He looked at Philopoemen.

'We'll be cautious, and quiet. And if someone offers us violence, we'll answer with the same.' Philopoemen smiled thinly. 'I'm not *that* much of a Stoic. Everyone wear a sword.'

'Maybe we should try Abdera,' Philopoemen said. 'I thought I'd be meeting someone here.'

He seldom displayed frustration or defeat, but two days in the fleas and lice of Zone had rendered him all too human.

'This is without a doubt the most depressing place I have ever visited,' Alexanor said.

He was looking at a huddle of blonde Thracian women, none of them more than fourteen years old. All were blank eyed, and they stood, or sat, with their faces turned towards the fortress wall.

'They fuck like bunnies,' the slave owner called. 'And they will bear strong sons to work in your fields. Every one of them can work with linen or wool all day and pleasure you all night. Come on, gentlemen.'

Philopoemen kept walking. Lykortas paused.

'I've never seen bunnies fuck,' he said to the slaver. 'How do they do it?'

'Uh-oh,' Syrmas said.

'All the Thracian sluts are hot for it, you'll see. I'll let you try one out for a drachma. Here, try this one.'

The slaver was himself a Thracian, tall, heavy with muscle and fat, and his whole body covered in intricate tattoos. He glared at Lykortas.

'I like to choose for myself,' Lykortas said. 'And I don't want your slave girl.'

'Prefer boys? Or just another impotent Greek? Here, I'll fuck her myself, and you can watch.'

The man had sensed Lykortas' disgust, and was *enjoying* it. He stripped the girl with one hand.

She didn't even flinch.

Lykortas kicked the Thracian slaver in the knee. It was a trained *pankration* kick, and the knee snapped, and the big man fell, roaring with pain.

And chaos came to the Ditch.

The slaver had guards – a dozen or more men like himself, coastal

Thracians who profited by the slave trade. And there were a hundred other small dealers and customers all around the periphery of the fortress, like an agora dedicated to the sale of Thracian women, and stolen Thracian cattle. It smelled of urine and despair.

And in a heartbeat, every head was turned.

A spear shaft caught Lykortas in the side of the head, knocking him unconscious in a single blow. The spearman reversed the spear to finish the young man, and Alexanor took the shaft in both hands and threw the man over his back. Another Thracian stabbed at him with a spear, and Leon tackled the man, arms around his waist, and dragged him down into the muck.

Alexanor turned, the spear in both hands, and used it as a shaft, body-checking a running man and then dropping him with a blow from the butt of the spear.

The slaver's guards were pushing forward. Syrmas drew his *kopis* even as Philopoemen wrapped his *chlamys* around his arm in a single, practised flip of the fabric. Alexanor blocked a thrust from another spear.

He took a stride forward and stood over the fallen student. He had a moment; he thrust ruthlessly at the man and killed him, the first man he'd killed since he went to Epidauros. Leon scrambled off the corpse and backed away. Alexanor glanced back at him and saw Philopoemen.

Philopoemen had paused, looking at the chaos, the men running. Alexanor never forgot that moment; Philopoemen was calm, measured. *Thinking.*

Syrmas cut a spear shaft in two with a single blow, broke a man's nose with the horse-head pommel of his sword, and then cut off another man's hand. He pushed forward, so that he was next to Alexanor.

Then Philopoemen moved. Alexanor was suddenly too desperate to follow the Achaean's fights. The only instant he could afterwards remember was Philopoemen's rising cut with his *xiphos*, withdrawing the blade from a falling man's throat to cut *up* into an unguarded man's chin, then passing his sword hand around the wounded man's head and throwing him into two more guards by the turning of the head, snapping his neck in the same motion.

The crowd fell back. Half the slaver's guards were down, and Alexanor didn't need to speak Thracian to understand that the survivors were demanding that they be shot down with arrows. Leon pressed against his back, a broken spear shaft in his hand.

'They are going to charge us,' Syrmas said. 'Fucking Thracians!' He shouted something.

Men shouted back.

Syrmas went mad, or so it seemed. He began a chant, and Alexanor could tell he was taunting his foes. He pointed at his crotch and screamed something.

Philopoemen was covered in cuts. His right arm was red to the elbow. He glanced at Alexanor.

'I don't think that's helping our cause,' he said cheerfully.

Alexanor parried a thrown spear. The Thracian slavers were hesitant to charge them.

Syrmas spoke a long sentence, punctuated with pointing at the slavers on the ground.

The slavers made up their minds, roared, and charged.

Alexanor had never fought like this without the benefit of an *aspis*, the big round shield that Rhodian marines still carried, for all that the Macedonians thought them old-fashioned. He felt naked without a shield, and he took a wound immediately; he never saw the weapon that scored his side, and he was only saved from instant death by his enraged adversary's poor practice. The point went in, but the blade cut the skin and the spear fell free, and Alexanor's panicked back-blow dented the side of the man's head.

Philopoemen's foes fell at his feet. He'd killed two of them in two blows.

Syrmas picked up a big man, raised him over his head, and threw him into the crowd.

Alexanor fell to his knees. The pain was intense, and blood was flowing out of his side. Leon stepped past him and used his half-spear like a woman would use a broom, slamming the saurauter down on the Thracians.

'Damn,' Alexanor heard himself say aloud. 'I'm dead.'

'I need you to get up, if you can,' Philopoemen said. It was the voice of command, and it sounded reasonable.

Alexanor pushed himself to his feet.

There were screams from around the corner of the Ditch, by the gate, and the sound of horse hooves. The crowd, which had been pushing forward, suddenly scattered, men barging into the slave pens or throwing themselves at the stone-lined walls of the great ditch.

'Hold!' Philopoemen roared.

He was almost perfectly still, his cloak held up with his left arm, his sword point tracing slow and bloody arcs in the air at eye level.

Alexanor leant in, covering his side. Leon stood beside him.

But the Thracians were not attacking, and the last slave guard threw down his spear and ran just as a trio of horsemen burst around the corner. The lead man wore a hat like a sack, well back on his head; his beard was dyed bright red, and he wore enough gold to purchase a ship. The young men behind him were wearing mail shirts. That was all Alexanor saw before the red-beard's horse was rearing over them, its shadow on Philopoemen's unmoving guard.

'Fucking Getae,' Syrmas muttered. But then he spoke, in Thracian, and Red Beard answered. The man's contempt was obvious.

Alexanor had to lean his weight on Philopoemen to keep standing.

More Getae trotted up the Ditch – an overwhelming force, forty horsemen, with bows.

Syrmas spoke again.

Red Beard laughed. He waved. In Greek, he said, 'This man speak for you, *Hipparchos?*'

He pointed at Syrmas, and Philopoemen nodded.

'Yes,' he said, standing straight from his crouched fighting guard.

'Eight drachmae a day?' the man asked. 'I'd fight my fucking brother for that. And a hundred tetradrachmae for me.'

Alexanor knew the crisis was past, and so did his knees. He fell.

'You're hired,' he heard Philopoemen say, as if at a great distance.

CHAPTER THREE

Mytilene and Crete

221 BCE

'This is not our bargain, brother,' Philopoemen said.

He was standing with a bowl of soup in one hand and a comb in the other, and behind him was Dinaeos, smiling nervously.

Alexanor wriggled, fretting at the pain of his recovering body.

'How so?' he asked.

He was frustrated with his body, and frustration made him peevish. He was the worst patient he'd ever met.

'*I* get wounded. You heal *me*.' Philopoemen smiled. He'd been endlessly patient, had made it through two medical tirades unfazed, and now that they'd sailed to Mytilene, he continued to wait on his doctor as if he was a slave. 'Next, you'll be commanding cavalry.'

'Never,' Alexanor snapped. 'I will never fight anyone ever again. What a foolish waste of life. We killed how many men? Innocent men?'

'Innocent rapists and murderers,' Philopoemen said.

'Lykortas?' Alexanor asked, rather than admit that he agreed.

'Lykortas was knocked unconscious. Nothing more. He has headaches, which he treats by drinking unwatered wine and having sex as promiscuously as possible.' Philopoemen smiled.

'Damn,' Dinaeos said, entering with more soup. 'I need to get knocked on the head more often. That sounds wonderful. Is this a new part of the whole Stoic thing that you've been hiding from me?'

'I don't want soup,' Alexanor said.

'Interesting, since Leon prepared and prescribed it. As many bowls as we can make you take.'

'Leon! That quack ...' Alexanor knew he was going too far.

'Eat your nice soup, there's a good boy,' Leon said cheerfully, appearing in the doorway.

Alexanor knew that ruthlessly cheerful tone; he used it himself. He resented it ...

He recovered very quickly, once his body had made up the blood loss; indeed, he was only bed-bound one day on Lesvos, and then he was moving around the house that Philopoemen had rented. In fact, he'd rented an entire farm – a small plain along the beach and a hillside full of olive groves. Alexanor could go to the windows, open them, and walk out into the brilliant sunlight, and he did, breathing the sea-scented air just touched with the smell of the distant pines. On the plain, the cattle and sheep had been penned so that seventy cavalrymen could drill. Alexanor sat wrapped in a cloak and watched his friend cajole, demand, mock, and laugh as forty assorted Greeks and thirty Thracians moved up and down the little plain and then up into the olive groves. Alexanor had assumed that the cavalry couldn't move easily among the rocks and trees, but the Getae seemed to flow through the trees like water and the Achaeans were almost as nimble.

'He plans so far ahead,' Leon said. 'It's terrifying. I imagine the gods must be like this.'

Alexanor glanced at his assistant. 'I'm very sorry for my behaviour as a patient.'

'And you should be,' Leon said, but his smile took the sting out. 'It was as if you were in an Olympic contest to be the worst patient ever born of woman.' He shrugged. 'Luckily, the one benefit of my former life as a slave is that I am immune to master's little ways.'

He spoke without bitterness, but Alexanor was shamed.

'You speak more plainly ...' He wasn't sure what he was trying to say.

'Less like a slave?' Leon asked, an eyebrow raised. 'I'm free. And as you and Philopoemen treat me as a peer, I thought I'd respond. Should I be silent?'

Alexanor drank soup and pondered slavery.

But Leon didn't leave him to writhe.

'Never mind all that. What I was trying to say was that Philopoemen rented this place before we arrived. Dinaeos was already here. Everything was already paid, already done.'

'Yes,' Alexanor said. 'But it's easier to plan this way when you are as rich as Croesus.'

'True enough,' Leon said. 'But the Getae chief? Thodor? Philopoemen took him at Sellasia. I think he had already sent for him … I want to learn to ride like that,' he said as a Getae leapt a downed pine tree and swarmed down a steep slope of stone, with Aristaenos and Philopoemen's servant Arkas side by side a horse length behind. They moved like centaurs over the broken ground, an expertise shared by Achaeans and Thracians.

During the entirety of Alexanor's recovery, the cavalry continued to train. Alexanor was used to practice – the rigid practice of detailed ritual, the memorisation of training routines in *pankration*, the memorisation of texts from the great medical writers – yet he was surprised to find that soldiers trained so hard.

'The greatest thing is that they have to ride well,' Dinaeos said.

'The most important thing is that they have to trust one another,' Philopoemen said. 'It is a sad comment on mortals that the bonds men forge in war are often the closest they will ever know.'

Alexanor winced.

Philopoemen shrugged. 'What would you have, brother?'

'I'd have a man's bond with his wife stronger than one forged in blood.'

He realised that he'd said the word wife, and paused. No one spoke of wives before Philopoemen, by tacit agreement.

The Achaean glanced at him, face unreadable.

'I've often wondered if we shouldn't encourage women to be warriors,' he said. 'It would change the way men perceive them.'

'What a radical you are!' Alexanor said.

'What a spoilsport!' Dinaeos said. 'Don't we go to war to get away from our wives?'

'No,' Philopoemen said. 'If my wife was alive, I would never leave her to make war.'

His face worked; he turned away.

The silence was made of iron.

Training was not merely physical. Every evening the officers, including three of the Thracians, gathered on couches and lay in the heated *andron* of the country house like men around a campfire. While they ate and drank, they talked about making war, and Philopoemen encouraged every man present to tell stories of combat and heroism that he himself had witnessed.

Other men came and went from the country house: merchants from Mytilene, who brought supplies – swords, armour, good horses, oats, olive oil. But they also brought news, and Alexanor, as the man always in the house, realised early on that Philopoemen had organised an entire network of merchants to report to him about politics in Crete.

'You have a very secret mind,' Alexanor said with a smile, one afternoon in the second week.

Philopoemen was covered in dust, wearing his armour as if it was light clothing, his dark red cloak almost white with local dust. He stood in the entrance of his rented country house, reading a scroll that a messenger, no more dusty than the captain himself, had just handed him.

'I have, too,' the *hipparchos* admitted. 'If you aspire to be the New Achilles, you must work in secret so that the effort is invisible. No one fancies a hard-working Achilles. It has to appear effortless.'

'How many men in your network?' Alexanor asked, when the messenger had been paid, rewarded, and dismissed.

Philopoemen gave him a thin-lipped smile. He looked out at the Thracian, Syrmas, drilling the other Thracians in close-order formations.

'Why do you assume men?' Philopoemen asked. 'Women hear everything.'

Alexanor shrugged. 'An expression—'

'Words have power,' Philopoemen said. 'A priest should know that. Regardless, you give me too much credit. It is Phila's network. I thought you knew that.'

Alexanor felt himself flush. 'I do not enquire too closely into her life. She doesn't belong to me.'

Philopoemen gave his friend an odd look, as if he was confused.

'I didn't mean anything like that.' He shrugged. 'At any rate, she has an extensive network of friends. She told me that last year she made more money selling financial advice to shippers than she did ... with her contracts.'

Alexanor narrowed his eyes. 'She talks to you a great deal,' he said carefully.

'I've seldom met a woman with such a grasp of the world. And she's Stoic. Indeed ...' He glanced at Alexanor. 'What's wrong?'

'You are in love with her?' Alexanor blurted out.

Philopoemen frowned. 'No. Why?'

The two men looked at each other, and Alexanor had to look away. His hands were shaking.

'I should be getting to my temple,' he said. 'I'd have left before now if I hadn't been wounded.' He looked away. 'And I intend to visit my father, on Rhodes.'

Philopoemen opened his mouth to speak, and then thought better of it.

'I thought we might land at Lentas together,' he said.

Alexanor was prey to a rip tide of conflicting emotions.

'I should get there first. Too much surprise could work against us.'

Philopoemen nodded. 'You'd know best, of course. But at least stay and meet our new recruit. He's from Crete.'

Philopoemen's new recruit was the oldest man of the *taxeis*, a Cretan from Gortyna, tall, athletic, and with immense dignity and a body that told of hard exercise every day. Scars on his sword hand and arm spoke of a life as a soldier.

'This is Antiphatas,' Philopoemen introduced him. 'He is the leader of the *Neoteroi* among the exiles of Gortyna. He will ride with us when we land.'

Antiphatas clasped hands with all of the officers.

'What a fine body of men,' he said to Philopoemen.

'Coming along,' said Dinaeos.

'Let's all sit and hear what Antiphatas has to say,' Philopoemen said, and all of the officers sat or reclined: Thodor lay with his tanist and nephew, the strikingly handsome Dadas; Alexanor with Leon; Dinaeos with Lykortas; Kleostratos with Syrmas; Aristaenos lay alone, because he was sharing his *kline* with Antiphatas.

The Cretan stood by an ornate bronze lamp stand with a figure of Aphrodite rendered in ruddy bronze. The Thracians had started the custom of touching her breasts each time they entered the room; it was apparently a Thracian custom, and after just a week of training, her breasts were polished to a near-perfect gold.

Antiphatas glanced at the figure of Aphrodite and smiled.

'I'll do my very best to distract you from the Mistress,' he said, and the soldiers chuckled. Several made religious signs.

'A good many things have changed since we sent a delegation to King Philip,' the man continued.

'Who's "we"?' called Thodor, the Thracian chief.

Philopoemen nodded. 'Good point,' he said. 'Please explain.'

'I am from Gortyna,' the man said. 'Gortyna and Knossos are the richest cities on Crete – perhaps in the Greek world.'

Lykortas laughed. 'Richer than Athens? Richer than Pella?' He was dismissive.

Antiphatas nodded. 'Yes. I don't think you foreigners have any idea of how rich Crete is. Leave it – you'll see soon enough. Knossos and Gortyna are the two main cities, but there are dozens of others. Knossos and Gortyna are in a state of almost perpetual war.' He shrugged. 'Cretans take war very seriously. It is the principal occupation of men. What else makes men worthy, or good?'

'Love?' Dinaeos asked.

'Philosophy?' Lykortas said.

Antiphatas waved a hand dismissively. 'The only reliable measure of a man is war. But I'm sailing away from my port, to use a Cretan saying. My point is that warfare is our daily routine, and it is conducted honourably – raids and counter-raids, so that men can show their courage, test their skills—'

'Accomplish nothing,' Dinaeos muttered.

'Let the man speak,' Philopoemen said.

'Two years ago, the *Presbyteroi* came to power in both Knossos and Gortyna.'

'What's a *Presbys* when he's at home?' Dinaeos asked. 'It just means "old man".'

'Among us, it is used for the old aristocrats. Oligarchs really. A few hundred families who own ... almost everything. Their ownership of property has increased to the point where other families are being excluded from the warrior classes. As their estates grow, the number of free farmers in the hoplite class declines.'

'That's true everywhere in Greece,' Alexanor said, and Lykortas nodded, as did Philopoemen.

'In Knossos, they allied themselves with some of the poorest people, however unlikely, and formed a political party, and then they moved on Gortyna. Now, with the help of Aetolian soldiers, they have pushed all of the *Neoteroi*, the so-called "new men" out of the cities. My people have been hoplites for twenty generations. I am now an exile with no income, excluded from rank or political office in my own city.' He shrugged. 'There's nowhere in central Crete not subservient to the oligarchs. Only Polyrrhenia and a handful of other towns are still free.'

'Aetolians?' Dinaeos asked. 'Zeus Soter! They're everywhere.'

Philopoemen nodded. 'So they are. What do they want on Crete?'

'Money, soldiers and slaves,' Antiphatas said. 'Crete is rich. But it is also a source of troops – Cretan mercenaries are valued everywhere—'

'If you all spend so much time making war, and you export mercenaries,' said the young Thracian, 'why do you need us?'

His accent was guttural, but his grammar was good, and his tone was a little sarcastic, and most of the soldiers laughed.

'First, we have almost no cavalry,' Antiphatas said. 'You'll understand when you see Crete. It's all rock,' he added cheerily.

'But rich ...' muttered Dinaeos. 'This bastard is about to sell me a rug, I can just feel it coming ...'

'Dinaeos,' Philopoemen said.

'Second, the Aetolians ...' He shrugged. 'They do not fight the way we fight. They execute every man taken. No one is ransomed. Their combat is ignoble. They decline single combat, they only fight when they have overwhelming odds, they pursue the defeated ruthlessly and execute the survivors.' He was red with anger. 'They are cowards!'

'They sound very effective,' Philopoemen said. 'How many men has Aetolia sent?'

'A thousand cavalry. A thousand!' Antiphatas took several deep breaths. 'How many do you have, *Hipparchos*?'

Philopoemen smiled grimly. 'A hundred, give or take.'

'Philip promised us two hundred Achaean horse!' Antiphatas said.

'He'd have been more honest if he'd sent you Macedonian cavalry,'

Philopoemen said. 'I, too, have been promised two hundred Achaeans. No one ever suggested that they would be cavalrymen.' He looked around. 'I doubt they'll reach us before spring.'

Antiphatas looked around. 'A hundred men?'

'I understand,' said Philopoemen carefully, 'that there is, at least in Gortyna, a large faction of discontented, disenfranchised men.'

'All of the leaders are in exile. Many are in Aegypt.' Antiphatas shrugged. 'I came to Mytilene ...'

'Some are in Antioch, too,' Philopoemen said. 'I have letters from several of them. Including your son, who is on his way.'

'Yes,' Antiphatas admitted. 'And in Macedon.'

'So your "New Men" are further divided into factions,' Philopoemen asked.

Antiphatas slumped. 'Yes. And no one trusts Macedon.'

'Least of all the Achaeans in this room,' Philopoemen said.

'Or the Thracians,' Kleostratos said.

'So, having requested military aid from Macedon, you don't have the unity to support it?' Philopoemen said.

'You mean, since we are receiving less than half the support we were promised, which was itself less than a tithe of what we requested?' Antiphatas spat back.

Philopoemen gestured to Arkas and Lykon, his personal servants, and they bustled through the room, serving bits of roast lamb and barley rolls and more wine.

'Is there support for us in Gortyna?' Philopoemen asked.

Antiphatas shrugged. 'I haven't been back in months. And as you have a hundred men, I can't imagine—'

'Imagine,' Philopoemen said. 'Imagine I can seize the main gate at Gortyna. Imagine that ...'

'How will you get there?' Antiphatas asked. 'Gortyna is forty stades from the sea—'

'I know,' Philopoemen said. 'My father and my stepfathers knew it well. I know where it is, how far from the sea, and even how well some of the gates are guarded. Are you willing to try?'

'An insane risk,' Antiphatas said. But then he smiled. 'But I'm sick of being an exile, and my son deserves to grow to manhood as a warrior, not someone's serf. I suppose the worst outcome is that I'll be spreadeagled and executed. Ugly, but, merely death.'

'That's the spirit.' Philopoemen stood up. 'Starting tomorrow we'll practise attacks on towers.'

'On horseback?' Thodor called out.

Philopoemen laughed. 'Of course. Although you'll have to teach me how to ride up a ladder.'

'Where are these Aetolians?' Dinaeos asked.

'I'll learn more,' Antiphatas said. 'Some will be in the garrison at Knossos and others at Gortyna, at least.'

'If the Aetolians fight so much against the customs of the country,' Alexanor said slowly, 'do you think any of the *Presbyteroi* might turn against them?'

'They don't even want to fight,' Antiphatas said bitterly. 'They just want money. More and more money, until we are all serfs and slaves, and they own everything.'

Much later, when most of the officers had gone to bed, Philopoemen surprised Alexanor, as he often did, by helping his slaves and servants tidy and clean. Two slave women emerged from the kitchen, the sort of drab, middle-aged slaves that were invisible. Philopoemen knew their names, smiled at them, and then joined Arkas in carrying dishes.

Leon rolled off his side of the couch and began moving the side tables that had carried the food.

'Who are those women?' Alexanor asked, carrying a single dish.

'They came with the house,' Philopoemen said. 'The taller one is Mari, and the shorter Hannah.'

He grinned at the two women as they reached out to empty his arms of wine cups.

Alexanor followed his friend back to the *andron*.

'Rhodes and Rome will have an investment in those Aetolians,' he said.

Philopoemen paused, and his blunt features seemed to sharpen as his face took on the look of intelligence that Alexanor had come to know.

'How so?'

'Half the piracy in the Inner Sea comes from Crete. That's where the riches come from, and the slaves.'

Philopoemen began to pick up the little bowls of nuts.

'Of course,' he said. 'I should have known that. So much to know.'

'Rhodes and Rome want open seas and no piracy,' Alexanor went on.

He was collecting all the wine things, the strainer, the measuring cups ...

'Rome,' Philopoemen said. 'I would like to go there. A whole new world, run by barbarians.'

'They are not so barbaric. Their merchants are always on Rhodes. When I was a marine, we supported a Roman squadron. I've never seen anything like their military organisation.'

'And rich?' Philopoemen asked, squeezing past Leon with his arms full of silver vessels.

'Richer than you can imagine,' Alexanor said. 'Listen, brother. Rhodes has bet on Rome. Over the Seleucids, over the Aegyptians or the Macedonians.'

Philopoemen unburdened himself on the vast, well-scrubbed kitchen counter and turned.

'I'll bear that in mind. And Rome is backing the Aetolian League?'

'Backing is too strong.'

Alexanor had the uneasy feeling that Philopoemen already knew the answer. *Is he testing me?*

'What's your role in all this?' Philopoemen asked suddenly. 'A Rhodian serving Macedon?'

'I serve my god,' Alexanor said.

Philopoemen nodded. 'You have saved my life many times, brother. You will hear no carping from me. But tell me the truth. You report to Rhodes?'

Alexanor almost dropped the wine gear; the great mixing *krater* slipped.

He caught it. 'Perhaps informally.' He steadied himself. 'I'm not a spy.'

'You wouldn't let me ride into a trap, would you?' Philopoemen asked gently. 'Because I'm going to war, and the faction I'm supposed to back is fighting against your Rhodes. And you want to go there and visit your father.'

Alexanor was appalled. 'Never!' he said. 'How could you imagine ...'

Philopoemen nodded. 'I'm very sorry. You know there was a Rhodian warship at Sounion when you went off into Attica, yes?'

Alexanor turned away to hide both anger and hesitation, and began to walk back along the ill-lit hall to the *andron*, glad that Philopoemen could not see his face.

'Yes,' he said. 'I used it to send a letter to my father.'

'And Rhodes is providing both monetary and military support to the Aetolian contingent on Crete,' Philopoemen said, following him down the hall. 'So you see why I might have some concerns.'

The *andron* was clear; eight men and two women had made light work of clearing it. Alexanor turned and looked at his friend.

'I should probably leave,' he said. 'As you do not trust me.'

'And if I say you could not leave?' Philopoemen said pleasantly. 'Consider, *brother*, that if I do not trust you, I can hardly allow you to land in Crete ahead of me.'

'I have nothing to do with Rhodian policy. I don't even know that Rhodes is supporting these Aetolians – I only heard that from you.'

Alexanor was angry, but also afraid. Afraid that somehow he had forfeited this man's good opinion.

Philopoemen put a hand on his shoulder.

'Well, it scarcely matters,' he said. 'I do trust you. And what we do in Crete is bigger than Achaea or Rhodes, who ought to be allies anyway. The day is coming when the small states will have to unite to withstand the great empires, exactly as the small landowners need to unite to face the oligarchs.'

'So I am free to go?' Alexanor asked.

'Yes.'

'Are you sleeping with Phila?'

Philopoemen whirled. 'What?'

'If you can ask me if I'm a spy,' the priest said, 'I can ask you an equally horrible question.'

Philopoemen raised an eyebrow. 'Fair,' he said. 'No,' he added. 'We're allies, not lovers.'

Alexanor wasn't sure he believed his friend, but he wanted to.

'I need more wine,' he said.

Philopoemen sighed. 'Me, too,' he admitted.

He walked off, his bare feet slapping on the mosaic floor, and came back with Arkas and a fine amphora covered in beautiful decoration.

Arkas poured unwatered wine into two Boeotian cups, handed one to each of the two men, bowed, and withdrew.

'It strikes me,' Alexanor said, 'that we love each other, and that you want to believe I am not going to betray you to Rhodes, and I want to believe that you are not sleeping with Phila, and that in each case, our desires are irrational. I am a loyal Rhodian. You are free to engage Phila as a *hetaera*, or she to take any lover she wishes. We are—'

'Fools? Listen, brother. Some day, I may meet a woman who stirs me, but all that ...' He shrugged. 'It died with my wife. There, it's said. No man or woman has stirred me since ...' His eyes narrowed, briefly. 'Since she died.' He choked, physically, speaking those words.

Alexanor turned and put an arm around him. Philopoemen, so imperturbable, was unable to speak.

But he mastered himself. He shrugged again. Wiped his eyes, cleared his throat.

'Phila is engaged, as a Stoic, in a war on the slave trade, especially the trade in women.'

'She never told me that,' Alexanor said bitterly.

'Perhaps you were always busy doing something else,' Philopoemen said, smiling. 'You say I am a secret man, but you spent a year at the court of Macedon, and none of us really know why.'

Alexanor sat back on the *kline*, his wine cup balanced on his stomach. He looked at the white ceiling and sighed.

'But Achaea is an ally of Macedon,' he said.

'*Aratos* is an ally of Macedon,' Philopoemen said. 'He's harnessed to them now. He's taken their money, and he's guest-friends with Philip, and his whole policy is dependent on Macedonian support. He's wagered that Macedon will do his fighting for him, so that he can dismantle our army and make deep tax cuts, which will ensure that the richest part of the citizens will support him.' Philopoemen drank a healthy amount of unwatered wine and sat down. 'I'm playing both sides,' he admitted. 'I need Macedon's support to even land this expedition – after all, you put me in this role. But in the long run –' he took a deep breath – 'I want Achaea out from under Macedon's boot, as she was in my youth, before Aratos sold Corinth.'

'We are both playing complicated games,' Alexanor said. 'We live in complicated times. I pass things to my father that will benefit Rhodes, or protect her. I suppose that I still seek his good opinion. But not in everything. I am a priest of the god first. My first loyalty is to my temples and the priests who trained me.' He smiled. 'And right now, they are getting a great deal of support from young Philip, who seems determined to be the richest donor in the Inner Sea.'

'I'm going to guess that Philip believes he can have it all. All of Greece – the islands, Crete, maybe even Syria.' Philopoemen swirled his wine in his cup and drank it off. 'Are we good?'

Alexanor sat up. 'I feel better,' he admitted. 'I already have two masters. You are a third.'

'I am not your master,' Philopoemen said.

'You are working to save Greece. No one else is.' Alexanor raised his cup. 'I liked your speech to young Lykortas. I am a doctor, of course I want to make the world better.'

'We can do it,' Philopoemen said. 'But not if we have hangovers.'

'This from you?' Alexanor asked, but he was pleased.

CHAPTER FOUR

—◆◆◆◆—

Rhodes and Crete

220 BCE

Alexanor and Leon landed on the same great mole that Demetrios the Besieger had failed, bloodily, to take when he attacked the city of Rhodes just a hundred years before. The Rhodian marines trained there, and every morning at dawn they stood on the mole in formation watching the sun rise out of the sea. Every ephebe was reminded of the fight on the mole before their morning run.

It wasn't morning, but a late summer afternoon, and the sun beat down on the pale stone and reflected back on the passengers coming ashore, grilling them like the sardines and anchovies in the tavernas along the civilian waterfront. To his right, under the walls, there were ship sheds and military equipment instead of tavernas, and the citadel towered over all of it, visible from every point in the city.

Alexanor hadn't even shouldered his sea-bag when a slave took it off his shoulder and his father embraced him hesitantly, and then both of his brothers embraced him with more force and affection.

'We heard you were coming,' Menes said. He was two years younger, and still struggled to have a beard.

'The harbour master told us,' Lysander said. He was the youngest, and still an ephebe.

'It seems like a long way round to go to Crete,' Philokles said with a smile, an hour later, at the family table. Alexanor had not been home in six years, and his eyes filled with tears every time he looked at his mother, Antigone, who couldn't stop placing food in front of him.

'You're so ...' she said again.

'Big?' his father asked. 'He was always a big man.' He pounded his son's arm. 'Lot of muscle for a priest.'

'Is that a wound?' Menes asked, looking at his arms. 'By Poseidon, brother! You're covered in scars!'

'I was in a bit of a fight,' he admitted.

'You took on a pair of pirate ships single-handed!' Philokles said, his voice warm with praise. 'We heard all about it from a merchant navarch, didn't we, boys?' He smiled at his son as if he'd never reproached him for failing to die in battle. 'And now what, the Macedonian fleet single-handed? I thought that you were a priest?'

'I was with my friend Philopoemen,' Alexanor said. 'We were attacked in a market. In Zone.'

'Zone?' his father said, spluttering. 'That mud hole?'

'The place where pirates sell their slaves?' Menes asked.

Lysander crossed his arms.

It took two days for him to tell them all his stories, and by then, his brothers were far too curious about his time at the court of Macedon. He had too many secrets; his father already seemed to know them all, and wasn't particularly good at keeping them.

Philokles had problems too.

'No matter what I do, I seem to bleed gold,' he said one evening, in irritation. 'I made a fortune on the grain from the Euxine Sea last autumn, and it is gone.'

Indeed, the whole time he was in the house, his brothers and his mother grumbled about money.

'Your father works like a dog,' his mother said. 'And has too little to show for it. He's getting bitter.'

'Agepolis treats him like a dog,' Menes said quietly. 'Pater ought to tell him to fuck off.'

'Menes!' their mother said. 'Keep a civil tongue in your head.'

'He's stealing from us,' Menes insisted. 'Fucking Agepolis.'

Agepolis, the man who had married Aspasia. His name made Alexanor shiver with distaste.

It wasn't just his father's financial difficulties that made his time stressful; his sisters came in, first Lydia and then Nestoria, his favourite sister, slipping away from their own families and households to see him. Both of them demanded his stories and seemed to know too much of his travels.

'Are you the youngest high priest in Greece?' Nestoria asked.

Alexanor smiled. '*Acting* high priest. I may be out on my ear in a year.'

'So modest,' Nestoria said. 'When will you get married?'

'Most priests of Asklepios don't marry,' he said.

'Really?' Nestoria asked. And then, as if changing the subject, she said, 'Aspasia still talks about you.'

Alexanor had thought of Aspasia every few minutes since landing on Rhodes, but he hadn't imagined he would hear of her. Her name went through him like a warm wind.

He spent the next morning fishing with his brothers, and the afternoon meeting his sisters' children, dandling babies ... and practising medicine for them. But that evening Philokles took him to an evening with friends, and he was brought face to face with her, the woman he hadn't married, now the young wife of his father's business partner, Agepolis.

She frowned at meeting him.

'I'm afraid I don't remember your name,' she said with a false smile. 'Tell me again?'

It was like a sword blow – cold and painful. It was deliberate, and he was cut to the bone at her deliberate slight.

She didn't even glance at him again, and while she made small talk with other guests, she was apparently uninterested in conversation with him. His eyes followed her, surprised to find that six years hadn't changed his reaction to her. She was tall, broad-shouldered, deep-breasted and beautiful, and maturity had only refined her presence. And now he missed her smile and her wit, neither of which were on display. She had been Nestoria's best friend. She welcomed the male guests to her husband's house, all very modern; she sat in a chair with the men for a little while, made some stilted jokes, and then sat in silence, except to motion to the slaves for more wine.

The talk immediately turned to the war in the Bosporus. Patrokles, a Euxine Sea grain merchant, and Nicodemus, one of his father's friends, spoke eloquently of their determination to see the war to its conclusion even if the city of Byzantium was destroyed.

'Nothing can be allowed to interrupt commerce,' Patrokles said with the air of a man saying a prayer.

'I haven't even heard of this war,' Alexanor said.

His father shook his head. 'My son forgets he is from Rhodes. Listen, my child.'

Philokles used the word *pais*. Alexanor hid his reaction; the last man to call him *pais* had been Chiron.

His father continued, 'Byzantium attempts to tax our grain coming from the Euxine Sea. They demand a tax merely for passing what they claim as "their" waters. They threaten our entire grain trade.'

Aspasia smiled. 'It's not really "our" grain, is it?' she asked. 'It is grain belonging to farmers in the Euxine.'

The men ignored her. 'We will crush them with sea power,' Nicodemus asserted. 'And then I would suggest we send the fleet to Crete.'

'Crete?' the host asked. He was looking at his wife, who sat, blank faced.

'The so-called *Neoteroi* are just pirates and terrorists,' Nicodemus said. 'We should help Knossos crush them. Deny Macedon a foothold, and improve trade with Aegypt, all in one.'

'How does killing men in Crete improve trade with Aegypt?' Aspasia asked, her voice clear.

'How many ships would it require?' Patrokles asked.

'Six should do it, and a strong marine contingent,' Nicodemus said.

Aspasia stood up. 'Good evening, gentlemen,' she said, her voice tight.

Alexanor started to rise, but his father's arm pinned him to the couch.

'Men's affairs are as dull to women as women's are to men,' Agepolis said, to cover his wife's withdrawal.

Philokles laughed. 'She's a brave little thing, your wife,' he said. 'No woman can really be happy in company. She braves it out, but what would she talk about? War?'

The other men agreed. 'It's a foolish custom,' Patrokles asserted. 'What can a woman bring to a party? I mean, except ...' He made a lewd gesture.

Alexanor looked away.

Agepolis cleared his throat. 'I am almost insulted. My wife welcomed you to my home.' He looked around. 'Alexanor, you have travelled widely. What do you think of this custom?'

Alexanor thought of Philopoemen, and of Phila.

'I like it,' he said. 'I am the youngest man here. I am hesitant to speak out of turn—'

'He's unmarried,' said another guest. Alexanor thought he was the Rhodian admiral, Polemecles, and wondered why the navarch had been silent on the subject of war. 'He hasn't had his fill of women's prattle yet.'

'Maybe we can speak of wool winding, or spinning,' said another.

Everyone laughed, except Alexanor and Agepolis.

'It is a Macedonian custom, is it not?' asked Nicodemus. 'Alexanor, haven't you been to Macedon?'

'Has he, though?' asked Agepolis. 'I didn't know that!'

Oh, Pater. What have you done?

'I spent some time as a physician to the king of Macedon.'

Alexanor hadn't expected to have to say this in public. Every head turned.

'Ha, ha, and then he died! Well struck, marine!' called out Nicodemus.

There was general laughter. Slaves moved among the couches, delivering wine, the prettier slaves writhing to avoid the men's hands while not spilling their wine.

Alexanor, who had watched a hundred Macedonian evenings, complete with men and women coupling in couches, extravagant kissing contests, and lewd demonstrations of every sex act conceivable, some surprising even to a physician, merely smiled.

'There are women at Macedonian feasts,' he allowed. 'Women share *kline* with men.'

'*Hetaerae* and *porne*?' his father asked.

'Yes, but also married women,' Alexanor said.

'Gods,' Philokles said. 'Degenerate filth.'

Behind him, Nicodemus had a slave girl pinned to the side of his couch while he groped her.

'Later, honey,' he said, pushing her away, and she ran, blushing furiously. She was blonde, buxom, and her flush showed all the way down her back as she ran.

'Thracians,' Nicodemus said. 'Always hot for it.'

Alexanor thought of the slave market in Zone and the slave factor. He got up. He never really thought about it, he just got to his feet. Something had snapped; he was done.

His father was stunned, and reached out, but Alexanor was quick, and determined.

'I don't feel well,' he said.

'You haven't even had wine yet!' his host said.

Alexanor slipped past the host's couch and towards the door.

'You can't just go!' Agepolis called out.

He paused in the doorway, aware of his own anger; aware, too, of the complexity of his father's friendships and business relationships. He bowed.

'My apologies, gentlemen,' he said. 'I am truly unwell, and I don't wish to embarrass myself or you!'

He slipped out through the curtain of beads, hoping that he had sounded the right note of urgency, and for the sake of verisimilitude, he made a beeline for the privy at the back of the lot, across the inner courtyard.

He emerged to hear gales of laughter from the men at the front of the house. He was obviously forgotten, and he nodded, and made his way to the courtyard's gate, which was, of course, closed and latched. It was dark; he ran his hand up and down the gatepost.

'You are leaving,' Aspasia said.

He turned. There was no light; she was more of a shape than a person. He was stunned – elated, terrified.

'Yes,' he said. 'I feel ill.'

'Really?' she asked, the sarcasm evident in her voice. 'Or are we just too barbaric to entertain someone as cosmopolitan as you?'

That was a little too accurate. He thought for a moment. He should not be talking to another man's wife, especially his father's partner's wife. Slaves might talk.

'I should go,' he said. Except that he wanted to ask her, *why so rude to me? I loved you, once.*

'Go, coward,' she agreed. 'Run away. Again.' Her bitterness was obvious.

'I didn't run away.'

'*You ran away from me!*' she said.

'My father ordered me not to see you again. He told me that your marriage was arranged.' He didn't bother to stop himself. 'Is it true? Did you think I was a coward?'

Silence.

He could hear her breathe.

His fingers found the simple wooden catch that freed the bar on the gate.

'You left,' Aspasia breathed.

'I left so that I would not make trouble. *For you.*' He paused. 'And, come to think of it, Aspasia, I'm leaving for the same reason now.'

'Always so kind. Such regard for the little people. You personify arrogance, to me. *You left me.* To this!' She all but spat.

He knew the sound of her anger.

'You think they behave badly?' she asked. 'The evening is young.'

He would have liked to make a graceful exit, but the bar wouldn't move. He cursed. And turned.

'And just for the record, I didn't run from the pirates. I fought them until I fell. I just happened to live.'

Aspasia made a sound in her throat. 'I never thought you a coward. I know you too well.' She looked away. 'Until you abandoned me to be the whore of this old man.' She didn't sob. Then her head bowed. 'There I go, again. I knew you had to leave ...'

'Fine,' he spat. 'Well, I'm a coward now. I'm not brave enough to stay and tell them what I think. Listening to them plan a war on people they don't even know so that they can make more money – and watching my father's friends paw your slaves is revolting.'

'I know,' she said softly. 'I just put my Thracian to bed. In the barn, where no one will find her. I am mistress here – my women are not for bedding.'

'May Aphrodite bless you,' he said, making a religious sign with his fingers.

She laughed. 'You, a priest,' she said, and reached past him.

Just for a moment, he thought she was going to kiss him, and then she moved something on the gatepost with her outstretched fingers. The bar came loose.

'And no, I didn't leave you to this. My father told me he would

197

disinherit me if I came to see you.' He was whispering. 'You were waiting out here for me,' he said with sudden realisation. She'd always been a plotter.

'I knew you'd leave,' she breathed in his ear. 'Or maybe I just hoped you would.'

His arm was around her waist, and he hadn't put it there ... Her body pressed against him. It was their second kiss before his brain worked at all.

I am a fool, he said in his head. *What am I doing? We can both be killed.*

She broke away, and he let her go.

She laughed. 'Go,' she said. 'You kiss much better than you used to.'

She pushed him and he stepped out through the gate, and he heard her latch it. And then her footsteps, as she ran across her courtyard and vanished into the house.

'Son of a bitch,' he said to the night.

If she hadn't thought him a coward ...

He stood in the dark street, listening to the sound of his father's friends laughing like satyrs, and the realisation dawned that Philokles had pushed him away from Aspasia simply so that his partner, Agepolis, could have her. That was how it had been done, and rage and betrayal flashed through him like a bolt from Zeus, and wounds that had spent six years healing burst open in his memory. She hadn't betrayed him. Perhaps his father had never actually thought him a coward.

Instead, his father had sold his son's bride to a fellow merchant, probably for some financial favour. And he could see how, to Aspasia, he had behaved badly, meekly fleeing instead of fighting for her.

'This can't be true,' he said aloud, except that with Aspasia's kiss burning on his lips, he could think of no other reason.

He turned, and walked back to his parents' house, where he woke his mother to kiss her. He found his bag, collected a few things he'd loved as a child, and then woke Leon.

'You can't just leave!' his mother begged.

'We're leaving,' he said.

Leon nodded. He rose and put on a *chiton* and asked no questions.

They walked to the beach. There, before the party at his father's partner's house broke up, they were on a fishing boat, bound for Kos.

As soon as he reached Kos, he found a professional letter-writer and paid the fisherman in silver to put his letter directly into Aspasia's hands.

The letter begged her to explain exactly how her marriage had taken place.

And then he and Leon went to the temple. It was not an easy interview, as Alexanor was not the temple of Kos's choice for Lentas.

But, three days later, they were bound for Crete.

CHAPTER FIVE

—⟐⟐⟐—

Lentas, Crete

220 BCE

He landed on the beach at Lentas without any ceremony, having given them no warning. Instead, he paid off the boat that had run him down the Dodecanese and walked up the beach like any pilgrim, sick or well, with his bag over his shoulder, and Leon at his side. They used the baths to cleanse the salt and sweat of the voyage away, and both of them watched the slaves, who were stony-faced, and the attendants, who were *timid*.

The massage was ineffectual; oddly tentative, as if the man rubbing them down was afraid of breaking them.

Alexanor had intended to announce himself as soon as he was clean, but after a whispered conversation, he presented himself to the priests, showed the wound in his side, and asked for the priests' intercession with the gods.

Alexanor's first impression wasn't helped by the long line he had to endure waiting for the single priest on duty.

It was also, perhaps, unfair that Alexanor immediately judged the duty priest for being fat. His weight made Alexanor question the man's devotion, as priests of the god were supposed to pay attention to their own bodies; but equally, it was possible that he had a disorder and he struggled with it. Alexanor was aware that his anger from Rhodes was making him petty.

'And what have you brought as an offering to the god?' the man asked.

Like the man's obesity, it was possible that the man merely had a poor bedside manner. Rich pilgrims were requested to make donations at every temple of Asklepios. But the request for a donation should never have preceded the man's diagnosis of a new patient.

'My wound,' Alexanor snapped.

The fat priest smiled. 'Bless you, lad, but I don't need your attitude. Why don't you go out and wait a while and start through the line again. Perhaps you'll find some manners.'

The priest snapped his fingers and a pair of large slaves appeared with staves.

Alexanor allowed himself to be escorted out.

He found Leon, not in the portico of the elegant baths, as he'd suggested, but on the beach.

'Slaves are only welcome when their masters are paying customers,' he said bitterly.

'You are no slave,' Alexanor said.

'I wasn't exactly going to announce myself as a priest, was I?' Leon shrugged. 'I said I was your slave. Bastard hit me with a stick.'

'Something's wrong,' Alexanor said. 'I shouldn't have gone home,' he added.

Leon was nursing a bruise.

'Want to talk about it?' he asked.

Alexanor was looking at the magnificent stone formation, the 'Lion', which towered over the sanctuary. The beach was very small – only big enough for three or four ships – but the water was clear and remarkably blue.

'I think that I just discovered that my father betrayed me,' he said, and his voice choked. 'Somehow, that's worse than imagining that he thought me a coward.'

Leon clasped his hand for a moment.

'Mine sold me as a slave,' he said.

Alexanor laughed bitterly. 'That puts it in perspective, doesn't it?'

'No. Betrayal is betrayal.'

Alexanor was looking up at the sanctuary, and the magnificent round temple.

'Philopoemen lands in fifteen days,' he said. 'Now, do I just walk in there and tell them I'm the new high priest?'

Leon looked at the bruise on his shoulder before re-pinning his *chiton*.

'I think we need to know the score first,' he said. 'Something's rotten. And people who do bad things don't take kindly to change.'

Alexanor nodded. 'My thought exactly.'

A day later, the two men had talked to every resident who would talk: to the man who kept the taverna across the agora from the sanctuary entrance; to the two foreign slaves who sold statues of the god outside the gate; as well as to a pair of sailors who'd been left by their captain on the outbound leg of a voyage from Crete and were waiting for their ship to pick them up on the return journey.

'Fucking dogs'll get you more healing than the fucking priests,' grumbled one.

'Took our money, put us in beds, left us to dream,' said another.

'And then put us to work washing floors,' said the first. 'Poseidon's sacred dick. Parasites.'

'Fakes,' said the second sailor, watching a young woman washing laundry.

It appeared that Pausanias, the high priest, was greedy.

'He's not really the high priest,' one of the slaves complained. 'But the great temple on Kos never sent a replacement.'

'It's because the masters are having a spat,' Bela said. She was older, and much respected among the temple staff. 'Kos and Epidauros, fighting over who owns us. Fools. When masters fight, everything goes wrong.'

'He wasn't so bad at first,' another slave put in. 'But a year ago, when it was clear he was really in charge, he just sort of ...'

'This used to be a place of healing, brother,' another man told Leon, assuming he was a fellow slave. 'We used to do good work here.'

The priesthood were mostly from Gortyna. Lentas wasn't the chief port of Gortyna – that was Phaistos, a *parasang* off to the west along the rocky, cliff-bound coast – but it was a valuable town with trade links to Aegypt. The sanctuary was also an important place for travellers, with two very modern fortified towers with engines that could reach into the bay. Alexanor walked past them on his third day, having paid his 'fee' at the sanctuary with an ill grace, playing the part of a wealthy and greedy man who resented paying for anything. He felt that his imposture was fairly broad, and he based it on the greedy Aegyptian merchant in Menander, but everyone around him accepted his poor manners and stingy treatment of his slave as genuine. The walks the two of them took were their opportunities to exchange information, and they stood under one of the towers, Leon apparently cowed and bullied by his master.

'It's surprising how gullible people are,' Alexanor said.

The performance of a greedy, immature person wore on him. He wondered if he had this evil man inside him; if, in another life, he might be that man.

Leon shrugged. 'People see what they want to see. People love to see merchants as greedy, rapacious, and ill-mannered. At the moment, all the slaves pity me.'

Alexanor reached up and touched the tower base. 'Recently built,' he said.

'The so-called "City Fathers" ordered them constructed. There's a garrison.' Leon smiled. 'I went to a brothel with some slaves,' he added. 'Pausanias' father is one of the *Presbyteroi*. And he's on the ruling council, the *Boule*, in Gortyna.' Leon shrugged. 'Or that's what I heard.'

'At the brothel,' Alexanor said.

'Yes,' Leon said. 'Research.'

'You are enjoying this too much.'

'Don't hit me, master,' Leon said, pretending to cringe. 'Some of the slaves are stealing from the temple. That said, given the example their "betters" are showing—'

'There's a great deal of rot. This is outside my experience. Any suggestions?'

'None, really. But – maybe one. The garrison are mercenaries, mostly Boeotians and a few men from Athens. Do we have money?'

'Not much,' Alexanor said bitterly. 'My father ...'

Leon nodded. 'Well, the garrison doesn't love the high priest, and the garrison commander served the Achaean League at Sellasia. I'll wager he'd consider a flat fee to hand over the towers.'

'You are much better at this than I am.'

'You play a pompous miser to perfection,' Leon said cheerfully. 'Now smack me. Everyone watching will expect it.'

Leon winced as he walked down the hill.

Two small merchants came in at dusk, showing stern lights, and anchored in the shallow water beyond the surf instead of beaching. A handful of men climbed over the low sides of the round merchant ships and swam ashore; the weather was perfect and the air warm.

Alexanor was waiting. 'Welcome,' he said.

'You're not dressed like the hierophant of a major temple,' Philopoemen said.

'Nothing has gone well. Tell me, is it worth half a talent of silver to buy the defences of this town?'

'The two spanking new towers with the torsion engines? Absolutely.' Philopoemen raised an eyebrow.

'Get me the silver. I have none. I'll see to that part. And then we'll go and meet the current high priest.' Alexanor couldn't describe how happy he was to see Philopoemen.

'Arkas?' Philopoemen turned to his groom. 'Give me the purse.'

The younger man was naked, but he had the heavy purse around his waist. He emptied the water from it and held it out.

He opened it. 'There's about forty minae of silver here,' he said, holding up a bag.

'You carry that much?' Alexanor asked.

Philopoemen shrugged. 'Money helps, in war. Let's go.'

Arkas swam back to the ships, and Philopoemen walked up the darkening beach, dressed as a religious pilgrim. The sun was setting in the west, and the red light permeated the place and made the giant stone promontory to the east look like a living lion.

'Thank the gods you are on time,' Alexanor said. 'I was running out of nasty small talk.'

He described what he had learnt of the sanctuary.

Philopoemen shook his head. 'Our world is dying,' he said in the red light. 'Men no longer choose to do what is excellent merely because it is excellent.' Then he smiled. 'If they ever did. Sometimes I doubt the utter wisdom of our forebears.' He glanced at the trail up to the tower and then back at Alexanor. 'Can these mercenaries really be bought so easily?'

'The commander loathes the high priest, which is no mystery. The man's an arse. Also, none of the garrison have been paid. Ever.'

Leon came around the corner of the tower, with a small man behind him in good bronze armour.

Philopoemen was looking at the tower walls. 'These towers are sloppy work, but the stone's good.'

'Probably robbed from older work,' Leon said. 'This way. Periander, this is your new employer.'

The Boeotian mercenary smiled. 'Money first,' he said. 'Now by Ares, you are younger than I am, *despotes.*'

Philopoemen nodded. 'Achaean League. *Strategos.* Can you live with that?'

Periander looked at the younger man. And at the ships in the bay.

'I haven't dropped a forty mina stone on your ships, have I?'

Philopoemen nodded.

'I want to know the whole deal,' Periander said. 'Sorry, but my lads could be massacred for this. So I either need to be hired by you, or your word of honour in front of the god that you'll ship us home to Attica.' He smiled nastily. 'Are you here to stay?'

'Perhaps,' Philopoemen said.

'I'd love to gut the high priest, if that's on the table.' The Boeotian's anger showed in the red light.

Philopoemen weighed the purse in his hand.

'I have forty minae of silver here,' he said. 'The weight of one of your heavy stones.' He glanced at his ships. 'How many men?'

'I have a hundred and sixty here, and another hundred at Phaistos.'

'Can you sell me Phaistos too?' Philopoemen asked.

'No, worse luck. Most of the garrison is Aetolian. Some Illyrians.'

The mercenary shrugged. It was getting darker, and his face was hidden in shadow.

'How long do you serve me for forty minae?' Philopoemen asked.

The Boeotian looked thoughtful. 'We're owed that in back wages, and more.'

'Unfortunately, I'm not the one who owes you wages. Also, you might as well know, I'm not very tolerant about indiscipline. No looting. At all.'

'So you are going to fight.' The man rubbed his beard. 'Forty for the towers and my men here. We'll serve you until the *Pyanepsia* in Athens. You know it?'

Alexanor, who, as a priest, memorised all the festival calendars, calculated on his fingers.

'Almost seventy days.'

'A generous offer.' Philopoemen handed over the purse. 'You are now in the service of the Achaean League.'

Periander bowed. 'And not for the first time, *Strategos.*'

An hour later, there was a knock at the gate to the courtyard of the high priest's residence. A slave came and ordered whoever was knocking to be gone. There were some shouts, and then the slave was knocked unconscious from behind.

The Thracians opened the courtyard gate, and Alexanor walked in. He was dressed head to foot in white. He wore white sandals and he carried no weapon. Leon was with him, wearing identical robes.

Periander's men moved into the courtyard. They were *thureophoroi* in the truest sense, with Celtic-style shields and short spears. Only the officers had armour, but they had the expensive new chain-mail shirts, also a Celtic innovation. Their drill wasn't very good, but they were willing enough, especially in storming the high priest's house.

All of Philopoemen's officers were present. They were there to prevent a massacre, or any looting.

The force went through the house – the palace, really. There was an outer yard and an inner colonnade with a fountain; two sets of elaborate bedrooms, kitchens, offices, a private bath.

Alexanor walked through the columns into the inner garden just as a scuffle announced the seizure of the high priest. He immediately began to scream, convinced that he was being robbed.

Periander dragged the fat man into the garden, one arm locked painfully behind his back. He dropped the man in front of Alexanor.

The high priest raised his head. There were two torch bearers behind Alexanor, and his white robes seemed to glow in the dark garden.

'Whose house is this, Pausanias?' Alexanor asked.

'Mine!' the priest spat. 'Who the fuck are you?'

'Priests of Asklepios live in barracks, Pausanias. Whose house is this?' Alexanor's voice was like stone.

'Mine!' screamed the man.

He wasn't terrified. He was angry – the anger of a pampered man who always got his way.

Alexanor turned to Periander and Syrmas, who stood close.

'You may loot the house to the walls. No rape – no slave to be touched.'

Periander smiled. The Thracian chief grinned. Out in the yard, a Greek voice said, 'That's the fucking way, mates! We get the loot!'

'That's the way! That's more like it!'

The officers dispersed, mostly to prevent theft from becoming murder.

The priest got up. 'Who are you?' he asked.

Alexanor pointed his staff at the man. It was a plain staff of cornel wood; indeed, he had cut it on the hillside that afternoon. He'd cut it, trimmed it with a sharp knife he wore around his neck, and stripped the bark.

Only high priests carried a staff.

'I am your master,' Alexanor said. 'Do you remember your oath?'

'I'll have you beaten by slaves, you whore!' the priest bellowed. 'Master my arse. You are the stupid merchant!'

'I am the man your priests refused to serve,' Alexanor said with a certain cold satisfaction, 'until I had paid an exorbitant fee. A fee far beyond that permitted by the rules of our order. I say it again, priest of Apollo and Asklepios. Do you remember your oath? Because you have done harm, and you will atone.'

'Really?' The man shrugged. 'You can't afford to have that butt-boy Periander around every day. My father will come here and crucify the lot of you. Or worse. Won't you lot look fine with a spear rammed up your arse.' He looked at Alexanor and he didn't cringe. 'Oath? Grow up. This is the world of men. If the gullible—'

Alexanor had little fear of blasphemy, but his hate rose to choke him – hate, and the latent anger at his father's betrayal and a dozen other things ... Before he thought, his staff struck – not once, but five or six blows – and the man lay at his feet, hands over his head, whimpering.

Later, Alexanor would regret the blows as unworthy of the first use of his staff of office.

But at the time, he turned and ordered Periander to take the whimpering mass to Philopoemen. Philopoemen had a brief interview with the high priest and came back to where Alexanor stood in the temple sanctuary.

'I can take him off your hands. If his father is one of the city fathers of the new government of Gortyna, he'd make an excellent hostage.'

'He is, for all his sins, a priest of Apollo. And Asklepios, although as far as I can ascertain, he's never been trained as a doctor. I don't even know how that could happen.' Alexanor shrugged.

'What will you do with him?' Philopoemen asked.

'I like the spear in the arse solution,' Dinaeos called from the scroll table. He and Leon and Lykortas were all writing messages at Philopoemen's dictation.

Philopoemen winced. 'No thanks.'

'Sends a clear message,' Dinaeos said.

Alexanor thought that Dinaeos enjoyed shocking his friend.

'I will send him to Epidauros, to the sanctuary. For trial.' He shook his head. 'Chiron and Sostratos will not thank me. I'm not even sure there's a process to try a priest of Asklepios.'

'Just kill him,' Dinaeos said. 'Save time. Effort. Money. Besides, Periander will pay to do it. I like that man. What'd the priest do to him?'

'Took his men's pay. But it's personal, too. Do we need to know?' Leon said from the table. 'I have friends among the former garrison.'

'From trips to the brothel.' Alexanor tried to hide his disgust.

'There's a brothel?' Dinaeos asked, sitting up like an eager cat at feeding time.

Alexanor was looking out at the first tinge of pink in the eastern sky. He forced his thoughts back to the situation before them.

'I'm not sure ... I have no instructions about this. And there's politics – Kos, the great temple of Asklepios, and my home temple at Epidauros, are apparently at odds. But I'm quite certain that Chiron meant me to support you, so if you need his worthless carcass for a bargain, be my guest. If you send him back to his father, I'll ...' He took a breath. 'I'll strip him of his priesthood.'

Philopoemen's eyes widened; a man who was never surprised took a step back.

'You can do that?' he asked. 'I mean, pardon, brother, but men and women are born to the priesthoods, surely.'

Alexanor shook his head. 'Would you ever want that man as your healer or counsellor? Would anyone? Would the great god Apollo want this man making sacrifices at his altar? Do we not clean ourselves of ritual impurity before we make sacrifice? Today, I will order every altar washed. I will order every priest to go barefoot, and I will wash everything. If I wash the altars, will I not also wash the priests?'

Philopoemen bowed. 'Pardon me, brother. I should not have doubted you. You are a true priest.'

Before the sun was over the rim of the world, the junior priests and free servitors of the temple were standing under the eyes of the Thracian cavalry in the sanctuary. Alexanor walked out to Kleostratos.

'Thanks,' he said. 'But I don't need a show of force.'

Kleostratos grinned. 'Just drying off the horses, so to speak.'

He saluted with his whip and led the Thracians out of the precinct. A horse defecated on the white marble, his heavy turd falling with a *plop*, audible because the priests were completely silent.

Alexanor walked to the middle of the sanctuary, his white sandals slapping on the marble floor.

'I greet you from your brothers and sisters at Epidauros *and* Kos,' he said quietly. It was the opening of the speech he'd intended to give under other circumstances.

Behind him, outside the sanctuary, he could hear Periander shouting commands in Attic Greek. The *thureophoroi* were drilling.

The staff looked at him, most of their eyes wide with fear.

'I come to you from a temple that serves every pilgrim,' he said. 'At Kos, and at Epidauros, every man or woman who comes sick to the feet of the god is sent away healed, at least, if the god so wills and to the best of our ability.'

He looked at them. He already knew a number of them: the pudgy priest who'd declined to serve him, now looking as if his bulging eyes might burst from his head; the slim young priest with the large eyes who had never appeared in the sanctuary in four days; servitors and slaves he'd met under the guise of a greedy merchant.

'You have been poorly led by a bad shepherd,' he said loudly. This was not his prepared speech. It was coming from his mouth, but he felt that perhaps the god was at his shoulder, putting words in his head. 'It remains for me to see if you yourselves have turned to evil, or whether you merely obeyed the bad shepherd. You will clean every surface inside the sanctuary – you will use clean, fresh water, hyssop and incense, and you will leave no place unpurified. To my eyes, this place looks like this.'

His staff pointed at the horse manure.

The staff tip rose and pointed at the pudgy priest.

'You,' he said. 'Remove this. Now.'

The man's face puckered and collapsed, as if he was going to cry, and he fell on his knees.

'I will be a better priest!' he whimpered.

'Then the god will forgive you,' Alexanor said, steel in his voice. 'In the meantime, clean this floor with your own hands, *priest*.'

One of the slaves tittered.

Alexanor walked over to the slave.

'You have been blameless?' he asked quietly. 'You have not stolen incense and sold it in the agora?'

The man blinked, suddenly too scared to speak.

'Work!' Alexanor roared. 'Make this place clean, and you will cleanse yourselves. Tomorrow, we will serve pilgrims, as the god intended.'

'Greedy merchant, spy, and acting hierophant,' Alexanor said bitterly.

He was sitting in the high priest's apartments inside the sanctuary. Philopoemen and Leon were writing messages for the *Neoteroi* in Phaistos and Gortyna.

Leon said nothing.

Philopoemen glanced at him. 'We all play roles, brother. Right now, I'm playing the role of great commander – the very pillar of confidence. Men can trust me – my troopers can die for me.'

He smiled and went back to writing his draft in wax.

Leon's stylus moved smoothly across the papyrus, copying the wax into a message ready to travel. Antiphatas, booted and ready for riding, was talking to Periander in the moonlight, getting instructions on contacting his *phylarch* among the mercenaries at Phaistos.

'I made them afraid. It was as if I was another man. I enjoyed it!' Alexanor said, his voice full of anger.

'I enjoy command,' Philopoemen said. 'I worry that this is how tyrants are formed – it is so much simpler to command than to discuss. Ah, Antiphatas – are you ready? This is a brave thing you do.'

'Essential,' Antiphatas said. 'I can be in Gortyna before dawn, and Phaistos tomorrow.' He looked at the stars outside. 'I wish that I knew that no one from here escaped. You did good work taking that worthless clod, Pausanias. His father, Zophanes, is the one who ordered my exile. He is one of the chiefs among the *Presbyteroi* and even he knew this son was worthless.'

'No one ran,' Philopoemen nodded. 'Not even a shepherd. Kleostratos is the best cavalryman I've ever met. His people were out all night. So was Syrmas and so was Thodor.'

'Someone from the temple might have escaped,' Antiphatas said. 'I'm sorry, but it's my neck.'

Alexanor shook his head. 'This place is decadent, but they have records. I'm not missing anyone, not even a washerwoman.'

Antiphatas bowed. 'I'll go then. But I won't breathe a safe breath until I'm back here.'

Philopoemen smiled, radiating confidence. 'See you in two days. Everything is ready.'

Antiphatas took the satchel of incriminating letters, bowed, and withdrew.

Philopoemen put his head in his hand. 'Here we go,' he said.

Leon looked up. 'Surely the threads of your fate were measured when you landed on the beach,' he said.

Philopoemen sighed. 'Yes,' he admitted. 'But now people will start to die.'

BOOK III

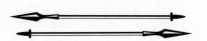

THE LYTTIAN WAR

CHAPTER ONE

—◦◦◦—

Lentas and Gortyna, Crete

220 BCE

Like a pebble sliding down a steep ridge, collecting sand and gravel until larger stones join the charge and the whole wave of rock becomes an avalanche, the arrival of the Achaeans at Lentas started a cascade of violence beyond the dreams of the handful of cavalrymen camping on the beach below the sanctuary.

Four days passed. Periander was drilling his Attic mercenaries on the narrow plain above the sanctuary. It was the cool of the evening; the horses were all ashore, picketed in long lines across the stubble of the summer fields along the coast. Most of the Thracian horses had already restored the lustre on their coats, but the Greek horses were responding more slowly than the hardy steppe ponies.

Alexanor had his priests and novices practising medicine on cavalry-men. Like any body of lower-class men and barbarians, they had their share of disease, abscesses, old wounds, ingrown toenails, and other ailments that reduced their good humour or fighting spirit. As most of the pilgrims had fled in Philopoemen's ships, taken to Kos at the Achaean's own expense, Alexanor used Philopoemen's men as training subjects for an intensive course in the human body.

Nor was he entirely disappointed in what he saw. The fat priest was Nazistratos, from Chios; the thin, androgynous one was called

Omphalion and came from the Odrysian Kingdom of Thrace. Both of them were competent, and both were working like dogs to prove themselves. Most of the young novices were local boys from aristocratic families – useless, but cheerful and hard-working so long as they were watched. Alexanor was teaching two of the boys to splint a broken finger, its owner injured in the taking of the high priest's palace, when a third boy called out.

'Horseman!' he shouted.

Philopoemen, who had been watching the lesson on broken bones with every evidence of attention, leapt to his feet. Dinaeos, who had been flirting idly with one of the few pilgrims to remain, joined him.

The pilgrim, a widow from Gortyna, smiled. 'I think I've been replaced,' she said to Alexanor. 'What will happen now?'

Later, it occurred to Alexanor that watching the horseman ride down the switchbacks of the mountain behind the town was one of the most unbearable periods of tension he had known. He found himself praying, as if the events that would be reported by the messenger hadn't already happened. And the messenger's horse was tired and the descent from the mountains behind them was steep; he stopped and rested his mount, and the men around Philopoemen groaned aloud.

'It's not Antiphatas,' Kleostratos said. 'I'll wager a tetradrachma. This one rides better.'

'Younger, too,' Thodor agreed.

'Let's parade all our people,' Philopoemen said calmly. 'We may have to move fast.' He glanced at Dinaeos. 'We'll want *kontoi*.'

'Lances? Will there be a cavalry charge?' Dinaeos shook his head.

Philopoemen smiled. 'Lances.'

'The ships are gone,' Alexanor said. He was aware that this was unnecessary; the words just fell out.

'And our backs are to the sea.' Philopoemen's voice was strong. 'Yes, if this goes badly, we're in a tight spot.'

His men, bandaged or not, saluted and scattered.

An hour later, the messenger arrived. He was a young man on a very tired horse.

'Telemnastos,' he introduced himself.

He saluted Philopoemen like a soldier. The Achaean's whole force was waiting: the cavalry all standing by their horses, the pages with remounts ready to move and a dozen of Philopoemen's slaves with the little force's baggage train of donkeys. The Attic mercenaries were formed close by, as if acknowledging that they would share the Achaean's fate.

'*Strategos*,' the young Cretan said. His smile told them everything. 'My father sent me from Phaistos.'

'You are Antiphatas' son?'

'Yes, sir. Here it is, sir. There's a lot of news. It's as if you used magic on the whole island. At the news of your landing, the men of Lyttos marched on Knossos and defeated them, yesterday. The Aetolians wouldn't move to support them because they were out looking for you. Then other Knossians attacked Lyttos and stormed it, or that's what we're hearing from the survivors.'

'Where in Hades is Lyttos?' Dinaeos asked.

'About one hundred stades east of Knossos,' Telemnastos said.

'Sir, my father says you must move quickly. The Aetolians are trying to cover the Knossian army – the Lyttians are refugees. Everything is chaos.'

'But Gortyna?' Philopoemen's voice betrayed his anxiety.

'Is ready,' Telemnastos said. 'I have men ready to fight, and weapons, although I could use more. The oligarchs disarmed my friends after I went into exile.'

'How much risk do you run, passing the gates?' Alexanor asked.

The young man shrugged. 'Some. Not enough to prevent me from trying. The Lyttian victory has stung them, regardless of what happened after, and Knossos is like a hornets' nest after a boy kicks it, or so one of our spies claims. Another thing – Hermes, it's hard to remember everything, and we couldn't write anything down. There's another rumour – Illyrians landed down the coast, at Polyrhennia.'

'Allied to us?' Philopoemen asked. 'Illyrians?'

'Who's paying them?' Dinaeos asked.

The young Cretan bowed. 'It is a rumour. But it will keep the Aetolians busy another day, at least, while they try to figure out what's going on. We're fanning the flames. My father has sent a spy into Knossos claiming that Philip of Macedon is landing on the north coast.'

Philopoemen nodded. He didn't seem surprised, and Alexanor wondered if his friend was more deceptive than he seemed.

'Do you know the ground in the centre of the island?' he asked.

Telemnastos nodded.

Philopoemen tugged at his beard. He looked at Dinaeos. He looked around at all the officers – Kleostratos, and Thodor and Dadas and Lykortas. He summoned Periander with a wave, and the Boeotian ran up, his armour gleaming.

'We are about to move very fast,' he said. 'How long to Gortyna?'

'Seven hours walking,' the younger man said. 'Maybe four hours on horseback.'

'Before midnight, then,' Philopoemen said. 'And beyond Gortyna, is there a fort? On the road to Knossos?'

'No,' the Cretan said.

'A hill we can hold? With water?'

'What are you thinking?' Dinaeos asked.

'I'm thinking that if we are going to provoke a change of government in Gortyna, we also need to block a counter-strike,' Philopoemen said.

'If we hold the walls of Gortyna,' Telemnastos said, cautiously, a younger man among older warriors.

'War is really about emotion,' Philopoemen said. 'Men are only rational when they have time. If the *Presbyteroi* see an Aetolian army under their walls, they'll hold firm. If it appears no relief is coming, even if the Aetolians are just forty stades away ...'

Dinaeos nodded. 'I see it!'

'There's Petra,' Telemnastos said. 'It's a big rock. Not much in the way of water, but men have held it before this. There's a low wall at the top.'

'Garrison?' Philopoemen asked.

'No.'

'Full canteens and spare water bottles. How long to get to your rock?'

'Six hours on horseback.' The Cretan was unsure. 'In the dark?'

'The boy's right,' Kleostratos said. 'Even for Thracians, riding over this country in the dark ...'

'We need some help from the gods,' Philopoemen said. 'Let's get up the mountain before darkness falls – that'll help. Telemnastos can guide us. Alexanor, do you have some local boys who can help as guides?'

Alexanor went and talked to his novices, every one of whom

volunteered. Before the sun had fallen into the western sea, the column was moving up the switchback trail on the cliff, the cavalry in front already outdistancing the Boeotians, who had their own guides. Alexanor was with Philopoemen.

'Are you sure you want to participate in this?' Philopoemen asked.

'I'd just as soon be hanged for a lion as a lamb,' Alexanor said. 'And if you are taking six of my novices, someone should be here to watch them.'

Midnight on the plain of Gortyna. The moon was nearly full; it provided enough light that the cavalry force had managed to reach the valley floor without a loss. The Attic mercenaries were somewhere on the ridge behind.

There were a few lights in the city; one burnt high up on the acropolis, and others just inside the wall.

Philopoemen had his officers together; grooms held the horses, with cloaks over their heads so that they wouldn't call out or whinny.

'Kleostratos, Thodor – you'll each take a third of the squadron. Ladders, escalade. Just as we practised. Dinaeos, on me, we go for the gate when Telemnastos shows a torch.' He looked around. It was light enough that Alexanor could see his face, apparently animated and excited, but not apprehensive. Apparently. 'Any questions?'

Dinaeos laughed. 'Easy as kissing a widow,' he said.

'We should have a rearguard watching the road to Knossos,' Thodor said.

'We should, but we're spread as thinly as a slave's *opson* on his bread,' Philopoemen said. 'All or nothing. If the Aetolians are already here, or on their way, we're lost.'

'We could wait for Periander,' Kleostratos said.

'Every moment we sit here in the dark with seventy horses, we could be discovered,' Philopoemen said. 'Anything else? Let's go.'

Alexanor, who had recently vowed to do no more fighting, found himself crouched amid the hovels of non-citizens outside the gate. A dog was barking wildly on the Knossos road; another dog started up.

He could hear a woman crying in the house behind which he hid. The hut was built of rubble and clay; the walls were thin and her despair was all too evident. He could also hear snores.

And another dog.

'Ares,' cursed Philopoemen. But that was the only sign that the long waiting wore on him.

The night wore on. The woman's weeping quieted; the dogs stopped barking. Off in the darkness, a horse gave a shriek of anger, and another horse answered it.

'Fuck,' muttered Dinaeos, whose shoulder was against Philopoemen's back.

Then, in the gate tower above them, a voice. A shout; the clear sound of a spear clattering against a floor.

A torch on the wall. The signal.

'Go! Go!' Philopoemen roared in a voice of bronze.

Somewhere to their left, the sound of a ladder scraping against mud-plaster. Then he was running, Philopoemen's backplate of figured bronze ahead shining dully in the moonlight. The main gate was open wide enough for a single man to slip through. Alexanor just had time to imagine that it was all a trap and then he was following the Achaean into the Stygian darkness of the gatehouse.

The inner gates were open a hand's width, but the darkness under the gate tower was so deep that the moonlight seemed as bright as an oil lamp. Alexanor ignored his fears and sprinted for the inner gate. He got one door as Dinaeos got the other and both of them pulled, even as Lykortas and Philopoemen got the outer doors open with a hideous screech of metal on metal that sounded louder than a trumpet call.

Arkas and Lykon were in the gateway, spears up and ready, when the garrison came tumbling down off the wall. Armoured men, shouting the alarm.

Dinaeos put one of them down immediately, striking unseen from the shadows, and the Achaeans began to form a line. A dozen men of the garrison formed up in the square behind the gate and charged. Suddenly the darkness of the gatehouse was full of war; sparks flew as steel blades caught each other, and men shouted, cursed ...

Alexanor defended himself with a spear, and then covered Lykon when the man went down. Off to his left the darkness was punctuated by Cretan war cries. The garrison were quite expert, but so were Philopoemen's Achaeans, and the fighting was vicious in the darkness. Men grappled, blind; one of the garrison officers stabbed one of his own men in the back with a spear, and then died on the sword of another opponent.

But through it all, Philopoemen moved like the God of War. His arm was around one man's neck, throwing him; he kicked a second, took his sword and used it on a third, as if he moved in a different river of time than his opponents, as if he could see clearly while the others were fogged with terror and the darkness.

Philopoemen was the balance of the fight. The Cretans were as good as the Achaeans, man for man, or better, and they had shields, a man's best friend in the bronze-shot darkness and the hail of steel, which the cavalrymen lacked. But Philopoemen swirled through like a squall tearing through the ocean, and the Cretans broke. The mounted men who had waited beyond the gate rode down the survivors.

Telemnastos roared '*Stasis!*' at the top of his lungs – the signal for revolt, known and feared by every citizen in every Greek city. He had torches in both hands and he was on the wall, running along it up the hill towards the acropolis.

Philopoemen was kneeling on the blood-sticky marble of the gateway road. But he was looking at the wall above them, where Kleostratos was waving a spear, the head like an arc of silver in the moonlight.

'The gods are with us,' Philopoemen said. 'Now we need a little time. And Periander.'

In the town, there were horns, drums, men shouting and women screaming. Lykortas came riding back. He shouted, his voice pitched high, and Arkas raised a trumpet and blew the recall. There were three dead Achaeans in the gateway; one was Lykon, the cook. Another man had lost his sword hand, cut clean off. Alexanor bound the stump.

'I'm fucking dead,' the man said.

Alexanor shook his head. 'No,' he said. 'I can save you.'

'And I'll see you never starve, Simos.' Philopoemen knelt by the wounded man. 'A farm, and slaves of your own to be your hand.'

The man nodded, gritting his teeth.

Philopoemen got up, glanced at the dead cook, and turned his head away.

'Out of the gate. Get mounted. Telemnastos, we're going to need a guide.'

The Cretan had come off the wall. His father ran up, a bloody *xiphos* in his hand and an old *aspis* on his left arm.

'When my son said you were coming *tonight* I thought my ears were playing tricks,' the older man said.

'Surprise is everything,' Philopoemen said. 'What happens now?'

'Our people already have the agora,' Antiphatas said. 'We're forming the citizens there, at least those who still have arms.' He nodded. 'Our people have taken most of the oligarchs. We have Zophanes, for example.'

'No executions, I beg you,' Philopoemen said. 'We are here to create the League of Crete and to restore democracy – we are not initiating a new terror.'

Antiphatas nodded. 'I'll do this your way, *Strategos.*'

'Good. I'm taking the cavalry away,' Philopoemen said. 'I have other plans, but also ... I don't want to tempt the Thracians beyond their ability to resist.'

'May the gods bless you for your foresight,' the Cretan replied. 'I hear fighting. I must go.'

'Go!' Philopoemen said. 'Periander will be here any time now, I hope, to hold the gate. I beg you not to massacre the *Presbyteroi*, if you take them. I *beg* you.'

The Cretan's grim smile didn't make any promises, but he nodded.

'I understand you, *Strategos*. My father hates Creon, the *Primarch* of the oligarchs, and Zophanes, who exiled him,' Telemnastos said as they mounted outside the gate. 'He has to go.'

Philopoemen may have disagreed, but he was impassive in the moonlight.

'We need to ride,' he said. 'Dinaeos? Are you wounded?'

'Just tired,' the man admitted. 'Phil, if it's so bloody important to keep these bastards alive we should leave someone to keep the Cretans from butchery.'

'Antiphatas gave his word,' Philopoemen said.

'Brother, you are too good to be among the mortals,' Alexanor said. Dinaeos nodded.

'I can't spare a sword!' Philopoemen said.

'Leave Leon. And one good blade. Syrmas, perhaps,' Dinaeos said. 'Leon is smart, and Syrmas has a cool head.'

'Do it,' Philopoemen said. 'We're out of time.'

And then they were off into the moonlight – fifty men, a hundred horses, tearing across the fertile plain of Gortyna, past the magnificent temples, past the dark olive groves and sleeping sheep and barking dogs, pounding hooves making the earth shake. No more stealth; now it was a gallop in the darkness. Gortyna had good roads, and the cavalrymen followed one, the Knossos road.

At the base of the next ridge, they halted and slid off their horses, drank water, pissed. Kleostratos and Dadas and half a dozen Thracians stayed mounted and rode ahead.

'Change horses,' Philopoemen ordered. He looked at Alexanor.

Alexanor was wrapping Dinaeos' arm, because, of course, the Achaean was wounded.

'Are we winning?' he asked.

'We've reached a point where everything is insane. I'm wagering, simultaneously, that the *Neoteroi* will win the *stasis* in the dark, *and* that Periander will arrive and hold the gate, *and* that I can win the race to this Petra fort before the Aetolians know we're in a race.'

He was smiling, his teeth white in the pale light of the moon.

'You enjoy this,' Alexanor said.

'I'm beginning to think that I live for it. Thanks for dragging me out of my valley. I needed to be here. This is my war.' Philopoemen's teeth flashed in the moonlight. 'It certainly does focus the will.'

Half an hour's rest; the men who had fought in the gateway were beginning to sag. Alexanor and his novices served them sesame seeds in honey, a well-known restorative for tired men, and they got back on their horses.

And then they began to climb the ridge.

The ridge went on and on. Alexanor, who had only defended himself in the fighting, began to dread everything. He was so tired that every turn on the road seemed fearful in the darkness, and from the grumbling, he knew he was not alone. Up and up, the road narrowing in places to a mere trail, *just* wide enough for a single cart. Then they passed through a grove of oaks and there was the whole valley of Gortyna laid out below them like a mosaic floor decoration, Gortyna herself a mountain in the midst of the valley. And that mountain was on fire.

'Dammmmnnnn,' cursed Dinaeos. 'That does *not* look good.'

'Too late to worry about that,' Philopoemen snapped in a voice that betrayed his own worries. 'Telemnastos! How much farther?'

'Six stades?' the man said, his voice carrying his own uncertainty.

'Or sixty,' muttered Kleostratos.

'I'm too old for this,' Lykortas snapped. He was the youngest man present, and the troopers laughed.

Up, and up, out of the woods and on to a broad ridge with scrubby pines standing like enemy sentinels in the darkness.

Thodor loomed out of the shadows of the mountain trees like a dark apparition in the moonlight, and horses started, ears laid back, tails lashing.

'Nothing,' he said. 'We've been all the way to the head of the next valley. There's a herd of sheep, a big herd with six shepherds, just as you cross the ridge crest there. We took a dozen of them, started fires.'

'Fires?' Philopoemen snapped.

'*Behind* the crest. We're Thracians. We know how to eat someone else's sheep,' the Thracian lord laughed. 'Better than Greeks.'

The shepherds were terrified of the Thracians, and their fears were not mollified by half a hundred cavalrymen emerging from the darkness.

'There's Petra!' Telemnastos said, the relief clear in his voice. 'Next hill. Right against the stars.'

The huge rock rose above the road a few stades to the north.

'Dinaeos, on me with the Achaeans. Thodor, as soon as your men have eaten, come and relieve us. Better yet, bring us some cooked mutton.'

'And water,' Dinaeos said. 'That rock will not have water, whatever the Cretan boy says.'

The first rays of the sun breaking over the eastern edge of the world showed all of the cavalrymen carrying stones and branches. The rock was not so high that walls wouldn't make it better, and sixty men can build a rubble wall with astonishing rapidity.

The rising sun also showed the dust of a column moving up the next valley from the north. On the road to Knossos.

'That's a lot of men,' Dinaeos said.

'Not a thousand, though,' Philopoemen said.

He didn't look tired, and he hadn't taken a wound. He and Alexanor were just getting around to eating their shares of the mutton, which was half-cooked, bloody, and, as Alexanor found, utterly delicious.

Philopoemen shared a little sheep's horn of salt, which made it even better.

'You're sure those are the Aetolians?' Alexanor asked.

'I'm sure of nothing,' Philopoemen said. 'I don't even know if there's any point in holding this post. If Antiphatas lost the *stasis* in Gortyna, we should be running. but, since no one has sent us a message ...'

'I could go find out,' said Telemnastos. He was as young as Lykortas, and he had been awake longer than any of them. The dark circles under his eyes made him look old.

Philopoemen shook his head. 'No. We all knew this moment would come *if we were successful enough to earn it*. Your father will send word when the city is secure. If he fails, hopefully he will still have a gate to retreat through, and Periander to support him in retreat. I left them six horses – someone should come and tell us what's happening.'

'Or we'll be surrounded by laughing Aetolians and massacred,' Dinaeos said. 'Bastards don't take prisoners, right?'

'True,' Philopoemen said.

Dinaeos nodded. 'Well, I have wine. Anyone want a gulp?'

Philopoemen took the skin. 'Now I think that *you* are the best of the Achaeans.'

Dinaeos grinned. 'If I'd been a hero in the *Iliad*, I'd have been the most *practical* of the Achaeans,' he said.

The Aetolians didn't parley. They weren't in a cheerful mood; the Thracians had ambushed their scouts and killed them all, and then rolled some rocks on the column. The avalanche hadn't killed anyone, but it had broken the legs of a dozen horses.

They dismounted a stade or so along the ridge.

Philopoemen waved his men into a huddle in the middle of his hasty fortification, leaving just two sentries.

'It is traditional, before a battle, to give a speech,' he said. He grinned with that infectious cheerfulness that was his hallmark when things were bad. 'So here it is. I brought you here to win, not to lose. We're not fighting for our homeland, but for someone else's. I could spin you a tale that we're part of a wider war and you're all fighting for the ones you love, but really, would any of you believe me?'

Men laughed nervously.

'What we're fighting for right now is a pocketful of silver and the thanks of the good citizens of Gortyna. And survival. Let's face it, friends, if we break, we all die. So hold the line, for your own hide and your brothers', and we'll be richer tomorrow.' He grinned. 'The Aetolians aren't worth a fuck, anyway, as fighting men.'

He stepped down off the rock.

'You don't believe that,' Alexanor said. 'You aren't here fighting for a few drachmae.'

'Maybe you need to hear Sostratos talk about battlefield speeches a few more times,' Philopoemen said. 'Sufficient to the day, brother. You'll fight?'

'I love my skin as much as the next man,' Alexanor said.

A dozen of the Thracians had Scythian bows. As soon as the Aetolians were all dismounted, Philopoemen told the archers to loose. They took their time, but every shaft fell into a mob.

Twenty men went down in a minute.

'We are very fortunate they don't have any actual Cretans with them,' Philopoemen said, watching under his hand. 'Most of their military class train with the bow – heavy bows, like these.'

Even as he spoke, one of the Aetolian officers in a fine bronze breastplate and a crested helmet came forward to look at the wall he was facing, and fell with an arrow right through his bronze.

Thodor gave a whoop. He waved his bow over his head, and the Aetolians, without any orders, charged.

'That's about the best we could hope for,' Philopoemen said aloud, as if he was chatting with Ares about the theory of war. 'No order.'

He turned. 'Get ready!' he roared. 'Form close!'

The Achaeans had long spears, held in both hands. The Thracians mostly had heavy javelins, with a sprinkle of bowmen in the rear rank. It didn't look terribly well organised, at least to Alexanor, but he had to assume they had practised, because Philopoemen practised everything.

The archers continued to shoot until the very last moment, down lanes left by their mates. They didn't seem to hit anything; the wave of enraged Aetolians came at them, unstoppable, apparently uncountable.

Then men fell, and other men fell over them. They had hit the little rubble field in front of the low walls that Dinaeos had encouraged his men to create by throwing stones too small for the wall out in front of it – round volcanic stones and sharp flakes.

The archers shot and shot again.

The horde of Aetolians went over the men who fell with twisted ankles and the victims of the Thracian archery, and came up the last rise of Petra, the Rock, which was steeper than it appeared from a stade away: an almost sheer rise a little bit higher than a man's waist, topped with the new wall of rubble and olive branches.

The Achaean spears began to reap men. The Aetolians were cavalry-men too: they didn't have shields. They had to watch their footing and climb into a forest of close-order spears. Their weapons could only just reach the rubble wall and the bronze-armoured legs of the Achaeans were safe behind it.

It was very one-sided for what seemed a long time. Men pushed and shoved below him as Alexanor's spear plunged into them, every stab down drawing blood from unprotected necks and shoulders.

Then their numbers began to tell. The men safely at the back re-alised that the Achaean force could not defend all four walls at once. They began to flow around the fighting, looking for a safer way in, as the Aetolian casualties were already terrible.

Then the fighting became close, personal, and deadly. Once a few Aetolians were at the rubble wall to the sides and rear, there was no line, and the chaos Alexanor had experienced in the fighting in the darkness of the Gortyna gate fell on the struggle at Petra.

Alexanor hadn't realised that Philopoemen had held back from the fighting until he heard his war cry of 'Zeus, Zeus!' The pressure on the front of the Achaeans was gone; no one wanted to face the spears and the climb. Alexanor turned and saw Philopoemen facing a crowd. The Achaean's heavy spear licked out, caught a man in the cheek and went *up* into his brain and then, as the man's knees folded in death, seemed to pull him from his feet. A second man, determined, leapt in to grapple.

Somehow, Philopoemen's left hand had a dagger readied, drawn, and thrust in a single motion straight into the man's nose, even as he one-handed his spear into a third man with his right hand. Before the tide could overwhelm him, Dinaeos and Alexanor were there, and then Lykortas, and Thodor, loosing shafts over Lykortas until the fighting was so close that the Thracian lord thrust an arrow under the brow of a man's helmet and drew his sword.

And then the Aetolians broke. Alexanor never knew exactly why. One moment, he was pressed so close that the fighting more resembled *pankration* than spear fencing, the next he was breathing like a blacksmith's bellows and Thodor and Dadas were cursing their lack of shafts.

The dew had not yet burnt off the olives, but already the base of the wall was so thick with dead and dying men that the shape of the slope had changed.

Alexanor wanted to sleep. Instead, he forced his hands to release the spear. They felt like an old man's hands: his joints ached, and his knuckles were bruised. He didn't even remember using them.

'You should rest,' Philopoemen said. He was watching the Aetolians.

'We will see to the wounded,' Alexanor said proudly. 'Including the Aetolians.'

Philopoemen looked at him for a moment, and then managed a tired smile.

'You are a good man,' he said. 'I admire you. But I beg you to wait until they either mount to ride away, or charge us again.'

'No,' Alexanor said.

He crouched, flexing his knees, and then called for his terrified novices. One had a bloody dagger, another a javelin. One was dead. Two were sitting, stunned, as if they couldn't function. The eldest was missing two fingers from his left hand, and Alexanor started with him, bandaging his hand carefully before all of them went to look at the other wounded.

'Come,' he said.

They clambered down a section of the wall where there were fewer bodies and Alexanor began the process of triage. He was looking for someone to save. He needed someone to save. He felt ill at the killing, at the ease of it.

He found a young man bleeding out – a simple cut to the thigh. Absent a fire and a red-hot iron, he could do nothing for the boy. He let him die and went on to the next, and then the next, until he found a man with a cut he could close, and then another.

'Brother,' Philopoemen said.

Alexanor was crouched over his fifth or sixth stab wound, a grown man weeping over the pain in his groin, just one of his four wounds. None of them had to be mortal.

'Go away,' Alexanor said. 'Linen thread, boy.'

One of the novices, his own hands gory with blood, fumbled to make a loop in the thread. Philopoemen took it from him and made the loop.

'The Aetolians are requesting permission to bury their dead,' Philopoemen said. 'And they hope to reclaim their wounded.'

'We should execute every fucking one of them,' Telemnastos said. His eyes were too bright – fatigue, the daemons of combat, terror, courage and too much killing, all in one man.

Dinaeos shook his head. 'Nah. This is one thing I've learnt from Phil. War needs good manners, and you don't teach manners to clods by out-clodding them.' He was standing by the heap of dead men. 'By Demeter, we killed a lot of them.'

'A hundred,' Alexanor said. 'Give or take.'

Deftly, he slipped the loop over the man's artery and closed it, saving the man's life.

The Aetolians declined his offer to continue caring for their wounded: it was clear they thought him mad, or lying, when he claimed he would save whomever he could on both sides. So he worked on Lykortas, and then men he didn't know as well, until his novices were all but weeping with fatigue. He washed in water that Thodor brought with his own hands, and saved a young Thracian with a spear thrust in his shin, right through his fancy metal greaves, and then . . .

He was finished.

He looked at them all again, and Dadas brought him wine.

'Men send you their ration,' he said in his careful Thracian Greek. 'Men give up wine after fight. For you.'

Alexanor drank the wine, watched the valley for a little while, and fell asleep.

When he awoke, there was a fire, and wine. And the wonderful smell of roasting mutton, a harbinger of the wonder of the meat itself, warm, salty, and delicious.

Philopoemen crouched by him, waving a leg of mutton under his nose.

'Get up and eat dinner,' he said. 'Come on, Alexanor.'

The priest raised his head. His whole body ached; he had been sleeping against the stone wall. There were flies everywhere.

'What's happened?'

'Gortyna is ours,' Philopoemen said. 'Periander is in the citadel. We have a hundred hostages. The oligarchs surrendered when the town was burning around their ears.'

Alexanor nodded dully, looking at the flies, and the blood.

'We buried our dead,' Philopoemen said. 'I lost eleven men. Almost all of them men I knew. My tenants.' He turned away.

You woke me up because you needed someone to talk to, Alexanor thought with the annoyance of a tired man woken too soon.

But he enjoyed the mutton and stale bread and watered wine, and then he slept again. And the next morning, he helped curry horses. There was no longer any point in holding the rock; they were leaving as soon as they had watered the horses.

Alexanor walked down the hillside alone, looking for a spring that Telemnastos said was there. Instead he found the dead man.

He was older, and had probably been very tough. He had good armour, and a fine sword still sheathed in a silver-encrusted scabbard under his arm. The *chiton* under his bronze armour was beautiful, or it had been before it was soaked in blood and intestinal fluids – red, embroidered with doves and roses by a loving wife.

A chance spear-blow had opened his throat; the man's hand was at his neck, trying to hold his life in. He'd crawled a long way in the underbrush, and then fallen down a little cliff and died.

Alexanor's immediate intention had been to see if the man was alive; his second was to take the fine *xiphos* at his side. But then he tugged away the breastplate and the backplate, a looter with a solid knowledge of the paralysis of death and how to strip a body.

And then ...

And then he had a nearly naked man before him who was clearly dead. His eyes had already been pecked out by ravens; maybe that made the difference.

Alexanor paused and prayed.

Then he drew his sharp neck knife from its scabbard and traced a long cut from pelvis to throat with the point. He had a feeling of guilt – of sacrilege. But his curiosity overwhelmed his scruples; and he had questions.

He took the man's arms and dragged him to a flatter space, and then traced his cut again, and he prayed. He prayed to Zeus, and to Asklepios, and then he said, 'Brother, I do not know who you were, but I ... I only do this to save others.'

Even then, his knife hand trembled as it never had with a living patient, and he hesitated for perhaps fifty heartbeats.

And then he cut. He opened the chest, and found the heart, and then opened the abdomen and found the intestines and the stomach. He knew them from opening animals, but in a man they had an element of the sacred that he had never ascribed to a cat or a deer carcass. He went to the spring, washed, and returned to open a shoulder, but he could not make sense of the incredibly complex workings of the shoulder muscles and tendons.

An hour later, men were calling for him, and he was covered in blood. He had more questions than he had started with. He clambered down to the little spring again and turned it red, then climbed back to where an angry Philopoemen towered over him on his big horse.

'You kept forty tired men waiting in the sun,' Philopoemen said in a quiet voice.

'Maybe someday that time will save all their lives,' Alexanor said.

He mounted, feeling filthy, and rode through the beautiful day in a black mood. The image of his friends as living, animated corpses, mere machines of sinew and gristle and sticky blood, would not leave him.

'All of us are but corpses,' he said aloud.

'You are so much fun,' Dinaeos said.

Gortyna did not improve his mood. Everything smelt of smoke; there were scorch marks on the Temple of Apollo, and no priests could be found, because Creon, *Primarch* of the *Presbyteroi*, had been high priest of Apollo. There was no one to purify the temple, and the temple slaves sat in huddles.

Alexanor spent a day arranging the affairs of someone else's temple, finding responsible priests who were not tainted by the oligarchy and would continue the sacrifices. A day later, he himself had been purified, and the temple operations were running, if not smoothly, at least regularly. Alexanor found Philopoemen in the agora, dispensing justice. He sat on a camp stool, surrounded by soldiers, looking a little too much like a statue of a tyrant for Alexanor.

Leon saw him and beckoned him forward, and Alexanor realised that the man currently standing, glowering, between two of Periander's men was Zophanes, the father of the former high priest.

'I have no need to defend myself, since you, a foreigner, have no status in law,' Zophanes said.

'Kill him!' roared the crowd.

Philopoemen shook his head. 'My father and grandfather were both citizens of Gortyna—'

'*Honorary* citizens!' shouted Zophanes.

Philopoemen shrugged. 'I might say, Zophanes, that I'm the one in command of this city and you are perhaps the most hated man in it, after Creon.'

'Should I care, that dogs and crows dislike me?' Zophanes said proudly.

'You are winning yourself no friends, Zophanes,' said Antiphatas.

'*Kill him!*' roared the crowd. A few voices called '*Achilles!*'

'Exile him,' Alexanor called out.

Philopoemen turned and looked at him. 'If we exile him, he will simply go to Knossos and work against Gortyna.'

Alexanor nodded.

'I propose that he maintain full citizen rights and remain here, inside the city. Not free, but under house arrest until such time as the Assembly restores his rights.' Philopoemen looked at Antiphatas.

The Cretan frowned.

'Do better to him than he did to you,' Philopoemen said. 'He may yet serve the common good.'

'What if he's as venal as his son?' Lykortas asked quietly.

Many of the citizens had reservations, and it was obvious that the crowd wanted blood, but Zophanes was led away to his own house.

'You are merciful,' Alexanor said.

'Merciful nothing,' Philopoemen said. 'In a few days they will awaken from rage, and be happy that we did not begin the new democratic government in a thunderstorm of blood. You are returning to Lentas?'

'I have no place here – there are factions in the temples and I want nothing to do with them. I need Leon.'

'Leon is a fine thinker. I could use both of you in government,' Philopoemen said.

Alexanor nodded. 'Perhaps when my temple is on a surer footing.'

CHAPTER TWO

—⟶◦◦◦⟵—

Lentas and Gortyna, Crete

220 BCE

For all his feelings of disgust at the hasty dissection he had performed, the first thing he did on returning to Lentas, after a long hot bath, was to sit and sketch the bodily formations he had seen under the skin. The heart. The muscles of an arm. The coils of intestines, in as much detail as he could remember. He sat in his cell, watching his own left arm raise and lower a bar of iron, and he thought of the gristle and meat under his sharp knife in the bright sun of the hill of Petra. His gorge rose, but he kept drawing. He tried to make sense of the shoulder; he played with a chicken leg that night at dinner. He had begun eating meat. His Pythagorean beliefs were falling away in the presence of so much violence.

For a few days, he promised himself he'd never dissect again.

But a week later, when a dog died in the town, he made his preparations. And he began to consider what he might do when a poor pilgrim died.

And then, as summer turned to autumn, a letter arrived from his father. It took him three days to raise the courage to open it; nor had he been wrong. It was a tirade of anger and accusation. His father assumed that he was a child, and treated him as one, for leaving an important party, for leaving his mother to worry, and for failing to report on important events in Crete.

'Important interests, business interests beyond your comprehension, hinge on our victory on Crete,' his father wrote. 'Your silence suggests that your loyalties to Rhodes have been affected by your other senseless behaviour. If you do not reply immediately, I will have no choice as a father and citizen but to disinherit you and erase your status as a citizen of Rhodes. This is in my power, as I am your father and under law have absolute rights over you.'

Alexanor put the letter aside. He reread it several times in the next days, but he made no move to respond, and he moved about his work pretending to himself that the letter had had no effect. Instead of allowing himself to think about it, he trained his novices and, with his priests, he did his best to heal the sick, or at least take them where the god could heal them. Days passed into weeks; festivals were celebrated, and incense and holy water began to clean his internal wounds. The flow of pilgrims increased dramatically, and the novices showed promise, and he sent word to Gortyna that he needed six more boys and two girls for the shrine.

A runaway slave died in the town. The body lay where the man had died for half a day, gnawed by dogs. Alexanor was tempted to try dissection again, but he resisted. Instead he fetched the corpse with his own hands and the temple paid for it to be burnt. He sent the ashes in an urn to the cemetery and took no further action. He sent for books on anatomy from Alexandria, and gathered oregano on the hillsides, and watched the stars at night.

He heard rumours, of course. His novices were local; they had family in Gortyna. The war was not over: Knossos was raiding Gortyna daily, had destroyed the city of the Lyttians, had attacked Polyrrhenia by land while the Rhodian fleet attacked it by sea.

He also heard that the Rhodian commander, Polemecles, was advocating for negotiations. Philopoemen sent for the former high priest, and then sent him back, with an apology.

'Best send him to Epidauros,' Philopoemen said laconically in his letter.

So when the next pilgrim ship from the Peloponnese landed, Alexanor sent it back to Epidauros with a request for another senior priest, and a long series of four scrolls documenting the former high priest's crimes. He sent along a sanctuary freedman as a witness, and two of the Boeotian mercenaries who were once again the garrison of the towers; witnesses against the accused and jailors too.

When his books came from Alexandria, they arrived with the news that the Spartan king, Cleomenes, had committed suicide after a failed attempt to take Aegypt for himself. Alexanor winced at the idea of the man's suicide, but filed it in the dead place in his heart with his father's letter. Instead of considering his father, Alexanor devoured Herophilus' *On Pulses* and all eight of his other works on anatomy.

But the next time a slave died and his body was unclaimed, Alexanor did not hesitate. He took the body with Leon's help, carried it to the palace that the former high priest had used, and the two of them dissected it for two days under the *stoae* amid the untended roses and unwatered rhododendrons. He and Leon took turns cutting and drawing, and the impiety, as well as the risk, brought them still closer together, so that when they were done, any lingering division of rank was buried with the slave's corpse.

Alexanor felt guilt; Leon, apparently, none.

'Poor bastard led a rough life,' Leon said, early enough in the dissection.

The man was not as old as he had seemed when Alexanor first inspected him; abuse and neglect, poor diet and long hours had forced him into age.

'In death, he performs a noble act, saving others,' Leon said.

Alexanor thought that Leon was making a sophistry, a rationalisation, but when he looked up from the man's abdomen, he saw that Leon was crying.

Alexanor reached out a bloody hand, and Leon blinked slowly.

'Sometimes it's fucking bad,' he said. 'By Zeus who saves, Alexanor. May you never know ...'

Alexanor nodded. But as the cuts went deeper – as they lifted organs from the cavity of the abdomen, guessing their function – Alexanor found that he was describing to Leon his father's anger, his letter. And his own failures with Aspasia. And Leon told him too much about slavery – about the petty humiliations and the endless betrayals and the casual abuse.

After two days, Alexanor began to train his novices to dissect frogs from the marshes to the east. He used the little creatures to show them the flow of blood and the fine tissues that supported muscle and tendon.

A hunter brought them a boar from the mountains, as an offering, and Alexanor purchased it, ostensibly for his table. He and Leon took it to pieces carefully, examining the muscular processes and marvelling at the linkage of muscle to bone. Alexanor was very tempted to ask one of the masseurs on the staff to join them; only massage professionals seemed to exactly understand the way the mechanical process of the body functioned.

And eventually circumstance, or the gods, sent a drifter who died in the agora and the temptation was too much for both of them; Alexanor took the body and they dissected it in the former high priest's rose garden. They both had duties they could not abandon, and they could not reveal what they were doing, and so, when the fine tissue had begun to decay in the heat, and dogs bayed outside the palace courtyards, smelling the corpse, and Alexanor could stand it no more, they closed the man up and buried him in the temple's cemetery with honour, washed carefully, and then drank wine together while they discussed how to teach their priests what they had learnt.

'I feel as if I know *less* than before,' Alexanor said.

Leon smiled. 'Well, I know now how the hand works, and I had no idea before. It's like the first time you see a woman undress ...'

'That's the oddest allegory I can imagine for the world inside that corpse.'

Leon laughed. 'I don't feel like a slave today. I feel like a priest of the god. Thanks, Alexanor.'

'I don't feel like such a fool,' Alexanor said slowly. 'Thanks, Leon.' He shrugged, and washed his hands again.

Over the next week, he and Leon began to teach their people the wonder of muscle processes. Teaching them helped him understand the processes himself, and he found that he didn't agree with everything the master taught in his essays. To him, it was clear that the brain was the seat of reason: a man hit in the head lost the ability to think; a man hit in the heart simply died, often with clear eyes and full cognitive powers.

'If Herophilus had spent more time on battlefields,' Alexanor said with a smile, 'he'd have understood even more.'

Theophilus was the best of the novices. He was the big lad who'd used a dagger in the fighting at Petra. He had the strongest stomach and the best mind, and his passion for Omphalion drove him to feats of medical emulation and piety unequalled among the other novices.

'He is a superior boy,' Omphalion would say, amused, in his high-pitched, feminine voice.

More than once, Alexanor wondered if Omphalion was a woman in disguise; it had happened before at the school on Kos. But whatever Omphalion's gender, he was the best of the priests at treatment, and the only one acceptable to most women.

Epidauros and Kos had female massage professionals and female assistants, and Kos had women priests. Alexanor wrote a pair of letters, one to Chiron and one to the hierophant at Kos, requesting a female priest for Lentas. Many of the women pilgrims had complaints that were purely academic to men. Alexanor wanted to do better.

Word reached the sanctuary from a Messenian pilgrim that the Achaean League had been defeated by the Aetolians near Messene; that Sparta's new king Lykourgos had attacked the Achaean League.

Autumn passed into winter, and Alexanor heard that Philopoemen had mounted a series of raids into Knossian territory; that he'd seized Petra again and used it as a base to steal thousands of heads of cattle and sheep from the valleys around Knossos.

Alexanor also received six new male novices, but no girls, and a polite letter from Philopoemen, praising his work, mentioning, in the most flattering terms, the new fame of the sanctuary, and signed 'Hipparchos of Gortyna.'

The messenger was Lykortas. He had Kleostratos and another Thracian as companions, and Kleostratos went straight to the baths and then to Omphalion to have a cut on his right bicep taken care of, as it was infected.

'Hipparchos?' Alexanor asked.

'He could call himself Tyrant and no one would complain.' Lykortas sat back, his riding boots stretched out before him. 'He is, to all intents and purposes, ruling Gortyna.'

'How did that happen? He's not even a citizen.'

'We're all citizens now. If you ask, you can be, too.'

Lykortas leant so far back that his head rested on the wall, and Alexanor thought the younger man might go to sleep.

'And is he good at ruling?' Alexanor asked.

Lykortas sat forward. 'Too good, if you ask me. He's like one of the ancient Greeks – like Solon the Lawgiver, or Lycurgus the Ancient. He speaks, they listen. He thinks, and suggests, they obey. They wanted to execute all the oligarchs – he advocated for ransoming them to Knossos. The Knossians declined to ransom them.' Lykortas shook his head. 'So Philopoemen sent word to the Rhodian admiral, of all people, and suddenly the Knossians changed their tune. It turns out that Phila told him that most of them owed huge amounts of money to banks on Rhodes. Of course the Rhodians paid their ransoms! They can't afford the financial loss. So now the treasury is full, and the citizens of Gortyna have a radical at the helm.'

'Phila ...' Alexanor said aloud, before he could clamp his teeth on her name.

'She's coming to Crete in the spring. Perhaps even sooner. Oh my. What an attractive young man.'

The soldier was looking out the window at Theophilus.

Alexanor raised an eyebrow.

'Any reply? I'd rather not ride back today unless I must,' Lykortas said. 'Kleo needs a rest, and that wound ...'

'I agree. Have dinner with me,' Alexanor said.

After the young Athenian was gone, he sat staring out of his open window at the sea. He thought of Phila, and Aspasia, and his father, and the idea of Philopoemen as a politician. Then he took a stylus and wrote his friend a letter, requesting citizenship in Gortyna.

Winter closed their little port. A handful of small ships still came; they received an entire shipload of sick men and women from Cyprus in the coldest month, and Crete was sufficiently close to Africa that there was always sea traffic, sails visible from the port. The soldiers changed their guard and held exercises, the older novices taught the younger, and his two priests read their way through Herophilus and dissected small animals with barely concealed distaste. Alexanor wrote several replies to his father, but sent none of them.

And then the jasmine burst into flower on the hillside, and the tufts of yellow flowers were picked by swains, and girls wore flowers in their hair. Alexanor tried not to stare as every young woman seemed more beautiful than the last, and threw himself into work; pilgrims arrived like the burst of water flowing down the hillsides. The little harbour was full of ships. A ship came from Kos, full of news of the world, and with two newly minted priests, both young, arrogant, and yet eager to please. Alexanor put them to work.

A few days later the pace began to slow. Alexanor put the lectures on a more orderly basis and had Leon and the new priests take turns teaching. It gave him time to read, and to do some diagnostic work with the pilgrims.

Another week and the oregano was in bloom, and every member of the order who was not actively teaching or healing was out on the hills, picking the herb; they used the blossoms in almost every concoction. Most of them were on the hills whenever they could be, gathering the blossoms, competing with the matrons of the town, who wanted the same blossoms for cooking.

He came in from a beautiful morning picking oregano and went straight to giving a lecture on improved diet to a room full of overweight men. They didn't listen, and he went back to his small cell and workroom, feeling frustrated, and sat at the long table he used as a desk. Sitting in front of his chair was a scroll tube that someone had placed on his wax tablets.

Leon leant in. 'He couldn't wait – said he has a cargo for Polyrrhenia. Name Diophanes. Said he was a marine with you.'

There was a note on Aegyptian papyrus attached to the scroll tube: 'Hope I've done the right thing. Buy me a cup of wine some time. I'm a *metic* in Alexandria now. Diophanes.'

Alexanor smiled. 'I haven't seen him in ten years,' he said to Leon, who was leaning in the doorway, scratching lecture notes on his own wax. 'Only four of us ... survived. I thought Diophanes died of his wounds.' He smiled. 'Gods! What a wonderful thing. If only he could have stayed.'

'He said he'd be back this way later in the sailing season,' Leon said. 'He was very happy to know you were here, and a little put out that we wouldn't bring you out of the treatment rooms.' He shrugged. 'I'm sorry – those are *your* orders.'

'So they are.'

Alexanor had opened the scroll tube. There was no address, no top note, and no heading.

He'd never seen the writing before – very careful, and very neat.

He read a sentence, stopped, looked at Leon, and blinked.

'You look like you've seen a ghost,' Leon said. 'Is it Kos, telling us we'll never get another senior priest?'

Alexanor let out a breath and took another, counted, and then tested his pulse.

Alexanor,

I risk my life writing to you, but my life is worthless anyway. Perhaps you never think of me; I think of you every day. I can no longer sit silently at my loom and dream. If you feel as I do, talk to me again! I am not Medea. I have no children to abandon, no friends, and no life here. I would as soon be a slave to a bad master as queen in this house.

I have thought a hundred times about what we said at the gate. Listen, then. Your father sold me to my husband for two warehouses on the waterfront and a house in town; my husband is a cheat who takes your father's money in every transaction. Imagine, then, what my life is.

I imagine it would be death, if this letter was found. So be it.
Aspasia

Alexanor read the letter three times. Then he put it down, stripped, and went for a run. He swam out of the bay and back, walked dripping up the beach, his head still a tumble of thoughts.

He sat through an interminable town meeting on the need for repairs to the roads and emerged without a thought in his head.

He emerged to find that Lykortas was holding court in the yard of the sanctuary. He was sitting in the sun, flirting with Theophilus while another slim young man gazed with admiration at the sacred statues. Most of the novices were standing about awkwardly; it was the break between lectures in the afternoon, and even the temple cats were awake.

'Shouldn't you be working?' Alexanor said gruffly, feeling like a hypocrite. Theophilus blushed and ran off to his studies.

'Must you be always corrupting the youth?' Alexanor asked.

Lykortas shrugged. 'I'm bored. Besides, I was only corrupting one. And he's very pretty.'

'How can you be bored, with me around?' the slim young man asked. Alexanor looked, and it was not a man at all. It was Phila, in a short *chiton* and *chlamys*.

Alexanor noted the increase in both his pulse and respiration, the outpouring of sweat, the moistening of his palms.

'Phila,' he said with false calm.

'It became clear you weren't coming to visit me,' she said.

She stepped up and kissed him on the lips, in front of most of his novices and an immediately fascinated Omphalion, who turned away with a barely hidden smile.

Phila, in a *chitoniskos* that barely covered the swell of her hips. Phila, her slight weight against his chest.

'Philopoemen needs you,' she said. 'Lykortas failed to fetch you. I thought I'd have a go.'

'So you rode all the way here …'

'I was hoping for a reward. Perhaps some medical advice.'

'My memory is that you healed me,' Alexanor said.

'Perhaps we could arrange an exchange,' she said with a smile, and he noted that his heartbeat leapt.

Two hours later, she lay across him on his narrow pallet.

'Now that we've made love, will you come to Gortyna?'

He sat back and ran his hands through her hair.

'I want to. But I have so much to do here …'

'Do you, though?' she asked. 'The whole place seems to run like one of those amazing mechanical devices that follow the movements of the stars and tell us festival dates. Leon can direct anything – don't deny it. He's more organised than you are. Why are you hiding?'

'I'm not hiding. I am the acting high priest of an important sanctuary …'

She rolled over and looked at him. 'I left a household with forty slaves to help Philopoemen win Crete. I own a dozen businesses and I run a spy network bigger than bloody Rhodes. I built it to run without me. You have a sanctuary with ten novices and four priests. Hmm?'

'And you made love to me just to get me to come with you?' Alexanor asked.

She looked at him for a moment. 'Yes. Besides, you needed it. Diagnosis: personal confusion, depression, denial of self, hiding from the world. Prognosis: if not dealt with, patient might develop into a self-important mediocrity. Treatment: conversation, straight talk punctuated with sex.' She ran a hand steadily down his abdomen. 'And I'll repeat the treatment until you recover.'

Alexanor shook his head. 'Tsk, tsk, young woman. One of the very first lessons a priest learns is not to threaten the patient with a repeated treatment he will enjoy more than recovery. Why do you think we make the opium taste bad and make massage a little unpleasant?'

'Unpleasant for who?' she whispered.

Alexanor emerged in the morning to find his students wreathed in smiles. Leon laughed aloud.

'I'm glad everyone is so ... relaxed,' Alexanor said testily.

Leon raised both eyebrows.

'Amused!' Alexanor snapped. 'I ...'

Leon put a hand on his shoulder. 'Are you going to Gortyna?'

'Yes,' Alexanor said.

'Good. You are an excellent high priest – but we need a break and so do you.' He physically turned Alexanor and gave him a gentle shove out of the lecture hall. 'Go and prepare your horse and I'll pack for you.'

Alexanor came back to his cell to find his military pack ready, and his sword and riding tunic laid out.

'Why is *everyone* smiling at me today?' he asked. 'Even the slaves in the stable?'

Leon handed him his heavy cloak, rolled tight.

'Sound carries inside the sanctuary,' he said. 'Have a good trip.'

CHAPTER THREE

―⟋⟋⟍―

Crete

SPRING AND SUMMER 219 BCE

Philopoemen sat at a table surrounded by wax tablets and scrolls under one of the four great *stoae* in the precinct of Apollo by the agora of Gortyna. He didn't look like a tyrant. He looked more like an athletic scribe, or a professional letter-writer. His table was surrounded by men, most of them young; Alexanor recognised Telemnastos and Dinaeos, but there were dozens of others of all ages, and a handful of women too, and all of them seemed to be speaking at once.

Phila knew them all, and they made a space for her as soon as she walked in.

'Welcome to the Revolutionary Council of Crete,' she said.

'We don't call it that, Phila,' one of the men said.

'More's the pity,' said a tall, dark-skinned woman with blue-black hair and a rakish look. Her eyes were dark; she had heavy eyebrows and long legs heavy with muscle, but she was thin as a farmer's fence rail.

Philopoemen looked up and saw Alexanor. He shot to his feet and threw his arms around him, pounding his back.

'She had persuasions I apparently lacked,' Lykortas said, and the dark woman barked a laugh.

Alexanor found himself deeply moved by Philopoemen's obvious demonstration.

'You are in charge here, I find,' Alexanor said.

'Never,' Philopoemen said. 'There is a council of thirty and a citizen assembly, and we've restored everyone here to full citizen rights. We're writing the laws for a real *thētes* class, like Athens, lower-class men with actual voting rights. And while we're at it, giving *metics* some rights, too.' He was all but glowing with vitality, and his eyes seemed to pour beneficence. 'Which reminds me.'

He went back to the big work table. Antiphatas chuckled and handed him a scroll tube, and Alexanor found that he was suddenly holding a writ of citizenship.

Tears came unbidden to his eyes.

Dinaeos came and embraced him. 'It's only a four-hour ride from Lentas,' he said. 'Too far to come and visit your friends?'

'I had work to do ...' Alexanor said.

'So do we!' Telemnastos said. 'We're going to change the world.'

'We are?' Alexanor asked.

'Who is this man?' asked a blond giant.

'Plator,' Lykortas said, 'this is Alexanor, High Priest of Apollo and Asklepios at Lentas. Alexanor, this is Plator, commander of the Illyrians sent by Philip.'

The two men clasped hands. 'Acting high priest,' Alexanor said.

'And perhaps you remember Aristaenos?' Philopoemen said.

'You healed me,' said a young man, who was both bigger and more mature than Alexanor remembered him. 'I will never forget that.'

'Aristaenos came with the Achaean military expedition,' Dinaeos said. 'Two hundred men.'

'The worst infantry on Crete,' Aristaenos said.

'Not any more, after a winter of drilling with Periander,' Dinaeos said.

'I will teach them to fight with horse,' Thodor said. 'To *ride*.'

'And we have our own phalanx now, and our own archer corps and we're working on forming a federal league, with laws,' Telemnastos said.

'Even for women,' said the dark-haired woman. 'I'm Cyrena. No one ever introduces me.'

She stuck out her hand like a man, and Alexanor clasped it.

Phila smiled. 'I'd have got to you in time. Cyrena organised the *porne* as spies during the *stasis*.'

'I want women to have a voice in government,' Cyrena said.

Antiphatas rolled his eyes. Telemnastos beamed.

Alexanor grinned. 'I've missed this.'

'Good,' Philopoemen said. 'You hear a good deal of news down at Lentas and I need to know what's happening in the world. Phila's information came like a breath of fresh air, but I need more. Do you know where Philip is?'

Alexanor shook his head. 'No,' he admitted. 'But I have heard that Knossos sent a thousand men to fight in Aetolia. The Aetolians and the Macedonians are locked together. My last batch of pilgrims came from Sicily. There's a rumour at Syracusa that one of the Carthaginian nobles has broken the treaty in Iberia.' He paused. 'That could be important.'

'That means no Romans at our end of the Inner Sea for a few years,' Dinaeos said. 'Good news if true. They say Hannibal is thirsting for war with Rome.'

'Despite which,' Phila said, 'I have an unimpeachable source who says that one of the two Roman consuls for the year has received Illyria as his theatre of operations.'

'I just received two new priests from Kos,' Alexanor added. 'One of Ptolemy's generals defected to the Seleucids. I gather that Aegypt is in chaos. You know that Cleomenes is dead?'

Philopoemen coloured slightly at the mention of the Spartan king's name.

'Yes,' he said. 'I would rejoice, except that his successor, Lykourgos, seems determined to carry on his work. Spartans are burning the farms around Megalopolis. Again.'

'But we are here,' Cyrena said. 'Not in the Peloponnese, not in Arkadia, not in Elis or Sparta. We are *here*. Peasants are dying *here*. Women are raped *here*.'

She crossed her arms, and then, head high, tapped the pile of scrolls, like a schoolmistress recalling an errant schoolboy to his work. Alexanor expected an explosion, but Philopoemen smiled.

'Your remarks are just,' he said.

Later, Alexanor lay with Phila. 'Are they lovers?' he asked, incredulous.

'Yes,' she said.

'Surely, he could have any woman ...'

246

'Sometimes you sound very like a misogynist, my dear. And in this case, I'd say that Cyrena had him.'

'But she's a *porne*! A whore!'

Phila rolled over and looked at him. 'Interesting.' She rolled off the *kline* and walked to the window.

'I didn't mean that!' Alexanor exclaimed.

'Mean what?' Phila said over her shoulder.

'You are being difficult.'

'You just made your views on women who provide sex for money very plain. I name you *hypocrite*.'

'You ... I didn't mean you. And besides, I didn't "make my views plain".'

'Didn't you?' Phila asked.

Silence, and darkness, lay between them.

'I suspect that you mean that she is neither as beautiful as I am, nor as well-educated.' Phila rustled; out in the darkness, she was putting on a *peplos*. 'A cheap whore, rather than an expensive one.'

'I didn't say anything like that. You are making up words I didn't say,' muttered the priest.

'Am I? When a patient is obese and short of breath, do you need him to use words to tell you what is wrong? When I saw you in your sanctuary, did I need words to tell me what you wanted from me?'

'Phila!'

'Alexanor!' she said, mockingly.

He thought that she was leaving, and he was desolated. He rose, but she pressed him down.

'No, no. I'd rather stay and educate you than leave you to mull over your many failings,' she said. 'Cyrena was taught *pankration* – as a slave, she gave demonstrations against other women slaves. It titillated men in Alexandria. Apparently, your friend had never seen a woman who could fight. He's ... obsessed. Also, her very origins, as a freed slave, a foreigner, an African, all fit his current political ideals. Which, if I may be direct, are my own.' She lit an oil lamp from the coals in the crock by the bed. 'Also, she is ridiculously beautiful, for a woman of her size. You just can't see past her skin colour.'

'I care nothing for her skin,' Alexanor protested. 'It is her accent!'

'Alexanor, we're having a revolution. We are overthrowing the old

247

oligarchs and restoring democracy. We're not doing it just so that people from "the best families" can enjoy their political rights.'

'I am *not* a farm boy from Pella!' Alexanor said. 'You do not need to patronise me like this.'

'Don't I?' she asked. 'You should have heard yourself when you called her a whore. I promise you, she loves your friend. And we need spies, Alexanor, something that you, of all people, should understand.'

'I told you that in confidence, not so you could throw it at me. Besides, I told you, I don't send reports to Rhodes any more.' He sounded petulant, and he regretted it.

'My dear, we're lucky to have her – doubly lucky she's such a noble soul. Frankly, I'm surprised a woman who has lived her life, been abused, been raped a hundred times, been sold, can *love* anyone. But she does. Perhaps she sees him as the saviour of the slaves. Perhaps he sees in her the slaves he means to save.'

She shrugged, her face beautiful in the lamplight, like a distant goddess.

'Do you believe that women should have political rights?' Alexanor asked.

She laughed. 'Yes. But it won't happen in my lifetime, so whatever Cyrena believes, I won't alienate the very men I need to save the world by forcing them to give me the franchise now. Bastards.'

Alexanor took a deep breath. 'Where's she from?'

'Somewhere south of Aegypt. Far to the south of Alexandria.'

He shook his head. 'I'm afraid of your revolution. What will be left?'

She shrugged and lay down again. 'What's left now, my dear? At the current rate, in a few years a handful of kings and extremely rich men will own everything – here, Macedon, Aegypt, Syria, Rome, Carthage ...' She leant over him. 'Philopoemen says that to have a strong city, we must build on strong foundations – justice for every class of men. All Cyrena and I want is for the men to remember women.'

Alexanor thought of his father. And his mother. And Aspasia.

He sighed. 'I'm sorry I said whore,' he admitted.

'I know that. That's why I am still here.' She looked at him fondly. 'I'm thirty now. Too old for customers, mostly. Lines in the skin of my eyes, no?' She gazed at him. 'And what happened when you went to Rhodes? A little bird tells me that you walked out on a dinner party.'

'Aphrodite!' he spat. 'Are your spies everywhere?'

'Well, you went to a party with some old men who hired a pair of flute girls for entertainment,' the *hetaera* said. 'So you needn't be shocked that I know what happened.' She put a finger on his chest. 'Except that I don't know why you left. Were you sick?'

'Sick with anger,' he admitted.

And then, without fully intending, he was telling her the whole ugly story, from his first trysts with Aspasia, to their betrothal, to his father's dissolution of their impending marriage, and then on to the dinner party.

'He ... wanted my Aspasia for his friend,' Alexanor said. 'She was the only child of a very rich man. I'm sure she stood to inherit some ... wonderful warehouses.'

Phila kissed him. 'So this is why you ran away from your family?'

Alexanor lay looking at the darkness. 'Bodily intimacy makes for easy confession,' he said.

'How astute of you, doctor.'

'Have you ever done something so ... bad ... that ...' He shook his head.

'You? Did something bad?' she asked. 'In a way, you cheer me up. I'm so glad to know you can do something bad. You're always so stable.'

'I am?' Alexanor asked. 'No, I mean something ... against the law of the gods.'

'I'm not sure I recognise any laws of the gods. You killed your father? No, I'd know.'

He shook his head. 'No. I dissected a man.'

'Dissected?'

'I cut him up. Carefully.' Alexanor said it with a bitter pride.

'Was he ... alive?' she asked.

'Zeus – no! What do you take me for, a monster?'

She shrugged, her body tight against him now. 'No. So ... you cut up a dead man. For ... science? Don't they do that in Alexandria?'

'Yes. But you understand, it is forbidden ...'

'Forbidden?' She shook her head, and he felt her hair against his chest. 'This is your crime against the gods? Cutting up a dead man?'

Alexanor lay back.

'Where is your lady-love now?' she asked.

'I find it very odd to talk to you about her.'

'That's because you equate us. But I promise you, I feel no jealousy, now or ever, and to me, she is just another misused woman.' She breathed out. 'One of thousands.'

Alexanor enjoyed voting in the Assembly. The citizens of Gortyna were not revolutionaries; most of them were middle-aged men, farmers and merchants, not unlike the citizens of any other Greek polity. They were a little more efficient than most, as if their recent brush with loss of their citizen rights had reminded every one of them to do a better job. In a day of voting in the Assembly they summoned the citizen phalanx to its duty, voted a long series of taxes on themselves for the war, and then got down to the drudgery of voting on temple repairs, theatre costs, festival liturgies and everything from flowers to wood for cremations. The budget lists took an hour to read out and five hours to vote, men rising to discuss the cost of torches, or who made better ones, or just speaking to hear the sound of their own voices, or so it seemed to Alexanor.

One of the most frequent voices was Creon, who disagreed with everything that cost money, and was outraged when he was handed the largest set of temple liturgies and theatre productions, to be paid for out of his own funds.

The second loudest voice was Zophanes. He was more of a wheedler than an orator, but he was just as outraged to be taxed for the upkeep of roads, which he proclaimed repeatedly neither he nor anyone else needed or used.

'If the farmers at the east end of the valley want a better road, they should build it themselves!' he said. 'It's only fair. If the men of Phaistos want a good road to Gortyna, let them pay for it.' He looked around. 'It is unfair to ask me to pay for things I do not use.'

Very few agreed with him.

Philopoemen only rose twice – once to defend the military budget, and once to insist on funding to improve the paving of roads outside the city.

'The roads are everyone's property,' he said. 'They are for the common good. This is why we *have* government – so that we, collectively, can act, like hoplites in the phalanx, for the good of our state. Who can fight alone on a battlefield? Who can build a road alone?'

He received an ovation, and Zophanes glared.

During an 'interval', Alexanor read the laws of the city, carved into stones, along with lists of slaves freed by vote of the Assembly and men granted citizenship. He was pleased to find his own name, immediately after Philopoemen's.

'They are fine men,' Philopoemen said.

'I agree. I love it here.'

'As do I,' said the Achaean. 'I will probably never go home.'

'What?' Alexanor asked.

'Aratos and Philip have ruined the Achaean League. These men are still capable of ruling themselves. They can work, they can fight, they can debate. This summer, when we face Knossos, we will have a citizen phalanx – the first one on Crete in fifty years. The first in Greece since ...' He shrugged. 'Since the Lamian War.'

He stood looking at the lists of laws of Gortyna.

'How old are they?' Alexanor asked.

Philopoemen shrugged. 'The laws? More than two hundred years old. Does it ever occur to you that we live in the ruins of the lives of our ancestors, and they were better men than we are ourselves? Look at what they built. Look at Socrates and Plato. Look at the Parthenon in Athens.'

'I might say, look at the theatre in Epidauros,' Alexanor said. 'Read a modern medical text – watch a good surgeon cut.'

'And in politics?' Philopoemen asked, crossing his arms.

Alexanor nodded. 'I concede that the Spartans and Athenians and Thebans of the past seem the better men,' he admitted.

'The men of Attica and Boeotia seem to me fewer, weaker, and less capable,' Philopoemen said. 'They live among the monuments of their greatness like keepers in a graveyard.'

'You may be doing an injustice to the Attics and the Boeotians.'

'Maybe. You know that Aratos has been defeated in battle twice now? Some of the Achaean federal states have raised their own armies, because they despair of the Federal army ever defeating the Spartans. It's Sellasia all over again. Aratos will invite Philip to do the fighting, and Philip will demand concessions, and in the end, Aratos will disband the Achaean Army.'

'And, of course, Aratos has no time for you,' Alexanor said.

Philopoemen glanced at him with a smile on his lips.

'I think you accuse me of ambition,' he said. 'But in truth, friends in Megalopolis have suggested that I may be exiled.'

'Exiled?' Alexanor asked.

'For serving a foreign power. This is the way of the world. Aratos sent me to Crete, and now, apparently, he tells people that I have abandoned my homeland to serve Philip of Macedon. In this way, he makes it impossible for me to return.' Philopoemen shrugged.

'That's insane!'

'Welcome to Achaean League politics. No one can rise to the level of the great Aratos, or they will be cut down. He was a great man once – a lesson to us all. Regardless, I will be happy to be a citizen of Gortyna. I will hold office here, too.'

Alexanor shrugged. 'I, too, am delighted to be a citizen of Gortyna. My father is disinheriting me. I will no longer be a citizen of Rhodes.'

'Oh, gods,' Philopoemen embraced the Rhodian. 'That's terrible.'

'It's a long story,' Alexanor said.

After that, Alexanor began to shuttle back and forth between Lentas and Gortyna. He prepared Theophilus and Omphalion to accompany him to war, and then added Leon and two more novices after consultation with Philopoemen. He went to testify before the Council of Ten on matters of sanitation, and again to vote in the Assembly about the war and covering the harvest.

Philopoemen was in the field, using his cavalry and the Illyrians as a hammer and a surgical knife to raid the great valleys around Knossos, first from Petra, and then from the west, using the superior horsemanship of his cavalry troopers to ride through rocky mountain passes that their opponents deemed impassable. Once, in late spring, Alexanor rode along on a raid. His clearest memory was that wherever he rode, there were Illyrians high above him, moving as fast on foot as he could move on horseback. They returned home with hundreds of head of sheep and cattle.

'One of my many worries is that the Gortynians will become so adept at this raiding that they'll never want peace,' Philopoemen said.

'It is not a very Hellenic method of war,' Alexanor muttered, possibly because his thighs were so sore.

'Perhaps not in Athens or Sparta,' Philopoemen said. 'But in Arkadia or Thessaly, this sort of thing is our bread and oil.'

'Thrake, too,' Thodor said, and all the Thracians laughed.

Dadas pointed mutely at the Illyrians in the rocks.

'I stand corrected,' Alexanor said.

Early summer rolled into late summer. Ships from Greece reported that the Illyrian prince, Demetrios of Pharos, had been badly defeated by the Romans and fled to exile in Macedon. Philip himself was reported to be hard-pressed, with Macedon invaded by Dardanians and Aetolians; confusing stories, and there was no word from Philip himself, even though he was the ostensible paymaster and head of the alliance of the *Neoteroi* on Crete.

'We are forgotten,' Dinaeos said.

'Sadly, we are not the centre of operations,' Philopoemen said. 'And yet the Aetolians continue to remember Knossos. When our citizen levy is stronger, we might consider sending a contingent to fight with the Macedonians,' he suggested.

Cyrena nodded, her magnificent eyes narrowed. 'This is good thinking. If he looks on our soldiers every day, he cannot forget that we are his allies.' She looked around. 'Listen, brothers. I am afraid we have ... traitors. In our midst.'

'Traitors?' Philopoemen said.

Alexanor sat back. He didn't want to dislike the African woman, but she was strident, insistent, too direct. And he feared she harboured political views more radical even than the Stoics. She had spoken openly of levelling: taking the property of the rich to help the poorest class, freed slaves and labourers, an idea that Alexanor found abhorrent.

'Someone paid a slave to go to Knossos,' she said. 'I don't know who, yet, but I'm in contact with the slave.'

'Someone?' Alexanor asked.

'Whoever did it was cagey enough to use a cut-out,' Cyrena said. 'He paid a tavern owner to find him a messenger. I'm still looking into it.' She put a badly stained square of cut papyrus on the table. 'But I did get the message. The slave sold it to us.' She smiled nastily. 'The slaves are with us.'

The message consisted of the recent voting in the Assembly,

itemised, and a neat list of all of the military resources of the city, followed by a well-written paragraph on the new 'League of Crete'.

The so-called Neoteroi *intend to form a League, or Federation, of* all *the cities of Crete on the model of the Achaean League or the Aetolian, with a single army and a single coinage, and a uniform administration of the whole island, by a Federal Assembly. I do not need to tell you how small our voice would be in such a Federation, or how much injury it will do to our commerce. Philopoemen of Achaea is the wellspring of all this; he must be dealt with immediately.*

Philopoemen glanced around. He was smiling.

'You know that you are doing the right thing when the oligarchs hate you,' he said.

Later, Alexanor was eating in Phila's home. She had freed Thais, but the younger woman continued to serve them at table.

'I still find it hard to like her,' Alexanor said, speaking of Cyrena.

He was lying on a *kline*, facing Phila who lay on another, looking at him over her folded arms.

'She certainly speaks her mind,' Phila said.

'She speaks as if she understands politics and war.' Alexanor raised a hand. 'I am *not* saying that a woman cannot understand such things. I'm saying that *she* is ignorant of these things – a North African slave who no more understands Cretan politics than we understand the actions of the gods.' He shrugged. 'Damn it, I'm not even sure *I* understand Cretan politics.'

'Philopoemen loves her.' Phila shrugged. 'Love is an odd thing, don't you think?'

'But she wants to democratise *everything*. You cannot democratise art. You need excellence for art. You cannot democratise philosophy. The discovery of the world of the mind, or nature, requires careful study. Which reminds me ... may I take your pulse?'

Phila smiled her enigmatic smile. 'What is a pulse?'

When he had demonstrated, she became excited.

'So this is how the blood serves the body?' she asked.

'I believe it is pushed through the body by means of the great pump which is the heart. Here,' he said, putting a hand on her chest above her left breast. 'Here, feel my heartbeat.'

He put her hand inside his *chiton*, on his chest.

'I feel it,' she agreed.

'Now feel my pulse here at my wrist,' he said.

'I have it!' she said. 'Amazing.'

'When we make love, I will take your pulse and mine—'

'How romantic,' she said with a wry smile.

'Last night I felt mine elevate. No, listen – when you disrobe, my pulse rises. The emotion feeds the heart, and the heart works harder, providing more blood. The excess of humour is transformed into my erection, yes? And in a woman—'

'You will rob love of all mystery, strip it and make it a science.' She made a face. 'Sounds dull. I hope I am more than an elevation of the humours.' Her thumb began to trace one of his nipples under his *chiton*.

'But, my dear ...' he began.

She called to Thais. 'Please put a wax tablet and a stylus on either side of my bed, there's a dear. We'll be taking notes.'

'How exciting,' Thais said, with just a little sarcasm.

'For science and the study of philosophy,' Alexanor insisted.

'Oh, *of course*,' Thais said.

'But this kind of thinking,' Phila went on, her hand going deeper into his *chiton*, 'is exactly what you and Dinaeos seem to dislike in Philopoemen and in Cyrena.'

'How so?' Alexanor asked, trying to keep his mind on matters of the intellect.

'Innovations. Science. Careful examination of conditions instead of accepting the assumptions of the past.' She lifted his *chiton* off him.

Alexanor answered her by putting his lips to her neck. She laughed.

'Wait,' she said, pushing him away. 'You need to take my pulse.'

He grabbed at her.

'Fie, sir!' she said. 'What has happened to science?'

In the Assembly, men were openly questioning the conduct of the war. As the Assembly had been re-established specifically so that men of small estate could speak freely, Philopoemen had to answer every question put to him. Most of the complaints centred around the cost of the war. Philopoemen had entered a motion to purchase two hundred horses so that he could convert Aristaenos' Achaean League soldiers to the cavalry they should have been to start with, and dozens of small farmers complained bitterly of the costs associated with having them.

Zophanes rose to his feet and decried the very existence of the war, claiming that it could be settled in a simple peace conference.

'This mercenary Achaean,' he suggested smugly, 'who you have mistakenly included in our citizen body, is here only to make his fortune. He and his "Achaean allies" – nay, friends! Achaean *mercenaries* is what we should call them. They are richly paid with *our* money. Illyrians, Boeotians ... we are paying good money while they get fat. We can settle our differences with Knossos in a day. This long war of constant raiding only enriches and empowers these foreigners!'

Men shouted him down, although the term 'Achaean mercenaries' had been planted like an evil weed in the Assembly.

But Zophanes was not the only man against Philopoemen's policies. Another farmer, a veteran hoplite, rose to his feet.

'Give us a proper battle,' he said. 'Us against them, eh? Let's fight the damn thing and get it over with. Not this endless raiding.'

There was some debate on that, as other farmers were growing prosperous on stolen sheep and goats. But the older man would not be shouted down.

'No!' he roared. 'Fuck all this shilly-shally fake war! Philopoemen and his friends were all very well when they came, but now they are just stringing it out to stay in power. Send the heralds, line up the phalanx, and go for their throats. One big fight and we'll be done.'

Hundreds of voices were raised in approval. And the next day, the same man spoke from the rostrum; he asked the same question. When he was done, and thousands of men had roared their approval, the farmer turned to where Philopoemen and his friends stood.

'I am not against you, *Hipparchos*. Appoint us some officers, form the *taxeis*, and lead us to battle. We'll get this done, and we'll vote you thanks.'

'Hear him!' roared the crowd.

Philopoemen tried to walk to the rostra to speak, but the crowd kept cheering the farmer.

'Battle! Battle!'

The roars shook the walls.

*

That evening, Phila told Alexanor she had invited Philopoemen for wine.

'And a few other worthies,' she said with an enigmatic smile.

Philopoemen was the first to arrive, with Cyrena and Dinaeos. Dinaeos threw himself on a *kline* and called for wine. Philopoemen lay down next to Alexanor. He was silent, even when Dinaeos began to tease Thais.

'Now that you are free, you can marry,' he said. 'I'll bet you have a dozen suitors.'

'They only want one thing,' she said. 'And that's my money.'

'I'd marry you myself ...' Dinaeos said.

'Oh, no. Red-haired children? I couldn't stand for that,' Thais said. 'More wine, gentlemen?'

Phila took Cyrena's cloak herself, and then put an arm through the other woman's and took her off into the house.

Philopoemen looked around. 'Phila must think things are desperate,' he said.

'That farmer who advocated battle is not alone,' Dinaeos said. 'In a few days they'll start calling us foreigners.'

Philopoemen drank wine, tugged his beard, and said nothing.

Alexanor leant forward. 'Can you tell *me* why you can't just force a battle? Or answer the complaint?'

Philopoemen nodded slowly. 'I'm finding that some things are very difficult to discuss in the Assembly. Every man has his own interest – most of them aren't even rational in their arguments. It's not at all as I expected it to be.' He frowned. 'I think the logic is obvious, but I find I can't bring myself to tell them that if we fight a battle, they might lose.'

'I agree that won't do our cause much good,' Alexanor said. 'But I'm also not sure I understand your logic. Why not fight a battle?'

Philopoemen sat back. 'Why do battles happen, Alexanor?'

The priest looked at Dinaeos, opened his mouth, and closed it. After a moment, he shrugged.

'Because cities send each other heralds?' he asked.

Philopoemen nodded. 'And you are a highly educated man. Dinaeos?'

'Battles happen because both sides think they can win the war with

257

a decisive engagement,' Dinaeos said, like a schoolboy reciting a lesson. 'That's what Philopoemen says.'

Philopoemen frowned. 'What do you say?'

Dinaeos shrugged. 'You're usually right,' he admitted. 'But I've been in four battles, and honestly, I can't tell you why men fight them. Cleomenes ... hmm. Fair enough. He thought that he could stop Doson at Sellasia. But when the Spartans sacked our city ... we didn't fight because we thought we could win.'

'We fought because we had no choice.' Philopoemen nodded agreeably. 'And we lost. Like Leonidas at Thermopylae.'

'Except that many of us survived!' Dinaeos said.

'Many of the men, with armour and horses, survived.' Philopoemen didn't flush, or show anger, but his voice sounded dead. 'Women and children died.' He sat up. 'I'll allow this as a codicil. Sometimes, men fight battles because they are left no choice, except slavery and degradation.'

There was an interruption – people at the door outside. Soon after Lykortas came in with Kleostratos, Aristaenos, and Dadas.

Philopoemen laughed. 'Phila is holding a symposium.'

Phila appeared, dressed regally in a long *himation*. Thais brought two chairs, and then Cyrena came in. She wore a rose-coloured *himation* with a *peplos* covered in embroidery. She looked like a queen, and Alexanor was shocked at the change in her. She held her head differently; she stood differently, and when she sat in a woman's high-backed chair, she did so with a dignity she never showed squatting by a table in a wine shop.

He rose from his couch and bowed. 'Good evening, *despoina*.'

She smiled and nodded, but said nothing.

When the new guests were seated, and had honeyed almonds and watered wine, Phila raised a hand. In it she held a fennel stalk.

'This is a council,' she said. 'Philopoemen, matters in this city are coming to a head. We are your closest friends – we love you. But you need to explain your strategy. Because if we don't understand it, the farmers on the plain and the herdsmen in the hills can be forgiven for not understanding it.'

Philopoemen *smiled*. 'I would like nothing better,' he said. 'Mistress Phila, thanks for this opportunity.'

He rose to his feet and stood like a philosopher delivering a lecture.

He turned to Alexanor. 'Tell me, brother, what is the principal political difference between Gortyna as she is presently constituted, and Knossos?'

Alexanor had a moment to see Cyrena master herself, so desperately did she want to answer the question. *Phila has begged or ordered her to say nothing, and she is taking the injunction literally.*

Alexanor sat up on one arm. He took a sip of wine to moisten his mouth.

'I suppose that the principal difference is that Gortyna is ruled by an assembly of citizens – several thousand. And Knossos by a council of oligarchs. A hundred?' He looked around.

Cyrena winked. Lykortas nodded.

'Exactly,' Philopoemen said. 'Now, brothers and sisters, why do Greeks fight battles?'

Dinaeos shrugged. 'Battles happen when both sides—'

Philopoemen interrupted. 'That's the answer to a different question. Why do Greeks, specifically, fight battles?'

Lykortas finished his first cup of wine and waved for the *hipparchos'* attention.

'Achilles,' he said. 'Greeks want to be like Achilles.'

Philopoemen smiled. 'Yes. That plays a role. Heroism, and the emulation of heroism. But let me suggest, friends, that Greeks fight battles because they want to get wars over with in a hurry. Like our farmers. And why? Because war is an interruption to the life of the community – sowing, reaping, cooking, festivals. War interrupts, and farmers want it over with. *We have no warrior class.*'

'The Spartans ...'

Philopoemen waved Lykortas off. 'And further, because cities discovered that they need a fair number of soldiers to fight decisive battles with a phalanx, they had to grant citizen rights to a great many men. But, by the same logic, a defeat in battle kills many citizens, and thus their army is defeated. Whereas, the defeat of an army of *professional* warriors changes little or nothing. Perhaps that defeat exposes the farms of the losers to looting. Perhaps it means that the victorious army can lay siege to the city of the defeated. But in the old way, in the contest between two citizen militias, the battle *itself* decided the issue. The voters of one assembly killed the voters of the other assembly until the issue was settled.'

The men looked at each other. Cyrena smiled. Alexanor wondered if this line of logic had come from her. What happened behind those dark eyes?

'Knossos is ruled by a tiny council of fabulously rich men who can hire mercenaries forever. Gortyna is ruled by an assembly of the very men who will form our army, with the exception of perhaps a thousand foreign auxiliaries. If we force a battle –' Philopoemen's eyes were very dark – 'victory will win us *nothing*. And defeat will be catastrophic.'

'This is a new way of thinking about war,' Alexanor said.

Philopoemen shook his head. 'No. No, pardon me, brother, but it is not new. Have you read Thucydides?'

Dinaeos sighed and rolled his eyes. Alexanor shook his head. Kleostratos took more wine and translated for Dadas, who laughed.

Lykortas nodded. 'Yes, I have,' he said.

'Well?' Philopoemen asked.

Lykortas shrugged. 'There are many battles in Thucydides.'

'But what did the Spartans do in Attica?' Philopoemen said. 'Athens tried to fight the war at sea. And they tried to undermine the Spartans at home by coercing the helots to revolt. They refused to face the Spartan phalanx in open battle.' He looked around. 'Instead, the Spartans built a fort near Athens and used it to raid and plunder the whole plain of Attica, daring the Athenians to come out and fight. The situation is different here – we are the democrats, and our adversaries are the oligarchs. But we need to fight a war without a decisive battle, if we can. I have built my fort at Petra. I raid the plains and valleys around Knossos.'

Alexanor shook his head. 'I still think this is a new way of looking at war,' he said. 'As a science.'

'This from you?' Phila asked with a very knowing smile. 'Shall I tell you my pulse rate right now?'

Alexanor could not help but grin.

'I do not know that the process of making war can be described as a science,' Philopoemen said. 'But some things are predictable. Alexander of Macedon proved that. Some victories are repeatable – some armies will reliably win. I do not want glory. I want Gortyna to win. I want our reforms to have time to take hold. This is not an empty war fought for possession of a few olive groves. This is a war for men's happiness.'

260

'And women's,' Phila said, before Cyrena could explode.

Philopoemen nodded. 'I know a little about how armies make war on women and children. We are making war on cattle. I agree that other people will be killed. War is terrible – we know it.'

He paused, drank wine, and Cyrena reached out a hand to him, and Alexanor, for the first time, felt an urge to like her. So she knew of Philopoemen's loss ...

Philopoemen took a deep breath. 'I can do no better than to minimise the horror, and do my best to make sure it happens in the valleys around Knossos, and not in the Vale of Gortyna.'

He sat down.

Dinaeos rose. 'Philopoemen, I understand. *I understand.* I am not a rock. I know what will happen if we lose. But I'm going to say to you as someone who is, perhaps, formed of a more common clay, I understand these men, and their numbers grow every day. You need to fight a battle. And while I admire your logic –' he smiled – 'I think you miss something that great Alexander of Macedon understood. Men are not rational creatures. Flesh and blood men –' he nodded to Cyrena – 'and women are creatures of spirit and emotion. If we win a battle –' he waved out towards Knossos – 'the oligarchs will feel it, and feel insecure, regardless of the logic of their position. And by the gods, Philopoemen, however rich they are, they cannot make war forever.'

'And if we lose?' Philopoemen said. 'Let me tell you what happens. Gortyna will fall. The oligarchs will restore their own. There will be hundreds of executions, including, I would guess, everyone in this room. The common men and farmers who demand a battle now will be deprived of their liberty and then of their property, and *all of that can be avoided.*'

'Better win the battle, then,' Dinaeos said. 'Because the time to fight the battle is while our citizen farmers are baying for it like dogs cornering a stag.'

'There is another thing,' Phila said into the silence.

Everyone turned to look at her. Even in the liberal atmosphere of Gortyna, it was rare for any woman to speak out in a political discussion.

'Cyrena?' Phila said gently.

'Zophanes is trying to sell us to Knossos,' Cyrena said.

'You *know* this?' Philopoemen said.

'Soon I'll be able to prove it. And it is *not* Creon, although ordinarily I'd be the first to say that birds of a feather—' Phila shot her a look, and she shook her head. 'Never mind. Zophanes sent a letter to Mineas of Knossos. Two, now. I have intercepted both.' She looked around. 'I would like to send them now. They will do us little damage, but perhaps we will see who else is involved. But he means to betray the city.'

'And if we act against him ...' Dinaeos said.

Lykortas shook his head. 'It will look like politics. Given how often he argues against us ...'

Dadas shrugged. 'Just kill him,' he said.

Cyrena smiled bitterly. 'I think we'd do better to watch him. Learn who follows him.'

'Internal divisions are another reason to fight soon,' Dinaeos said.

Philopoemen looked at his friend for a long time, and there was no sound. No one ate or drank. Later, Alexanor wondered if anyone had moved, or even breathed. Time seemed to stop.

'Well,' Philopoemen said. 'That's me told. Friends, I'm *afraid*. Battles are in the hands of Tyche. We could lose. We could lose for reasons beyond our control.'

Lykortas stood up. 'You of all men take too much on yourself,' he said. 'We will not lose.'

Dinaeos stood up. 'I agree with Lykortas. We have a fine body of men and good officers. We will not lose.'

Philopoemen looked around. 'If I agree to this battle, will you agree that it happens when and where I say?'

'You think you can determine the timing and location of a battle?' Dinaeos asked. 'Are you going to send the oligarchs a herald, in the old way?'

'Not exactly,' Philopoemen said.

CHAPTER FOUR

‒‒◦◦◦‒‒

Knossos and Gortyna

LATE SUMMER TO WINTER 219 BCE

Alexanor went back to the sanctuary the day after the Assembly summoned the phalanx of Gortyna. He loaded a baggage train of medical supplies and took Omphalion, Leon and all ten novices, leaving only two priests and the best-trained slaves to see to the pilgrims.

By the time he took his train of donkeys back over the mountains, accompanied by fifty Aegyptian horses brought by a smuggler and all of Periander's mercenaries, he was late for the muster. When he arrived before the city gates, the 'Army of the Federation of Crete', as it was called, had already marched for the mountain passes.

Alexanor was surprised at how robust the garrison left behind was.

'He left almost two thousand men,' Phila said. She had forage ready for his medical team's animals, and water skins, and wine. 'And he left a garrison in each of the port towns.'

'He recalled my lads,' Periander said. He shrugged. 'And replaced them with locals.'

Alexanor had doubts, but he kept them to himself, and he and Phila and Periander and Leon rode to Petra.

There, thousands of men camped on the ridge overlooking the valleys around Knossos. The camp was organic, but carefully organised; the tent lines were not straight, but conformed to the contours of the

263

hills. The front of the camp was covered by three large forts dug into the hillsides, covering all three of the easy approaches to the ridge.

Lykortas escorted them to their assigned camp area and showed Leon where to site the military hospital.

'So he's going to fight here?' Alexanor asked.

Lykortas shrugged. 'No idea,' he admitted. 'Dinaeos is out with all the cavalry, somewhere to the east. Another raid? A reconnaissance?' The young man shrugged again. 'And Plator the Illyrian, and Telemnastos with the new archer corps, are off to the west, linking up with the Polyrrhenians and stealing more cattle.' He pointed at the camp at their feet. 'There's our phalanx in the centre – on the right are the Lyttians. You know they are Spartan colonists, eh? Anyway, Phil and Dinaeos assume they'll fight like lions as they've lost their city.'

'It is a strange war that Philopoemen is on the same side as the Spartan colonists,' Alexanor said.

'It's odder than that. Sparta's new king has sent a contingent to the Knossians. Quite a sizeable contingent – Spartiates and mercenaries.' Lykortas steadied his horse, which was tormented by the ever-present flies, and shrugged. 'I have trouble remembering what the sides are.'

Phila waved an arm over the valley. 'It's everyone who detests oligarchy against the oligarchs,' she said. 'And we'll accept any ally who will help us. For now.'

'Maybe you should be *Strategos*,' Lykortas said. 'You certainly look like a goddess on horseback.'

'Where is Philopoemen?' Alexanor asked.

Philopoemen was far down the valley towards Knossos when Alexanor found him, the only man on horseback with a hundred *peltastoi* and Cretan archers. The archers were the only genuine federal troops; the League of Crete, established by Philopoemen in Philip of Macedon's name, had put together a *taxeis* of the selected *epheboi* of all the cities opposed to Knossos, trained archers with excellent armour, the kind of men usually sent overseas as mercenaries. They were paid by the 'Federation'. They wore some armour; the richest wore maille cuirasses and good bronze helmets, but they carried the heavy bows favoured by Cretan archers. They also had swords, and light bucklers.

They were moving down the valley. Ahead was a village – twenty white buildings shining in the sunlight, and a small temple to Hera, its sacred precinct defined by a wall of stones culled from the fields around it by farmers.

'Basileus,' Philopoemen said. 'I've been through before.' He smiled sadly. 'I doubt they like me.' He pointed north. 'Three valleys converge here.'

There were, in fact, steep, knife-edge ridges towering over the village.

'Three?' Alexanor asked, dismounting. He was not used to riding and his thighs hurt. Again.

'They're all roughly parallel and fairly narrow,' Philopoemen said.

Ahead, the archers moved forward carefully, exploring every wall, every stand of trees.

'The Knossians have hired a Spartan commander,' Philopoemen said. 'Nabis. Remember him?'

Alexanor smiled. 'He wanted to defile the sanctuary at Epidauros. And then you crushed his cavalry at Sellasia.'

'Yes, well, now he has lots of men and, let's admit it, he's quite competent.'

Philopoemen rode on in silence, his light troops scouring the fields. A handful of federal *epheboi* moved into the village proper, and then six of them went into the temple sanctuary.

'Abandoned,' Philopoemen said. 'Good, in a way. Fewer civilian casualties.'

'You plan to fight here,' Alexanor said, realisation suddenly dawning.

'No,' Philopoemen said.

A young man with blond hair emerged from the temple and waved. All of the archers relaxed.

'No,' Philopoemen repeated. 'I just want this Nabis to *think* I plan to fight here.'

The Boeotian mercenaries and the Achaeans, some of them now mounted on the Aegyptian horses Alexanor had brought, moved forward in the early afternoon to Basileus.

Philopoemen had his horse tied to a pine tree just outside the sacred grove. His light infantry were mostly asleep in the shade of the olive groves, with a handful of sentries thrown out to the north, and two men, changed every hour, on the highest ridge above the town. Periander marched in and occupied the houses.

Alexanor noticed that the mercenaries were better armed and

armoured than they had been the year before. Chain maille *thorakes* were now everywhere; new bronze helmets sat on every brow.

'I should bring up the hospital,' Alexanor said.

Philopoemen was reading from a pair of scrolls, his back to the temple precinct wall.

'No need,' he said. 'We won't fight here.'

Out on the plain of the valley, the fifty newly mounted Achaeans rode up and down, instructed by Aristaenos and Kleostratos. Most of them were just learning to ride.

They raised an impressive cloud of dust. They also entertained the *epheboi* who were awake by falling off, and other antics.

'But you brought up more men,' Alexanor said.

'I'm a deceptive bastard.' Philopoemen smiled. 'By the gods, I hope I am. We'll know in a couple of hours.'

'But ...'

'The Achaeans are here to raise a dust cloud. The Boeotians are among my most trustworthy infantry. You know what is hard? Retreating. It demoralises, and it seems pointless, and men desert, or lose cohesion. It's all right here.' Philopoemen held up the scrolls. 'Xenophon.'

'Ah, Xenophon,' Alexanor said. 'I read some of his *Memorabilia*.'

'This is *Anabasis*. Ten thousand men retreating across Asia.' Philopoemen smiled. 'If this works, we will need to get out of here in a great hurry. I can't have amateurs, and I need the men here to trust me.'

The sun began to sink into the hills in the west.

Philopoemen was obviously nervous. To add to his apprehension, messengers began to come in from Lykortas, and from Antiphatas, requesting permission to bring the phalanx forward.

'Gods, no!' Philopoemen shook his head.

He called for Arkas, his groom, and then turned to Alexanor.

'Everyone knows you. I need you to be my voice. Go back and make them stop. I do not want the phalanx here. I am not fighting here.'

Alexanor had seldom seen his friend so emotional.

'Of course,' he said.

He mounted the fine gelding that Philopoemen had given him two years before and rode back along the main valley and then, as quickly as he could manage, up the ridge to the lines before Petra. Arkas rode with him, silent.

Antiphatas was waiting at the edge of the fortified camp, fully armed. He had his helmet up on the back of his head and his heavy *aspis* at his feet.

'We're ready to march,' the Cretan said. 'It's late in the day. Does he still intend to fight today?'

Alexanor slid from his tired horse.

'He begs you not to advance. I believe he is setting a trap for the Knossians. He does not intend to fight down below, and he ordered me not to advance with the hospital.'

'All he has down there is fuckin' foreigners!' an angry hoplite spat.

'We want to do our own fighting,' said another.

'He is deceiving the enemy,' Alexanor called out. 'And all he took were the men best at running away. I assume he doesn't think you men are any good at running away.'

'Nicely said,' Arkas whispered. 'Damn, sir.'

Alexanor watered his horse, drank some himself, and ate bread and olives with Phila.

'I want to be down there. What's he doing?'

'Everyone wants to be down there. I think he's doing something underhanded and he doesn't want witnesses,' Alexanor said. 'I'm still not convinced he means to fight a battle.'

'He can't go back now!' Phila said. 'The phalanx would crucify him.'

'I'm not convinced that Philopoemen always knows what the rest of the world is thinking,' Alexanor said. 'I'm going back. I beg you not to come. If a woman—'

'I know,' Phila said. 'If a woman comes to a battle, it's the end of the world. I'll just wait in camp and see who wins, and then I can die ingloriously.'

'In this case,' Alexanor said, 'I mean that if you come with me, Antiphatas and all the rest will insist they must come too.'

She handed him a Boeotian cup of unwatered wine.

'Fine. But please tell me everything when you return.'

'I promise,' Alexanor said.

He and Arkas slipped back down the ridge as the shadows of the trees became long stripes of shade across the barren ground. There

267

was dust in the valley – a haze over Basileus – but also puffs of more distant dust, lit red by the setting sun, over towards Knossos, twenty stades beyond the tiny village.

Once they were clear of the rocky slopes, Arkas led the way at a gallop and Alexanor got his weight forward and survived. He was a far better rider than he had been at Sellasia, but he didn't gallop very often, and staying on was the limit of his ambitions.

He could measure Philopoemen's mood by the speed with which the commander shot to his feet when he saw the approaching horsemen.

Alexanor saluted like a soldier. 'They're still in camp,' he said.

He noted that Dadas was there, covered in dust and looking like a cat who had eaten the family cream.

'They're so late I thought they weren't coming,' Philopoemen said, pointing at dust clouds in the direction of Knossos. He rubbed his hands together. 'I feel like a boy about to kiss his first girl. Never let anyone tell you that command is a wonderful thing.'

Alexanor guzzled some water and wished he hadn't drunk Phila's unwatered wine.

Dadas rode away into the gathering gloom, headed north, towards Knossos.

'Must you be as mysterious as a playwright?' Alexanor asked. 'Is this some hitherto concealed flair for drama?'

Philopoemen turned his horse and watched the hills either side of the central pass above them.

'For three days I've been baiting the Knossians to come out and fight,' he said. 'And now, too late in the day to actually fight, they're coming out.'

'So they don't intend to fight,' Alexanor said.

'That's my guess. It's fine with me – I didn't intend to fight today either. Maybe Nabis is smarter than I expected.'

'Maybe the oligarchs are merely cautious?' Alexanor said.

'Why? None of them are doing the fighting.'

'Rich men think of these things differently,' Alexanor insisted, thinking of his father. And Aspasia. *I really need to do something about that*, he thought, before dismissing it from his mind.

Suddenly, the head of the pass seemed to erupt with dust. Cavalrymen began to crest the pass and ride down the long road to the village. There were more than a hundred of them.

'Tell Periander to get moving,' Philopoemen said to Arkas, who cantered away to the village.

The Boeotian mercenaries piled out of the houses of the town, set fire to two of them, formed sloppily, and began a hasty retreat up the valley.

'Now Aristaenos,' Philopoemen said.

He motioned to Alexanor, who, reduced to the role of messenger, ran across the hard-packed fields. As soon as Aristaenos saw him waving, he looked up, saw the cavalry coming, and his trumpeter sounded a long call. The Achaeans filed off, already better horsemen, and headed towards the distant, looming rock of Petra. They raised even more dust than the Boeotian mercenaries.

The oncoming cavalrymen, clearly Aetolians, gave hunting cries and broke into a gallop, riding hard in pursuit.

'Are we in danger?' Alexanor asked, riding back to his friend. Philopoemen was alone in the little agora of the village, and the Aetolians were just a stade away.

Philopoemen no longer looked apprehensive. He was calm.

'No,' he said.

The Knossian advance guard swept into the outskirts of Basileus, and the federal archers who had been hiding in the long grass stood up and loosed a volley of arrows into them from very close; most men shot two or three shafts. A few missed, and a handful of Aetolians, accompanied by horses without riders, broke away from the front of the town. Other horses put their heads down and began to munch at the grass, ignoring their dead or dying masters.

There were forty men dead. One older man screamed and screamed like a woman giving birth. Ravens began to gather from the west.

Philopoemen rode over to one of the archers and prevented him from lofting a shaft at the fleeing survivors.

'Let them go,' he said.

'You are merciful,' Alexanor said.

'Not really. Let's go.'

The Cretan archers plucked the shafts they had prepared by sticking them in the ground at their feet, and dropped them back into ready quivers. Then the entire *taxeis* began to trot back up the ridge, abandoning the town. They moved more quickly than Alexanor would have thought possible – as fast, or faster, than the Achaean cavalry.

'Fit young men,' Philopoemen said, watching Telemnastos sprint past. 'That was our part. The rest is up to our opponents, and Dinaeos.'

The Cretan archers ran on, vanishing into the rising dust of the retreating Achaeans. Alexanor reckoned they must be invisible from the pass above.

'One thing you learn about on cattle raids is dust,' Philopoemen said.

Then he was quiet as they trotted along the road towards distant Gortyna, beyond Petra and the high pass.

Looking back, Alexanor saw a scarlet-cloaked figure emerge from the mouth of the pass of the central valley. He raised an arm imperiously and bronze-clad figures began to tumble down the slope towards the village. Other men, shrouded in dusk and dust, rolled out to the left and right, staying on the heights. The enemy commander was marshalling his light troops carefully, sending *peltastoi* well around the village to make sure the hills were clear of any traps. They passed the mouth of the first valley and nothing happened. Alexanor was getting a pulled muscle in his neck from turning to look, and he was sending confusing signals to his gelding.

Philopoemen got up the first serious slope of the long ridge towards Petra and turned his charger, looking back. Alexanor rode to join him. When he turned, there were Knossian dust clouds all around the village. From their new position above the valley's flanks, the setting sun shone bright on their road. But down in the valley, the light was blocked, and swirls of dust spiralled in the murk and gloom, fattened by the Aetolians and the Knossian light troops.

'When …?' Alexanor turned his horse. 'Where is Dinaeos?'

Philopoemen shrugged. 'Twenty stades away, I hope.'

The Knossian professionals had now blocked all three valley entrances.

'That man is capable,' Philopoemen said. 'A little cautious, but he's made sure he cannot be ambushed again.' He smiled, slapped Alexanor on the back, and turned his horse. 'Let's go. We won't know anything for hours.'

'I don't know anything now,' Alexanor said, and rode behind the commander.

*

Dawn.

The magnificent wheel of the sun crept up over the distant rim of the world. From the very top of the rock of Petra, Alexanor greeted the sun with a prayer. Beneath his feet, the various *taxeis* of the Cretan League were forming across the sheepfolds and barley fields of the ridge top. To the south, they could see the smoke of breakfast fires from Gortyna, and, far away, at the edge of darkness, a glimmer of the sea. To the west, the rising sun lit the mountain tops of central Crete, running like waves on a windy day away and away. And to the east, the valley floors were gradually catching the orange light; the wheat and barley in the fields seemed to glow.

Alexanor sang the invocation to Helios.

At his feet, the men of Gortyna were arrayed by Antiphatas. The army was forming in a rough crescent, with the Lyttians at the far right and the new Achaean cavalry still exercising on the left, almost six stades away. The ridge was too small for the whole League force.

The rising sun gradually lit the hillsides to the north, over towards Basileus, and then, a little at a time, the empty valley floor.

There was no enemy army facing them in the long valley to the north.

'Someone's going to be very disappointed,' Lykortas said.

Indeed, the discontent of the phalanx could be heard all the way down the ridge.

Dinaeos laughed. 'Only an amateur is sorry to miss a battle,' he said.

'You're back,' Alexanor said.

'So I am. Thodor is still out there. I just brought the news.' Dinaeos yawned.

'Which is?' Alexanor asked, impatient. 'Men have been strangled for less.'

'I'll help.' Lykortas pinned Dinaeos' arms as the man laughed.

Philopoemen rode up. 'Do you need rescuing?'

'They want to know all your secrets,' Dinaeos said.

Philopoemen gave them his odd, lopsided smile. The one that meant he knew something.

'Come and listen to my speech,' he said.

Fifteen minutes later, Philopoemen sat on his magnificent Thessalian charger, his armour glowing in the rising sun, in front of the Gortynian phalanx.

'I hate to disappoint you, gentlemen,' he called out, 'but our friends in Knossos have declined to meet us. It's a little like being left alone at a symposium. We had a very small fight yesterday – a small affray, a few cavalrymen ambushed.' He paused. 'All theirs.'

Men laughed.

'So we'll wait here for a day or two. I've a mind to march down the valley and perhaps burn the standing crops. But they won't come out this year. The oligarchs are going to cower behind the towers of Knossos. Their army is half again as large as ours, and *they will not face us.*'

Philopoemen's horse flinched at the cheers, and he turned it in a tight circle.

He motioned to Arkas behind him, and the man led a pair of donkeys forward.

'On a more positive note,' he said, 'we did capture most of their baggage train. Including a great deal of newly minted coin. I wonder what they're using to pay their mercenaries tonight!'

'So no battle?' Alexanor said quietly to Dinaeos.

'Not this year,' Dinaeos said with evident satisfaction.

Winter, and Alexanor had made the trip over the mountain to see Phila and enjoy the company of his friends. There were fewer than a dozen pilgrims at the sanctuary. Once again, he lay on the *kline*, this time with Phila. Philopoemen lay with Cyrena, and Lykortas with his latest conquest, a local girl close to his own age named Andromache. Dinaeos shared his couch with Dadas, the Thracian, who could not take his eyes off Cyrena.

'We got in behind their rearguard when they all pushed forward to storm Basileus,' Dinaeos said. 'I admit there was a good deal of luck involved.'

'Luck my arse.' Plator, the Illyrian chieftain, downed a whole bowl of watered wine.

His partner was Berenike, a local *hetaera*, tall, with a heavy, beautiful face. Alone of the women, she had come in revealing clothes and make-up, as if she'd expected a very different kind of party, but Alexanor noted that Phila was as welcoming to her as to the other women.

The Illyrian was dishevelled, to say the least, his tunic rumpled up to show his heavily tattooed thighs, his bare arms showing gold and dark ink together.

'We made a good plan and it worked,' the Illyrian said. He raised the empty cup in salute to Philopoemen. 'When I came down that hillside and saw all them donkeys, I thought, fuck, Philopoemen had that right!'

Penelope smiled automatically. She kept looking about, a little like a trapped animal, trying to decide what role the women in the room played.

Dinaeos shook his head. 'Still luck. Luck that their rearguard pushed forward and left all the beasts huddled on the road.'

'Good luck comes with careful planning,' Lykortas said.

'Make that up yourself?' Dadas asked.

'No,' Lykortas admitted.

'In the spring the citizens of Gortyna will demand another battle,' Alexanor said.

'Maybe not,' Philopoemen said. 'We covered a lot of bills with the gold we took. The farmers won't feel overtaxed in the spring, all of our mercenaries are paid. We have paid for more armour for the phalanx and more for the archers. *And* there's money left to pay for road improvements.'

Phila shook her head. 'If Philip is as hard-pressed as I hear,' she said, 'we'll be pushed to fight, but this time from above.'

'We could double the League's archer corps and then send half of it to Philip,' Philopoemen said.

'We could just fight,' Dinaeos said. 'You fooled us. You never meant to fight.'

'It's not a game,' Philopoemen said. 'I would have fought, if Nabis had been more of a fool – if he had pushed forward and camped below us at Petra, or better yet, tried to storm our positions.'

'In other words, if he was an idiot and you could have an easy win,' Lykortas said.

Philopoemen didn't take offence. 'Exactly. This is not a game. I am not actually Achilles. Instead of a bloody meeting, we took their money and left them unable to prosecute a war. Their farmers must be ready to revolt, and we didn't lose a single man. We bought time. Our phalanx is better trained now, our cavalry is better horsed.'

'And you keep your emergency powers,' Phila said. 'I'm sorry, dear, but that's what they'll say.'

Philopoemen shrugged. 'I could resign. But what's the point? I know what I'm doing.'

Phila turned on him. 'I'm sure you do, but your very cockiness is going to tell against you. And all the changes—'

'Changes you supported,' Philopoemen said, stung.

'Of course I supported them! But every change creates dissent, and there will be more of it when we widen the franchise to include the new *thētes* class.' She looked around. 'Your "reforms" are increasingly revolutionary.'

'The laws protecting prostitutes passed easily enough,' Lykortas said.

'Gortyna has always been fairly liberal that way,' Telemnastos said. 'Our old law code has the same stuff. You can read it in the stadium.'

Philopoemen's jaw was set. 'I won't fight a battle unless I have to,' he said. 'They're fools if they want to fight when we can just sit tight, steal their cattle, and wait for them to surrender.'

'You are ruining war,' Thodor said.

'You love cattle raiding,' Philopoemen said.

'I love riding on a moonlit night, fooling my foe, taking his cows, and slipping away leaving some throats cut,' the Thracian said. 'Your way is like stealing a baby goat from a little child. They—'

Suddenly Philopoemen got up, leaving Cyrena, and walked out.

After a moment of stunned silence, Alexanor got up and followed him.

The *hipparchos* stood in the alley behind Phila's house. He was looking at the stars. There was snow on the hillsides, bright in the moonlight.

'I feel like I'm talking to children,' Philopoemen said.

'I'm sorry you think we're like children,' Alexanor said. 'In fact, I think we're all telling you the same thing we told you the last time we were together. You have to pay attention to what men *want*. It is not entirely rational. And Phila is right – Philip will demand that we finish Knossos.'

'Knossos is richer and more powerful than we are, especially with Rhodes and Sparta paying the bills.' Philopoemen continued to stare into the darkness. 'Do you remember what Aratos said? His goal was that we should form a Cretan League and create a stable ally for the Achaean League.'

'My memory is that all he wanted was to appear to support Philip.' Alexanor shrugged. 'But I know what you're saying.'

'Yes, well, in three years we've accomplished it all. In the fullness of time, Knossos will fall, from *inside*, when their farmers topple the oligarchs, and we will be prosperous and free. Without a battle. The odds were impossibly long, and it's all but finished, and all of you want a *battle*.'

'I do not particularly want a battle, brother,' Alexanor said with a smile.

'Philip hasn't even covered the cost of the mercenaries the last year.' Philopoemen sounded plaintive. 'Why should I care what he wants?'

Alexanor said nothing.

'I've built the best rough-terrain fighters in the Greek world, and we have, effectively, made it impossible for our opponents to leave their walls. We don't even need to lay siege to their city. We'll never cut off the head of the Hydra, but we can bleed it with a thousand tiny, controlled cuts.'

Alexanor shrugged. 'I am here to tell you that we all trust you, and Phila is on your side. You don't need to walk away.'

Philopoemen nodded, and then turned and threw his arms around his friend.

'I'm sorry,' he said. 'I thought ... I felt ...' He let go. 'Never mind. Damn, it's easier to walk out than to walk back in.'

'I know,' Alexanor said.

Later that night, Phila turned to him.

'I'm leaving,' she said.

'Leaving me?' Alexanor said. He'd known it was coming.

'Leaving Crete. Philopoemen is right about most things. The war here is done. The laws are passed. The Cretan League is built.' She sighed and stroked his neck. 'I thought Philopoemen might be the man to change the world, but I think he plans to make a life here on Crete, settle down, and play the big fish in a very small pool. I've played the great woman here. I'm going back to Athens.'

'Why?'

She smiled. 'The bigger war is not over. Change is coming. Crete is only the beginning.'

'Am I, too, only a means to an end?' he asked. It hurt far more than he'd expected.

She grinned. 'You, my dear sir, are my winter's entertainment.' She smiled. 'Seriously – you encourage me to monogamy. I have had no other lover in quite some time. Maybe I'm growing old.' She drank a little wine and shook her head. 'I'm not a wife. I enjoyed playing house, especially with a man who was away on the other side of a mountain most of the time. But in the spring I'll go back to Athens. Why don't you rescue your lady-love?'

'Rescue her? She's married ...' He didn't want to discuss Aspasia. He wanted Phila. In that moment, he realised, too late, that he loved her.

'So what?' Phila smiled lazily. 'You live openly with a notorious woman, my friend. Living with someone else's wife will hardly wreck your reputation. And you're a priest. You have no political career to ruin, do you?'

'My lover is giving me advice on my next lover,' Alexanor said. He knew enough to keep the tone light, although his body was as tense as it would be before combat. He made himself relax. 'Besides, I will have enough trouble being confirmed as high priest without adding "seduction of a rich man's wife" to the crimes of "revolutionary" and "Stoic".'

'Goodness, my dear, I've counselled men about choosing brides, this is nothing.' She shrugged. 'She deserves a life.'

'Would *you* marry me?' Alexanor asked suddenly.

She rolled over atop him, planted herself on his chest, and kissed him, long and deep.

'No,' she said. 'I would if I were Aspasia, but not as Phila.'

'Why not?'

She shrugged. 'We can spend tonight arguing. Or we can do other things.'

'Never?' he asked.

'Never,' she said.

'Will I see you again?'

'Of course!' she said. 'I need you and your Rhodian connections for my war on the slave trade.'

'That's hopeful,' he said. 'When does that start?'

'I've already begun,' she said.

BOOK IV

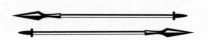

THE MAN-KILLER

CHAPTER ONE

—⟨◦⟩—

Lentas, Crete

218 BCE

Spring. Water on the hillsides, and water threatening the foundations of the north-facing sanctuary wall. More rain than Alexanor had ever seen on Crete, and a consequent explosion of colour; flowers everywhere.

Diophanes sailed out of the east with a cargo straight from Kos: two priests and two priestesses. And a heap of scroll tubes, as if all the columns of a miniature temple had collapsed on his work table.

Among them was another letter from Aspasia.

Why am I unhappy? she concluded. *I am not beaten; I have food, wine, and money. And yet, the words "your weaving is marvellous, my dear" are not the summit of my ambitions. I am considering writing a book,* Antioeconomicus, *a book on how a woman should train her husband to his duties. Write to me! Tell me a tale from outside my house.*

His head still hard from a long night with Diophanes in which they refought every action in which they'd participated, mocked their superiors, wept over their dead and derided almost every aspect of modern politics, Alexanor sat down to write to her. At first it was difficult, but once he allowed himself to write about the near collapse of the retaining wall above the sanctuary, he soon found that he'd filled six sheets of joined papyrus with incident and scenario: the fight at Petra; his friend Philopoemen; his horror at dissection. He almost lined that section out, but in the end he did not. Instead, he closed with a summing up of his own situation.

I am master of a small temple, and I love my work. I have found
an area of research too great for one man, or even one team of men,
in one lifetime, but we heal people here, with the god's help, and
I find myself happy, when I allow myself to think at all. And yet,
despite my peers and my little wars, sometimes empty, too.

He stared at those words, surprised. Again, he thought of scraping them clean or lining them out, but he realised they were true. And when he allowed himself the time for self-examination, which he seldom did, he realised that this emptiness was what Phila saw.

He stared at the papyrus until Leon came in.

'Are we going to tackle all those scrolls today, or just drink more?' Leon said. He was smiling.

Alexanor drank some water. Then he and Leon dived into the mound of scroll tubes, which included everything from the official notification of Leon's elevation to the rank of senior priest to an indemnity for twenty sacrificial sheep owed as a tithe to the mother house on Kos.

Alexanor looked up. 'What year was Antiphilus *Archon Basileus* in Athens?' he asked.

Leon pursed his lips. 'No idea,' he admitted.

'Most of these tithe bills are dated based on Athenian festivals,' Alexanor said pettishly. 'Thrasyphon? Is that even a Greek name?'

'Thrasyphon was the *Archon Basileus* of Athens in the last festival cycle but one,' said a woman's voice. Alexanor looked up, prepared to be annoyed.

The woman was short and very muscular; his age or a little older. He rose.

She bowed. 'Hierophant,' she said, and knelt.

No priest had ever knelt to him. He laughed nervously.

Leon offered the woman a hand, but she rose to her feet effortlessly, and with athletic grace.

'We aren't much for bows here,' Alexanor said.

'Hmm,' the woman sniffed.

'I am Alexanor of Rhodes.' He offered the woman a masculine handclasp.

She accepted it hesitantly, but her smile was solid.

'Lysistrata, daughter of Artistion. Of Athens. I am here with the priestesses you ordered from Kos.'

'Lysistrata.' Alexanor smiled.

'I have taken shit about my name all my life,' the woman said. 'She is an ancestress, though. High priestess of Athena.'

'So you know the Athenian festival calendar?' Leon asked.

'Intimately. I was a priestess of Nike, as well, before I left for Kos. Here, let me help. On Kos, they say that Lentas is behind on its tithes – more than a decade behind.'

Alexanor leant back and steepled his hands.

'I understand that there is some bad feeling between Kos and Epidauros. I have sent my tithes to Epidauros. It is my understanding that this place was founded from there.'

'Trust me,' Lysistrata said. 'You do not want to get involved. It's petty beyond all comprehension. I thought I'd seen it all on the Acropolis, but this isn't even about money or power. It's ...'

Leon nodded. 'That's what I thought. Alexanor, to the best of our ability, we should do what each asks, and be silent.'

'So ...'

'Send the sheep to Kos. They asked. And twenty sheep seems a fair trade for four new priests.'

'Ouch,' Lysistrata said. But she smiled, and Alexanor already liked her.

The arrival of the priestesses changed many things. Suddenly, the local aristocrats were happy to send their daughters to the sanctuary to serve, and a host of women pilgrims appeared looking for health. Some of the older priests muttered about 'women's complaints' but Lysistrata and her partner, Antigone, leapt into the work.

They taught the latest developments in medicine: Antigone had attended a long series of lectures in Alexandria, and so had one of the new priests from Kos, Diodoros. The barracks was full, and the priests' table every night was a rapid-fire symposium on blood vessels and heart rate, hair growth and fingernails, hygiene and trauma.

Diodoros had witnessed the dissection of a criminal at Alexandria. Midway through his exposition, using almonds and peaches to lay out body parts on the communal dinner table, Alexanor pushed his bowl of lamb stew away.

'You must be joking,' he said. 'Or I misheard you. You suggested this man was ... alive.'

'Oh, yes,' Diodoros said.

Antigone nodded. 'It's true. I was there, although I was ... disguised.' Diodoros looked at her, as if to ask, *you were?*

But then he turned back. 'Yes, the king gives the philosophers hardened criminals – rapists and murderers. The philosophers dissect them alive. They are given heavy drugs.'

'Gods,' Leon said, pushing his bowl away.

'They are terrible men,' Antigone said. 'Who commit terrible crimes.'

'And we learn so much,' Diodoros said. 'I have seen a heart beating inside a man's chest.'

'But what if the men are not guilty?' Alexanor said.

'Even if they are, this is *hubris* of the most outrageous kind,' Leon said.

Lysistrata nodded. 'I'm inclined to agree with you, but I'm old-fashioned. The world is changing. People care only for what works, now, immediately. No one cares for a more measured pace and respect for tradition.'

'And yet, with the knowledge we gain from these criminals, we can heal wounds and save people,' Diodoros said.

Theophilus nodded. 'I agree, sir. Is it not our duty to heal the sick?'

'Our first duty is to the gods,' Alexanor said, and he felt both pompous and hypocritical.

'Don't you find a little power awakens the petty tyrant in all of us?' Alexanor asked.

He was sitting opposite Philopoemen in the older man's favourite wine shop, a small taverna high on the slopes of the acropolis of Gortyna with a stunning view, good wine and excellent olive oil. Spring was a riot of colour beyond the walls, and Alexanor had just led the procession by which Apollo and Demeter welcomed the new growth, winding through all the streets of the upper town, blessing the doors and promising fertility. It was the first time he'd been invited to take part.

Philopoemen smiled. That spring, he seemed to smile all the time. Antiphatas had just been elected *Archon* by the Assembly, and Philopoemen had been elected *strategos*: a public office which merely confirmed the role he had played the year before. Aristaenos, not Dinaeos, had been chosen as the Cretan League's *hipparchos*. Aristaenos had politicked hard, explaining as if ruefully that as he was the Achaean League officer, not Dinaeos, he needed to be in command of the Achaean League forces. It had been the sole moment of dissension that spring – a little introduction of faction in an otherwise unified front.

'My petty tyrant is a dangerous animal at all times,' Philopoemen conceded. 'Once you allow yourself to believe that you know better than your fellow man about anything, there is no limit.'

'And yet—'

'And yet a fair number of them are utter fools,' Philopoemen said. 'Listen, brother. Is it true that you have priestesses now? Are they also healers?'

'Yes. Remarkably well-trained. For the moment they will only practise on women, though. I find Cretans even more ... hmm ... traditionally minded ... than I am.' Alexanor shrugged. Phila had changed him.

Philopoemen nodded. 'I am the revolutionary here, and yet, there are things that I hear that make me wonder ... Never mind. I hope that one of your priestesses will attend Cyrena. She is pregnant, and she is so thin I fear ...'

'Every husband since Priam fears for his wife,' Alexanor said, his bedside manner long practised. 'But you will like Lysistrata. A fine woman from one of the oldest families in Athens. Probably a better doctor than I am myself.'

'Ha, never say it. Most of the old troopers think you can raise the dead.'

Philopoemen waved, and Dinaeos joined them, with Lykortas at his heels.

'This season, we'll have three hundred horse,' Dinaeos said. 'And another hundred Thracians if Thodor has found them.'

'What's the prospect for this season?' Alexanor asked.

'You tell me,' Philopoemen said. 'I just watched you make the sacrifices.'

'Damn it, *Strategos*!' Alexanor said. 'I'm a doctor, not an seer! Come to think of it, *you* are a priest of Zeus.'

A young man came in, glanced around, and asked the door slave a question. Alexanor watched the man; he had the too-bright eyes of a man with a disease of the mind. And when he left, he appeared to be talking to himself.

But his train of thought was wrecked when Cyrena, round in the belly, tall and still a little feral, stalked in. She smiled brilliantly, and indeed, her skin had a flush of health that Alexanor knew was pregnancy, but which suited the African woman. Philopoemen rose and kissed her, one hand on her belly, and she laughed up at him.

The men rose. Women were not generally seen in wine shops unless they were relatives of the owner, or slaves, or prostitutes.

Lykortas passed Philopoemen and kissed Cyrena on both cheeks, a very recent innovation in greeting.

'You are bold.'

'I am a retired strumpet. Not the first time I've been in a wine shop, though it might be the first time all the patrons stood when I entered. Hello, Alexanor! You looked like one of the gods themselves, giving the sacrifice today.'

Alexanor flushed and made a sign to avert the revenge of a jealous god.

'You say such things,' he said. 'But I'm glad I looked my part.'

She raised an eyebrow. 'Ain't you an odd one, though. I'm not just painting you in honey, love – you are the best priest I know.' She sat on Philopoemen's lap, smiling beneficently, like a dark-eyed Aphrodite, but then she leant over, her face severe. 'Listen, gents. One of the sisters has sent me some news from Knossos.'

All of the men leant forward, and she spoke quietly. 'Nabis is assembling his forces. Right now. That is, yesterday about this time. He had all his Illyrians formed in the agora and all his Aetolian cavalry. But they are waiting for something.'

'Waiting for something?' Philopoemen asked.

'He has quartered his Spartan mercenaries on the merchants and he's asked the Rhodians to land their marines on his command,' she said.

Dinaeos made a face and chewed on his moustache.

'That goes with what I saw,' he agreed.

'Saw?' Alexanor asked.

'Dadas and I rode pretty much to the gates of Knossos yesterday,' Dinaeos said. 'We saw soldiers, but they were going *in* the gates.'

'Could Nabis intend to overthrow the oligarchs?' Lykortas asked. 'He'd hardly be the first Spartan mercenary to kill off his employers.'

'Maybe that's it,' Philopoemen said. 'Regardless, we should summon our forces.'

Arkas came out of the back with the owner and put a pitcher of wine on the table, and then went back behind the curtain.

'The farmers are sowing,' Lykortas said.

'I know,' Philopoemen said. 'I am a farmer. I even have a farm. It's a terrible time to summon the phalanx.' He looked around. 'But we have our Illyrians, three hundred cavalry, and the archers – that is, we can have them in five days. Less, maybe.'

'Periander ...'

'Periander has been offered a great deal more money than we can afford to go and fight for Antiokos,' Philopoemen said. 'We can't count on him. I need to talk to him, man to man, anyway. He owes us something for all the new armour we got him last year.'

Philopoemen rose. 'Where is Periander?' he asked Dinaeos.

'Phaistos,' Dinaeos said. 'With Kleostratos, reviewing the fortifications.'

Philopoemen stepped away from the wine-stained table, and Cyrena rose.

'You can't just leave, honey,' she said.

'Lykortas, are you up for a ride?' Philopoemen asked.

Lykortas began to rise, and the wild-eyed young man who'd come in and left earlier walked to the doorway, turned, and beckoned at the street.

Alexanor was still drinking his wine. He looked up when Cyrena shoved Philopoemen hard into the table, the force of it moving the table towards Alexanor, pinning him against the wall.

Alexanor was sprayed with blood, and he still didn't know what was happening. He tried to kick the table back, but Philopoemen was lying on it and blood was pouring out of him; his weight held the table against Alexanor's gut.

285

'Finish him!' roared a voice.

A man with a *kopis* charged into the group. Dinaeos was pinned with Alexanor. Lykortas had his *xiphos* clear of the scabbard and had buried it in another man. Dadas was wrestling with a third attacker.

Cyrena threw herself on the *kopis* wielder. He cut at her, his weapon chopping two fingers into her skull; but she clung to him, holding him, and he fell backwards with the pregnant woman atop him.

Blood was everywhere – blood and spilt wine.

Alexanor and Dinaeos managed to overturn the table. Dinaeos exploded from behind it. He was as big as a Titan, and Alexanor was not much smaller. Alexanor had no weapon but the razor-sharp knife he wore on a cord around his neck – more of a scientific instrument than a weapon. He nonetheless used it like a dewclaw, opening Dadas' assailant's thigh to the groin, severing both of the main blood vessels.

Dinaeos caught Cyrena's assailant as he rose from the floor and broke his neck.

'Ware!' Lykortas called.

There was a man in the doorway, enveloped in a charcoal-coloured *himation* like a caul of smoke.

Alexanor turned.

The man had a *gastraphetes*, the heavy crossbow that snipers used in sieges. He raised it.

Cyrena, blood from her head wound running down her face, pushed herself to her feet. The crossbow bolt caught her in the chest, between her breasts. She didn't fall backwards; she simply subsided to the floor like an upper-class woman in a faint, with dignity.

Philopoemen, on the floor, had another such bolt in his gut. He was screaming in pain.

Dinaeos ran into the street, chasing the archer and bellowing for help.

Alexanor knelt by Philopoemen. Then he looked at Dadas, who had a bad cut right to the bone in one hand, where he'd caught a sword; the cut had almost severed his left thumb. Lykortas had lost an ear.

'Apollo!' Lykortas said. 'Is he dead?'

'*She* is,' Dadas said. 'Gods, why?'

Alarms were sounding through the town.

'Arkas!' Alexanor roared.

Philopoemen's groom appeared a minute later, with hot water and linens.

'Is he ...?' Arkas was white as parchment. 'Oh, gods,' he said.

Cyrena was obviously dead, lying in a pool of her own blood. Flies were already gathering. Lykortas, with some foresight, sat by the door with his sword across his lap, watching every passer-by, blood streaming down his face.

Alexanor went to Cyrena. She was dead, as he feared, and his first examination showed that her baby could not be saved; too young, too soon. Moving without apparent volition, he cleaned and bandaged Dadas before turning to Lykortas.

'Save him,' Lykortas said.

'I cannot,' Alexanor said. 'It would require a miracle, the very will of the gods.'

He bandaged Lykortas' head, and then went to Philopoemen. The Achaean was on the floor, curled around the crossbow bolt in his gut, but he had managed to crawl the half a pace to Cyrena, coating the left side of his body in blood from the floor. He had her outflung hand in his.

'Save her,' he croaked to Alexanor.

Her staring eyes were beyond saving.

'She tried to save *you*,' Alexanor said.

'Oh, the gods ...'

Philopoemen lay still, his chest rising and falling too rapidly. His pulse was rapid, but scattered. Suddenly he stiffened, as if in pain. His eyes opened, hot with intelligence.

His bloody hands grabbed Alexanor's head.

'Listen to me!' he spat through gritted teeth. 'Thissss! This is ... Nabis!' He groaned aloud. Thrashed in pain, and curled up tight, like a child with a tummy ache. Then again: 'Listen! This is what they are waiting for!'

'You heard that?' Alexanor asked Lykortas. Philopoemen's bloody hands were still clenched on his head, as if he were the Spartan enemy.

Lykortas stood. 'That makes sense. Who else would do this?'

Alexanor felt Philopoemen go. The body passed from rigidity to a flaccid relaxation.

For a moment, he thought the Achaean was dead. But he had only fainted.

'I need to move him. I need my things. Things I have in my travelling kit. He's dying. I want to extract the arrow. And then ...'

Arkas appeared. In five years, the groom had grown from wiry adolescence to wiry manhood; he could lift his master.

'I've got him.'

A dozen of Telemnastos' archers walked with them. People came out of their homes; men swore revenge. A dozen men followed them, openly weeping. Antiphatas threw his *himation* over his head and turned away.

Lykortas, drawn sword still in his hand, followed.

'Antiphatas!' he shouted. 'His last words – this was planned. Planned! Now Knossos will attack.'

Antiphatas stood still, as if this was more than he could understand.

Alexanor ignored them. Later, he would remember that walk through the streets of Gortyna as a nightmare – the steep alleys rising above them, the footing treacherous, he, dreading that his friend would die at any moment, unable to put down the body sticky with his blood – and over it all the fear that the dark-cloaked man with the *gastraphetes* was still out there. Lykortas thought the same; he didn't stop for a moment but walked, sword in hand, next to the body.

He operated on Philopoemen on the clean tiles of what had once been the *andron* of Phila's rented home. He washed the entry wound as well as he could with the hot water Arkas provided, and then he took his arrow spoon in hand. But after three tries, he couldn't get any of its three shapes around the head – it was buried deep. He pressed against Philopoemen's back with his left hand and felt the sharp point of the bolt *through* his skin.

'Apollo,' he said aloud.

He wished he had even one of his novices. Anyone with whom to share the decision.

Then, as if his hands were guided by someone else, he cut the short bolt close to the entry wound, grasped the shaft of the bolt firmly, and *pushed it through* the flesh of the lower back. Once engaged, he was like a fighter in combat; he didn't stop to think, only acted. He cut the unbarbed bolt-head, heard it drop with a *clink* to the floor, and then, with one steady pull, drew the whole shaft out of the wound.

He noticed, with grim professionalism, that there was little blood, and the same kind of clear fluid he'd observed the first time he'd been inside Philopoemen's abdomen. By some grim irony, the bolt had struck almost exactly on the old scar, penetrating at the same angle.

He was kneeling on the tile floor. He looked up.

They were all around him: Lykortas, Antiphatas, Arkas, Aristaenos and Telemnastos, Dinaeos, and a dozen other officers. They had been standing silently, or holding things. He hadn't even noticed them.

'Any chance at all?' Dinaeos asked. 'Give it to us straight.'

'Yes,' Alexanor said. 'Yes. One chance in ... fifty.'

'Will he awaken?' Dinaeos asked. 'I ask, not as a friend, but as his officer. Nabis is marching.'

Alexanor shook his head. 'I don't know. Perhaps in an hour – perhaps never.'

Dinaeos looked at the others. 'Anyone else want to take command?'

Antiphatas frowned. 'I am in command,' he said.

Dinaeos looked at the older man. 'What are your orders, sir?'

Antiphatas was looking at Philopoemen.

'Do what you think he would have done,' Antiphatas said.

'Did you get the assassin?' Alexanor asked.

Dinaeos shook his head. 'No.'

Alexanor felt the man's pain. 'He may never wake.'

Dinaeos nodded. 'Get me Periander and Kleostratos. And send to Plator over the mountains. Those were his last orders. We'll stick to them.'

'Gut wounds recover more often at sea,' Alexanor said to Leon. 'I read it somewhere.'

'So put him on a ship,' Leon said.

'My plan exactly,' Alexanor said bitterly.

Gortyna's nearest port was forty stades away over a steep mountain range; travelling over the mountains was a sure death sentence.

'He survived the last time,' Leon said. 'And that was after his friends threw him over a horse and rode all night.'

Alexanor shook his head.

'You saved him ...' Leon said.

'I was young and arrogant, then. I took chances ...'

'You are older and just as arrogant now,' Leon replied. 'Listen, my friend. If I had a wound in my belly, I'd take you over any other doctor or priest in the world. I brought you some boiled wine and all the Smyrnan honey. What else do you want?'

'Incense – I want to cense him. I need the intervention of the gods. This is beyond me, and if there's any man I have ever met who is a friend of the gods, it is this one. Maybe he has some immortal ichor in him. Maybe he has the fortune to survive. Maybe the threads of his fate are not yet cut.'

Alexanor washed and made himself ritually clean; then he went and made a sacrifice at the altar of Apollo in the great temple, aided by twenty other priests as interested in the outcome as he was himself. Then he hurried back, censer in hand, afraid at an almost atavistic level that his friend had died while he was out, convinced irrationally that the incense could do to Philopoemen's humours what he could not do himself.

When he came in, Philopoemen was still breathing, and Alexanor censed him thoroughly, so the scent of frankincense permeated the house.

But there was no change in the patient. Night came, and Alexanor fell asleep in Phila's chair, by the couch.

When he awoke, Leon was there, with a six-wick lamp lit.

'He spoke,' Leon said.

Alexanor rose, his senses wrecked by fatigue; and yet, some of the ancient authors suggested that it was between sleep and wakefulness that man was closest to the gods and the supernatural. Alexanor had some of that feeling, as if the veils between the worlds were drawn, and he was seeing more deeply into the darkness around him than was quite right.

Philopoemen seemed to glow in the lamplight. He lay on a *kline*, head up on the backrest, legs folded, but no longer curled around his wound.

Alexanor bent over the Achaean.

Philopoemen managed the faintest trace of a smile.

'I hoped you'd save me,' he whispered. 'That's why I keep you around.'

'You are not saved yet,' Alexanor said.

'Oh, I'll make it,' Philopoemen said, as if he had private knowledge of the workings of his intestines.

Alexanor could imagine them all too vividly – the coils of glistening rope, flaccid and yet curiously resilient. But a single nick in the walls of the intestine and Philopoemen was a dead man. He smelt the wound, examined Philopoemen's colour and breath ...

'Has Antiphatas summoned the phalanx?' Philopoemen asked.

'I don't believe so,' Alexanor said.

'Tell him I said to summon the phalanx,' Philopoemen whispered. 'My death must be the signal for Nabis to attack.'

'Who is going to command the army?' Alexanor asked. 'Dinaeos?'

Philopoemen closed his eyes. He was silent for so long that Alexanor feared the worst, but when he held a little mirror in front of Philopoemen's mouth, there was vapour on it, and then the man's eyes opened.

'I will,' he said. 'Where is Cyrena?'

Alexanor was ready for that.

'She's not here right now,' he said. 'She took a wound.'

'Will she recover?' Philopoemen raised his head, and then sank back.

Alexanor stood silent until his friend fell asleep.

'He'll find out soon enough,' Leon said.

'If he believes, utterly, in his heart that he will recover, that we need him to face the army of Knossos ...' Alexanor shrugged. 'You know as well as I do that engaging that kind of passion is the key to recovery.'

'You think that if he knows that Cyrena is dead, he'll let go?'

Alexanor shrugged again. 'The balance is so fine, I don't want to take any chances. Listen, Leon – he could be dead in an hour. In the morning. Or in a week.'

'You saw that the wound fell on the old scar tissue. Lightning struck twice in the same place. It didn't kill him last time.'

Alexanor shook his head. 'I would like to believe.'

The next day, Philopoemen was awake at midday. There was a crowd outside the doors – a hundred men and women, or more, standing silently.

'Clear broth,' Alexanor ventured. 'Chicken. Let him have some and let's see what eventuates.'

'What's your theory?' Leon asked.

Alexanor stared into the brazier they'd lit to heat the broth.

'Either the intestine is damaged or it isn't. If it is damaged, it should leak, and there should be intestinal fluids, and chicken broth. If not, he should digest normally. Or as normally as a patient can who's had an extreme trauma.'

Leon scratched his balding head. 'Why risk the broth at all?'

'If the intestine is damaged,' Alexanor said, 'he's already dead. In a way, I wish I had never looked inside a body. The body is tough, and yet, once damaged, very weak.'

'Knowledge is power.'

'Sometimes knowledge only leads to an understanding of the horizon of ignorance.'

Dinaeos came in, wearing boots and a cavalry *thorax* of brilliant bronze.

'Can I speak to him?'

'Briefly,' Alexanor said.

'Lives depend on it,' Dinaeos said.

'His life may depend on it. Go ahead.'

Dinaeos stood by the bed. Philopoemen's eyes opened.

'Dinaeos,' he breathed.

'*Strategos*,' Dinaeos said, 'Nabis has seized the fort at Petra. He beat us there, and already he has raiders in the valley, burning farms.'

'Damn it,' Philopoemen said.

'It's not all bad. Periander caught one of the raiding parties, all Illyrians, and smashed it. Took prisoners, got the booty back. Most of our cavalry is out in the fields, hunting raiders.'

'Nabis learns quickly,' Philopoemen said. 'Have you summoned the phalanx?'

'Antiphatas says you told him not to,' Dinaeos said.

'That was ... before.'

Philopoemen began to breathe rapidly, and then his forehead broke out in a sweat.

'Enough,' Alexanor said.

'Tell him to summon the phalanx,' Philopoemen whispered. 'Tell him to ... get the ... farmers in ... We ... cows and sheep ... not free farmers.'

'I'll tell him. He's terrified, Phil. He's ... not dealing with this well.'

Dinaeos leant forward, but Leon took one of his arms.

'Enough,' Alexanor said, more fiercely.

'Tell him I ...' Philopoemen raised his head. 'Begged it!'

His head fell.

'We could kill him with this,' Alexanor said.

Dinaeos turned to Alexanor. 'It's worse than I said, Alex. It's bad. We could lose the whole countryside. Nabis has got more men than I would have believed. He's put a blocking force out by the main gates of Gortyna and he's starting to destroy the countryside. Lykortas said he caught a party of Spartan helots stripping the bark off olive trees. He's burning every village he takes.'

'That's barbaric,' Alexanor said.

Dinaeos shrugged. 'These are barbaric times. We've made Knossos look bad for three years – now they're in a hurry. We will have to fight.'

'Is anything going well?' Leon asked.

Dinaeos smiled. 'Well, I wasn't born yesterday. The Spartan hasn't covered all our gates, so I have cavalry patrols dogging his raids. All our messengers made it out last night, so we're probably going to get help in the next day or so.'

'You have done something ...' Alexanor guessed.

'I'm making a big wager with the gods, yes. But it's what *he* would have done, if he was with us.'

'What?'

Dinaeos looked around, as if he might be overheard. 'I sent Telemnastos and the whole archer corps to take Petra back. I'm guessing that Nabis thinks the war has moved into the Vale of Gortyna, now.'

Alexanor smiled. 'I am no soldier, but that sounds quite brilliant to me.'

'It means that for the next day, this city is virtually empty of real soldiers. Only the gods would save us if Nabis tried an all-out assault.' Dinaeos shrugged. 'By tomorrow night I'll have Periander's mercenaries here, and probably Plator's Illyrians. Plator will probably take command – he's senior.'

'But not the elected *strategos*,' Alexanor said.

'I'm the elected *strategos*'s friend and officer, but I'm not even the *hipparchos*, remember? That's Aristaenos. He's in the field with his Achaeans.' Dinaeos shrugged. 'And I'm going out, too, as soon as I arrange for Antiphatas to summon the phalanx.'

*

The next day was, in its own way, as long and tortuous as the trudge up the acropolis carrying a wounded Philopoemen had been. Every grumble of his patient's stomach, every twitch of his face, every movement of his legs, was cause for anxiety. Alexanor unwound the bandage on the wound and sniffed it. He tried to time how long he imagined food would take to reach the injured spot, and realised that he knew too little about the function of the stomach or the intestine. He didn't even have his books.

He guessed. And worried. Paced.

'Eat something,' Leon said. 'I'm going out. This house is empty – we need everything, including food. And I don't really fancy being returned to slavery. I'm going to grab some weapons.'

He returned an hour later – an hour in which Alexanor discovered that sitting *alone* with a wounded friend is much, much more wearing than sitting with another priest of Asklepios.

'Antiphatas has summoned the phalanx,' Leon said, carrying two big bundles and wearing his *chiton* unpinned at the shoulders like a small Herakles. 'There are hundreds of armed men in the agora, and more in the stadium.'

'Thank the gods,' Alexanor said.

'Thank Dinaeos. I just spoke to Lykortas, and he said that Aristaenos, for whatever reason, tried to argue against summoning the phalanx. Lykortas thinks Aristaenos is grasping for power.'

Alexanor shrugged, uninterested. 'He hasn't awakened. Do you have any idea how long digestion takes?'

Leon frowned. 'Half a day, I think. Remember Sostratos? He used to time men from their first food in many days to the first stool. Water is surprisingly quick, especially in a dehydrated man, but food is much slower.'

'Dehydration!' Alexanor shook his head. 'We haven't been giving him much water.'

Leon shrugged. 'Why not? As you say, either the wall of the intestine is pierced, or it isn't. And the water will pass through him much faster.'

'By Apollo, I wish I knew ...' Alexanor turned away. 'Anything! Anything. I'm so ignorant that it's pure *hubris* to even practise.'

The two of them gave Philopoemen water when next he awoke. His eyes were almost instantly clearer. He spoke better, too.

'Ahh,' he said. 'I was dreaming of water.'

Alexanor was watching the bandage.

'Will it grow damp?' Philopoemen asked with apparent interest. 'Am I leaking?'

'We hope not,' Alexanor said. 'Drink this and go back to sleep.'

'I haven't had this much sleep since I was a child.'

'On the contrary, brother.' Alexanor allowed himself a small smile. 'You slept this much at Epidauros.'

He made some notes and then joined Leon in the kitchen, where the former slave was making something highly spiced, with chicken.

'I think he is better,' Alexanor said. 'I was foolish about the water. Thanks for putting me right.'

Leon smiled but kept chopping herbs.

'I'm sorry,' Alexanor said.

'Sorry?'

'When you were gone today, I realised how much … I rely on you. And treat you …' He took a breath. 'Like a slave, still.'

'Not always,' Leon said with a smile. 'Know how to pluck a chicken?'

'Of course.'

Leon handed him two.

Alexanor plucked. Time passed; a fine down of chicken feathers began to float in the afternoon sunlight.

'You are a fine physician,' Alexanor said. 'I ought to consult with you more often.'

Leon shrugged. 'You are brilliant. I am merely studious. Perhaps I'm dull.'

'No. I tend to ignore you, even though … you often know more than I do.'

'Well,' Leon said, 'it's true that I was at this some years as a slave before you appeared at Epidauros.'

'I regret …'

Leon turned to him, a meat cleaver in his hand. 'Don't. Listen, Alexanor. You raised me from slavery and brought me to the company of men like Dinaeos and Lykortas and even Omphalion. I am over fifty – but now I have respect, even love, from worthy men.' He smiled with a trace of bitterness. 'You know that the sage Solon said "count no man happy until he is dead"?'

'Of course,' Alexanor said.

Leon nodded. 'Perhaps in my case, you could say "count no man *unhappy* until he is dead". I was a slave at thirteen, and let me tell you, it was brutal. Now, at the other end of life ... Listen – more and more, you all speak to me as if I am one of you. This is the best reward. Because I *am* one of you.'

Alexanor sighed, thinking of many things.

Outside, there was a scream, and the sound of a bronze bell.

'Alarm!' roared a sentry, not far off.

'Shit,' Leon said.

Alexanor grabbed one of the spears Leon had brought and then paused.

'Someone has to stay with him,' he said.

Leon shook his head. 'He won't die – or if he does ...'

The shouts were constant now. The city wall was just a block away, off to the north. The alarm fire was burning on the tower.

'We're trained men,' Leon said. 'We have to go.'

'Why here?' Alexanor asked the darkness as he ran. Their section of wall was high on the hillside.

He felt like a fool, running into the darkness, leaving his patient, but, as Leon said, trained fighters were in short supply, and Dinaeos' words were echoing in his head.

Only the gods would save us if Nabis tried an all-out assault.

Up a narrow street to an alley. Philopoemen had ordered the wall-street that ran around the walls to be cleared of all shops and hasty shelters rigged against it; here it had been done. The city wall rose three times the height of a man. The stone had been exposed by weather, the old plaster broken away, and the wooden steps running up to the top of the wall were in poor repair. The alarm fire on the near tower gave the scene a golden glow.

Alexanor had no armour and no shield. He got his heavy wool *chlamys* on his arm and ran up the steps, the whole wooden frame groaning under his weight.

He looked up, and there was a man ...

Bronze ...

Cloak. Red.

Alexanor slashed at the man's armoured legs and put his shoulder into the man's groin, taking him completely by surprise. He continued forward, slammed the man into the front face of the wall, and took a punch to the head. Then they were grappling. The other man grabbed for his nose and eyes, his hand pressing blindly into Alexanor's face. Alexanor turned his hips, slammed a knee into the other man's groin, stepped back, missed his hold, and then caught the other man's failed punch and threw him off the wall, down into the houses.

There was a ladder against the outside of the wall. It was full of men. There were men trying to storm the tower, and other men on the wall. They had torches. Alexanor took all that in with one hasty glance, and then his sword was in his hand and he was facing a Spartiate with an *aspis*. The man charged him, and all Alexanor could do was back away, but the Spartan was a veteran, and backed him into a corner by the tower. One blow Alexanor deflected, but his attempt to tangle the man's spearhead with his cloak failed, and he took a long gash on his 'shield' arm.

Then the Spartiate's face relaxed, and he fell. He collapsed in silence, his arm back for a killing blow, and there was Leon, a spear held in both hands like a man boar hunting.

'Cover me!' Alexanor yelled

He knelt, wrestling with the dying Spartan for possession of the big *aspis*. After a moment, life left the man's eyes, and Alexanor took the *aspis* off his arm and put it on his own. He picked up the Spartan's heavy spear.

Leon was facing two men on the catwalk. They were *not* Spartans; they were helots, or light-armed mercenaries, and they were not eager to face the priest and his spear. They threw half-hearted attacks from out of distance and called to men below them on the mountainside to come up the ladder faster.

Leon covered their attacks with his spear.

The Spartans attacking the tower began to notice that there were suddenly defenders on the wall.

Alexanor roared the war cry of the Rhodian marines and charged the two *peltastoi*, and they ran.

The Spartans attacking the tower abandoned their attempts to take a doorway and turned on Alexanor.

Leon picked up a stone, stored there ready for the purpose, and threw it down the ladder.

Alexanor charged the Spartans. There was no other choice. He had an *aspis*, and years of training told him: better to be going forward.

The Spartans had the same training. He went shield-to-shield with the nearer man, their *aspides* cracking together in the darkness. Alexanor had no helmet and had to be cautious; but he was strong, larger than his opponent, and he went to win the shield push, using the round face of his *aspis* with the cunning his *hoplomachos* had taught him. He turned the force of the other man's charge, channelled it, turned his hip, struck with the spear.

The Spartan raised his shield to cover ...

Alexanor exploded into him, one sudden push with all his weight behind it; the spear attack had been a feint, and the Spartan fell off the wall.

The second man thrust hurriedly, and his thrust tore at Alexanor's scalp.

'Trouble!' Leon roared.

Alexanor nicked the other man in the knee, slammed his shield forward, kicked again, thrust ... The Spartan stumbled back. Alexanor was relentless, kicking with both his feet – one-two – and the copper studs on his outdoor sandals scored the man's ankles and made him flinch. But the Spartan was well trained. He set his hips and pushed back, and suddenly his *xiphos* appeared, licking around the shield like a steel viper, and it bit into Alexanor's left bicep.

Alexanor punched, the spear in his left hand too long for the close fight. He used the shaft to clear the sword off his shield, reversed his hand as the man stumbled back, and thrust from the left side, using the *saurauter*, or butt spike of his weapon. He'd meant it as a feint, a clearing blow to buy a moment, but the bronze spike went over the Spartan's shield and into his face, and the man went down without a scream.

Alexanor turned. Leon was gone; there were a dozen new men on the wall behind him.

'Damn,' he said, and set his feet, prepared to sell his life as dearly as possible.

But the new men were not Spartans. They had javelins and narrow shields, and one of them rifled his spear at Alexanor. Instinct, or training, saved him, although the javelin only glittered for a moment, catching the beacon light.

Alexanor got his *aspis* on it. It clattered away into the darkness.

'Behind you!' Leon called.

He was in the street below, having been driven off the wall.

Alexanor turned. There were the two *peltastoi* he'd chased earlier. They were both facing him. As he took a step towards them Leon got one with a javelin – a fine throw.

The other man threw himself on Alexanor in desperation.

Alexanor was off balance, and his back was naked. As soon as the other man's arms caught him, he felt his weight go, and the two of them fell, struck the wooden steps, and fell onto the cobbled street below.

He lay, stunned.

The other man was dead, his neck broken at a horrific angle by Alexanor's borrowed *aspis*.

Leon ran to him. 'You alive?' he asked.

'So far,' Alexanor managed. 'Aphrodite! My ankle is … Fuck. It's my hip.'

He lay against the cobbles, the stone still warm from the heat of the day.

There were men running, and the steps groaned.

Alexanor tried again to rise, and the pain was too much. He retched and lay back.

Close by, he heard the unmistakable *thwack* of a bowstring on a heavy bow, and then another. He turned his head, and there were half a dozen Cretan *epheboi*, their red *chitons* bright in the firelight.

Leon's hands were probing his side.

'It's not broken,' he said. 'Let's get out of here.'

The archers were clearing the wall, and the *peltastoi* had nowhere to run except back down their ladder. There were also arrows coming from inside the tower above them, and the archers in the tower couldn't distinguish friend from foe. Arrows rattled off the steps and the cobbles.

'Come on,' Leon said. 'Get up on the left leg. Push.'

Alexanor powered up, and the pain wasn't bad until he tried to put weight on his right foot.

'It's the leg that's broken,' he said.

'I disagree.'

'Whose leg is it?' Alexanor spat.

'We're about to be in the middle of a storming action,' Leon said.

He began to hobble away with Alexanor, and two women came, and put Alexanor on a board, and lifted him. One of the women had water, and gave some to each of them, and then most of the women hurried on, their long dresses kirtled up and full of stones and roof tiles.

'Give me your sword,' one woman said to Alexanor.

He handed it over, and the woman took it grimly.

'Let me see.'

Alexanor got his hip into a crevice in one of the wall-side buildings. He looked up.

The Cretan *epheboi* had cleared the wall but were hesitant about going back onto it.

Alexanor looked at Leon. 'Take my shield. Lead the women up the steps and throw rocks,' he said. 'Anyone in the ditch will assume the wall is held.'

The group of women were hesitating at the base of the rickety steps. The wall looked like a theatre scene of carnage – dead men, and blood glistening in the distant firelight, trickling off the wall and onto the cobbles.

'I knew you would say that.' Leon took a deep breath. 'Well – it's the first city that ever made me a citizen.' He took the *aspis*. 'Fuck.'

'Just stay behind it,' Alexanor said. 'Let your enemy fight the shield.'

'Whatever,' Leon said.

But he stood straight, grasped his spear in the middle, and shrugged both shoulders, as if throwing off the last yoke of his former slavery.

'All right, ladies,' he said. 'Follow me.'

One of the *epheboi*, bolder than the rest or perhaps shamed by the courage of the women, picked up the dead *peltast*'s shield and javelins and followed the women up the steps.

The women gave shrill screams as they came up the steps, but they were bold on the wall, hurling their stones and tiles down into the ditch, and the men in the tower gave a cheer that was echoed farther away.

The *epheboi* ran up the steps, and Alexanor worried that they'd collapse, but they held on, swaying under the weight of the adolescents.

Three of the young men and two women with stolen spears converged on something in the dark, and with a sudden scream, they threw down the enemy ladder. Alexanor, across the street, heard the enemy ladder burst on the rocks below, and men screaming, their cries different from the triumph of the women.

Alexanor sat in the fire-shot dark, waiting for the next wave of attackers.

But that was the last of the fighting.

Three hours later, Alexanor was lying on a couch. He was next to Philopoemen, and the other man's wound showed no leakage. He was asleep. In a minute, so was Alexanor.

He awoke when Leon leant over him with soup.

'He's already awake,' Leon said.

Alexanor rolled over, and the pain in his hip was sharp, but not as bad as he'd feared.

Philopoemen was *sitting up*. On the other side of the *Strategos* was Dinaeos, with Lykortas and Thodor.

'We held,' Alexanor said.

Dinaeos shook his head. 'Talk about miracles.'

Thodor nodded. 'You were betrayed,' he said. 'We know some things about it.'

Dinaeos shrugged. 'Later,' he said. 'I find it hard to imagine that anyone here would actually offer to let the town be sacked. But maybe. Regardless – Nabis didn't try hard enough.'

'One force – they sneaked up past the gate towers and tried for the wall ...' Lykortas smiled at Leon. 'Well, you know. You were there.'

'Leon!' Alexanor exclaimed. 'You are a hero!'

Leon shrugged. 'You made me go. It was just duty.'

'And the women,' Alexanor said.

'Women?' Lykortas asked.

Philopoemen shook his head. 'You all underestimate women,' he said. 'Never mind. What *now*?' He looked at Dinaeos. 'Tell me what's happening?'

'I ordered Telemnastos to take Petra back,' Dinaeos said.

'Excellent,' Philopoemen said. 'Exactly.'

'Telemnastos took it last night. Nabis had left fewer than two hundred men to hold it.' Dinaeos was pleased with himself.

'Excellent. Now Nabis has to take it back.'

'Up that trail? Telemnastos has half the federal archer corps and a hundred Illyrians holding it.'

Philopoemen closed his eyes. 'Damn. You don't need me at all.'

'I almost lost the city,' Dinaeos said.

'Almost doesn't count in war,' Philopoemen said. 'More soup.'

'What now?' Alexanor croaked.

Philopoemen glanced at him. 'Now we fight a battle. I don't think we can avoid it, although if anyone listens to me, we'll put it off as long as possible.'

'Put it off?'

'Nabis needs to fight to win. But the longer we leave him out there in the plain, the harder he'll find it to get food or water.'

'And the more farms he'll burn,' Thodor said. 'This Spartan likes fire.'

Philopoemen took a deep breath and then coughed as the pain in his gut hit him. He spluttered a little, drank some soup, and then shook his head.

'We can afford to lose farms.'

'Tell that to the farmers,' Alexanor grumbled.

'There are already factions proposing surrender,' Lykortas said. 'Sorry, sir, but that's what I heard this morning.'

'I'll bet those women don't want to surrender,' Philopoemen said. 'Damn it, I wish Phila was here. Where's Cyrena? She'll mobilise the women for us.'

The silence went on for too long.

Philopoemen looked around. 'Alexanor?' he asked, plaintively.

Alexanor swallowed. Hard. 'She's ...'

Philopoemen looked at Dinaeos.

Then back at Alexanor.

Alexanor gathered all the shreds of his moral courage.

'She died saving your life,' he said. 'She took the second bolt meant to finish you off. She tackled one of the attackers and ...'

Philopoemen burst into tears. And then, suddenly angry.

'You *hid her death*?' he screamed.

And then his wound was too much for him, and he subsided, lying with his face to the headrest, sobbing.

Alexanor reached out for his hand, but at his touch Philopoemen flinched and pulled his hand away.

'She's dead and no one told me ...' he moaned.

Leon caught the wounded man's shoulder.

'Philopoemen!' he said. 'You think we can afford to let some farms be burnt to save everyone!'

The *Strategos* turned his head away.

'She's dead!' he mourned. 'Oh gods. Dead, and in the ground ...'

Leon slapped him. 'Get with it,' he snapped. 'She died so that you could save this city, which she loved. Which I love. Grieve later. Now is not the time.'

Even Alexanor was astounded at Leon's fierceness. But he did not relent, and Philopoemen met his eye.

'We have no other choice but to fight,' Leon said. 'And you are the man everyone will follow. I have her body – it is tended to but not buried.'

Alexanor was ashamed that he hadn't thought of any of that; Leon had.

Philopoemen shuddered. 'I'm sorry,' he said in a small voice.

Philopoemen's bedside became the command council of Gortyna, and indeed, after Plator's arrival and the *Strategos* of the Lyttians, Idomenaeos, it was the command council of the League of Crete, the whole force of the *Neoteroi*.

'Nabis is a very capable adversary,' Philopoemen announced.

He was wearing a purple-red *chlamys* wrapped around him; he lay on the couch while most of the other men stood, dust-covered and in armour.

'He's found a new way over the mountains,' Dadas said. 'We can raid his convoys, but he has re-established contact with Knossos.'

'And he's offering terms,' Lykortas said.

'Also a brilliant move,' Philopoemen said. 'We could lose through political manoeuvring as thoroughly as losing on a battlefield. Where is his camp?'

'He's withdrawn up the valley to the east,' Dinaeos said. 'To cover his new supply line.'

'And you are raiding into his territory?' Philopoemen asked.

Dinaeos looked smug. 'Of course. Aristaenos went the day before yesterday, all the way to the gates of Knossos, but that's just my feint. To cover Plator. He's moving along the mountains—'

'Along the mountains?' Alexanor asked.

'From Petra! East along the ridge, trying to find where the Knossian convoys run. If a goat can make it through those mountains, the Illyrians can do it.' Dinaeos had made heaps of almond shells to represent terrain. 'Here, I expect.'

'We need to make sure all of our mercenaries are paid up,' Philopoemen said.

Antiphatas spoke up. 'Why? We pay at the end of the season—'

'Nabis is backed by the Rhodians,' Philopoemen said. 'He will try and buy our mercenaries.'

'We won't have the money to pay our citizen levy,' Antiphatas said. 'Men always say you are yourself a mercenary, and you take care of your own first.'

'You may withhold the pay of the Achaean League troops, if you like,' Philopoemen said. 'But I promise you, the closer we get to the day of battle, the more Nabis will try and use silver to win for himself.' He looked at Dinaeos. 'How many men does he have?'

'Maybe fifteen thousand,' Dinaeos said.

'By Zeus,' Philopoemen said, stunned. 'That many?'

Dadas shrugged. 'When he retreated from our walls and went to cover his convoys, I lay in an olive tree and counted. Thracians count the stars and their enemies and all their enemies' horses. We know how to count.'

'Fifteen thousand men,' Philopoemen said. 'That's a lot of food.'

'An incredible amount of food,' Dinaeos said. 'We need more cavalry.'

'We won't be receiving any,' Philopoemen said. 'So we have what … nine thousand?'

'If you count every ephebe in the Federation and all our allies,' Antiphatas said. 'Then maybe eleven thousand.'

'We need to starve him for two weeks,' Philopoemen said.

Lykortas nodded. 'We need to arm our peasants and make them prey on his foragers,' he said. 'And maybe we need to try and buy *his* mercenaries.'

'We have no money!' Antiphatas cried.

'They don't know that,' Lykortas said. 'How underhanded am I allowed to be?'

Philopoemen smiled grimly. 'I know I'll regret this, but do whatever damage you can, Lykortas.'

Lykortas stretched. 'Does anyone doubt that Zophanes arranged for the killers who attacked Philopoemen?'

'Zophanes?' Philopoemen asked. He grabbed at his cut, doubled in sudden pain from his own rapid movement. 'Gods. I want him dead, then.'

'I have a better use for him,' Lykortas said.

Philopoemen's face took on an unaccustomed look of sheer hatred.

'If Cyrena were here, she would agree with me,' Lykortas begged. 'Let me use this traitor for our own ends. I can help save the city. Let me do this.'

Philopoemen looked away. 'Do it,' he said.

Lykortas smiled.

'We need time,' Dinaeos said.

'Ask this Nabis for his terms,' Alexanor suggested.

They all looked at him.

'We should ask this Spartan for terms?' Dinaeos asked.

Alexanor shrugged. 'Surely the discussion of when and where to hold the discussion will take a day or two.'

Philopoemen nodded. 'I feel that we are at the limit of what might be allowed by the gods,' he said. 'But we will listen to whatever Nabis offers, and we'll undermine the peace party in the city. I agree.'

'Will you put it to the Assembly?' Lykortas asked.

'No!' Leon said.

'Yes,' Dinaeos said. 'Telemnastos would insist if he was here.'

Philopoemen agreed. 'What are we, if we lose faith in our own institutions?'

The next day, Philopoemen sat at home while Dinaeos addressed the Assembly. It was a very military assembly; most of the men present had been summoned to the phalanx and wore their armour. They listened to Dinaeos, and then to Antiphatas and to Alexanor, who rose for the first time to address the Assembly on anything but a medical matter.

Zophanes looked at him suspiciously, but did not rise. Afterwards,

305

when the Assembly had voted to send a delegation to the Knossian army, Zophanes accosted Alexanor under the *stoa* of Apollo.

'Where is my son, priest?' he asked.

'At Epidauros,' Alexanor allowed.

'I want him back,' the older man said. 'Or I will see to it that your life becomes very difficult indeed.'

'You seem to me to be in a weak position to make threats.'

'I know your father,' Zophanes said. 'I found him. We have exchanged a letter or two. And I know people on Kos – that's how I got my worthless son his office. I can have you replaced. Or I can allow you to continue to hold your new office. But you need to shut up and make way for native men who know their business to rule here. And I've told your father all about your dealings with this Achaean and his mercenaries.'

'Then it seems to me we have nothing more to say to each other,' Alexanor said. 'I care nothing for your dealings with Kos, and as to my father, he has disinherited me. We are nothing to each other. Your son is beyond my control. He broke the laws of gods and men and will be punished for it.' He bowed. 'Good day to you.'

'Revel in it,' Zophanes called out, to his back. 'At best, you lot have a few days left in power.'

From Leon, he heard that their arrangements for the conference were taking longer than anyone expected. Alexanor had plenty to do seeing to his patient, and he spent his spare time in exercise, because his hip and right thigh, although not broken, hurt like blazes. He did what he could for himself, and fed Philopoemen, but even he had to admit that the miracle had happened a second time.

'You must live a very clean life, or the gods love you,' he said.

'If the gods loved me, Cyrena would still be alive.' Philopoemen's voice was flat; his face had acquired its set, statue look, the look he'd worn on his farm in Arkadia.

Alexanor walked to the window and opened it.

'Look outside,' he said. 'Come. I'll support you.'

He put an arm around his friend and helped him to the balcony over the street.

There were two hundred men and women below them.

'Look!' Alexanor said.

Men looked up; a woman pointed. Philopoemen waved.

'There he is! Alive! He cheats death!' called a man.

'Achilles! Achilles!' called a dozen voices, and then the chant was taken up, and it rebounded off the walls and seemed to fill the very air with sound.

'Achilles! Achilles undying. Achilles Athanatos!'

Alexanor took him back to his *kline*.

'Now tell me the gods don't love you,' he said.

Philopoemen shook his head. 'What am I to say to them?'

Alexanor had no answer for that, so he was silent a while. Then he looked at his friend.

'Will you ride to meet this Nabis?' Alexanor asked.

'I was going to ask you the same,' the Achaean replied. 'Of course I want to hear what he has to say. And I want him to see that I'm still alive. I wonder if he remembers us?'

'I remember him well enough, thank you.' Alexanor was taking Philopoemen's pulse. 'I only remember him as a figure in good armour, though, and then as a golden figure, fleeing. Does he know you?'

'No better than we know him.'

'Oh, I suspect I know him better. I remember when he threatened to invade the sanctuary of Asklepios at Epidauros.' Alexanor smiled. 'To answer your question, I believe that you can ride. Need I tell you that you are taking a risk, even a sizeable risk, and your wound could open at any time? Then the disorder of the humours will set in, and rot, and you will die.'

'So I can ride?' Philopoemen asked.

'Sometimes I feel you are not listening to me,' Alexanor snapped.

'I am listening, but events are moving and I have lain on my back for eight days.'

'Seven days.'

'And I want ... Damn it, Alexanor. They sent a killer to murder me. They killed Cyrena. And now they'll just meet us at a peace conference.'

'Nabis might say that he had nothing to do with your murder. That it was all done here, in Gortyna, without his authority.' Alexanor shrugged. 'Zophanes hates us – you and me both.'

Philopoemen sighed. 'Do you know what Lykortas is doing?'

'No,' Alexanor said. 'But he's quite gifted, in a bent way.'

'That's what worries me. If I ride out to meet Nabis tomorrow, will you come?'

'As your bodyguard, no. As your physician, of course.' Alexanor clasped his friend's hand.

CHAPTER TWO

—◦◦◦—

Gortyna, Crete

217 BCE

The two parties met at the sanctuary of Herakles, well out on the plain of Gortyna, almost halfway between the Knossian encampment by the mountains and the city to the south and east.

Alexanor knew Nabis immediately. He was older, more dignified, and his armour was, if anything, richer, but he was the same man, and his face still wore something of the habitual sneer that had decorated it six years before. He came with an escort of Thessalian cavalry; two of them looked familiar to Alexanor. In addition, he had a pair of officers in the red cloaks of Spartiates, as well as an obvious Illyrian and half a dozen other men, all well mounted and wearing riding clothes.

Nabis' cavalrymen went through the entire sanctuary, lined up the slaves, and examined everything, including the sacred inner rooms of the temple.

Dinaeos then entered the sanctuary with Antiphatas' escort, and did the same, searching every room. Only then were the principals invited to enter.

A table had been set up under the sacred pines, where it was cool. The grove was beautiful, with the mountains of central Crete as a backdrop. Antiphatas sat on a stool that Dinaeos had brought for him.

'Who are you?' Nabis said. 'Where is your pet Achaean?'

Antiphatas sat back. 'I am the *Archon* of Gortyna. I am here to

309

listen to your proposals on behalf of the Polis of Gortyna. Aristaenos is here to listen on behalf of the Achaean League, and Telemnastos is here for the League of Crete.'

'You are joking,' Nabis said. 'I am not going to deal with some flunky of your so-called democracy.' He looked around, but did not sit. 'Where is Philopoemen? Or is he even alive?'

He looked at Dinaeos. 'You, I know,' he said.

Dinaeos smiled. 'Philopoemen is alive, Nabis,' he said.

'Philopoemen is *Strategos*,' Antiphatas said. 'But he is not the head of government. And you, sir? Who are you? I do not know you.'

Nabis shrugged. 'I am Nabis of Sparta. I command here.'

'So you, and not the Council of Knossos, are leader of the *Presbyteroi*?' Antiphatas asked. 'You have been elected leader of the *Boule* of Knossos? You are perhaps Tyrant?'

Nabis shrugged. 'I'm done here. I came to hear you democrats crawl. Surrender, or die. Those are your choices. I thought Philopoemen was man enough to come and answer in person. Apparently not.' He sneered. 'Goodbye.'

'I am right here, Nabis,' Philopoemen said.

He was wearing armour and standing next to Antiphatas' chair. The cheek plates on his cavalry helmet hid his face, and, as Alexanor had found with some experiment, the tight bronze *thorax* actually supported the wound.

Nabis looked Philopoemen over. 'There you are at last,' he said. 'You know, I politicked to get this mission just so that I could be the one who put you down. So, do you surrender?'

'What are the terms?' Antiphatas asked.

'When I want to speak to the master, I do not address his dog,' Nabis snapped.

'I find it interesting,' Philopoemen said quietly, 'that you lord it over these men just as they seek, using you, to lord it over Crete. Do they have minds and mouths of their own?' He looked at the Knossians in their riding clothes.

'We are not here to make speeches,' Nabis said.

'Aren't we, though?' Antiphatas was relaxed, even cheerful. Alexanor found time to admire him. 'We're politicians.'

'Are you here to surrender?' Nabis asked.

Antiphatas shrugged. 'I have to hear your terms.'

Nabis looked at Philopoemen. 'There are no terms. You surrender without condition, and I, personally, will guarantee the lives of all of the Achaean soldiers and their property.' He grinned. 'Except Philopoemen. Sparta wants him.'

Philopoemen nodded. 'You make this sound as if the war is between Sparta and the Achaean League.'

'So it is,' Nabis said. 'What else is there?'

'Interesting that you are so bold as to admit it. Convenient, too. You take away their citizen rights, and then send their sons to Aetolia to fight, so they cannot revolt.' Philopoemen shrugged. 'As I am only here as a guard, I have to decline to respond to your offer. Aristaenos, here, is the commander of the Achaean forces. Do you agree to these terms?'

Aristaenos shook his head angrily.

Antiphatas smiled. 'So I suppose the answer is no, we won't accept an unconditional surrender.'

Nabis looked puzzled. 'Then why are you here?'

Antiphatas met his gaze and held it. 'Listen, Spartan. We are citizens in a city, as you used to be. A city with laws, and with a constitution, and with an assembly—'

'Spare me,' Nabis said.

'No, I will not. Your fabled lawgiver, Lycurgus, learnt his wisdom *on Crete*. Everything that made Sparta great *came from Crete*. Today, you are representing a tyranny of rich men. I represent an assembly of free men.'

'Are you through?' Nabis yawned. 'I was told you were ready to surrender. I can tell I was misinformed.'

'Surrender?' Antiphatas asked. 'I was told you had terms to offer. The Assembly voted to hear them. I will report them to the Assembly, but I must tell you that it seems unlikely to me that anyone in the city will accept them. Even Creon, when he hears how you silenced his allies.' He rose.

'You have wasted my time,' Nabis said.

'Supplies running low?' Philopoemen asked.

Telemnastos, who had sat silent, grinned. 'Running out of Illyrians?'

'Why don't you come out and fight, and see what happens?' Nabis asked.

'Why don't you go home?' Philopoemen asked. 'Have you even

told these gentlemen that you lost the fort at Petra? Or that there is smoke over Knossos?'

The Knossians, silent until then, all looked at each other.

Nabis was unmoved. 'Do you know that there is a Rhodian fleet on your south coast?' he asked. 'Or that they are landing at Lentas?'

Alexanor felt as if he'd taken a knife in the gut.

Nabis shook his head. 'Well, so much for talk. When we storm your city, there will be no mercy. Indeed, there is talk of massacring the population and resettling with Spartan colonists and helots.' He made a brushing motion with his hand. 'You are dismissed.'

'Speaking of storming,' Philopoemen said, 'we have the bodies of three of your Spartiates. Would you like them returned?'

Nabis froze. Then his eyes seemed to catch fire.

'You know I would, you bastard, ' he said.

'Excellent,' Philopoemen said. 'Then send a herald, as is customary, *when one is defeated.*'

'I should have gutted you when I had you under my hand,' Nabis spat.

Alexanor spoke for the first time. 'You never had him under your hand, Spartan. Chiron, our high priest, threw you in the dust, remember? How's your arm? Shall I look at it?'

'Ah, the Rhodian traitor,' Nabis said. 'Your turn is coming.'

Antiphatas rose. 'I see you offer nothing but taunts and threats,' he said. 'The saddest thing is that I, a democrat, should find that you will not even allow my actual enemies, the oligarchs of Knossos, to speak. I pity them.'

'Enough speeches!' Nabis called. 'Come out and fight, or be branded cowards.'

'Cowards?' Philopoemen asked. If his wound hurt him, he showed no sign. 'Cowards? When you send a hired killer to murder a woman, you have the effrontery to call *me* a coward?'

Nabis sneered. 'No idea what you're talking about,' he said, without even trying to appear truthful. 'Anyway, my sources inside your walls say that only some black whore died. Don't get all pious at me.'

Philopoemen was livid. His hand went to his sword ...

Alexanor had seen it all – the escalation, the tone. Philopoemen found his sword hand gripped by his friend, and Telemnastos took his other shoulder.

'Friend of yours?' Nabis asked. 'Come on, break the truce and attack me.'

Antiphatas shook his head. 'You are an ignorant man. And as the gods love justice, you are about to receive your punishment. But it will be in an open field.'

'Last chance, *Archon*. Surrender and we don't kill everyone in your town.'

Antiphatas turned to the oligarchs. 'If you should reconsider,' he said, 'we would welcome all of you as free men and Cretans.'

'This parley is at an end,' Nabis said.

His Thessalians closed in around him. The Knossians dignitaries were left unguarded, to shuffle out of the sanctuary on their own.

'That was no parley,' Antiphatas said bitterly. 'Is this all personal, between you and Nabis?'

'Me?' Philopoemen hissed. 'I scarcely know him.'

'He killed your wife,' Antiphatas said. 'Or so I hear.'

'No,' Philopoemen said. 'Other Spartans killed my wife. Machanandas and his mercenaries. Believe me, I know. Nabis was busy trying to kill me at Epidauros.' His voice was flat. 'I put the good of our city ahead of any personal quarrel. And the Spartan never intended us to accept the terms. He meant to gauge our resolve while he bought time for damned Rhodian marines to land.'

'That is a bitter blow,' Alexanor said. 'And they landed during a truce – surely an affront to the gods.'

'Perhaps,' Philopoemen said. 'But I confess that we only wanted time, as well, and we've been moving people during the truce, too. If it was a truce. I swore no oath, and my legal quibble is that since Nabis never sent a herald to collect his dead, we're still fighting.'

Alexanor looked at his friend, and thought *you never used to quibble at all.*

They rode carefully back to the city. Philopoemen was pale and quiet, but he appeared well enough. He led them up onto the walls of the citadel, a long climb even for a healthy man.

'You should not—' Alexanor began.

'I need to see,' the *Strategos* said.

And indeed, long before they were at the top, they could see columns of smoke away to the east – four of them.

'Try that, Nabis,' he said.

'What are we seeing?' Alexanor asked.

'Several hundred low-class citizens led by Simos.' Philopoemen waved, and then winced as he hurt his wound.

'The man who lost a hand in the first fighting?'

'Exactly. A good leader. Of lower-class men like him. I sent the farmers and labourers back out onto the plain. They know the olive groves – they're attacking Nabis' foragers. And burning anything that the enemy tries to steal.'

He was white as parchment, and unsteady.

Alexanor caught him. 'This is an ugly kind of war, brother.'

'All kinds of war are ugly. We will fight a battle, outnumbered almost two to one. I'm making sure that my opponent has little sleep and no food.'

'Those men will die,' Alexanor said.

'They are all volunteers. Many of them volunteered because of Cyrena. They are earning their full citizen rights. And because of Cyrena, we have the lower-class men and women with us. They aren't observers, Alexanor. They're people, and we're making them into a force.'

'You are full of righteousness, I find.'

Philopoemen looked at him and nodded. 'I agree. I fear it too.'

The next day, Nabis moved forward towards Gortyna. He linked up with four hundred veteran Rhodian marines.

'Shouldn't we have prevented that?' Alexanor asked.

He was very bitter about facing his own. Once again, they were watching from the wall.

'He's stretching his already stretched supply line to Knossos,' Philopoemen said. 'Today, unless everything goes wrong, Plator will take his daily food convoy from Knossos. He'll have to leave more than five hundred men to watch his supply lines and his camp. Maybe more.'

'We won't have the Illyrians ...' Alexanor began. 'If we fight a battle in the next few days.'

'I don't tell you how to operate—'

'You never trained as a physician,' Alexanor said. 'I *was* a hoplite.'

'Quite a good one, given your fight on the wall. Leon makes you sound like Hector come to life.'

'I prefer to think of myself as wily Odysseus,' Alexanor said. 'But I admit to being proud. I have never fought better. Falling off the wall wasn't too clever, though.'

'You walked away alive.'

'Limped.'

'Alive. Listen, brother. The Lyttians are a day's march away – the best hoplites on Crete. Rumour says that the Polyrrhenians are coming behind them. We're going to face this army. But I'm going to do everything I can to take the sting out of Nabis before I face him.' Philopoemen pointed. 'There they are. He's forming the whole army, to show us his power.'

'You seem pleased,' Alexanor said.

Philopoemen gave him a wry smile. 'Now I know what his fighting order is. Dadas is out there right now, counting everything.'

'Is it tomorrow?'

Philopoemen shook his head. 'Ask Lykortas,' he said enigmatically.

The next day, the Knossians formed at the head of their camp and marched out onto the plain. Antiphatas drilled the phalanx inside the city. Dinaeos drilled the Allied Cavalry behind the city, to the west, towards Phaistos, and then returned suddenly, the dust of his rapid passage rising into the still late-summer air. Hidden in the dust were two thousand Lyttians, all wearing their own armour. They'd lost their city, but they were unbowed.

Kleostratos and the Thracian cavalry, reinforced with another hundred mercenaries paid by the Cretan League, were out amid the olive groves, harrying the Knossian foragers and supporting the small farmers and labourers. They were winning against Nabis' light troops, but Nabis had taken to putting any man caught on a stake, or crucifying them on large crosses. A few had their heads removed and thrown at the town walls. The dying men screamed their lives out within sight of the city.

But instead of cowering, the new Gortyna *psiloi* struck back. Any Knossian straggler, any man found too far from the Knossian camp, men relieving themselves, or looking for food, were killed, their throats slit, or worse.

'We should not be letting these men behave thus in our name,' Antiphatas said.

Philopoemen shrugged. 'This is war. Our opponents have no rules. We must answer in kind.'

'Must we?' Alexanor asked. 'You didn't always believe that.'

Philopoemen frowned.

Alexanor dreamt, that night, of men he knew, men he'd served with in the marines, being dissected alive by Cretans. It was a terrible dream that reflected all his own fears, and he worried that it was a god-sent.

Late in the day, Nabis set up a battery of heavy engines.

In the night, Dinaeos stormed them and burnt them.

They went up to the wall nearest the house, the same stretch of wall that Leon and Alexanor had defended, to watch the engines burn. After they had been reduced to glowing embers, they walked back through darkened streets. There were barricades of carts and paving stones at some cross streets, and an impromptu militia of men and women who called out in the darkness for passwords.

'The city is alert,' Alexanor said.

'The whole city is fighting,' Philopoemen said. 'Not just the rich.'

Leon supported Philopoemen, who was already tired, while Alexanor let them into Phila's yard.

'I'm going to lift weights,' Philopoemen said. 'I am sadly out of shape.'

'You bear a strong resemblance to a Titan, I find,' Alexanor laughed. 'More like Herakles than most of us.'

Philopoemen smiled. 'I feel as if my whole body is slipping away since this wound.' He sat down with lifting stones. 'Tell me what I can do?'

'You can do any exercise that doesn't hurt. I still fear that a little too much strain and we could open the wound, or worse. It is a miracle that you have survived two abdominal wounds. You must not strain it.'

Philopoemen nodded, an odd smile on his face. 'I can't lie around and do nothing any more,' he said.

Then he began to lift the stones, favouring the left side over the right, protecting the wounded area.

A quarter of an hour later, there was a banging at the outer door, and Arkas went to answer it. He returned with Lykortas, who was beaming like a boy with his first sword. He had a roll of parchment.

'Our traitor has served us very well,' he said.

Philopoemen looked up. He was still exercising, sitting on the mosaic floor, lifting stones.

'How?'

Lykortas was smug. 'I arranged for him to see all the gold we have prepared to buy Nabis' mercenaries.'

'We have gold?' Leon asked.

Lykortas shrugged. 'Not much, but we made it look good. And Zophanes' steward, Niceas, was placed to overhear what he apparently thinks was a meeting between Telemnastos and the man who commands the enemy Illyrians, Rhaeterios. And Arkas, here, sold him a set of notes ...'

Arkas blushed.

'... in Philopoemen's own hand, describing negotiations with two Aetolians and two of the Knossian oligarchs.' Lykortas smiled. 'I think my favourite part of the whole plot is that I used the gold he paid Arkas for our supposed "secrets" to create the scene he saw himself. All the gold, ready to buy our enemies. Oh, by the way, about an hour ago, he slipped out of the city with his steward. I made sure he escaped.'

Philopoemen smiled. 'Just for a moment there, I thought Arkas had actually—'

'I would *never!*' Arkas said.

'I know,' Philopoemen said gently. 'Will it work?'

'We had some luck,' Lykortas said. 'The gods were with us that we captured so many Illyrians yesterday, when Plator hit their convoy. But it is a pleasure to use Zophanes' arrogance and his assumptions against him.' He smiled unpleasantly at Alexanor. 'I promise you, his idiot son is truly bred by his father. Greedy and gullible.'

'Strangely just,' Philopoemen said.

'Most of us are punished by our own errors,' Alexanor agreed. 'So now we fight?'

'Now we fight,' Philopoemen said. 'Tell the *phylarchs* and get some sleep.'

CHAPTER THREE

—◦✈◦—

Vale of Gortyna

217 BCE

A little after the sun crested the mountains to the east of the Vale of Gortyna, the city's west gate, facing Phaistos, opened, and the army began to march out. As the army of Knossos faced the east gate, it clearly puzzled many of the Gortynian hoplites, who complained as they marched. Indeed, the west gate faced hilly country and a set of deep valleys, requiring the army to toil along the paths below the walls headed west, almost away from the Spartans. But the *epheboi* and the *psiloi*, the men from the poorest classes, moved easily along the difficult ridges above them.

Before they came back to the plain at the Temple of Apollo, the army turned to the north and marched up one of the many gullies that led up the ridge that faced the city.

Once, the long climb up a steep trail on horseback would have taxed Alexanor's skills, but now it no longer even gave him pause. He leant well forward, supporting his weight with his thighs, easing the back of his horse as the beast did the work of cresting the long ridge. Behind him, the men of the Gortynian phalanx sweated in the crisp, late summer morning air, and complained loudly of the fatiguing march and a hundred other things that helped them cover their fears.

Alexanor had spent enough time with soldiers and marines to know the sound of the morning before a fight: voices a little shrill; arguments too heated; men bragging or posturing, a few openly expressing fear. The younger men betrayed their emotions with too much excitement, too much bright chatter, an insistent edge to every word. Older men, veterans of a dozen fights, were more silent, or simply hid their fears in a torrent of complaint.

'Fucking Achaean aristo, up and down fucking hills and what for?' muttered a voice close to Alexanor. The man meant to be heard; free men on Crete were never afraid of speaking up.

Alexanor smiled and looked at Philopoemen.

'That's what the hymn to Ares should sound like,' he said. 'The grumbling of the veteran hoplite.'

Philopoemen crested the last of the ridge and turned his horse off the line of march. The Gortynian phalanx was advancing by pairs of files from the left of the formation they'd made when they mustered in the agora. Ahead of them were the men of Lyttos, men who'd lost everything – their wives, their homes, their city. They had been hosted in Gortyna, but they were silent, withdrawn men. They didn't grumble or complain, but marched along, two files wide, carrying their own shields, whereas the Gortynians, closer to home, often had their spears and shields carried by their sons, or their slaves.

Away behind the phalanx of Gortyna were the white leather *thorakes* of the men of Polyrrhenia. Gortyna's best ally in the war with Knossos had supplied its whole citizen levy, minus enough men to hold their town in the event of a disaster or sudden attack by the Rhodian fleet.

Philopoemen looked back at the city, rose-pink in the rising sun.

'I don't believe in praising Ares in any form,' he said. 'My patron is Zeus.'

'I was attempting humour, however weak,' Alexanor said.

'Oh,' Philopoemen remarked. His face was pale, his lips tight.

'Are you in pain?' Alexanor asked.

'Yes,' Philopoemen snapped.

Alexanor watched the phalanx go past. Most men lifted an arm and waved at Philopoemen, and a few even reached out and touched his horse for luck.

'Take us in, *Strategos!*' called one young man.

'Achilles Athanatos!' a whole *taxeis* chanted as they marched by, and Philopoemen flushed red.

'No worries, mate,' called another man. 'Show me the fucking Spartan. I'll show him a fight.'

'You aren't *worried*, are you?' asked Alexanor, fascinated. 'If I saw any other man behaving like that, I'd say he was—'

'Of course I'm worried!' Philopoemen snapped, his voice low. 'I'm a *fucking* imposter.'

'What?'

'I've never commanded a battle before . . .'

'You won Sellasia,' Alexanor said. 'Where is this trouble of spirit coming from? Let me see your abdomen.'

'Do you go to the theatre, Alexanor?'

'You know I do,' the priest replied.

While more and more of the phalanx strode past, Alexanor un-hooked the pins in the side of Philopoemen's cavalry breastplate of bronze and iron, holding them between his lips for safekeeping. He turned Philopoemen and his horse so that the marching men wouldn't see the wound, and he looked at the bandages. There were brown stains in two places; the wound was still leaking fluid.

'I have been known to attend the theatre,' Alexanor said again, somewhat muffled by the pins. 'I'm partial to Menander. You know that.'

Philopoemen nodded. He ignored the priest's actions, his eyes on the valley, still a little dark, far below them. Smoke rose from the poorer sections of the city. Bronze-clad sentries walked the walls; the eastern gate had a garrison so large that, as they drilled, they raised a dust cloud.

Out on the plain, a line of light marked the sun's progress through the olive groves and fields. The Knossian camp was visible, with a long line of earthworks and an abattis of felled olive trees covering the whole front of the army. A cavalry patrol passed along the front of the camp, headed out onto the plain to the west.

'Do you ever watch a play and think, damn it, I could write better than that? Do you ever hear a speech and think, no, the mercenary shouldn't sound like that, he should curse more?'

Alexanor laughed. 'Yes.' He was re-wrapping the wound. He smiled to himself. 'Yes, I'm always a critic.'

'Because you can improve on the play, do you think you could write one?' Philopoemen asked.

The Knossian cavalry patrol, probably Aetolians, were riding north, not west, headed for the foot of the ridge on which Philopoemen's army was marching.

Alexanor closed the *thorax*, popping the two halves together, getting the catches that held the pins into their slots, and then taking the pins out of his mouth.

'In my next life, I'll be an excellent *skeurophoros*,' he said. 'I know how to wait on a man in fine armour.'

He could feel Philopoemen's pulse. It was rapid.

'I take your point,' Alexanor said. 'It's one thing to see the enemy error at Sellasia, and another thing to plan the whole battle.'

Philopoemen's pulse ran even faster.

'Are you all right?' Alexanor asked.

Out at the edge of the sun, the Aetolian patrol turned onto one of the farm roads and began to trot, raising dust, headed east.

Alexanor felt his friend begin to breathe.

'I have taken a ludicrous, enormous risk,' Philopoemen said.

'Your hands are shaking,' Alexanor said.

'Tell me something I don't know. Your talent for expressing the obvious is unmatched.'

'I could give you a little lotus flower, perhaps ...'

'I'd rather be irritable and in full control, thanks.' Philopoemen's pulse had slowed as soon as the cavalry turned away.

'You are afraid that this stealthy movement will be discovered?' Alexanor asked.

'We will definitely be discovered. It's all about when. If I can get the *psiloi* and the Lyttians down off the ridge and onto the plain, then my risk will be ...'

He didn't complete his thought. A second cavalry patrol was emerging from the head of the camp. But they merely formed in four ranks and waited.

'Damn,' Philopoemen said. 'He's alert. If Nabis was a little less competent ...'

He rode ahead.

The next hour was long for Alexanor and, he suspected, even longer for the Achaean. Rain had washed out a section of the track they were following over the hills. The young shepherd guiding them along the ridge lost his way and led the Lyttians astray, and they took almost a quarter of an hour to backtrack.

Quietly, fiercely, Philopoemen demanded that they reorder their files.

'We could be fighting as soon as we enter the plain,' he said. 'You need to have the same files you had when you marched off.'

This was a level of discipline seldom attempted by Cretans, and it took time to unravel the mess made by some of the Lyttians turning and walking back to the correct trail while others countermarched and dozens of men simply clambered up the rocky ridge to the higher trail. The movement raised a telltale crescent of dust, ruddy in the early morning sun.

Alexanor wondered if Philopoemen would lose his temper, but instead, as the odds of discovery went up and the Lyttians argued, he became calmer. He dismounted, heedless of the pain of his wound, and took men by the shoulder, his tone light.

'I know it's silly, but you need to stand here,' he said to one man.

'Listen, is this the spot you started in?' he asked another.

'No, I was behind Philip,' the man said.

'Better not get too far from Philip,' Philopoemen agreed. 'He must miss you.'

The dour Lyttians managed to laugh.

And they moved.

Out on the plain, the sun was full on the valley, and the cavalry at the head of the Knossian camp were mounting.

'We walk all around the bleedin' city just so we can fight outside the fucking gate?' asked a *thētes*-class skirmisher. 'My legs are already done.'

'Maybe the Achaean thinks we need exercise,' muttered another. 'He's big on exercise, from what I hear.'

'Fucking aristos,' a third added. 'He has a horse.'

The three men trotted by, apparently oblivious that the *strategos* was behind them.

'Another quarter of an hour,' Philopoemen breathed. 'If you have the ear of the gods, this is the time for prayer. Zeus, saviour of man, I never imagined that this would take so long. And we haven't even begun to form yet.'

Below him, the *psiloi* were entering the olive groves on the lower slopes off the long ridge.

'We're spotted,' Philopoemen said.

Sure enough, a dozen Aetolian cavalrymen emerged from the olive groves and cantered across the open ground towards the Gortynian *psiloi*. They were distant figures; the shouts of the Aetolians were utterly disconnected from their actions, so that a man and mount accelerated to a gallop and then, after a delay, came his shout of 'Go, go!'

A handful of *psiloi*, a little clump of animated ants, sprinted into the open ground and threw javelins, the iron heads and polished shafts catching the brilliant sunlight.

A horseman fell. Another horseman turned in a swirl of dust to help his mate, and went down; at the distance, it wasn't obvious what had happened.

The *psiloi* all gave a cheer and went forward, pursuing the Aetolians, mistaking their return to camp for headlong flight. And the Aetolians, stung by their losses of just two men, ran, their galloping horses leaving thin lines of dust to hang like coloured smoke in the new sunlight.

Philopoemen was shaking his head. 'Well, that's not what was supposed to happen,' he said, as the *psiloi* cleared the olive groves and began to cross a belt of barley fields. 'I guess this is how battles go wrong. Here I go, brother. Wish me luck.'

Alexanor was going to say something, but Philopoemen put his charger's head at the slope and was off down it. To Alexanor, no longer a novice rider, it looked more like a controlled fall than a gallop. The horse ignored the trail and went straight down the hillside towards the distant *psiloi*.

Alexanor rode to the head of the Lyttians.

'Faster, gentlemen,' he said. 'There's trouble on the plain.'

The Lyttian commander, Xaris, looked back at his men.

'On me,' he called.

He broke into a trot, and the long file, like a bronze and iron snake that ran all the way back over the ridge, began to move faster.

Alexanor rode down the trail, passing the head of the files of *epheboi*, and breaking into a trot as he hit the shallower slope into the olive groves. He was still high enough on the ridge to see activity in the enemy camp, and a long double file of men on foot trotting towards him.

Then he was in the olive trees. There was now no one ahead of him; the *epheboi* were behind him, and he didn't see Telemnastos and his League archers anywhere.

He turned back to the south, leaving the farm track and riding down a series of terraces like shallow steps down the hillside. Halfway to the valley floor, his horse gave a great leap; he was caught unawares, but managed to stay on as they landed, and the horse ran on.

In heartbeats he was coming out of the olive groves. The sun was hotter on the valley floor, and his horse swished through the barley as if he was flying in a cloud of gold, and he could see Philopoemen ahead of him.

'There's men coming for you,' Alexanor said.

'Where away?' Philopoemen asked.

Alexanor, looking down, realised that the barley was full of men, lying flat.

'Right in front of us ...'

'*Peltastoi*,' Philopoemen said, kneeling on his horse's back. 'Well spotted. Here they come. Run.'

Alexanor turned his tired horse and leant forward, using his weight to urge the horse to speed, and they were away, riding back for the olive groves.

The *peltastoi* behind gave a whoop and followed, plunging into the barley fields.

'We can stop running,' Philopoemen said. 'Go and find Telemnastos and tell him to keep going east and not to be distracted by this.'

'But—'

'Go!' Philopoemen said.

Behind him, dozens of little men with rocks and javelins and little round shields rose out of the grain and began to savage the foreign *peltastoi*, most of whom were Greek mercenaries.

Alexanor tapped his heels, and his horse responded, and they were away, flying back over the golden grain. But once he was in among the olive trees on the lower slope, he had no idea where to find Telemnastos. He rode part of the way up the ridge, dismounted, found the Lyttians and finally found Telemnastos, so far to the east that the ridge was a distant memory. He arrived too late for his message to have any effect; Telemnastos had done the right thing without an order.

Telemnastos passed over a lower ridge and then turned his whole force of archers south, onto the plain amid the fields of grain. The fight between the enemy *peltastoi* and the local *psiloi* was three stades to the west, now. They were to the north of the enemy camp, and almost behind it, and the camp itself was like an ants' nest opened by the shovel of a farmer, with men going in every direction.

A few dozen enemy skirmishers were coming in a loose knot across the fields. Telemnastos formed his archers in a line, wheeled it to the right, and unleashed a single flight of arrows when the enemy *psiloi* were still two hundred paces away.

The volley struck the men moving across a wheat field, and the survivors broke and ran. Half of them were down.

'This is where he told me to be,' Telemnastos said. 'You want to ride back and say we're in place?'

Alexanor mounted again and rode back as the Lyttians trotted up in two long files. But Telemnastos waved, and even as Alexanor rode by, Xaris trotted to the right end of the archers, turned into the line, and stopped, his spear extended out to the right to indicate where his men should stand. The files began to come up, the Lyttian phalanx filling in like a water tank on a rainy day.

Alexanor passed the last files of the Lyttians coming down the low, second ridge, and then the Gortynians coming up the other slope. He waved at every group as he passed.

From the top of the low ridge, he could see dust in the barley fields, but that was all. But halfway down the line of Gortynians, he encountered Philopoemen, riding the other way.

'Hah!' Philopoemen called.

The anxiety was clearly gone; the man seemed larger, sat straighter. He was smiling.

'Hah?' Alexanor said. 'Telemnastos says that he is on the ground you assigned him, and the Lyttians were just forming their phalanx to the right of the archers.'

'Splendid,' Philopoemen said. 'I mean, not really what I had planned, but I'll take it. Antiphatas! Here!' he roared suddenly. 'This way!'

The commander of the Gortynian phalanx waved and followed Philopoemen.

'Not the line I thought we'd form on. Now we're making it up as we go along.'

Philopoemen trotted off, leaving Alexanor, who dismounted on the low ridge and rested his horse. He found a spring with a basin, gave his charger water, and drank some himself, while dozens of men from the Gortynian phalanx left the ranks, filled their canteens, and ran back.

An hour passed. The Gortynians formed loosely, with their servants, sons and slaves still among them. Off to the east, there was a cloud of dust. The Knossian camp began to spit out clumps of men, and then, almost as fast as a storm cloud brings rain, the enemy line began to form. Alexanor watched Nabis ride out, look at the Lyttians, and ride away, his dozen Thessalian bodyguards at his heels.

Aristaenos rode up at the head of the Achaean cavalry, now almost three hundred strong.

'Philopoemen told me to take the cavalry all the way to the left,' he said. 'I don't see it. I should cover the Gortynians. Was that Nabis, riding away?'

Alexanor looked at the younger man. 'Where did he tell you to go?'

'Past the archers. But now I think ...'

Alexanor nodded. 'I suspect you should do what he said,' he put in, as kindly as possible.

Aristaenos had a tendency to look for solutions when there was no problem to be found.

'What if Nabis comes back with cavalry while the Gortynians still have all their baggage handlers in the ranks?' he said. 'Besides, what do you know about war, anyway? Fill my canteen, will you?' he asked, reaching down to hand Alexanor a beautiful bronze canteen.

Alexanor shrugged. 'If the *strategos* orders you to the left of the line,' he said.

'I'm not even sure that Philopoemen *can* give me orders,' Aristaenos said. 'After all, I'm the commander of the Achaean cavalry. I'm not even a member of the League of Crete.'

'This seems an odd moment to refuse his orders.'

Aristaenos shrugged. 'He doesn't know everything. He was ordered to stay in the reserve at Sellasia and look what he did! I was there. Everyone praised him for it.'

And that's what you crave, don't you? Alexanor thought.

'Telemnastos was afraid of being outflanked,' Alexanor said.

'He was, was he?' Aristaenos shook his head. 'No, from this hill I can see everything.'

He turned and ordered the Achaeans to dismount. They were a curious mix of men, some young idealists and adventurers, proud to serve the Achaean League, excited to be 'overseas' on Crete instead of home in Arkadia, but for every one of these men, there were two less willing – farmers and labourers for whom 'service with the League' was preferable to arrest for debt, or other crimes. Many were expert horsemen, but a few were very poor; the unit had been sent as *peltastoi* and *thorakatoi*, or armoured spearmen, and only mounted on Crete itself.

Opposite them, a phalanx was forming. A squadron of cavalry-men passed behind the new phalanx – hundreds of men, their horses moving quickly, raising dust punctuated only by their spear points glittering in the now hot sun.

Alexanor thought his horse was better. He nodded to Aristaenos.

'I'm off to find my hospital,' he said. 'I think you'd be better off where the *strategos* posted you.'

Aristaenos smiled. 'So you keep saying,' he agreed.

Alexanor walked up the slope to the farm road near the crest. The Gortynians were all in their ranks, although not yet closed; the Polyrrhenian phalanx was forming from left to right. Three thousand men in a dozen ranks would only take up three or four hundred paces of frontage, but it took time. The enemy phalanx opposite had started later, but manoeuvring on the flat plain, coming out of a camp with interior lines, the enemy was forming twice as fast.

Alexanor mounted and rode back, past the last of the Polyrrhenians. Behind them were Periander and his Boeotians, and in among them the victorious *psiloi*, hundreds of them, far outnumbering the Attic mercenaries. And there was Philopoemen, giving orders. Leon and the priests and assistants from the sanctuary at Lentas were just coming by, along with Arkas and Philopoemen's household, leading a dozen sheep.

'There's a spring of fresh water about halfway up the hill,' Alexanor said, pointing to the green trees around the spring.

'I see it,' Leon said.

Indeed, the little stand of bright green, oaks and even grass, amid the golden brown of late summer on Crete, made the spring tolerably obvious.

'Let's put the hospital there,' Alexanor said.

Leon smiled at him, the look of a man who didn't really need to be told the obvious.

He nodded at the sheep. 'He must be the last man in the Hellenic world who actually plans to sacrifice to the gods before battle.'

'That's Philopoemen,' Alexanor agreed. 'I'll be with you ...'

Leon shook his head. 'If he falls dead, we're done,' he said, looking at the Achaean. 'You stay with him. I'll run the aid station.'

Alexanor wanted to protest, but he also wanted to stay with Philopoemen.

Leon shook his head. 'I'm afraid even to look at him. His face is almost grey.'

'His wound is leaking,' Alexanor confessed.

'Apollo, now?' Leon closed his eyes, and then opened them. 'I'll pray. Stay with him.'

'I'll pray, too,' Alexanor said. 'I don't think there's a human, medical solution.'

'Your line isn't straight,' Alexanor hoped his forced cheerfulness wasn't too apparent.

Philopoemen turned and looked back past the priest.

The Allied line was indeed angled. On the right, the Boeotian mercenaries under Periander were quite far from the enemy line, tucked well back in the little valley between the big ridge and the lower hill to the west.

When Alexanor looked back over his shoulder, he could just see the federal archers, well advanced, the Lyttians stepped back on the eastern flanks of the low hill, the Gortynians and Polyrrhenians stepped back further still.

'It's an echelon,' Philopoemen said. 'Alexander did it. So did Epaminondas.'

He looked back at the huddle of Boeotians and *psiloi* on their right. Beyond them, back on the big ridge, was Dinaeos with the mercenary cavalry, and a long tail of dust behind them indicating the baggage.

'Aristaenos is between the Gortynians and the Polyrrhenians,' Alexanor said.

'What?' Philopoemen shook his head. 'Where?'

'On the hillside. There. Where the two grain fields come together.'

328

Alexanor looked around. 'I think he has some notion of having an effect on the battle and being a hero.'

'Aristaenos is unlikely …' Philopoemen shook his head. 'He wants to be independent. He's just not ready.' He grinned. 'I may not be ready myself. Look, there's Nabis.'

A little below them, on the plain of Gortyna, Nabis had almost formed his army. It was formed perpendicular to his camp.

On his right, which was Alexanor's left, he had a body of cavalrymen with brightly polished bronze helmets and breastplates that flashed gold in the sun. Next to them was the phalanx, and it was not broken into different regional blocks. Instead, it stood in a single block of five hundred files, all in the Macedonian style, with small, rimless shields the size of a man's straw hat, and *sarissae*, long pikes.

Next in line was *another* huge phalanx, although this one was neither so deep nor so well-armed.

'Who are they?' Alexanor asked. The phalanx in question seemed to ebb and flow.

'That's the phalanx of Knossos,' Philopoemen said with some satisfaction. 'They aren't even sure they want to be here. After all, the *Presbyteroi* have taken away their citizen rights. How well would you fight?'

Next, almost directly across from Alexanor's position, was a loose line of men who also glittered with armour.

'Illyrians,' Philopoemen said. 'And next to them, Thracians. Very slow to form, which is good for us, because Nabis has half as many men again as we have.'

He watched for a little while.

'He's putting all the cavalry at the right of his line,' he said. 'A big, strong, Spartan alignment, just as he demonstrated yesterday.' Philopoemen began riding towards Aristaenos. 'All his best troops on the right – Aetolian cavalry and his mercenary phalanx. But he's moved the Thracians. Yesterday they were also on the right.'

He turned and looked under his hand.

'When will you attack?' Alexanor asked.

Philopoemen wasn't watching the enemy. He was watching Periander's men. His file leaders were pushing the *psiloi* into ranks behind the well-armoured Attic mercenaries, but the whole was still a confused mess. Opposite them, the Illyrians were pounding their shields with their spears and chanting. But here, the enemy was curiously far away. As Nabis had formed straight across the side of his camp, along a road that might have been laid out by a craftsman's ruler, his right was much closer to Philopoemen's left than his own left, which was several stades from Philopoemen's angled line.

'I think Lykortas' story about a traitor in the Thracians has indeed rattled his cage,' Philopoemen concluded. 'Or the Thracians would still be in the position of trust, on the right.' He turned his horse and began to trot.

'You put Periander in the position of trust,' Alexanor called, rising into the trot.

'I put my best on the left, facing his best.' Philopoemen looked back at Periander. 'As to attacking, it's Nabis who will attack.'

'Up this hill?' Alexanor shook his head, his thighs burning. 'Why would he do that?'

Philopoemen rode over to Aristaenos. 'Good morning,' he called out.

Aristaenos had dismounted. 'I'm here because it's the best place,' he said without preamble. 'From here, I can—'

'I need you to go and face the Aetolians,' Philopoemen said. 'Only you can do it. Your men have won a dozen skirmishes with them. I need you to cover the eastern flank of the Lyttians. If the enemy phalanx pushes them back too far, our whole line will crack.'

Aristaenos shook his head. 'No, what I think we need to do is get into the seam between his two phalanxes right there with the cavalry.'

Philopoemen nodded. He looked where Aristaenos was indicating for a long moment.

'No,' he said. 'Please go off and cover the left.'

Aristaenos' face worked, his cheeks moving like land in an earthquake.

'Please,' Philopoemen said.

Aristaenos shrugged. 'I think you're wrong,' he said.

Philopoemen nodded. 'Well, friend, I think you are wrong, too.' He grinned. 'But if I'm wrong about the left, I'm probably wrong about everything else.'

'We should attack,' Aristaenos said. 'Now, while Nabis is still disorganised.'

Philopoemen shook his head. 'Let him attack us.'

'He won't attack us! We have two hills – a better position. Even with his numbers—'

'Nabis is arrogant,' Philopoemen said. 'He has staked everything on a major battle. Now he will be arrogant. He assumes his mercenaries are better men than our Gortynians.'

'Well, I think you are wrong,' Aristaenos said. 'I think we could have won right here.'

'Noted.' Philopoemen's humour seemed unaffected.

Aristaenos made a great show of mounting in disgust. He didn't hurry to his men, and when he got there, they heard him tell the Achaeans that they 'had to move, because Philopoemen said so'.

'You are not tempted to eviscerate him on the spot?' Alexanor said.

Philopoemen ignored him, watching Nabis. The Spartan commander was apparently giving an oration to the mercenary phalanx.

'Why do you believe he'll attack you?' Alexanor asked.

Philopoemen pointed at the two hills, or rather, the high ridge on his right and the low hill round him that held his centre and part of his left.

'Doesn't it look like the Spartan position at Sellasia? I'm trying to get inside his head and give him the chance to change the past.' Philopoemen smiled. 'And anyway, you see that spring?'

'See it?' Alexanor joked. 'I drank from it. Here, have some.'

'It is the best water on this part of the plain,' Philopoemen said. 'We're on the flank of his camp, and we have his main water supply.' He smiled grimly. 'He has three choices – attack us, storm the city, or retire to the east.'

'Who did you leave in the city?' Alexanor asked.

Even from the low hill, he could see the glitter of steel on the gates of the city, but looking at the Allied array, the only troops missing were the Illyrians, away somewhere in the north on a raid.

'The city is empty,' Philopoemen said. 'There are women on the walls in all our spare armour – even trophies from the temples, polished and newly strapped.'

'Oh, gods,' Alexanor breathed.

'Relax. The risk was this morning, before we were formed. I told you that I intended to take every advantage I could. We have most of his water. Every minute he waits, his men are thirstier. That's not even my last trick.'

'And Aristaenos?'

'He'll fight well enough,' Philopoemen said. But he didn't sound so sure of himself.

Another hour passed. Nabis rode up and down his line, and then did so again.

'He knows perfectly well I've outmanoeuvred him,' Philopoemen said. 'That's a taunt, too.'

'Can he still march away to the east?' Alexanor asked.

'I guess he might. But if he does, the campaign is over, and he might as well march back to Knossos. His mercenaries might defect today.'

'Really?'

'Lykortas claims that he killed the Illyrian commander last night – executed him in his tent. We can only hope.' Philopoemen watched.

Nabis rode along the front again. He rode all the way from west to east, and then he placed himself with the Aetolian cavalry.

'And now we fight,' Philopoemen said.

Only then did he ride down the last of the slope to the front of the Gortynians. Their ranks were closed, and despite a large gap between their left and the Lyttians' right, they were well formed, on good ground, with a gentle slope in front of them, the ground falling away. The mercenary phalanx would have a long climb to reach them, in the full heat of the noonday sun.

Philopoemen rode to the very centre of the Gortynian phalanx.

'Comrades!' he roared.

His voice carried so well that heads turned among the Lyttians, and among the Polyrrhenians.

He turned his horse and pointed at the enemy.

'They have had neither sleep nor water,' he called. 'Last night we slept in our beds. Every one of you has water.' He waited a moment, and his voice echoed off the distant hillside. 'All you need to do to win is hold this hill. As long as you stand, men of Gortyna, your freedom is assured. No tyrant. No false laws. No one has the responsibility for your future but you yourselves. Win here, and Knossos will never face you again – at least, not in your lifetimes. Lose here, and your wives are slaves, your farms lost, and you, yourselves, will be dead.'

No one cheered.

'You wanted a battle,' he called. 'I have done what I could to make that battle *unfair*.'

Men laughed. Across the valley, the mercenary phalanx began to come forward. Trumpets sounded, and the enemy, a thousand files wide, came forward.

'All you have to do is hold!' Philopoemen said. 'And tonight, we will set up a trophy, and tomorrow, we will sacrifice for victory.'

Now they roared.

Philopoemen rode around the end of the Gortynians and dismounted where Arkas had a pair of sheep tethered and had built a rough altar of stone. He and a dozen other men had raised a big stone and set it on a base of smaller stones.

Philopoemen walked up and took a heavy knife from Arkas, a big knife shaped like a *kopis*. He took the rope round the whiter, cleaner sheep's neck, pulled it to stretch the animal's head, and then struck, his knife faster than Alexanor would have thought possible. The knife didn't slash down, but cut up, severing the sheep's throat and turning it so that it bled out across the altar even as its legs buckled.

Two men reached and lifted the sheep onto the stone.

Philopoemen opened its gut with a single slash. The entrails poured out, and Alexanor thought of the man he'd dissected at the spring by Petra, and about Philopoemen's wound.

Philopoemen looked up from his sacrifice. He looked from right to left, like an eagle looking for prey, and then he motioned with one bloody hand to Arkas.

'Bring me the other one. Unless you want to?' he asked Alexanor.

Alexanor shook his head. 'This is for a priest of Zeus. If you were to ask a priest of Asklepios, he might pray that both armies ran away and no one was killed.'

Philopoemen barely smiled. He was in another place, his eyes distant. Syrmas poured water over his hands, a hasty sacred washing, and again the knife flashed out, and the rumble of hooves to the east didn't interrupt the ritual. Even as the sheep bled out, the Thracian grasped it with Kleostratos and the two men all but threw it on the altar.

Philopoemen glanced at the sky. Off to the right, over the city, an eagle rose in lazy circles, the very best of omens.

Philopoemen raised his bloody hands and intoned the hymn to

Zeus, the Cretan hymn that was sung in Sparta and Arkadia and throughout the Dorian world.

The rumble of hooves became a roar to the east.

He added the second sheep's entrails to the first and stirred them with the tip of the *kopis*.

'Victory!' he shouted.

Every eye in both the Lyttian and Gortynian phalanxes was on him, and when he raised his bloody hands, a shout went up across the valley.

'Victory!' men shouted. 'Nike! Nike for Gortyna! Nike for Lyttos!'

And then he stood calmly while Arkas poured spring water over his hands, and he wiped them clean on a white towel.

When he turned to Alexanor his eyes were bright, and there was colour in his face.

'The gods help those who help themselves.' He put a hand to the centre of his gut and winced. 'I hate watching other men fight.'

'Nonetheless, your wound ... You cannot fight.'

Philopoemen closed his eyes briefly. 'Maybe I'm not meant to survive this,' he said quietly.

'You wouldn't make me look bad, would you?' Alexanor said, with false humour.

Philopoemen shrugged. 'I'd give my life to win this. I will, if that's what it takes.'

He rode along the front of the hill, watching the mercenary phalanx come on. Other officers were giving orations: Cirdas, Antiphatas' second-in-command, got roar after roar from the Gortynians; Xaris pointed down the long slope at the enemy and made the Lyttians growl with rage.

On the far left, the enemy cavalry was reforming. They had clearly failed in their first attack, and the Achaean horse waited in the open ground.

'That won't work twice,' Philopoemen said.

A little less than a stade away, Nabis' red cloak floated behind him as he rallied the Aetolians.

'The archers were interspersed with our cavalry,' Philopoemen said. 'He lost a lot of horses.' The Achaean nodded, as if talking to himself. 'And he should be wondering where I am. I should have put Aristaenos in my cloak.'

'Aristaenos is going to charge Nabis,' Alexanor said.

Philopoemen was watching the enemy commander. He glanced back.

'That would be foolish,' he said. 'Where he is, he has the archers— Oh, gods.'

Aristaenos launched his men across the valley floor. The Achaeans were well formed, a single squadron in a deep rhomboid.

But the Aetolians, however shocked by all the bows they'd run into, were old soldiers, veterans of other ambushes, and they rallied quickly. They outnumbered the Achaean horse almost two to one, even after a volley of arrows, and the clash was explosive.

Philopoemen watched, tight-lipped and silent, as the Achaean horse was routed. A few men broke out of the back of the mounted mêlée, and then more, and more, until the whole formation broke, and the Aetolians launched in pursuit.

'Oh, gods.'

Philopoemen seemed to deflate, and his shoulders bent forward and his head drooped as if he could not bear to watch.

'I should have been there,' he said bitterly.

'You should have been everywhere,' Alexanor said. 'Can Telemnastos save it?'

'No,' Philopoemen said.

And then, almost at his feet, Xaris ordered the Lyttians *forward*.

The small phalanx of Lyttians marched down the hill, their order perfect. They were the best of the allies – the descendants of Spartan colonists, they used the Spartan orders and trained to the *agoge*. The loss of their city rendered them both hopeless and beyond despair. Xaris acted on his own; he saw the victory of the Aetolian horse and chose to attack before his own flank was lost.

Aetolian horsemen and Lyttian hoplites passed within a stone's throw of each other, but the cavalrymen were on the phalanx's shielded side. The fleeing Achaeans were a safer bet, and the Aetolians pursued their defeated opponents instead of turning into the flank of the Lyttians. They, for their part, were only half as deep as the enemy mercenaries, and instead of being in a Macedonian formation, they were armed with old-fashioned *aspides* and spears only half as long as the enemy pikes.

And they flinched, even in their advance, when the pikes were close.

335

Alexanor heard Philopoemen cry aloud as the Lyttian line rippled and the pike heads struck home. Men died without avenging themselves, and the front of the Lyttians seemed to crumple as the unstoppable fist of the pikes slammed deeper and deeper into the Lyttians' formation. Men fell.

The Lyttians stumbled back. And back again. And back again. In a hundred heartbeats they were driven back almost as many paces.

Philopoemen began to ride forward. Alexanor caught his reins.

Philopoemen shook his head. 'I'd rather die here,' he said.

'I'd rather you didn't,' Alexanor said.

The Lyttians were still giving ground. Their bold attack had taken them out onto the plain; now, as they were pushed back, and back, they were being pushed back onto the lower slopes of the low hill. Their two hundred files began to bend to conform to the shape of the hill.

But the *rate* of their stumbling retreat began to slow.

Almost two hundred paces back from where their brave charge had begun, their rear rankers dug in their heels. Men leant into their mates. The pikes were deep into their formation; the moment of terror was past.

The men in the front ranks of the Lyttian formation had shorter spears, and then began to use them. Pikemen began to fall. The mercenary advance was slowed.

Without a word, Philopoemen began to ride to his right, towards the Gortynians. But Cirdas needed no instructions. Alexanor could hear him roaring orders over the clash of a thousand shields, and the left files of the Gortynian phalanx went forward, and then the whole block. The front was disordered. Antiphatas was out in front, bellowing for men to dress the line.

But the leftmost files slammed into the enemy mercenaries. They did so at a very slight angle, and their order was imperfect. They were armed in the old Iphikratian manner: Macedonian-style shields but short spears, just twice the height of a man. But the mercenaries had been too eager to finish the Lyttians, and their files were straining to reach the Spartan colonists. The Gortynian spears plunged into their ranks and suddenly the mercenaries were stopped dead and the Gortynian phalanx was pressing forward.

The whole battle was pivoting.

Alexanor came over the side-crest of the central hill and there below him was the phalanx of Knossos. However unwilling they had been before the contest, they were coming on now, passing the edge of the mercenaries and crashing into their traditional enemies of Gortyna, so that, whatever their political feelings, they were pushing with spirit. The right files of the Gortynian phalanx and the whole of the allied Polyrrhenians met the oncoming Knossians with a clatter of spears and shields that filled the whole of the Vale of Gortyna with a sound of bronze-throated thunder. Shields cracked and shattered at the impact; spears broke at the head, or halfway down the shaft. The men of Knossos had the same old-fashioned arms as the men of Gortyna and Polyrrhenia, and their traditional hatred fuelled the fire.

A hundred men died in a second. The line didn't move by a foot.

The two infantry centres were helmet to helmet. The men in the midst of the press could smell the breath of their enemies. In a forest of shattered spear shafts, men fought with swords and knives and bare hands. The Knossians were deeper; the Allies were uphill.

The dead began to fall atop the wounded.

Somewhere, a brave man gave his life, sweeping spear shafts into his own chest, and the Knossians pressed forward. The Polyrrhenians stumbled back five paces, and then held, again.

From his vantage, Alexanor could see from the end of the Polyrrhenians all the way to the leftmost file of the Lyttians. The whole line was engaged.

'Well,' Philopoemen said. He looked back, as if measuring.

The Aetolian cavalry was rallying behind the Lyttians. Telemnastos was loosing arrows into them, and knots of Aetolians tried to drive the archers off. But it was not in balance. Nabis had hundreds of cavalrymen, and the Lyttians were only just able to hold their part of the hill, their leftmost files already bent back, almost like a *lambda*, to keep the rightmost files of the mercenaries, who overlapped them, from turning their flank.

Philopoemen nodded. 'If they last a quarter of an hour,' he said aloud, and touched his heels to his mount. He wore boots, and spurs, and his charger, who was not used to being spurred, burst into an angry gallop.

Alexanor's horse followed, as horses will, and he almost came off in the first ten strides. Then he floated along the back of the mêlée

– twenty thousand men locked, head to head, face to face, on a front of four stades.

Down in the side valley, in the fields of barley where the *psiloi* had ambushed the *peltastoi*, the Boeotian mercenaries waited, their rear ranks filled with the 'little' men of Gortyna.

Opposite them, the Thracians and Illyrians came on – the Illyrians boldly, the Thracians hesitantly. The Illyrians outran their supports, bursting into a running charge through the golden barley fields.

Periander ordered the Boeotians to retreat. The whole block, Boeotians and their new rear-rankers, stumbled back, leaving the flank of the Polyrrhenians open, but the enemy Illyrians were bent on winning, their charge too wild to be controlled with fine manoeuvring.

Alexanor saw it in the moment before the Illyrians did.

The retreat of the Boeotians was to expose a ditch – a ditch that the *psiloi* and the labourers had had three hours to dig, and then to line with sharpened stakes. The Illyrians slammed into it and men fell; the screams sounded even above the thunder-crashes in the centre.

The rear ranks of the Illyrians piled forward, pushing their front ranks into the pit traps, until the Illyrians were across a bridge of their own dead and wounded, the injured shrill and desperate.

They met a wall of professional steel. The Boeotians killed the survivors of the ditch. They held their ground, shedding the Illyrian charge like a tile roof sheds winter rain. The Illyrians huddled at the edge of the ditch, a handful of beautifully armoured warriors trying to whip the rest back into a killing frenzy. The Boeotians kept their shields up, and behind them, the *Neodamodeis*, the newly enfranchised *psiloi*, stood firm, pushing against the backs of the Boeotians, handing up javelins to the professionals so that a steady rain of death fell on the Illyrians.

Alexanor followed Philopoemen. He rode right past the rear of the Boeotian *taxeis*, and then up the long ridge, through the first olive trees, to the far right of his line, where Dinaeos and his own cavalry waited, hanging off the end of the now utterly hesitant Thracians.

'I was going anyway,' Dinaeos called. 'How is Aristaenos doing?'

'Broken,' Philopoemen said.

'Don't you want to go and fight Nabis yourself?' Lykortas asked.

'My wants are neither here not there,' Philopoemen snapped. 'The Spartan is there, and we are here, and we can win this thing right now.'

Gone was the morning's hesitation, the grey face. Now he truly looked like Achilles, and the doctor in Alexanor wanted to know if his wound had stopped bleeding, too. *Even I think he is superhuman.*

Dinaeos nodded sharply. 'Yes, *Strategos*,' he said.

'Wait!' Philopoemen roared. 'Just walk them out. Let the Thracians see. We need them to run. We need to let Lykortas' rumour and his fake gold do their work, so that our own Thracians are fresh. We need to charge the Knossian phalanx, not the Thracians. You understand?'

Dinaeos nodded, his eyes on the enemy Thracians. 'Forward at a walk!' he ordered the cavalry.

Kleostratos blew the *Hipparchos'* trumpet, and every enemy Thracian head turned. They'd halted in a huddle when the Illyrians broke; now, the emergence of enemy cavalry on their flank panicked them. They turned and ran.

Lykortas whooped as if he was himself a Thracian.

'Best victory money can buy!' he called.

Philopoemen drew his sword. 'Companions!' he called. 'We need to break the Knossians faster than Nabis can break our Lyttians.'

'Not you,' Alexanor said.

Philopoemen shook his head. 'I'm done here. Win or lose, this was my plan. I will ride with the charge.'

He turned, and raised his hand, and Arkas tossed him a spear – a *longche*, with a heavy head and a long, double-tapered shaft.

Alexanor reached for Philopoemen's reins while he was distracted, just as Kleostratos put the trumpet to his lips. His fingers closed ...

On air.

Philopoemen whipped the reins out from under his reach as the whole squadron started forward, down the ridge. He looked back.

'You should come,' Philopoemen said, as if inviting Alexanor to a party.

That was how Alexanor always thought of him after: half turned, his horse gathered under him; the spear in his hand like a thunderbolt of Zeus; the cloak whipped back in the speed of his turn; bigger than most men, and larger still in his moment of glory.

'Come with me!' Philopoemen called, and he was away.

Philopoemen's veteran riders could ride through an olive grove and form at the trot into a deep line; the Thracian cavalry recruits had almost doubled their numbers.

Alexanor's horse was carried away, and Alexanor, having failed to grab Philopoemen's reins, was almost instantly tucked in, a horse length behind him, following Arkas, who was himself at the *strategos'* shoulder.

The horsemen on the outside leant in, even at a canter, so that the mass of horseflesh packed together. Alexanor, caught two horses behind Philopoemen, was pressed from both sides. His knees cracked against Kleostratos' knee on one side, and slipped behind Syrmas' knee on the other.

He had the most curious feeling, of belonging to a single giant organism, a huge beast of hooves and manes and bronze and steel. He couldn't really see; he could barely ride. He simply *was*; he rode with the charge. He was in the charge.

He was the charge.

At some point, the whole mass accelerated into a gallop.

Perhaps the leftmost files of the Knossians flinched. Perhaps men turned to see their doom and screamed; or perhaps braver men called for the end files to turn and face the threat. Perhaps, in desperation, there was heroism, or perhaps only despair, in the ranks of the Knossians.

The juggernaut was imperfect by the time the squadron struck. The ends had begun to fray out; older horses began to slow, balking at the collision.

But in the centre of the charge, around Dinaeos and Philopoemen, the charge went home, straight into the shielded flank of the enemy. Whole files were knocked flat, and the Thracians' horses were more deadly than their riders, and as the outer files collapsed, the ties of liturgy and piety and family began to fail, and the Knossian phalanx unknitted. Men turned to flee. Men struck their neighbours, desperate to escape the equine tide, the teeth and hooves, the swords and heavy spears.

Alexanor saw none of that. All he saw was Philopoemen, his arm faster than a cat's paw, stronger than an ox's horns; every blow ended in a spray of red. Philopoemen's magnificent horse passed Dinaeos, and then opened the way for the whole squadron, the way a craftsman's chisel opens a crack in a tree trunk for the workers to split off a plank. He went forward, his spear like the bolts of great Zeus, and men fell. Even the ones who flinched away were hit, and he was without mercy, free of restraint, deeper and deeper into the Knossian phalanx as it unravelled behind him and to the side. Suddenly Alexanor burst through, no longer restrained by the tide of bodies at his feet, or his comrades, and everywhere the enemy was running, and the *hippeis*, instead of being pressed, were inexplicably free.

For an instant, Alexanor was riding over open ground. He had just time to note that he was now in front, not behind, and then …

Then, for the first time, Alexanor was fighting. Men pressed around his horse in the blink of an eye – well-armoured men who had thrown down their pikes and were fighting with swords – and Alexanor fought, his horse pressed alongside that of Kleostratos. The Thracian pulled savagely at his horse's bit, made his stallion rear, and the enraged horse lashed out, scattering their foes. Alexanor finally got the mercenary who was trying to rip open his charger's belly, stabbing down with some dead man's sword.

He turned his horse, and tried to follow Kleostratos, but the Thracian was a far better rider. His horse took him away into a flaw in the enemy formation and left Alexanor alone.

Alexanor threw blows in every direction; his horse moved under him, and he struck. It had been his intention to merely parry and stay alive, but in the fight, he didn't control his sword arm, and he stabbed down into men's faces, their shoulders, the sides of their necks, with medical precision. His horse turned and turned, and at some point he realised that the armoured men he was fighting were the enemy mercenaries, not the Knossians, even as his wonderful gelding took a spear in the neck, and another in his belly, and, game to the last, slumped down. Even in death the horse was beyond praise, falling forward like a pious man kneeling before a statue of his favourite god, and then down, down so gradually that Alexanor dismounted and landed on his feet, well clear of his dying charger, and then he was in among the mercenaries.

There was no thought – no consciousness of fighting.

Alexanor had begun training in *pankration* when he was eight years old. He'd never had the body to be a champion – too small, too thin. But he'd never stopped practising; in the marines, he'd been considered so skilled they made him an instructor. And the priests of Asklepios had their own *pankration*, and he'd embraced it – a faster game that emphasised speed and precision in the delivery of punches and kicks to the weakest points in the body.

He didn't think of any of it.

It was black. But for the first time, there was neither terror, nor a flash on the corpses of his dead. His dead were at rest, and he was free.

He was there, in that moment, and he struck.

Men fell. He caught his own actions in bursts: a lock; a shattered knee, his kick passing through with a sickening crunch; a man's head under his rotating arm; his sword left in a man's armoured gut.

And then he was on his back, a spear in his thigh. Blood, and worse, had turned the ground to muck. He imagined drowning in the bloody ooze. He fell, and couldn't rise, and he raised a hand.

There was a man above him, and he was going to die. The man's spear went back for the killing blow, the head heavy, the shaft long and black, the man's lips peeled back from his teeth, his sweat shining on his face.

And then the man was gone, and there was a horse above him, the thing's belly wet. The stink of the horse passed over him; a hoof slammed into the earth with crushing finality. The man on the horse's back was larger than life, a Titan bestriding the world, challenging the very gods.

I've taken a blow to the head, and something is wrong.

And the horse was gone, and the sky above Alexanor was blue, and it hung, pregnant with immanence, as if somewhere a new god was being born. Far off, an eagle turned, and turned again, watching the battle. For a moment, Alexanor felt that he was one with the eagle, watching the tiny men far below, fighting and dying in the blood and the sand and the barley fields of the plain.

'Achilles! Achilles Athanatos!'

'ACHILLES!'

I cannot be seeing this, he thought.

But he was; circling above, safe, on the auspicious side of the sky, he saw the mercenary phalanx collapse as the Polyrrhenians and the Gortynians who had been fighting the Knossians turned, the pressure on their front suddenly released, and fell on the flank of the mercenaries, following the now scattered cavalry. The mercenaries were slow to fail; veterans, well aware of the consequences of defeat, they went back, and back again, bleeding men but refusing to break.

He looked down into the storm of death, and he imagined he found himself, and there he lay, Philopoemen and his heavy horse towering over him, fighting, fighting ...

The Gortynians were advancing, and they roared, now.

'ACHILLES!'

He seemed to fall from the eagle's height into his own body, a long plummet to consciousness. His head seemed to explode and he ...

Alexanor heard the noise of the battle before he regained full consciousness. He was on his back, and he was looking up into the belly of a horse, and he rolled, aware that his leg was hurt, aware of pain, fatigue, thirst, sweat, abrasions ...

He rolled onto one knee and got to his feet, digging the point of someone else's *xiphos* into the bloody dirt. His right leg was bad; it wouldn't take all his weight ...

An iron arm closed around his *thorax* and he was lifted off his feet.

'I thought you were dead,' Philopoemen said. 'Damn it, you weigh a hundred talents.'

And then he went out; darkness fell.

He awoke to pain.

'Catch him!' Philopoemen roared.

Alexanor felt himself being lowered and realised that he was going in and out of consciousness. He felt his knees crumple, and great pain ...

'Lie down,' Leon said. 'Lie down immediately.'

Alexanor struggled to rise to one elbow. He was lying on the sand and gravel of the hillside, near the spring. Below, the enemy mercenaries were well down the valley, holding together, stumbling away, but he could hear fighting, very close.

'The Lyttians,' Leon said. 'They held. They're still holding.'

Almost at their feet, just over the lip of the hill, a thousand Lyttians still stood. Their line was now bent all the way back along the base of the low hill, and they faced all of Nabis' Aetolians. They gave ground, and died, but would not break.

Above him, the shadow of Philopoemen fell across the wounded. When Alexanor looked up at him, the sun was behind him, so that a nimbus of unbearable brightness surrounded his head.

All around them on the ground lay the army's wounded – hundreds of men between life and death.

'Comrades,' Philopoemen called. 'I have no one left to ask, except you who have already given all you have. I know from your wounds that every man here is a hero. If your legs will hold you, rise. This is

343

the moment, and there is nothing that can stop us but fear, or death. You have already beaten fear, and brothers, death comes to us all.'

Around Alexanor, men – wounded men who had been dragged to the shade of the oak trees and the beautiful taste of clean water, men who had endured the fear and the pain and lived, men who had thought their task complete – rose. Some stumbled; more than one sank with a groan.

But more than a hundred rose amid the oak trees. And Alexanor was one of them, although he had to use Leon's priest's staff to walk.

The hundred walking wounded took any weapon near them and followed Philopoemen towards the back of the Lyttians. They shambled. They stumbled.

The Lyttians fell back again. Men died, but still, despite everything – the heat, the desperate enemy, the flailing hooves of horses, their terrible losses – still, the Lyttians *would not break*. They died for their lost wives, their butchered children, and for men and women they did not know. They died hard, for a city that was not theirs, because their own was lost.

Philopoemen's horse slipped into the Lyttian line, and the walking wounded came up behind the Lyttians and began to push, weary men pressing other weary men. The retreat stopped, and for as long as it would take a choir of priests to sing a hymn, the battle balanced: Nabis and his Aetolian horse pressing from in front, the battered Lyttians and a hundred walking wounded pushing back.

And then there was pressure against Alexanor's back. He felt it but never turned his head. He was pushing with one leg, trying not to think, waiting for the moment when the two Lyttians in front of him were dead and he had to fight.

He pressed forward a step against his will. A step, and another painful step, his hip feeling as if he must fall from the pain. A long cavalry spear caught in his crest, passed between his arms, and slammed into the ground, and Alexanor caught at it with his left hand and held it. Above him, the cavalryman, his snarl like a mask of hate, tried to take it back, but he only had one hand and his balance was limited. Then he was gone, and Alexanor had his spear, and the whole line went forward, first one step, then five, then ten, and Alexanor fell, his right leg unable to bear the stress. He lay and watched men pour past him, until two grinning peasants got him under his armpits and lifted him.

'We'll take you to the doctors, mate,' one said. 'They'll have you right as rain.'

He was surrounded by Boeotian mercenaries and the *Neodamodeis*, who appeared as if out of the air.

'Let me look,' he said.

The two men turned him, and he was high enough on the hill to see the Aetolian cavalry over the now-swelling ranks of the Cretan League. There was no order left; Lyttians who had lasted an hour against impossible odds simply sank to the ground, to be replaced by Boeotians and Gortynians and *epheboi* and *Neodamodeis*, all intermixed, all pushing together down the hill.

There was a last flurry, as the cavalry drew off and made a charge. Alexanor saw Nabis, his face red under his magnificent helmet, order another, but then, all the men around Alexanor were shouting.

In the olive groves to the east, behind the Aetolian cavalry, there was a sparkle of bronze.

Men stopped, and stared.

Even among the Aetolians, men turned to look.

A stade away, a tall man with three huge plumes stepped out of the olive trees like a predator stalking his prey, and he began to run at the Aetolian cavalry. A line of bronzed warriors burst into the sunlight behind him.

'Plator!' Alexanor called.

All around him, wounded men and rear-rankers took up the shout.

The Aetolians didn't break. But they and their officers took one look at the charge of the Illyrians, and the narrowing gap between the new enemy behind them and the road home to their employer's city, and they put their heads down and rode for it. Telemnastos, still out there in the trees and grass, now facing Rhodian marines in the broken ground, managed to empty a few saddles, but most of the archers had loosed their last shafts. Alexanor watched Nabis ride free, his cloak fluttering like a red wound behind him, his Thessalian escort close by.

Closer, the sun caught Philopoemen. He was slumped forward, his helmet gone. There was blood coming from under his breastplate. His hands were empty; at some point he'd lost his sword.

But his eyes were on the Aetolians, and Nabis. And a slight smile fought fatigue for possession of his mouth.

'Help me,' Alexanor said. 'I need to walk.'

The two *psiloi* were willing enough, and they helped him hobble forward a few steps.

'Get off that horse at once,' Alexanor said. 'You're bleeding, damn it. You should be flat on your back.'

Philopoemen looked down. 'You're a fine one to talk,' he said.

And then his eyes rolled. He seemed to collapse, and the two men helping Alexanor had to catch him as he fell.

BOOK V

EXILE

CHAPTER ONE

—◦◦◦—

Gortyna

217 BCE

Alexanor rode back into Lentas five weeks later. His fine bay gelding was dead, so he rode a mule. He thought about the horse that Philopoemen had given him all too often, and he cursed his own weakness: other men had given their lives or their arms or legs to defeat Knossos, and he had given a few measures of blood and a horse.

But he missed the horse.

And despite an awareness that wounds and illness made him a difficult man, he couldn't stop himself from snapping at Leon and at Philopoemen, who rode beside him on a fine Arab, the very picture of martial accomplishment.

'Why do you get a magnificent animal, and I get a mule?' he muttered.

Leon turned, one eyebrow raised. 'I'd swear that you insisted on it yourself,' he said.

Alexanor took a breath and tried to muster a crushing retort, but nothing came, and he was further infuriated by Philopoemen's smile.

'We could trade this minute,' he said.

'You know that's ridiculous,' Alexanor spat. 'You can't ride in to talk to the Rhodians on a mule.'

'I could, though,' Philopoemen said.

'Don't humour him,' Leon said.

Kleostratos laughed. 'You're a fine healer,' he said. 'But damn, you suck at being hurt.'

Below them, the sanctuary came into sight for the first time. In one beat of his heart, many of his anxieties vanished. He could see the Asklepion and the baths, untouched; he could see statues glowing with colour in the corners of the *stoa*. The Rhodians had occupied Lentas in the middle of the siege; they still held it. His people.

He smiled, despite himself.

Behind them, Periander's Boeotians marched along, singing songs from Thebes and Thespiae and Plataea.

'You really expect the Rhodians to just hand over the sanctuary?' Alexanor asked.

'Yes,' Philopoemen said. 'They're really very civilised.' He raised an eyebrow, and glanced at Leon.

'You are all conspiring against me,' Alexanor muttered.

'Try not to get wounded again,' Leon said. 'It's too hard on your friends.'

That afternoon, Alexanor was welcomed back into his own temple precinct by those of his priests who had not been with the army. Together, they made the rounds of the precinct walls, Alexanor limping all the way, and then they cleaned and censed the altars and Alexanor made a sacrifice, favouring his right leg.

Philopoemen met briefly with the Rhodian admiral, Polemecles. Later, Alexanor hosted an evening symposium inside the temple's sanctuary walls. It was a beautiful space, with a view out over the bay, where six Rhodian warships lay at double anchors in the shallow water. Their oarsmen and marines were camped on the beaches, and some of the marines were being treated in the Asklepion. There had been no violence in the town – no resistance offered, no one killed or molested.

Alexanor hadn't realised how deep were his fears of meeting the Rhodian admiral until the man clasped both of his hands.

'I came early, to have a talk,' Polemecles said. 'Let me begin by saying that I knew your father,' he added. 'May I pass my condolences.'

Alexanor felt as if he'd taken another wound.

'You didn't know?' Polemecles said.

'We were ... estranged,' Alexanor said.

The Rhodian nodded. 'I'd heard something like that. Our thanks for arranging this symposium. It's a bloody mess out there,' he added.

'Literally,' Alexanor agreed.

'What do you think of the Achaean commander?' Polemecles asked.

Alexanor shrugged. 'He is perhaps my closest friend. I cannot give you an unbiased judgement.'

'And yet, you are a veteran, a man of Rhodes, a citizen,' the admiral said.

Alexanor led him to a couch and Leon put a cup of wine into his hand.

'Not a citizen any more,' Alexanor said, with as little bitterness as he could manage.

'You are no slave,' the navarch said to Leon. 'I know you – you were with my wounded after the battle.'

The Rhodians, posted on the extreme right of Nabis' array, had spent the action trying to drive Telemnastos' archers out of the olive groves.

Leon smiled. 'I have been a slave,' he admitted.

Polemecles shrugged. 'That's true of many good men.'

Alexanor put a hand on Leon's shoulder. 'I thought it might be better if we had no other witnesses tonight,' he said.

Polemecles nodded. 'You are wise.'

He lay down and drank some of the wine he was offered, and Alexanor sat on the edge of his couch while Leon returned to the door in the yard, the perfect steward.

'This was a mare's nest from the beginning,' Polemecles admitted. 'And we were always divided in our councils. There are men on Rhodes who care for nothing but their profits, and they think it is their right to use the fleet for their own ends.' He shrugged.

There were other guests arriving. Polemecles glanced at the door and leant forward.

'For my part, I'd like to see the Cretan ports closed to pirates. And some of the Cretan ports *are* the pirates. Do you think there's any level on which I can engage your friend?'

'He's no friend of slavery,' Alexanor said, glancing at Philopoemen, who was embracing Leon.

'Well, that's something,' Polemecles said. 'Listen. Why do you say you are not a citizen? Did you relinquish your status because of . . . the war here?'

'No, my father stripped me of my citizenship,' Alexanor said.

Polemecles shook his head. 'I don't believe it. I think I'd know. I'll look into it.'

'Why would he say such a thing?' Alexanor asked.

Philopoemen was coming over, with Dinaeos and Kleostratos and Lykortas around him. Telemnastos was in the doorway, making a small sacrifice to the statue of Apollo in the niche at the door.

'Frustrated parents lash out,' Polemecles said. 'Wait until you are one. Believe me, the most surprising—'

He rose from his couch and took Philopoemen's hand.

'These are some of my officers,' Philopoemen said, introducing his friends.

Polemecles introduced two of his *trierarchs*: Demippos and Poseidonos. Both were men that Alexanor knew, if at a distance; both were instantly friendly to him, disarming any lingering notions that he was considered a traitor.

After they made sacrifices and had a tour of the temple, led by Leon, they reclined to a dinner of strips of beef, the fruit of the afternoon sacrifice of a bull, and a whole, magnificent tuna, brought in by Arkas and Syrmas and two cavalrymen. Alexanor carved the great fish, served his guests, and then sent the rest out into the courtyard, where most of Dinaeos' cavalry troop and all of the temple servants and some Rhodians fell on it like an avenging army.

When the fish had been consumed, and several rounds of wine, small cakes, sweets and nuts had made their rounds, Polemecles rose.

'Gentlemen,' he said.

The mosaiced room fell silent, although outside in the courtyard, there were loud shouts and louder laughter.

'Alexanor, our host, was kind enough to give me leave to speak,' the Rhodian admiral said. 'I'll be quick and to the point. Rhodes has no choice but to accept the new alliance of Cretan cities. But I hope to do more than accept it. Even now, while my squadron sits in this bay, somewhere in the Eastern Sea, a pirate ship is striking a village. Pirates take the women, break them to prostitution, and sell them. The men go to agricultural labour. They take our commerce on the seas and ruin our trade in ports that they destroy.' He shrugged. 'The Great

Council of Rhodes thought that they could end piracy from Crete by supporting Knossos, and that has failed, but my task remains. Is there any chance I can persuade you gentlemen to support me in fighting the pirates?'

'This seems like an about-face, even for a wily politician,' Lykortas said.

'Perfidious Rhodes,' muttered Dinaeos.

But Philopoemen leant forward. 'Slavery, and the threat of slavery, is the very death of our small farmers,' he said.

'Except when your small farmers take to boats and become the pirates,' Polemecles said.

'They are not, strictly speaking, my farmers,' Philopoemen said.

Polemecles gave a slight, man-of-the-world smile. 'You are the *Strategos* of the Cretan League in all but title.'

'I am a private individual with a troop of mercenary cavalry and –' Philopoemen smiled back – 'and a certain reputation. I will discuss the matter with Antiphatas.'

'Philip of Macedon will not support you, if you make an alliance with Rhodes,' Lykortas said. 'My understanding is that he is to be appointed the *Hegemon* of the League of Crete. He is no friend of Rhodes.'

Alexanor had not heard that Philip would hold the title.

'Is this true?' he asked.

Philopoemen shrugged. 'He paid most of the bills,' the Achaean admitted. 'The Polyrrhenians are very strongly pro-Macedon.'

'And you yourself?' the admiral asked.

Philopoemen shrugged and drank some wine. 'I think it best that I keep my views inside my teeth,' he joked. 'Let's leave it that I will speak to Antiphatas before I leave for home.'

'Home? So you will return to Achaea now?' Polemecles sounded disappointed.

Alexanor sat back.

'I've sold all three of my farms,' Philopoemen said. 'I was sent by the Achaean League to perform a task, and my task is complete, at least for now.'

'And, having cleaned the stables, you are off to kill the Lion?' Polemecles asked.

Philopoemen's smile was political. 'If by the Lion you mean

Macedon, I am more likely to be supporting him than stalking him. I rather expect to be elected *hipparchos* of the Achaean League.'

Polemecles nodded. 'With the consent of Aratos?' he asked. 'Listen, say what you will about Rhodes – we're the centre of the world, for trade and for gossip. My understanding is that Aratos is no friend of yours.'

Philopoemen was silent for a moment.

Lykortas sat up. '*Strategos*, he has you there. I confess that I am also puzzled. You expect to serve with Aratos next year?'

Alexanor had heard nothing of this. 'It might be dull here without you,' he said.

Philopoemen ran his fingers through his beard. 'I suppose that it's no secret. As I played no small part in the victory here, the king of Macedon has said that he will support my candidature for the *hipparchy*.'

Polemecles nodded. 'Well, congratulations. Please remember, if you achieve such rank in the Achaean League, that we Rhodians have neither horns nor tails, and that we would rather be allies and trading partners with the Achaean League than enemies. I fear that young Philip will link everything together, and demand that all of his clients follow his policy.'

Lykortas spoke up. 'Is it possible, Polemecles, that with Rhodes' great ally in the west, Rome, facing such enormous threats, you are looking for new friends?'

Polemecles smiled, although the smile never reached his eyes. 'Aye. Such a thing is possible. You have heard of the disaster Rome suffered at Lake Trasimene?'

'No.' Philopoemen sat up eagerly. 'Was this Hannibal Barca again?'

'Again. The man must be the darling of the gods – he's surely the terror of Rome. He caught the new consul, Flaminius, in a fog and destroyed his whole army – fifteen thousand dead. My source says the Carthaginian slave markets are full of Roman soldiers.'

'Ares,' spat Dinaeos. 'And so the Roman barbarians are destroyed. Good riddance to them.'

'Have you been to Rome?' Polemecles asked.

'Never,' Dinaeos laughed. 'I hear it's dirty.'

Polemecles shook his head. 'I won't hide that Rhodes fears for its ally. But Rome is greater than you can imagine. It is not a Greek state, swollen with silver and power. It is a vast agricultural power with endless reserves of manpower.'

Philopoemen listened, fascinated. 'And yet, how many disasters can this barbarian state endure?'

Polemecles shrugged. 'Indeed. So, if you go home to real political power, think of Rhodes. And the slave trade.'

Philopoemen glanced at Alexanor. 'What do you think, brother?'

'You are no friend to slavery,' Alexanor said. 'And Rhodes could be a good ally.'

'You hold no rancour?' Philopoemen asked.

'It appears that I am still a citizen,' Alexanor said.

'I'll consider all that,' Philopoemen said. 'In the meantime, I'd like to thank you, Polemecles, for preserving this town and this temple. Your marines have excellent discipline. I think it bodes well for our future co-operation that you did no harm.'

'First, do no harm,' Alexanor said. 'The first rule of Asklepios.'

When Philopoemen left Crete for Megalopolis a month later, Alexanor didn't expect to see him for a long time. They ate a dinner together, and embraced, and Philopoemen sailed away from Lentas, much as he had come, with his troop of horse and his friends.

A month later, before the winter storms closed the sailing season, and after the flow of pilgrims trailed off, Alexanor left his sanctuary in Leon's hands and sailed for Rhodes. The end of the war had reopened communications, and he had three letters from his mother and one from his father's factor. It was true, his father had never disinherited him, and his father's death left many legal problems that only the lead-heir could resolve.

And Alexanor had the vaguest feeling that if he didn't return, he'd never resolve whatever stood between him and his father.

He arrived in the port of Rhodes on a brilliantly sunny late autumn day, and was met at the ship by two of his brothers, both grown men. They embraced and went to the Temple of Poseidon and made sacrifices together, and Alexanor felt like a fool for imagining that he could ever live permanently estranged from his family.

It took a week to sort out the legal quibbles about inheritance. His father's will had been badly cast, and he had made attempts to alter it to exclude Alexanor. But he'd never registered the new will at the

Temple of Poseidon and, in the end, several senior members of the Great Council approached Alexanor privately and asked him to settle the will without a public fuss.

'It's better for everyone,' Nicodemus said.

Three years had not made him any less pompous; Alexanor couldn't stomach him, but he kept quiet, and in the end, when presented with a deed that settled the property, he signed.

'How is my father's friend Agepolis?' he asked. He thought Agepolis was on the Great Council.

The two men looked at each other.

'You really don't know?'

Alexanor shrugged.

Nicodemus barked a false laugh. 'Agepolis died last year. After he died, it became clear that he'd been swindling your father for years. It killed your father, and it's one of the reasons this estate is in such chaos.'

'Ah.' Alexanor didn't know what to feel. 'I assumed Pater made bad investments.'

'He did,' Nicodemus said. 'He chose a bad friend.'

'Will you stay and run the business?' Lykaeos asked. He was the other Great Council member, a secretive man who seldom spoke.

Alexanor shook his head. 'As you know, I am a priest of Asklepios,' he said. 'I am the acting Hierophant of Lentas. My brothers were trained to the business – they are both sailors and both competent traders.'

'Very proper,' Lykaeos said. 'You come with a *special* recommendation, from Polemecles.'

'Do I?'

Alexanor was almost amused, except that his mind had started to go off in a very different direction.

'We would ... appreciate ... anything you wanted to tell us. About your friend. And Macedon. And Achaea.' Lykaeos looked exhausted from talking so much.

Alexanor looked back and forth at the two of them.

'We assume you remain a loyal Rhodian,' Nicodemus said.

'I don't really fancy informing on my friends, if that's what you mean.'

Lykaeos nodded. 'No one does. Only ... Rhodes is weak, and has many strong enemies. Polemecles says you are a true enemy of the slave trade.' The smaller man leant on a staff and frowned. 'Information is power, Alexanor. Rhodes could fall, in our lifetimes. One long interruption of trade—'

'Rome could fall this winter,' Nicodemus put in.

Lykaeos raised an eyebrow, and glanced at his partner with distaste.

'The sky could fall. Please consider. This is not a dirty deal. We have prepared this solution to your father's will for the benefit of everyone concerned. But I did want to talk to you in person. The whole world is falling into chaos and war, Alexanor – the Seleucids and the Ptolemies, the Romans and the Carthaginians, from Iberia to Antioch. Little states like Rhodes, and even the Cretan League and the Achaean League need each other, or we will all fall alone.'

Alexanor nodded. 'I have heard the very words from Philopoemen,' he said. 'And now, if you gentlemen will excuse me, I have an appointment.'

In the end, he couldn't think of what to say, or what to take, whether to bring her flowers, or a condolence gift. He didn't even know if Aspasia had children.

He went to her gate and knocked. The house was shut up; the stucco had not been painted recently, and the second-floor balcony was sagging. There was a lot of broken tile around the gate, and the gate itself . . .

He heard the sound of plodding feet, and he thought of the last time he'd slipped out of this gate. She would be thirty-three now. Perhaps with grey hair.

The gate opened. He heard the bolt, and its catch.

A slave opened the gate. He had a heavy club in his hand.

'What do you want, Master?' he said.

'I'd like to see Mistress Aspasia,' he said. *I'd like to be twenty again, and do this over.*

'Mistress accepts no visitors,' the slave said, and closed the gate.

Alexanor jammed his priestly staff in between the halves of the rapidly closing gate.

'She'll see me,' he said.

The slave shook his head. 'No, she won't. Don't make me hurt you, Master. I don't want the trouble.'

Alexanor nodded. 'Neither do I, but I suspect I can take that club away. Listen – I'll make you a wager. You let me in to see your mistress. If I'm wrong, you can have this gold daric. If I'm right, and she's happy to see me, you can still have it.'

The slave scratched his jaw with the club. He was Thracian; fit enough, with tattoos around his ear.

'Let me see it?' he said.

Alexanor reached into the bosom of his *chiton*, took out his deerskin purse, and took out a gold coin.

'Toss it here,' the slave said.

Alexanor smiled. 'Let me in.'

The slave shrugged and dropped his club.

'You overpowered me,' he said, and held out his hand.

Alexanor dropped the coin into it and walked past him, into the yard. He crossed it, and passed the main house, but it was, as he'd expected, shut up, except for one door to the kitchen.

He looked in.

And there she was. As soon as he saw her, it was as if years fell away; he didn't see the lines on either side of her mouth, or the crow's feet at her eyes. The woman he loved was right there.

She looked at him for a moment. Then she wiped her hands on her apron and shook her head.

'If you are here for the money my husband stole from your father, we have none,' she said.

'I'm here for you,' Alexanor said.

'Oh, gods,' she said, and suddenly, she was trembling, and her voice failed her. 'Oh,' she moaned. 'Gods.'

He wrapped his arms around her, and she burst into tears. Behind her, a slave woman turned away, and a small boy ran out of the kitchen.

'I didn't even hope,' she said. 'I sent you that letter ... and then ... by Demeter ... when I knew he was stealing from your father, I thought the gods hated me.'

Alexanor just held her and listened to her voice.

'Maybe I was being punished for loving *you*. Maybe the gods take vengeance on a disloyal wife, no matter ... no matter ...' she muttered into his cloak.

'Marry me,' he said.

She looked up at him. 'Don't you want some fifteen-year-old virgin you can train to your every need?' she asked bitterly.

'Not especially. I'd like back the last fifteen years, but we can't have that. So why not make hay while the sun shines?'

'If this is an elaborate plot to make love to a poor widow, you really needn't go to so much effort.'

'You always make me laugh,' he said.

'I cannot believe you are here. You mean it? You'd marry me?'

Alexanor took both her hands. 'Listen, I'd need a dispensation. It would be easier if you became a priestess of Hygeia or one of the healing goddesses.'

'I'd be happy to! I'm devoted to cleanliness. It's the only comfort I have left.' She stood on her tiptoes. 'Oh, gods.'

'I won't be staying ...'

'Love, take me anywhere,' she said. 'I can leave tomorrow. Now, if you insist.'

The most difficult thing proved to be telling his mother.

'I knew your father did wrong in separating you two,' she said. 'He cursed us before the gods.'

Alexanor said nothing, since he agreed.

'But she is too old to have your sons. And anyway, you will take her away to some foreign place, and I will never see you, or her.'

Alexanor smiled and kissed his mother. 'Today, of all days, I rather feel things might come out right in the end.'

It took him two more days to divide the estate with his brothers. The easiest thing, as it proved, was Aspasia's house; his brother Lysander purchased it. He kept a little money but put the rest back into the business.

Nobly, Aspasia handed him back the full price of her house – a large sum, as good houses inside the city of Rhodes were very valuable.

'Your brother will take care of me,' she said. 'Perhaps this will make up for the gold my first husband stole.'

And later, in the privacy of his mother's best bedroom, she wriggled away from him after a long kiss.

'Listen, love,' she said. 'You may think me a harridan. But I'm going to do this right. Marriage.'

Alexanor didn't need his medical training to measure his reaction.

Aspasia laughed. 'You look like my cat when I take away his mouse.'

He laughed, and all the world had the rosy glow of her smile and the rising sun over the sea.

'At least this way I can look your mother in the eye,' Aspasia said.

'My mother loves you and gave you a private bedroom as far from her own as possible,' Alexanor said. Her *peplos* was unpinned, and one shoulder and one breast tantalised him.

'Just as I expected. You *are* just hoping to seduce a poor widow.' She leant back and let him kiss her neck, but when his lips slipped from her shoulder to her breasts, she pushed him away. 'Fie, sir!'

He had to laugh.

Alexanor had considered going to Kos; it was close enough, a mere day's sail away to the north and west. Now he had good reason, and he had money. Menes loaned him a family ship, a small round ship that was usually used in the coastal trade, moving tin and copper and small, valuable goods like perfumes and ivory. The captain was a freedman, Nestor, a jolly man unbroken by hard times, and they had a beautiful sail across a calm early winter sea.

Alexanor was well received on Kos, and his request to be married received an easier sanction than he might have imagined. The hierophant placed Aspasia in a class for matrons learning to be priestesses, and then summoned Alexanor.

Over sweet wine and barley cakes, he got to business.

'You are a famous man,' the hierophant said. 'You see that I make no difficulties about your wedding – the more so as your wife is so obviously intelligent. She'll make a fine priestess. Now on to other matters. I want you to go to Philip as my ambassador.'

Alexanor took a breath or two. 'When, sir?' He saw his wedding slipping over the horizon.

'Now. Tomorrow, if you'll go. Philip's quarrel with Rhodes has to end. Two months ago we had a pirate raid. *Here!*' The man was furious. 'Philip needs to understand that if he wants allies in the islands, he needs to help clear the pirates, not invest in them.'

'Invest?'

The hierophant shrugged. 'Word is he's funding the construction of a major fleet by allowing his captains to prey on shipping. Listen.

360

Chiron, at Epidauros, says you have a good head on your shoulders. And you know Philip, yes? You have visited him.'

'I was his father's physician for a while,' Alexanor said.

'Exactly. Perhaps I should send a younger man with you, in case Philip wants a priest of Asklepios. What do you think?'

I think my wedding is being ruined.

Aspasia shook her head. 'I just found you and you are leaving,' she said. 'On the other hand, learning something from actual teachers may be the most exciting thing I've ever done. Why didn't my mother send me to be a priestess?' She kissed him. It was a long, frank kiss.

Alexanor responded with interest, and the two of them drew a disapproving glare from a passing priest.

'Perhaps we could ...' Alexanor smiled.

'Don't worry. I'll be fine. I have Hygeia and Asklepios.' Aspasia paused, and glanced at him from mostly downcast eyes. 'You might hurry, though. I'm not getting any younger, and my teachers assure me that a woman of my age can bear children.'

'Really?'

'Really. And you'll never guess how children come about,' she said, a little breathlessly. She put a hand on his chest and kissed him. And then gave him a shove. 'Hurry.'

CHAPTER TWO

—◦◦◦—

Pella and Crete

216–214 BCE

The storm caught the round ship west of Chios and drove her for four days. Nestor never left the deck, eating rain-soaked bread and drinking neat wine with cheese grated into it. Alexanor helped as much as he could, taking the tiller for hours at a stretch as the east wind blew them down the sea, keeping the stern onto the rising waves. Twice in four days, the wind worked round from east to south, and they had haze and sand off Africa mixed in the wind. Once, a mighty gust tore the mainsail free of its lashings, so that it snapped the yard and they lost way. Then every man had to come to the deck, the sailors rowing on the four sweeps a side, desperate to keep her head downwind and the following seas under the stern while an elite crew of four men, led by Nestor, attempted to get a scrap of boiled wool sail on the mast. Later they saved the yard, which had not snapped, only given at the lashings, and ten men repaired it on the deck while sixteen pushed the heavy oars. Alexanor, doing his best to manage a sweep, was appalled at how heavy the small ship was.

He was too tired to be afraid, at first, and then later, fear and fatigue and desperation, thirst and hunger all came together into one long nightmare. They gathered what rainwater they could, but the ship was ill-equipped for ten days at sea. By the eighth day, the storm had blown itself out, but they had no food and little water.

They landed in the Bay of Marathon, of all places. Alexanor bought a small herd of sheep, and the crew feasted and sacrificed to Poseidon for their survival. Alexanor made sacrifice to the Heroes at the great Tumulus of the Athenian dead and then rode to Athens while Nestor engaged a dozen local men to build him a new mainmast and a new mainyard to hold the sail. He easily sold his cargo of perfume.

'It's an ill wind that blows no one good,' Nestor said to Alexanor. 'That's a year's profits in one voyage.'

Alexanor raised an eyebrow and looked at his own hands, scarred from encounters with ropes and oars.

'Bah,' Nestor said. 'If you will sail in winter, you will always find a storm. We lived. I'm loading some of these nice white-tawed hides. They'll sell well at Amphipolis. Even better at Kos. You'll end up with a pair of sandals made from them, priest! I can give you a week here before we need to set sail.'

'I only need a couple of days,' Alexanor said. 'I'm going to visit a friend.'

Phila received him with a kiss on each cheek and introduced him to a number of men; he was unsurprised that the *Archon*, Kallimachos, was her guest. She invited him to lie beside her at dinner, and he was not unmoved by her hips next to his, even as the men eyed him jealously and discoursed on politics and attacked the morals and military fitness of the young king of Macedon.

'He'll fuck anything that moves,' Kallimachos said.

'What a rare disability,' Phila muttered.

'There's a rumour he's dressing as a commoner at night and going out in the festivals, looking for love,' another Athenian said. 'How ridiculous.'

'He is quite young,' a third man said.

Talk turned to the disasters of the summer suffered in Rome. Despite years of alliance with Aegypt or Antioch, the Assembly of Athens had begun to make overtures to the Romans, but the series of disasters disheartened them.

'And now Philip will join in the feeding frenzy,' Kallimachos said. 'Or at least, that's what we hear on the wind.' The Athenian *archon* glanced at Alexanor. 'You are the Hierophant of Lentas, yes? You must hear all the news.'

'Perhaps not as quickly as Kos or Epidauros,' Alexanor said modestly. 'But I was just on Rhodes, and then Kos. I have indeed heard that there is contact between Hannibal Barca and Philip.'

Phila rolled over and gazed at him. 'Ordinarily, *I* know all the best gossip. Now everyone will come to *your* parties.'

The men laughed, but the *archon* was interested.

'Do you think Philip will back Hannibal?' he asked.

'It would not hurt Athens to see the Macedonian armies go over the sea,' another man said. 'Especially if they never came back.'

'On Rhodes, they don't think Rome is finished,' Alexanor said.

Kallimachos shrugged. 'I'd like to believe it, but if you come to the slave market tomorrow, I can show you fifty noble Romans going on the block for a song. Hannibal has flooded the market with Romans and their allies – by Ares, he's taken fifty thousand slaves, or more. How long can Rome take it?'

'We're better off making whatever peace we can with Philip and hoping he leaves for Italy,' another man said.

The conversation veered off into slaves, and slave auctions, and the price of good servants.

After a while, the wine stopped coming, and the men began to leave. Kallimachos showed signs of trying to outwait Alexanor but, in the end, despite his wealth and power, he showed good manners, bowed with a smile, and withdrew, his dozen slaves holding torches to light his way.

When he was gone, Phila kissed him lightly on the lips.

'So,' she said.

'I'm about to be married,' he said.

'I know, silly. As long as there are ships between Athens and Rhodes, I'll know things. Are you happy?'

'Yes!'

She laughed and put a hand on his chest in the familiar way.

'Men who are happy with their wives are a rare sight in my home,' she said. 'I was very sorry not to be in Gortyna for the celebrations. I hear it was a great victory.'

'It was,' Alexanor said. 'Have you seen Philopoemen?'

'He writes to me. I invited him here before he went to Pella, but he went straight to Amphipolis.'

She walked back inside. Slaves were clearing the feast and the drinking party from the side tables. Thais waved, and then walked about, pouring wine into a *krater* from guests' cups.

'But I thought she freed you?' Alexanor said to Thais.

'I like it here,' Thais said. 'Now she pays me.' She shrugged. 'Regularly.'

Alexanor poured himself a little more wine.

'Well ...' he began.

Phila looked at him and sat down on a *kline*.

'Has he sold out to Philip?' she said. 'I thought he was a radical. He certainly fought the good fight on Crete. But now ...'

'I think he found that he's very good at war,' Alexanor said. 'If Philip offers him a command ...'

She shook her head. 'He should have come here.'

'You would have turned his head?' Alexanor asked, raising a cup to toast her.

She was just as beautiful – perhaps more so, in Athens – wearing the most fashionable clothing, one perfect shoulder exposed, her eyebrows touched with make-up, bathed in the glow of her golden lamps. She was like an exotic creature, a goddess or a nymph, and not a woman at all. And he had not made love to Aspasia. He flirted with his own desire, and then put a spear in it.

Some things are worth a wait.

Phila smiled at him as if she could read his mind.

'With my feminine wiles?' she asked, her head thrown back. She batted her eyelashes. 'Perhaps – I won't pretend I don't fancy him. But no. I mean that I know things about Macedon that he doesn't know, and one of them is that no matter how good an officer he is, the other Macedonians will never, ever, let a Greek command troops.'

'I think his goal is to be *Hipparchos* of the Achaean League.'

She smiled. It was a bitter smile, full of knowledge. 'He's being gulled. Used.'

'What?'

'Aratos sent him to Pella,' she said, 'hoping that he'd take a command with the king of Macedon.'

She lay back, and Alexanor tried not to admire her breasts and her hips. And her lips.

'I don't like the sound of this.'

'Hades, I could be wrong. But I think Aratos, who has the ear of the king, is playing Philopoemen until his status as hero of the hour has worn off.' She drank some wine, and put the cup aside. 'My wedding present to your Aspasia will be not trying to seduce you. But I confess that having you here reminds me that we spent almost a year together. I've never put so much work into one man.'

He laughed. He got up and stepped away, so that he was sure of his own position.

'Every part of me is aware of you,' he said.

'Good, then. I'm not an old hag yet. Go to bed – Thais will show you to a room. Goodnight.'

She blew him a kiss and walked around, blowing out the golden lamps. He watched her for a moment, because she was so beautiful. But then the gods sent him a vision of Aspasia, in the moment she'd seen him in her yard.

He watched her for another moment, as she stretched to extinguish the last lamp. She glanced at him, a smile on her face.

He turned and went to bed. It was one of his bravest acts. One he looked to in other days, to remember that he was a good man.

In the morning he awoke, and smiled at the ceiling, and after a light-hearted breakfast with Phila, he kissed her and sent for his horse.

'No long goodbyes,' she said. 'I'm sending you with a couple of amphorae of wine for Philopoemen. After all, Macedon is pretty barbaric. I doubt they have good wine, unless they steal it from someone.'

He left her to her busy day and mounted to ride back to Marathon, but then he had an idea, and he turned and rode down to Piraeus. There, he visited the slave market, where cohorts of blank-eyed Roman slaves stood, or sat, or crouched in abject despair.

Alexanor was modestly wealthy. He walked up and down the market, listening to the prisoners speak in their barbaric tongue, and after speaking to the slave factors, he found two men who spoke Greek.

'What do you know about horses?' he asked the two slaves.

One man shook his head and turned to the wall of the market, lost in his own thoughts.

The other man met his eye. 'A fair amount,' he said. 'Although,' he added with his Latin accent and a fair amount of bitterness, 'I had a slave groom to do most of the work.'

'You were a cavalryman?' Alexanor asked him.

'My pater raises horses for the army.' The man shrugged. 'I volunteered. And now they say we were all cowards.'

'I'll buy this one,' Alexanor said. 'What's your name, lad?'

'Kaeso,' the young man said.

They sailed across the Aegean, untouched by the thunderheads they could see to the south. By the time they'd coasted around to Thessalonike, Kaeso's Greek had improved, his fear of Alexanor had dwindled and the haunted look had begun to leave his eyes.

They landed on the beach and sacrificed in the temple, stayed a night at a local inn, rented bad horses and then Alexanor rode up country to Pella. It was a strange experience being back in Macedon; they had no love for Greeks and never stopped reminding him of it, at stage houses and inns and tavernas.

As a mounted man with only one slave, Alexanor was assumed to be someone of no importance, and he was treated accordingly. He was assigned a room in a public inn in Pella and the wine was virtually undrinkable.

'So this is Pella,' his new slave said. 'It has a lot of fine buildings.' The Roman looked around. 'I'd like a new cloak, if you can get me one.'

'Cold?'

'Yes, sir. Master.' The boy laughed.

'You don't have to call me Master,' Alexanor said.

'Good,' the young man said. 'Can I have a cloak anyway?'

Pella was a fine city, laid out on a grid and with a magnificent, *stoaed* agora built in the centre for civic activities and shopping.

Kaeso looked around, a smile on his face. 'It's laid out like an army camp,' he said.

Alexanor raised an eyebrow. 'It is laid out according to mathematical principles, as determined by Hippodamus of Miletus,' he said.

'Oh,' the boy said. 'I thought Romans invented the grid plan.'

Alexanor wondered why barbarians always assumed that they had invented everything.

The shops in the *stoa* were good, and Alexanor bought himself a riding hat and a whole suit of clothes for Kaeso, and, after some patient shopping, saw what he really wanted – Arkas.

Philopoemen's groom was happy to see him, and they clasped hands.

367

'This is my new groom, Kaeso,' Alexanor said. 'Roman.'

'Rome!' Arkas grinned. 'That's amazing. Everyone's talking about invading Italy.'

'Wonderful,' Kaeso muttered.

'Where is Philopoemen?' Alexanor asked.

'We're staying on a farm outside the city,' Arkas said. 'I'm here doing some shopping for the *hipparchos*.' He looked around. 'We're very careful here,' he said with too much emphasis.

That Arkas should say such a thing told Alexanor a great deal.

'Can I follow you home?' Alexanor asked.

'Of course! The *hipparchos* will be delighted to see you.'

The three of them, with three slaves following them, rode out along a rain-swept road. Kaeso enjoyed his new cloak, at least until the pouring rain soaked it through, but he didn't admire the road.

'This is a terrible road,' he said to Arkas. 'If the kings of Macedon are so powerful why don't they build better roads?'

Arkas shrugged. 'To an Achaean, Macedonians are very like hill-tribe barbarians.' He shrugged. 'They hire Greeks to do everything.' He looked back at Alexanor. 'Except fight. They don't want us as soldiers,' he said, with surprising rancour.

Arkas glanced at Alexanor. 'What do you think of Pella, sir?'

'Sterile,' Alexanor said.

Kaeso laughed.

An hour later, Alexanor was embracing his friend.

'What brings you to gods-forsaken Pella?' Philopoemen asked. 'You are welcome, regardless.'

'The high priest of my order sent me to address Philip,' Alexanor said. 'But the steward at the palace treated me like a servant, so I'm unsure how to go about this.'

Philopoemen ushered him into a fine country house, with white-washed walls, red tile roof, a fine sweep of shuttered windows, and a roaring fire on the central hearth.

'You bought a house?' Alexanor asked.

'Rented. I imagined I might be here a while.' He turned and met Alexanor's eye. 'As it proved, I was wrong.'

'Wrong how?' Alexanor asked. 'By the way, I brought you a present.'

'I like a good present. But damn it, I've been had. Twice. I imagined that Aratos wanted me home. I was wrong. And I imagined that Philip wanted me as a cavalry officer.' He winced.

'You are insufficiently Macedonian?' Alexanor asked quietly.

'That about sums it up. And by Athena, brother, they're a vicious lot. Gossipy, nasty, mad as hares in spring, and violent like criminals while rutting like stags and rabbits. I can't stay here.' He shrugged. 'It was a mistake to come.'

Alexanor could not remember having seen the man so defeated since he lay wounded on the sand at Epidauros.

'Because Philip won't have you?'

'Because I allowed myself to be outmanoeuvred by Aratos, damn it.'

'Phila sends her regards. She said some of these things—'

'I know. It irks me that I could have visited her in Athens on my way here – I'd have known all the gossip.' He shook his head. 'I thought I was in a hurry. You know what happened last week? Philip ordered me to disband my troop of cavalry.' He shrugged. 'I'll be going back to Achaea. I probably won't win against Cercidas, but I'll run for *hipparchos* and make some trouble.' He shrugged again. 'I'm a bad host. Here's some wine.'

Alexanor tasted it. 'Not bad, but Phila sent some better.'

Philopoemen smiled.

In fact, it was the most military house Alexanor had ever visited. There were no women; not in the kitchen, not in the stable or the house. The food was military food; the 'servants' were cavalry troopers, most of whom waited on Alexanor with broad smiles, which was only fair, as he'd fixed most of them up. A broken nose he'd straightened brought him a second cup of wine; a compound fracture he'd set brought in skewers of goat meat, which they cooked on the hearth as if they were soldiers at a campfire.

Alexanor introduced the Roman lad, Kaeso. Philopoemen immediately began to question him, and the Roman narrowed his eyes.

'I don't want to tell you anything you'll use when you attack us,' he said.

'There's a lad with spirit,' Philopoemen said. 'I hope my men would speak as well, captured and enslaved. But listen, young man. I'm unlikely to invade Italy with all the armed might of Achaea.'

'What's Achaea?' the Roman asked.

'That about sums it up, doesn't it?' Lykortas asked. 'Hello, Alexanor. For whatever reason you've come, you should get the fuck out of here as soon as you can. It's a madhouse.'

'I lived here for a year,' Alexanor said. 'I know it.'

Lykortas shook his head. 'Who's this?' he asked, and the Roman slave was introduced.

They ate, and the troopers stood or sat along the walls and ate their food too. It was all fairly democratic; men spoke up when they wished, and Arkas, who'd grown to full manhood all of a sudden, spoke up often.

'Can you get me in to see the king?' Alexanor asked Philopoemen.

Philopoemen nodded. 'I think my credit at court is still good enough for that. But not much more. I have no interest in disbanding my troop and I think the king is foolish for wanting to invade Italy.' He smiled bitterly. 'Time to go and be a farmer, I think.'

In the morning, the rain had stopped. Alexanor woke on a pallet of straw; the farm had little furniture. He rose and went to the wellhead to have a drink, wrapped only in his winter *chlamys*, and at the well he found Arkas and Philopoemen.

'Going to run?' Philopoemen said.

Alexanor laughed. 'I got enough exercise to last me the rest of my life just getting here.'

Philopoemen shrugged. 'Brother, you are the doctor and I am the politician, but it seems to me we're reaching the time of life when men layer on fat, if they aren't careful.' He put a hand on Alexanor's belly. 'And Kaeso says you are to be wed. She'll want you hard.'

Arkas turned red and then turned away to bray a young man's laugh.

Philopoemen smiled sheepishly. 'Ah, I didn't see that coming,' he admitted.

Alexanor bit back various unfortunate replies. 'Fine,' he said. 'In fact, I agree. Let's run.'

It was cold, and they ran naked. After a few minutes, the cold fell away, and the sun began to rise in the east over Thrake. The day was beautiful, and they ran along the farm roads, chased a rabbit over someone else's field, and made a long circle up an oak-crowned ridge before running back down into Philopoemen's rented farmyard. All three men were covered in sweat.

'We have never had our *pankration* bout,' Philopoemen said suddenly.

Alexanor drank a cup of watered wine that one of the cavalry troopers handed him. Then he leant forward on his knees. They'd run much farther than he'd intended; something about Philopoemen made it impossible to say 'Are you serious' about a running distance.

When he was master of his own lungs, he shook his head.

'You outweigh me by what ... ten talents? Maybe more. I don't need a broken nose when I plead with the king.'

Philopoemen shrugged, but something in his face made it impossible for Alexanor to refuse. Philopoemen was not Achilles today. He was at the edge of a great darkness; Alexanor could see it as if written on his face.

'Fine,' he said. 'Three throws or three good blows.'

'Ah!' Philopoemen said. 'Now I feel bad, like a man pushing a slave girl.'

'I think you just called me an unwilling slave girl. After suggesting I might not be hard enough for my wife.'

'That was not my intention ...'

Alexanor had wrapped his heavy wool *chlamys* around his body as soon as they entered the yard, but now he tossed it to Alcibiades, one of Kleostratos' file leaders, and he unlaced his heavy winter sandals.

'No studded sandals,' he said.

Philopoemen untied his own. He was half a head taller and heavily muscled. The two wounds in his abdomen showed only as a deep pit, like a second belly button. Otherwise, his abdomen was as hard as an ephebe's, which Alexanor could not say for his own.

His arms were so long that Alexanor had a moment of real doubt. But he set his teeth, worked his jaw, flexed his hands, and then knelt and made a brief prayer to Apollo, settling his mind.

'Are you ready?' Philopoemen said.

'Yes.'

Alexanor was relaxed now, his muscles only pleasantly tired from running. He was warm and alert, and the morning sun was beautiful.

They circled while the cavalrymen in the courtyard called out to the late sleepers to come and see. Alexanor moved carefully, until he stopped thinking at all.

Philopoemen opened with a rapid attack, as Alexanor would have expected. Philopoemen used his reach and his long legs to cross the distance between them, his right hand brushing Alexanor's reflexive jab aside more rapidly than he could really believe, his left hand reaching for Alexanor's neck ...

Alexanor's snap kick was imperfectly timed, because Philopoemen was faster than he'd expected, and he knew how fast the man was. But it was still accurate, if slightly late. Instead of catching the charging Titan's knee, it caught his thigh, but it turned him slightly, and both of their complex intentions tumbled away to nothing as they traded jabs and broke apart.

Philopoemen flowed back like thick water, pivoted his hips, and struck again – a punch, a kick, a punch.

Alexanor caught the third punch, a thumb-down wrist block that was also a blow to the adversary's wrist. Despite the larger man's speed, his blow was good. He tried to grab the arm, but it was gone, and Philopoemen flowed back as easily as he'd flowed forward.

They circled, both men smiling.

'I knew this would be excellent,' Philopoemen said. 'Lykortas? Are you there?'

'I'm here,' Lykortas said. 'Usually he tosses me around every morning.'

'Or me,' Dinaeos said. 'Glad to have you here, Doc.'

They circled.

Finally, Alexanor stepped in. He intended to draw a kick, and he was startled when instead he drew a punch. He'd misjudged his distance, and the punch caught him above his nose and rocked him. He pivoted and threw a straight kick to cover his retreat; Philopoemen took his foot and pulled, and he was on his back.

Alexanor drank a little more watered wine while the cavalry troopers commiserated.

Then he went back on to the sand. 'Ready,' he said.

Philopoemen nodded, and moved in.

Alexanor backed away.

Philopoemen followed him around the circle of watchers for ten strides or more; men were beginning to laugh. And then Alexanor changed the tempo of his retreat. Philopoemen's kick was too late, and they were grappling, but Alexanor had the initial advantage.

He landed a punch, from quite close, covered the counter-punch with the same wrist block he'd made earlier, and this time he got the hand, or a piece of it, and he went forward, his whole weight and intention like a cavalry charge. His right hand didn't so much punch Philopoemen as palm his face. His fleeting hold on the reaching hand overstretched the man's balance. He pulled his knee-shattering kick, merely tapping the back of the Titan's knee to fold the muscle, and Philopoemen was down.

'By Zeus!' Philopoemen bounced to his feet and crushed Alexanor in a great hug. 'By Zeus!'

Other men came into the ring, slapping Alexanor's back.

Dinaeos said, into his ear, 'I've never seen him put down.'

Alexanor tried not to be smug.

He returned to where his cloak was, and crouched, ready for a third bout.

Philopoemen shook his head. 'I take it the knee kick would have broken the knee out sideways?'

'Yes,' Alexanor agreed.

'And if you hold my hand all the way to the ground, you unknit the whole shoulder?'

'Yes.'

Philopoemen shook his head. 'Well, that's two blows right there. We'll fight again when you have taught me that.' He reached out a hand, and they shook.

'I'm for a bath,' Philopoemen said. 'Damn it, I feel better than I have in weeks.'

'And then we see the king?' Alexanor asked.

Philopoemen nodded. 'If we must.' He leant over. 'Have I told you how much I esteem you, my friend?'

'Never,' Alexanor said.

They both laughed, the darkness averted for a while.

It was mid-morning by the time they arrived at the palace, which stood on a long hillside above the Temple of Herakles. Next to the temple, just slightly higher on the hill, was a magnificent, smaller temple that glowed, its white marble almost alive in the fresh winter sunlight.

'Alexander's temple,' Philopoemen said. 'Shall we make a sacrifice?'

They dismounted.

'To what goddess?'

Alexanor didn't recognise the statues, although the temple had military trophies everywhere – *aspides* and *pelti* and helmets and spears, as many as at Olympia, or more.

'It is a temple to glory,' Philopoemen said, his voice hushed.

'Glory?' Alexanor halted in the nave. He looked up at the decorations, and then shook his head. 'My family are descended from Herakles. I'll go and offer to my ancestor. But I won't sacrifice to glory.'

He walked out, watched by several Macedonians, and then went up the steps of the older Temple of Herakles, where he gave a sign to the priest and was admitted to the sanctum. He prayed a little, and then made a small sacrifice, just a pair of oatcakes, as was appropriate to the time of year.

'You are a foreigner?' the priest asked.

'Yes,' he said. 'From Rhodes.'

The priest nodded. 'Herakles' sons are everywhere.'

He offered his hand and, at the clasp, Alexanor offered him another sign, a sign of his order, and the man responded with a smile.

'I have also been to Delphi,' the man said, the correct response.

Alexanor could see Philopoemen waiting for him.

'Another time, I might ask you for some help in talking to the king,' he said.

The priest nodded. 'They are all sons of Herakles,' he said, 'the kings of Macedon. But this one never comes here. He worships glory.'

Alexanor shook his head. 'I can't really imagine anything more foolish to worship.'

The two priests looked at each other. And smiled.

The palace of Pella towered above them, a monument to the power of Macedon, built by Cassander, the front portico larger than the largest temple anywhere in Greece. It towered over them, the power of immense empire rendered physical, in stone.

'Don't pretend that you are impressed,' Philopoemen said.

'I lived here for a year,' Alexanor said.

They walked up the long steps, attended by Kaeso. Macedonian officers and Greek bureaucrats passed them without word or a greeting. A Paeonian chieftain, his cloak heavy with gold and his arms tattooed, passed them going down the steps and shook his head in silence, as if to suggest that they avoid the place, the way a traveller might shake his head at a man entering a bad inn.

Under the enormous portico, a great deal of the business of the Macedonian Empire was done. Men sat in the winter sunlight with tables and scrolls; a money-changer changed coins for Macedonian currency; a trio of tax-farmers argued their accounts with a tax official. There were hundreds of men under the portico, in among the colonnade, and some aristocrats strolled along, idly looking at the statues, many of which were loot from the east, from Athens or Thebes.

'Has there ever been a Macedonian sculptor, I wonder?' Alexanor asked.

'You must have been very popular here,' Philopoemen said.

They walked along the colonnade until they came to three sets of double doors. Alexanor expected that they would go to the right, into the private apartments, but Philopoemen led them off to the left. After crossing an impressive mosaic floor and climbing a short staircase, they emerged into another colonnade and beyond it lay the sands of a *palaestra*. A dozen pairs of men were out on the sand, wrestling or boxing. One pair was engaged in *pankration*, and forty or fifty men stood under the vaulted columns, watching the fight. In the midst of them stood Philip. Alexanor knew him immediately – of middle height, but very blond, his hair short and curled, his blue eyes everywhere.

He was not dressed for magnificence. His fine cavalry cloak was edged in the Royal Purple, but his *chiton* was merely elegant – simple, without gold or embroidery. His boots were practical, soldier's boots. Only the gold decorations on his belt and the superb ivory and gold work on his sword and scabbard marked out his rank.

He smiled when he saw Philopoemen, and then he saw Alexanor. Alexanor saw recognition strike the king.

He said something to the man closest to him – Antipater, who had been his father's trusted aide.

Antipater clearly disagreed.

The king shrugged, and beckoned, quite publicly, to Philopoemen.

Out on the sand, the two contestants were exchanging blows. It was a very different fight from the one that Alexanor had shared with his friend in the dawn light. This was two very big men standing head to head and trading heavy blows, with little deception or manoeuvre.

It might have been a different art; neither man blocked, parried, or evaded. The sound of their blows landing on each other's muscled flesh was the loudest noise on the sand.

'Our favourite Achaean,' the king said. Philopoemen made to bow, and the king caught his hands. 'No, no, none of that. I never seek to embarrass you stiff-necked Greeks.'

Philopoemen flushed.

'It is many years since you have graced our court,' the king said to Alexanor. 'I haven't seen you since my father died.'

Alexanor bowed. 'Your Grace, your esteemed father sent me on a mission.'

Antipater laughed. 'You mean, since you'd failed to save him, you thought you'd better go, eh?'

Most of the Macedonians laughed.

Alexanor knew his Macedonians. He laughed too. Then he said, 'It would be hard to blame me, since he never took one iota of my advice.'

Philip smiled. 'I know, Alexanor. Truly, I do.'

Behind the king, the two champions were beginning to hurt each other. The larger stumbled, swaying, but caught himself, and his great fist lashed out again.

'What brings you here?' the king asked.

'My lord, I was sent by the Hierophant of Kos ...'

Alexanor had a prepared speech, and he was ready to give it, however distracting the surroundings, but just then the larger contestant fell backwards, his knees folded and he was down.

Most of the court applauded.

'Well struck, Cortus!' the king shouted. He turned to Philopoemen. 'You're a great one for the *pankration*, Achaean. What do you think of our champion? He'll go to Nemea and then perhaps to the Olympic games.'

'What does a Greek know of fighting?' asked one of the courtiers.

Philopoemen shrugged. 'Well,' he said in a drawl that was a parody of his slight Arkadian accent. 'Well, laddie, I was fighting this morning. While you were still nursing a hangover.'

Even Antipater laughed. The king laughed so hard he had to turn away.

Alexanor had never seen Philopoemen trying so wilfully to please

376

someone, except Phila. He wondered at it. His friend was smiling. The Macedonian courtier was not smiling.

'Who were you fighting?' the king asked.

'This lout here dropped me,' Philopoemen said.

The Macedonians looked at wiry Alexanor.

'Oh,' said Antipater. 'I'd imagined that you were good, at least, for a Greek.'

'You note, Antipater, that our Achaean has made no comment about our champion. You don't think he's very good, do you?' the king asked.

Philopoemen shrugged. 'No,' he said simply.

The king frowned. 'You are very plain spoken. Why don't you like him?'

Antipater smiled. 'Oh please,' he said. 'Please tell us.'

Philopoemen shrugged. 'It's a matter of style and tactics. Your Grace, Alexanor wishes to approach you on a matter—'

'Alexanor is a *pankrationist* too, apparently,' Antipater said with ill-concealed glee. 'Why doesn't he tell us his views on Cortus?'

'His *Greek* views,' another man said. The courtiers laughed.

Alexanor smiled. 'Tell me,' he said, 'the name of the last Macedonian fighter to win in the Olympics?'

They looked at him.

He shrugged. 'I saw Agesidamos down Klosander a few years back. Klosander fought the same way as this man – he never touched Agesidamos. Too slow.' He turned to the king. 'Your Grace, may I give you my address?'

The king was slightly red in the face. 'This is the Macedonian style,' he said. 'We believe it is better training for real war.'

Philopoemen raised an eyebrow. 'You, the descendent of golden Alexander, who was the master of the deceptive attack and the counter-strike, are advocating this sort of stolid, dull offence?'

The silence that came after Philopoemen's remark had a tangible quality, as if every man present wanted to be sure that the king had heard the damning words.

The two men looked at each other, eyes locked.

Then they heard a set of sandals approaching. Heads turned, and the silence was broken.

The king said, 'Philopoemen, you are the harshest—'

'Ah,' said a round, unctuous voice. 'It is our Philopoemen. Must you always argue with the king, my boy?'

It was Aratos – older, greyer, and perhaps a little rounder.

Philopoemen's eyes didn't leave the king's. 'Isn't it my duty to correct power, if power has gone astray?'

Antipater shook his head angrily. 'No, Greek. It's your duty to do what you're told.'

Philopoemen smiled. Alexanor knew that smile. It was the smile he'd worn, watching Nabis run at Gortyna.

'Really?' Philopoemen asked. 'He has you for that, after all.'

Antipater reached for his sword. The men around him restrained him. Aratos was as white as a fish's belly.

The king smiled. His eyes were still locked with Philopoemen's.

'I suppose that it's useful to have a naysayer,' the king said. 'Do you think you could defeat Cortus?'

'Yes,' Philopoemen said.

The king nodded. 'Show me.'

Philopoemen nodded twice. Then he said, 'Your Grace, it's hardly a fair contest. He's bleeding, and tired.'

The king's smile was broader. 'All the easier for you, then.' He raised a hand. 'Cortus? I'd like you to fight this man – an Achaean.'

Cortus nodded slowly. 'Sure,' he said. 'Can I hurt him?'

The king looked at Philopoemen. 'How soft does he need to be?' he asked, his tone derisive.

Philopoemen sighed, as if the prospect annoyed him. 'He can play as hard as he likes, Your Grace.'

'You heard that, Cortus?' The king smiled at his court. 'Let's hear some bets, gentlemen.'

Antipater laughed. 'I'd like to bet on Cortus, but I doubt anyone will take my money.'

Alexanor glanced at Aratos, and caught a gloating look on the politician's features. *You hate Philopoemen as much as Antipater*, he thought.

'I'll take your wager,' Alexanor said.

'One hundred gold?' Antipater asked.

'For what?' Alexanor said. 'A clean win? A hold? A fall?' He shrugged. 'I'll wager you at one hundred to your one hundred that my man wins the first fall.'

Philopoemen dropped his *chlamys*, and unpinned his *chiton*.

'How many of us can you wager with?' asked another courtier.

Alexanor counted in his head. 'Three of you,' he said, a little too contemptuously. 'Decide among yourselves.'

The king turned his back on Alexanor. *I was the wrong man to send on this mission*, Alexanor thought.

Philopoemen walked out onto the sand.

'Begin,' the king said.

Philopoemen walked all the way to engagement distance without taking a fighting stance.

Cortus threw a blow, and Philopoemen passed around it like smoke. His kick was in tempo with his steps; he caught the other man in the groin. As the big *pankrationist* folded, Philopoemen caught his head and threw him.

Cortus lay, moaning.

Philopoemen walked back to his clothes, and the new pool of silence around the king.

He put on his *chiton*; Alexanor pinned it at the shoulder.

'You didn't even fight!' the king suddenly exclaimed.

'Your man doesn't know what a fight is,' Philopoemen said. 'I had every advantage – reach, height, wind. You even let me watch him fight his last fight.' He shrugged. 'I took full advantage of what I was offered.'

Kaeso picked up his cloak. 'That was amazing,' he said in his Latin-accented Greek.

Philip turned. 'Are you a Roman?'

The young man lowered his eyes, and then raised them. 'Yes,' he said.

Philip laughed. 'How apt! I'm about to make war on Rome.'

'Is he one of the slaves from Hannibal's victories?' Antipater asked.

'Yes,' Alexanor said.

'Good!' Philip said. 'Let's have him tell us all about the Roman armies. If there are any left for us to fight.'

Kaeso squared his shoulders. 'No, Your Grace. I am a slave, but no traitor. You'll have to find out for yourself.'

Antipater laughed. 'Talk about stupid. Let's put him to a little torture. We'll have it out of him.'

'Why?' the king asked. 'Who cares? I have all of Barca's notes, and

Demetrios here has fought them, too. I don't need to torture a slave.' He looked at Kaeso and smiled. 'I like your courage.'

Then he turned to Philopoemen, and his tone was much more dangerous.

'But now that you've made your point about our *pankrationist*,' he said, 'what do you think of my plan to make war in Italy?'

Don't say it, Alexanor wished.

Philopoemen frowned. And said nothing.

'Oh, come,' said Aratos. 'You have an opinion on everything, Philopoemen. Why not tell the king what you told me?'

Philopoemen looked ... betrayed. But only for a moment, and then he turned his head slightly, as if to study an adversary, except the man he was looking at was his fellow Achaean, Aratos. The *Strategos*.

'You *wish* this?' Philopoemen asked.

Aratos smiled broadly. 'I do.'

'Ah,' Philopoemen said. 'Too late, I fully understand.' He turned to Alexanor. 'I'm sorry.'

Alexanor smiled ruefully.

'I think it is a terrible, foolish notion, Your Grace, one you can only follow if you refuse to read the information available to you and instead believe your own propaganda.' Philopoemen bowed.

'Really?' The king flushed red, bright red. 'And you, a commander of some barbarian horse, feel that you can lesson me in military tactics?'

Philopoemen's eyebrows went up. 'Rome now has the most powerful fleet in the world. You have no fleet. Rome has endured two shattering defeats and is still raising armies.' He shook his head. 'None of that is what matters. The Illyrians, the Dardanians, the Aetolians and the Spartans all make war on your alliance, and remain unbeaten, and you want to go and fight *Rome*.' He pointed at Aratos, and Alexanor thought what a powerful orator he was, so unlike most soldiers. 'Those are the words *he* wants me to say. So that he can spurn me later, and yet the words will have been said, suiting his purpose.'

Aratos allowed himself a look of outrage.

The king was redder than his cloak.

'You are deceived if you imagine you can speak to the king of Macedon this way,' he said. 'You may go. Do not return.'

Philopoemen bowed.

'I will attack Rome if I want, and I will reap the glory and be victorious,' Philip said.

Philopoemen didn't reply. He only glanced meaningfully at the groaning figure of the Macedonian *pankrationist* out on the sand.

'Begone!' the king spat.

Alexanor stepped forward. 'Your Grace, may I collect my winnings first?'

EPILOGUE

―◦◦◦―

Gortyna, Lentas and Achaea

214–212 BCE

The first ship to arrive in the spring brought news that Philopoemen had been exiled by the Achaean League. The vote was close; clearly, some of the member states had a hard time swallowing the charge that Philopoemen was a 'tool of the king of Macedon' from Aratos, who had wintered at Pella.

Philopoemen took no notice. The buyers of his three farms on Crete had sold them back, and when Alexanor rode over to visit in the first bloom of spring, Philopoemen was, once again, naked but for a loincloth. He and Arkas and Kleostratos were raising an Achaean-style stone barn on the plain of Gortyna.

'Most people hire builders,' Alexanor called.

Philopoemen came and took his hand. 'I won't get my sweat on your nice cloak,' he said.

'It's the largest barn in Crete,' Alexanor said.

'My realm,' Philopoemen said. If he was bitter, it was not showing.

Later, over dinner, Alexanor asked about the exile. Philopoemen laughed ruefully.

'I tried to tell him,' Lykortas said.

'He did, too,' Philopoemen said. 'I thought he was being ... too ...'

'Underhanded. That's what you said. That I had worked in an under-handed way for so long that I could no longer see how honourable men ruled.' Lykortas drank some wine, and shrugged. 'It's not like it gives me any satisfaction.'

'I am so lucky to have good friends to tell me all my faults.' Philopoemen looked around. 'I thought that in the matter of war with Rome, Aratos was my ally. In fact, he was willing to use any issue to see to it that I fell from the king's grace. The exile was probably unnecessary.'

'It's not even legal,' Lykortas said. 'It wasn't voted at a legal session.'

Alexanor shook his head in surprise. 'Terrible,' he said.

'So you say,' Philopoemen said. 'It doesn't matter. My life is now here. I will farm on Crete. Perhaps I will run for office.' He smiled at Alexanor. 'What I have learnt is that politics is much more complicated than war. Perhaps this is why men prefer war. But enough of my exile – it will pass. Or not. What of you, brother?'

'I'm here to invite you to a wedding,' Alexanor said.

'I love weddings,' Lykortas said.

Kleostratos laughed.

'Mine,' Alexanor said. 'The Hierophant of Kos has approved my Aspasia for the priesthood, and approved my wedding.'

'Even though I wrecked your mission to Philip?' Philopoemen said.

Alexanor shrugged.

Lykortas sat back and laughed. 'Alexanor had an audience with Philip before we left,'

Now it was Philopoemen's turn to be surprised.

'I got to him through his physician, and through the priests of Herakles,' Alexanor admitted. 'He sent an ambassador to Rhodes.' He leant back. 'I learnt something too, brother. The ambassador was arrogant, and has since left, and nothing is accomplished. Macedon and Rhodes are virtually at war. But I did my part and the hierophant approved my marriage. This is how men become hardened to the ways of the world. It is as if it is not what we do that matters, but what we appear to do.'

Philopoemen drank some wine. 'Well, I will play a better game next time, if allowed. And I congratulate you on yours.' He grinned. 'I look forward to meeting a woman who you feel can replace Phila.'

'You can see them together,' Alexanor said. 'I invited Phila to the wedding, too.'

Philopoemen roared a laugh. 'And men say I am brave.'

*

Alexanor's wedding day finally came, and the chariot of the sun leapt into the sky over the Lion of Lentas. All of his fears fell away; his wife and Phila were equally amused at him, and the priests and novices of the temple cleaned until everything shone. The only cloud on his horizon was that Philopoemen hadn't come, nor had Lykortas.

The day passed in a blur of censers and ceremonies, and the smoke of their sacrifices rose to the gods. The sight of Aspasia in her rose-coloured veil and saffron-yellow *peplos* with a year of embroidery at the hem and across the breast inflamed him and struck him with the same awe that he sometimes felt in the temple when he served at the altar. He raised the veil and kissed her before gods and men, and two hundred voices shouted for them, and then they were walking down the steps of the temple, hand in hand, and there, at last, was Philopoemen.

Alexanor embraced him, but then there was dancing, and food, and another round of sacrifices, and Aspasia's formal introduction to the temple, performed as part of the wedding by the two priestesses of Hygeia.

It was during the latter that Alexanor clasped his friend's hand.

'I feared you were not coming,' he said.

Philopoemen looked tired, but he smiled. 'How would I miss this?'

When he went to fetch wine, Lykortas took Alexanor's hand.

'Listen, he almost did not come,' he said. 'All he does is go to Cyrena's grave.' He shrugged. 'The giant barn is finished and he has no more worlds to conquer.'

Alexanor was watching his radiant, beautiful priestess-wife coming down from the temple with two sheaves of wheat in her arms. Their eyes met; he was almost unable to speak.

Phila's voice came from behind him. 'Let's see what I can manage,' she said.

And when they were all reclining on a hundred *kline* to eat the wedding feast, Alexanor saw, not without a pang, that Phila lay beside Philopoemen. He was talking, and her head was lifted towards him, and she was laughing without restraint.

That night, Aspasia rolled over and surprised Alexanor by being awake.

'You are not the sort of man to be jealous of a friend?' she asked.

Alexanor laughed softly. 'No,' he said.

She ran a hand over his chest. 'Good. Because finding that man as a farmer on Crete is like finding a god in a cage.'

'You fancy him?' Alexanor asked.

'Gods, no! I merely say what I think. He is ...'

She shrugged, and wriggled, and soon enough, they were otherwise occupied than with politics.

It had, indeed, been worth waiting a year. Alexanor had never known a night like his wedding night.

A year later, Crete had the best harvest of olives she had had in a hundred years; the wheat harvest was as good, and the barley. Aspasia bore them a daughter, her first child, and her labour was easy and the birth quick, as befitted a priest and priestess of health. And the next year, the festivals were brilliant. Everyone had a little money, and the barns were bursting with barley and wheat, and Alexanor learnt about going without sleep and helping a nursing mother. Philopoemen was elected *Hipparchos* of Gortyna, and his only duty, besides being on the Great Council, was to lead the equestrian parade on feast days. On the Great Feast of Apollo, he led a procession – two hundred cavalry, a thousand infantry, two hundred priests and as many maidens and priestesses and much of the population of Gortyna – all the way from the city to the sanctuary at Lentas.

Alexanor had risen with the dawn after his longest sleep in a year, kissed his sleeping wife and tranquil daughter, and had gone out, in a plain brown *chiton*, with Leon and Omphalion, and they had polished all the gold and silver, and washed ritually. Later Aspasia and the other priestesses washed the altars, and then all the celebrants together cleansed them again with branches of sacred olive and laurel, sweeping the floors that were already clean enough to eat from, and then sweeping the three great altars themselves.

Alexanor went to the sacristy and prepared his censer. This one was solid silver, a donation from Philopoemen and Dinaeos, made by a woman silversmith in Gortyna – a work of art. The incense was from the east; the charcoal he had made himself, with the help of two wrinkled old charcoal men from the hills, from a tree struck by the lightning of the god.

When Leon told him that the horsemen were cresting the distant ridge, Alexanor lit his charcoal from the sacred fire. He and Aspasia walked through the gleaming temple together, censing the altars and the rooms and then the thousands of people attending the festival, in crowds along the avenue to the sanctuary, and the pilgrims, too. And then, as the riders came down the avenue between the young trees he'd planted, Alexanor blessed them: Philopoemen, of course, larger than life and magnificent in armour as he never was in his everyday clothes; Dinaeos, fresh from Achaea on a new, fine cavalry horse; Lykortas, in a cloak with more purple than the king of Macedon; Kleostratos, smiling, wearing a heavy arm ring of solid gold; and Arkas, who wore a sword with an ivory hilt.

Philopoemen, as a priest of Zeus, led one set of sacrifices; Alexanor led another, and Aspasia led the women in the sacrifice of the cakes, and then all of the celebrants danced in a stately ring. At sunset, almost the whole of the festival went to the sea to throw the sacred laurels into the water.

And then the wine was served, and food, and it was over. Or rather, the formal celebration was over, and the god's holiday began. Most of them leapt into the water, and the stately procession developed a very different tone, and Alexanor carried his priestess down the beach as she giggled like a girl.

'I wish he'd take a wife,' Aspasia said later. Philopoemen was swimming in the sea, with half the population of Gortyna. 'I could find him a girl on Rhodes. Your sisters would do the trick in a week. Some nice—'

'Fifteen year old virgin?' Alexanor watched his friend and shook his head. 'Not yet. He will when he's ready. He's still besotted with Phila,' he added.

'Who ran back to Athens as soon as she was bored with him,' his wife said bitterly.

Lykortas ran past, pursuing a young person in a cloak, both of them giggling.

'I think Phila had other ...' He paused, and decided that defending Phila to his wife was not going to be a winning ploy.

Aspasia shook her head. 'I find him a puzzle,' she admitted. 'And I can't love her.'

'Most people are puzzles, if you really get to know them,' Alexanor said. And then they were swimming in the warm water, and laughing.

*

When they woke, with hard heads for the first time in a year and too little sleep, there was a new ship in the bay: a two-masted round vessel, the kind that usually brought pilgrims from the mainland. Alexanor saw it when he got up to drink water, and again, later, when he got up again because he had duties, even the day after a major festival. His wife was trying to rise, but she, too, had been festive, and she lacked his experience.

He splashed water on his face, and then walked out. When he'd married, he'd left the priests' barracks and engaged a small house in the town – not a palace like his predecessor, but a fine house, with a central court and a good shed for storage and a big kitchen. Aspasia had brought roses from their home island, and their courtyard, instead of being a dusty mess, was a rose garden with some marble seats and a fine statue of Apollo – a restful place when their daughter wasn't testing her lungs.

As soon as he washed his face, he could hear voices in the rose garden. He threw on a *chlamys* and walked out, surer and surer as he walked of who he was hearing.

Phila sat at his marble table, wearing a light cloak and a conical straw hat.

Philopoemen sat opposite her. He wasn't sitting with her, but their hands were together, and their smiles betrayed intimacy, and, just for a moment, Alexanor knew a pang of jealousy. But it was ugly and unworthy, and he shrugged it off and walked forward to be kissed by Phila.

'Too late for the party,' she said. 'The captain was a mere atheist, I assure you. But I brought good wine, so you can repeat it all for me tonight.'

Alexanor glanced at Philopoemen. 'You knew she was coming back,' he said, with some accusation.

Philopoemen smiled his lopsided smile. 'I did, too,' he admitted.

'Well, you are welcome,' Alexanor said. 'I'm sure we can find some festival to entertain you ...'

'I've really come to take Philopoemen away,' Phila said.

'Wait until you hear her news,' Philopoemen said.

Alexanor sat down just as Aspasia appeared. She paused, and then she came forward as if it was nothing to her to have the greatest beauty in Athens on her doorstep at the dawning of the day. But as soon as Philopoemen touched Phila's hand, Aspasia gave Alexanor a significant glance. He shook his head, as if to say *tell you later*.

Eventually, they made it back around to Phila's news.

'Well,' she said, and paused dramatically.

The gate opened, and Lykortas came in. He had a wreath of somewhat tattered flowers in his hair, but otherwise looked as fresh as a new dawn.

'Phila!' he said.

'My favourite schemer,' she said, kissing both cheeks. 'After myself, of course.'

Lykortas turned to Philopoemen. 'Aratos is dead,' he said.

'That's my news!' Phila said.

Aspasia looked at her husband, and Philopoemen stood up.

'Aratos is dead,' Philopoemen said. 'My exile is lifted, and the king of Macedon has asked me to return to Achaea.'

AUTHOR'S NOTE

It is several years since I've written a novel about Ancient Greece.

Actually that's not quite true. All my novels are about Ancient Greece, really; if you read my stuff, you know that William Gold stops at Thermopylae and has a deed of arms with his friends ... real knights really did that. And you know that my fantasy *Cold Iron* is set in a sort of seventeenth century Hellenistic world ... In a way, it is always Ancient Greece somewhere in my mind.

Nonetheless. This is my first Greek novel in several years, since *Rage of Ares*, and going back to the Ancient world was, in fact, like going home. These two books, *The New Achilles* and *The Last Greek* are the product of years of research, some of it original. That's a bold assertion from a mere novelist, but I'll make it anyway; I read the inscription to Philopoemen at Delphi myself, while 'leading' my 'Pen and Sword' tour in 2015. I think these books were born that afternoon, in the perfect sunshine of a Greek autumn. I'd heard of Philopoemen, of course, and at one point I'd painted part of his Achaean army in 28mm. But there was this stone – and there was his name. I saw the name from fifteen feet away, and it was, really, as if a thunderbolt from Zeus had struck me.

Because history really happened. This book is a novel, and a great deal of it, especially the details, is made up. But Philopoemen really lived. And he really was so great a man that everyone, friends and enemies, honoured him when he was dead. He is, as a Classics professor once said, 'The greatest man you've never heard of.'

And another year, my Pen and Sword bus was travelling through Arkadia and we stopped at the battlefield of Sellasia. Now, here's the exciting part. Our guide and the local mayor of a very, very small town in the Peloponnese agreed it was the battlefield, but it's not the battlefield that is marked on tourist maps. That's where the 'original research' part comes. Our local guide took us to a place whose topography matched the battle account in Polybius. Polybius wasn't there, but his father probably was; Polybius' father carried Philopoemen's ashes at his funeral and the famous author probably knew a great deal about him and his battles. The topography is so exact ...

Right, anyway, we spent three hours on the battlefield. I could have wished for days ... and I will go back. But I saw it: the stream, the hills, the central saddle with the cavalry fight.

The same can be said for Crete. A great deal of this book takes place on Crete, and I went there two years ago and walked the battlefields, climbed the ancient acropolis of Gortyna, and visited the sanctuary of Asklepios in Lentas. All that is real.

All the political situations are real, too. I have tried, in these books, to avoid the simplicity of 'good' and 'bad'. I recognise that sometimes black and white world views make books easier to read, but anyone paying attention to our own world in the last forty years can see how unlikely such lineups really are. The Romans were not 'good'. The Spartans were not particularly bad. (Or good.) Greece was modern Syria – all the big players fought over her – and Hellenistic Greece in the second century BCE was not very much like the Greece of my earlier books. Archaeology suggests that the decline of small free farmers and the creation of large landed estates, combined with the constant drain of manpower as country boys went to get rich fighting in Persia, had the net effect of depopulating the countryside. Sparta could no longer raise an army of thirty thousand men to fight, as she did for Plataea. Sparta was lucky if she could raise fifteen thousand, and a third of those were mercenaries.

That is part of the charm of this story. This is not Hannibal and Scipio Africanus fighting over the fate of the Western world. This is a handful of free people trying to stay free as the iron vice of imperial oppression closes on them from all sides. Later Greeks would remember the Achaean League as the exemplars of what it meant to be 'free'. The founding fathers of the United States admired the Achaean League; it was one of the models for American federalism. And that brings up a thematic point in writing historical fiction; I like my novels to be 'about' something. One thing that these two novels are 'about' is best encapsulated by Shakespeare. 'The good men do is oft interred with their bones,' he said, but in this case, Philopoemen and his generation not only bought Greeks another three generations of liberty but created a model for the future – maybe a better model then Athens or Rome.

I had enormous support in writing these books. First, I'd like to thank Aliki Hamosfakidou of Dolfin Hellas travel, the best friend and travel agent I could have, and without whom I would have done no research, drunk no wine, eaten poor quality food, etc. Aliki does all the detail work on my Greek tours (which are also research trips … you should come!) and none of this would have happened without her.

I was also supported by a variety of Greek academics and history professionals: Nikos Lanser (who discovered the battlefield of Sellasia) and Aristotelis Koskinas (who knows more about the Battle of Plataea then anyone I've met); Dr Maria Girtzi, who led me through the Macedonian tombs and Bulgaria as well and without whom this would have been a different book; as well as the staff of the New Acropolis Museum (best museum in the world), and the Greek National Archaeological Museum, and the Archaeological Museums of Olympia and Delphi as well as the historical sites at Zone near Alexandroupolis (Archeologikos Choros Archea Mesimvria Zoni to be precise) and the Archaeological Museum of Pella and the Archaeological Site of Aigai – Macedonian Royal Tombs at Vergina. I was at those last sites a year ago today, imagining Philip's Macedon. I also managed to visit a number of tombs and historical sites in Bulgaria that, while not directly related to the events of Philopoemen's life, helped me understand the breadth and riches of the Hellenistic world.

I'd also like to thank my many friends in the world martial arts community, from Aikido to Armizare – most especially my own Hoplologia and my friend Greg Mele's Chicago Swordplay Guild. Fight scenes are enriched by regular fighting, despite the many artificialities of safe simulation. This year we had sixty people in a phalanx learning to use the weapons of the Hellenistic phalangite; next year, at the Hoplite Experiment, we hope to pit two groups of trained martial artists against each other in carefully controlled conditions to try and replicate phalanx combat in the early Classical period. Thanks to all of you, martial artists and re-enactors!

And last but by no means least, my wife Sarah and my daughter Beatrice, who ask questions and accept strange 'vacations' so that we can visit this or that site or maybe help someone plan a re-enactment that's really an experiment or an immersion ...

Actually, I also owe thanks to the vast team that helps me: my copy editor Steve O'Gorman; my editor Craig Lye; my agent Shelley Power; my map artist Steve James, and my friend and sometime research assistant, sparring partner, and general willing listener, Aurora Simmons.

Ah, and all of you who buy my books. I appreciate it deeply.

Christian G. Cameron
Toronto, October 2018

GLOSSARY

I am an *amateur* Greek scholar. My definitions are my own, but taken from the LSJ or Routledge's *Handbook of Greek Mythology* or Smith's *Classical Dictionary*. On some military issues I have the temerity to disagree with the received wisdom on the subject. Also check my website at www.christiancameronauthor.com for more information and some helpful pictures.

Agema: An elite Macedonian military unit; in Sparta, merely a detachment.

Agrianios: A month in the Rhodian calendar. In the ancient world, every city and state had a different calendar with different names for months, and feasts.

Andron: The 'men's room' of a proper Greek house – where men have symposia. Recent research has cast real doubt as to the sexual exclusivity of the room, but the name sticks.

Apobatai: The Chariot Warriors. In many towns – towns that hadn't used chariots in warfare for centuries – the *Apobatai* were the elite three hundred or so. In Athens, they competed in special events; in Thebes, they may have been the forerunners of the Sacred Band.

Archon: A city's senior official, or in some cases, one of three or four. A magnate.

Archon Basileus: The 'king archon' or chief magistrate, at least in Athens and some other cities, but not, for example, in the Achaean League.

Artemon: A sail, usually on the 'fore' mast of a trireme.

Aspis: The Greek hoplite's shield. (Which is not called a hoplon!) The *aspis* is about a yard in diameter, is deeply dished (up to six inches deep) and should weigh between eight and sixteen pounds.

Basilieus: An aristocratic title from a bygone era (at least in 500 BCE) that means 'king' or 'lord'.

Bireme: A warship rowed by two tiers of oars, as opposed to a trireme which has three tiers.

Boeotarch: A military commander of the Boeotian Federation.

Boule: One of the councils of Athens.

Causia/kausia: A Macedonian hat, flat brimmed and rolled, which resembles the modern Afghan *pakol.*

Chiton: The standard tunic for most men, made by taking a single continuous piece of cloth and folding it in half, pinning the shoulders and open side. Can be made quite fitted by means of pleating. Often made of very fine quality material—usually wool, sometimes linen, especially in the upper classes. A full *chiton* was ankle length for men and women.

Chitoniskos: A small *chiton*, usually just longer than modesty demanded – or not as long as modern modesty would demand! Worn by warriors and farmers, often heavily bloused and very full by warriors to pad their armour. Usually wool.

Chlamys: A short cloak made by a rectangle of cloth roughly 60 by 90 inches – could also be worn as a *chiton* if folded and pinned a different way. Or slept under as a blanket.

Corslet/Thorax: In 200 BCE, the best corslets were still made of bronze, and the 'muscle' style predominated. Another style is the 'white' corslet seen to appear just as the Persian Wars begin – re-enactors call this the 'Tube and Yoke' corslet and some people call it (erroneously) the linothorax. Some of them may have been made of linen – we'll never know – but the likelier material is Athenian leather, which was often tanned and finished with alum, thus being bright white. Yet another style was a tube and yoke of scale, which can be seen in Hellenistic Scythian and Bulgarian tombs. A scale corslet would have been the most expensive or all, and probably provided the best protection.

Daimon: Literally 'a spirit', the daimon of combat might be adrenaline, and the daimon of philosophy might simply be native intelligence. Suffice it to say that very intelligent men – like Socrates – believed that god-sent spirits could infuse a man and influence his actions.

Daktyloi: Literally 'digits' or 'fingers', in common talk, 'inches' in the system of measurement. Systems for measurement differed from city to city. I have taken the liberty of using just one, the Athenian units of measurement.

Dekarch: A military officer commanding at least ten men.

Despoina: Lady. A term of formal address.

Diekplous: A complex naval tactic about which some debate remains. In this book, the *Diekplous* or through stroke is commenced with an attack by the ramming ship's bow (picture the two ships approaching bow to bow or head-on) and cathead on the enemy oars. Oars were the most vulnerable part of a fighting ship, something very difficult to imagine unless you've rowed in a big boat and understand how lethal your own oars can be – to you! After the attacker crushed the enemy's oars, he passes, flank to flank, and then turns when astern, coming up easily (the defender is almost dead in the water) and ramming the enemy under the stern or counter as desired.

Doru or Dory: A spear, about ten feet long, with a bronze butt spike and a spearhead.

Eleutheria: Freedom

Ephebe: A young, free man of property. A young man in training to be a hoplite. Usually performing service to his city, and in ancient terms, at one of the two peaks of male beauty.

Eromenos: The 'beloved' in a same sex-pair in ancient Greece. Usually younger, about seventeen. This is a complex, almost dangerous subject in the modern world – were these pair-bonds about sex, or chivalric love, or just a 'brotherhood' of warriors? I suspect there were elements of all three. And to write about this period without discussing the *eromenos/erastes* bond would, I fear, be like putting all the warriors in steel armour instead of bronze ...

Erastes: The 'lover' in a same-sex pair bond – the older man, a tried warrior, twenty-five to thirty years old.

Eudaimonia: Literally 'well-spirited'. A feeling of extreme joy.

Exedra: The porch of the woman's quarters – in some cases, any porch over a farm's central courtyard.

Falcis: A sword, back-curved like a Gurkha knife.

Gastraphetes: A crossbow.

Helot: The 'race of slaves' of ancient Sparta – the conquered peoples who lived with the Spartiates and did all of their work so that they could concentrate entirely on making war and more Spartans.

Hestiatorion: A guest dining room.

Hetaera: Literally a 'female companion'. In ancient Athens, a *Hetaera* was a courtesan, a highly skilled woman who provided sexual companionship as well as fashion, political advice, and music.

Hetaeroi: Literally 'male companion' but usually used for military companions i.e. household troops, companion cavalry.

Hipparchos: A cavalry commander. In the Achaean League, the *Hipparchos* was the second-in-command of the League armies.

Hippeis: Cavalry, usually the richest men in a city.

Himation: A very large piece of

rich, often embroidered wool, worn as an outer garment by wealthy citizen women or as a sole garment by older men, especially those in authority.

Hoplite: A Greek upper-class warrior. Possession of a heavy spear, a helmet, and an *aspis* (see above) and income above the marginal lowest free class were all required to serve as a hoplite. Although much is made of the 'citizen soldier' of ancient Greece, it would be fairer to compare hoplites to medieval knights than to Roman legionnaires or modern National Guardsmen. Poorer citizens did serve, and sometimes as hoplites or marines – but in general, the front ranks were the preserve of upper-class men who could afford the best training and the essential armour.

Hoplitodromos: The hoplite race, or race in armour. Two stades with an *aspis* on your shoulder, a helmet, and greaves in the early runs. I've run this race in armour. It is no picnic.

Hoplomachia: A hoplite contest, or sparring match. Again, there is enormous debate as to when *hoplomachia* came into existence and how much training Greek hoplites received. One thing that they didn't do is drill like modern soldiers – there's no mention of it in all of Greek literature. However, they had highly evolved martial arts (see *Pankration*) and it is almost certain that *Hoplomachia* was a term that referred to 'The martial art of fighting when fully equipped as a hoplite'.

Hoplomachos: A participant in *Hoplomachia*.

Hypaspist: Literally 'Under the shield'. A squire or military servant – by the time of Arimnestos, the *hypaspist* was usually a younger man of the same class as the hoplite.

Katagogion: A pilgrim hostel.

Kerameikos: The potters' quarter of Athens, noted for its statuary.

Kithara: A stringed instrument of some complexity, with a hollow body as a soundboard.

Kline: A couch.

Kontoi: A cavalry lance.

Kopis: The heavy, back-curved sabre of the Greeks. Like a longer, heavier modern kukri or Gurkha knife.

Kore: A maiden or daughter.

Kykeon: A savoury mulled wine with cheese and herbs, sometimes considered magical.

Kylix: A wide, shallow, handled bowl for drinking wine.

Lembi (pl): Small boats.

Logos: Literally the 'Word', in pre-Socratic Greek philosophy the word that is everything – the power beyond the gods.

Longche: A six to seven foot throwing spear, also used for hunting. A hoplite might carry a pair of *longche*, or a single, longer and heavier, *dory*.

Machaira: A heavy sword or long knife.

Maenad: The 'raving ones', ecstatic female followers of Dionysus.

Mastos: A woman's breast. A mastos cup is shaped like a woman's breast with a rattle in the nipple – so when you drink, you lick the nipple and the rattle shows that you emptied the cup. I'll leave the rest to imagination ...

Medimnoi: A grain measure. Very roughly – thirty-five to a hundred pounds of grain.

Megaron: A style of building with a roofed porch.

Metic: A foreign legal resident of a Greek polity. Remember, even someone from the next city over was a 'foreigner' in your city.

Naos: The inner cell of a temple.

Navarch: An admiral (at least in Sparta) but also the owner of a ship.

Neodamodeis: Newly enfranchised men.

Neoteroi: The 'new men', a faction in government as contrasted with *presbityroi* 'the old men'.

Oikia: The household – all the family and all the slaves, and sometimes the animals and the farmland itself.

Opson: Whatever spread, dip, or accompaniment an ancient Greek had with bread.

Pais: A child. Sometimes a slave.

Palaestra: The exercise sands of the gymnasium.

Pankration: The military martial art of the ancient Greeks – an unarmed combat system that bears more than a passing resemblance to modern MMA techniques, with a series of carefully structured blows and domination holds that is, by modern standards, very advanced. Also the basis of the Greeks' sword- and spear-based martial arts. Kicking, punching and wrestling, grappling, on the ground and standing were all permitted.

Pelta: A shield, small and round or crescent-shaped, not as sturdy as an *aspis*.

Peltastoi: Soldiers; usually a form of soldier who could both skirmish and fight in close order, but in Hellenistic times sometimes special elite organisations.

Peplos: A short over-fold of cloth that women could wear as a hood or to cover the breasts.

Phalanx: The full military potential of a town or kingdom; the actual, formed body of men before a battle (all of the smaller groups formed together made a phalanx). In this period, a massive, unmanoeuvrable juggernaut.

Phalangite: A soldier armed with a pike or sarissa and forming in close order in a phalanx.

Phylarch: A file leader – an officer commanding the four to sixteen men standing behind him in the phalanx.

Polemarch: The war leader in most small states.

Polis: The city – the basis of all Greek political thought and expression; the government that was held to be more important – a higher good – than any individual or even family. To this day, when we talk about politics, we're talking about the 'things of our city'.

Porne: A prostitute.

Porpax: The bronze or leather band that encloses the forearm on a Greek *aspis*.

Pronaos: The vestibule in front of a temple.

Propylon: Part of the temple complex.

Psiloi: Light infantrymen – usually slaves or adolescent freemen who, in this period, were not organised and seldom had any weapon beyond some rocks to throw.

Pyrrhiche: The 'War Dance'. A line dance in armour done by all of the warriors, often very complex. There's reason to believe that the *Pyrrhiche* was the method by which the young were trained in basic martial arts and by which 'drill' was inculcated.

Pyxis: A box, often circular, turned from wood or made of metal.

Rhapsode: A master-poet, often a performer who told epic works like the *Iliad* from memory.

Sarissa: The long pike of the Hellenistic armoured phalangites.

Saurauter: The butt spike on a spear; on a phalangite's pike, it could be a very heavy instrument meant to balance the weight of the *sarissa*.

Satrap: A Persian ruler of a province of the Persian Empire.

Skeuophoros: Literally a 'shield carrier', unlike the *hypaspist*, this is a slave or freedman who does camp work and carries the armour and baggage.

Skeuotheke: A treasure house, or storage area for sacred things.

Spolas: Another name for a leather corslet, often used to refer to the lion skin of Herakles.

Stade: A measure of distance. An Athenian stade is about 185 metres.

Strategos: In Athens, the commander of one of the ten military tribes. Elsewhere, any senior Greek officer – sometimes the commanding general.

Synaspismos: The closest order that hoplites could form – so close that the shields overlap, hence 'shield on shield'.

Taxeis: Any group, but in military terms, a company; I use it for sixty to three hundred men.

Taxiarchos: Commander of a *taxeis*. Also the name of a play by Eupolis, now lost, that was about the god Dionysus reporting for forced military service.

Thētes: The lowest free class – citizens with limited rights.

Tholos: A round building. Tombs of the Mycenaean period were often 'Tholos' tombs and the form was still held special or sacred 1000 years later in Philopoemen's time.

Thorax: Body armour, usually bronze.

Thorakatoi: Armoured infantry, usually *Thureophoroi* (see below) in maille shirts or bronze armour.

Thugater: Daughter. Look at the word carefully and you'll see the 'daughter' in it ...

Thyreophoroi or **Thureophoroi**: Men carrying a Gallic-style long oval shield and javelins with or without a long spear; very much like early period Roman legions. Greek infantry of the third century often were armed this way, as it made the best 'all-round' soldier who could patrol, skirmish, fight from a wall, and also have battlefield utility. (We tend to forget today that in the past, soldiers were not just important for the day of battle – so the most efficient battlefield type might not be the best choice for a small city state ...)

Trierarch: The captain of a ship – sometimes just the owner or builder, sometimes the fighting captain.

Xenos: A foreigner.

Xiphos: A straight-bladed sword, often leaf-shaped and sometimes made of folded steel.

Zone: A belt, often just rope or finely wrought cord, but could be a heavy bronze kidney belt for war. Also a place near modern Alexandroupolis in what is now Greece. It was Thrake in 210 BCE.

'One of *the* finest historical fiction writers in the world'

BEN KANE

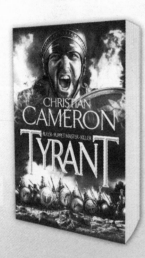

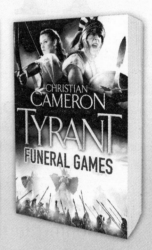

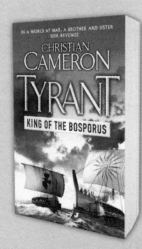

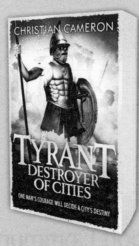

THE TYRANT SERIES

by CHRISTIAN CAMERON

Opening in the setting sun of Alexander the Great's legendary life, follow the adventures of Athenian cavalry officer Kineas and his family. When Alexander dies, the struggle for power between his generals throws Kineas's world into uproar. He must fight if he is to hold on to what is his . . .

Available now from Orion Books

THE LONG WAR
SERIES

by CHRISTIAN CAMERON

Arimnestos of Plataea is just a young boy
when he is forced to swap the ploughshare
for the shield wall and is plunged into the fire
of battle for the first time. As the Greek world
comes under threat from the might of the
Persian Empire, Arimnestos must take up his
spear to preserve his entire way of life.

Available now from Orion Books

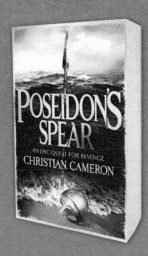

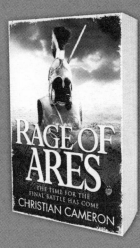

'This series promises to be a standout epic fantasy for the ages'

FANTASY BOOK CRITIC

THE TRAITOR SON CYCLE

by CHRISTIAN CAMERON
writing as MILES CAMERON

If you enjoyed Christian's Chivalry series,
you may also enjoy this knightly fantasy
cycle, following the exploits of the Red
Knight as he rises to fame using only his
wits and the edge of his blade.

Available now from Gollancz